A Scandalous Pursuit

AVA STONE

 Night Shift Publishing

AVA STONE

ISBN: 1517270464
ISBN-13: 978-1517270469

Dedication

For my dearest friends Tori and Becky ~ Thank you both for always being there for me through thick and thin, good times and bad. I love you both.

One

June 1814 – Prestwick Chase, Derbyshire

Lord Staveley's wire-rimmed glasses
Mr. St. Claire's sapphire cravat pin
Epaulette from Commander Greywood's uniform
Lord Carraway's pipe
Cravat with Beckford insignia
Captain Seaton's tricorn
Lord Carteret's signet ring
Gold button with Kelfield crest
Mr. Greywood's pocket watch

OLIVIA Danbury stared blankly at the list in her hands. Her friends had taken her simple idea of a treasure hunt and turned it into something quite impossible.

"You can't honestly be serious," she said with a shake of her head. There was no conceivable way to get any of these items. One couldn't just ask Lord Carteret for his signet ring or beg the wicked Duke of Kelfield for one of the buttons from his waistcoat. That was ridiculous.

"Where's your sense of adventure?" Felicity asked her as she linked her arm with Livvie's.

Adventure? Had her friends all lost their minds?

Cordie's green eyes twinkled. "Come on, Livvie, this is the most fun any of us have had since we arrived."

That was true. The house party at Prestwick Chase had been tedious at best. Still *this* charade was the most ridiculous thing Livvie had ever heard of. How unfortunate that it was her idea—at least in the beginning. She wasn't keen to take the responsibility for what this had become. "I don't even know how I'd go about acquiring any of these things."

Phoebe giggled. "Then I suppose Cordie and I will win."

"We have 'til dinner to get all the items. The team with the most will win."

"Yes, but—" Before Livvie could utter further protests, Phoebe and Cordie sprinted through the door, giggling the entire way. She turned a shocked expression to Felicity, her partner in this insanity.

Felicity looked quite determined, which was a rare look for her. Her blond curls bounced as she leaned in close to whisper, "All right. My cousin, Mr. St. Claire, will give me his cravat pin, no questions asked. I'll also take Lord Carraway's pipe. I know where he keeps it. We can get Staveley's glasses from Caroline. And I'll ask Jensen to get us one of Luke's cravats."

"Felicity!"

"There's no point in us wasting our time on Captain Seaton, since he's been making moon eyes at Cordie all week. Phoebe can get the ring from her Uncle James and the epaulette from her Uncle Simon. And I'm certain Matthew will give his pocket watch to them. Which means we'll be tied. So, all *we'll* need is one of Kelfield's buttons to win."

Livvie rolled her eyes. The idea that the arrogant duke would just hand over one of his buttons for a game was ludicrous. The man was completely unapproachable. If Felicity thought that Kelfield would help them win...

"And then I'll meet you back here," Felicity finished

Livvie shook her head. She must have missed something while she was woolgathering. "I'm sorry. What did you say?"

With an exasperated sigh, Felicity towed her towards the door. "Get some sewing shears, sneak into His Grace's room, and remove one of his buttons. I'll get the cravat pin, the pipe, Staveley's glasses and Luke's cravat. Then I'll meet you back here."

Sneak into His Grace's room and remove one of his buttons? "Absolutely not!"

"Come now, Livvie, don't be a spoilsport. I've got to sneak into Carraway's room for his pipe. I'd send you, but it would take too long to explain where he hides the thing. Besides, Luke has ordered me under no uncertain terms to go near His Grace *or* his room."

Livvie didn't know how Felicity talked her into participating in this ridiculous game. She berated herself for being a fool as she crept into Kelfield's guest room. However, it *was* the most fun she'd had since arriving at Prestwick Chase. She wasn't quite sure what that said about her, but the thrill of being somewhere she wasn't supposed to be had her heart pounding excitedly.

She tiptoed to a large wardrobe on the far side of the room and inhaled the duke's masculine, sandalwood scent as she pulled open the doors. It was almost as if he was there beside her, his silver eyes raking across her form. Chills crept up Livvie's spine and she glanced around the room to make sure she was alone—which, of course, she was. So, she shook her silly head and focused on the job at hand.

Inside the wardrobe were several fashionable waistcoats, and Livvie ran her hands across the expensive silk. Kelfield always looked so devilishly handsome. He had excellent taste—not that she made a habit to notice such things about the scoundrel. She quickly selected a midnight blue waistcoat and fingered one of the gold buttons. Before she had time to consider what she was actually doing, she snipped the thread with her sewing shears and pocketed the coveted button.

She started for the door, but froze when she heard footsteps outside the duke's threshold. Then came a thump against the oak door and a feminine giggle, followed by a hushed but very masculine growl. Slowly, the doorknob began to turn.

Panicked, and with her heart pounding viciously, Livvie looked around the room and dashed inside the wardrobe, just as the door flew open.

That was close. Too close. And what was she to do now?

The giggling continued and two bodies stumbled into the room. Livvie could hear kissing and moaning. Her curiosity warred with her fear of discovery. Curiosity won out.

Tentatively, she pushed the wardrobe door just a crack, so that she could see what was going on.

The Duke of Kelfield held a flame-haired woman against him. He was pulling down the edge of her serviceable gown, until her ample bosom spilled free from its confines. The duke took one nipple into his mouth and sucked. *Good Heavens!* Livvie shrank back against the edge of the wardrobe and closed her eyes tightly. How had she gotten herself into this situation? *Stupid treasure hunt.*

"Get on your knees," the duke ordered.

Livvie's eyes flew open. Oh, she shouldn't be doing this, but she didn't seem to be able to help herself. What was the man doing now? She edged closer to the opening of the wardrobe and peeked through the hole with one eye.

Kelfield stood with his back towards her, but Livvie could clearly see the red-haired woman, whom she thought she recognized as one of The Chase's maids, kneeling between the duke's legs, with her mouth around...*Merciful heavens!* Kelfield's head fell backwards and he let out a low, guttural moan. The sound that came from him was primitive. It reverberated through Livvie—her knees even weakened in response.

After a moment, Kelfield hauled his lover to her feet and yanked the gown completely over her head. Livvie gulped. She should not be witnessing this. Not any of it. But she also couldn't make herself step away. Most importantly, she couldn't let them discover her.

The duke was slowly kissing the woman and backing her against the four-poster bed at the same time. When her legs hit the bed frame, Kelfield easily lifted her up in his strong arms and dropped the sultry-eyed maid in the middle of the mattress. Then he discarded his own clothing in no time at all.

Livvie swallowed. Hard. Then she blinked. He was magnificent. She had no idea the male body could be *that* exquisite. His shoulder blades flexed as he tossed his shirt and then his trousers across the room to land on a chair. He had muscular, well-shaped thighs and an amazing bottom. Livvie hadn't realized that a bottom could be amazing—but his was like a work of art, sculpted from marble.

Heavens! She should not be here.

Kneeling on the bed before the red-haired maid, the duke held her legs open with his large hands and then he pushed himself inside her.

The sensual moan the woman emitted echoed around the room. Livvie couldn't watch anymore. She carefully edged herself to the back of the wardrobe to avoid detection. Though she doubted *anything* could distract the pair on the other side of the door.

The maid's moans turned to giggles, and Livvie tried to cover her ears.

The duke groaned loudly.

This was torture.

After what seemed like forever, Livvie's legs cramped and all she could breathe was sandalwood. Did the duke douse everything he owned in the scent? Her nose tickled and she tried to breathe through her mouth, but she was felt lightheaded. And still the giggles and groans went on and on. How long could the man keep up this sort of activity? People were probably already looking for her, for heaven's sake.

And then the worst possible thing happened.

Livvie sneezed.

Loudly.

The giggling and groaning stopped instantly and Livvie closed her eyes tight. If she prayed hard enough, perhaps she'd awaken in her own bed and this whole thing would be a terrible dream. Though she knew it wasn't the case. Her imagination had never been wild enough to conjure the images she'd seen today.

"Leave," the duke barked, and for a moment Livvie thought he was talking to her. But from the crack in the wardrobe she saw the man toss the maid her discarded dress.

Livvie's world went dark when Kelfield stepped in front of her hiding place and closed the wardrobe door. She felt a thump against the furniture and she imagined him blocking her exit with his body.

She heard the rustle of clothes and the maid grumble under her breath. A moment later the room fell silent, except for an irritated sigh that seemed so close, right on the other side of the door. "If that's you, Greywood," the duke growled, "I'll have your head."

Tears threatened to spill down Livvie's cheeks. Her life was over. The duke would surely kill her on the spot, and she was powerless to keep him from finding her. There was nowhere else to hide.

Then the wardrobe door wrenched open and Livvie squeaked in fear. She expected him to be furious when he found her, but when Kelfield's silvery grey eyes settled on her, he seemed more stunned than angry. His inky black hair was disheveled from his most recent activities, and he looked down his aristocratic nose at her. "Miss Danbury?" he asked in bewilderment.

Completely mortified, Livvie blushed deeper and redder than she ever had in her entire life. "Ex-excuse me," she stammered and tried to brush past him. Even after everything she'd just witnessed, she wasn't accustomed to conversing with naked men, no matter how impressive they were. And she especially didn't want to talk to *this* naked man. She didn't even want to converse with him fully clothed.

Kelfield chuckled and blocked her path from the wardrobe with his body and an outstretched arm. "I don't think so." Then his eyes narrowed and he inched closer to her. "Did you enjoy the performance, sweetheart?"

Wishing that the floor would open up and swallow her whole, Livvie pushed against his chest. His strong and very naked chest. She gulped as she met his silver eyes. "Please, let me pass, Your Grace."

The bedroom door suddenly opened behind them. "Alex, did I leave my spectacles in here?" Lord Staveley's voice preceded him into the room. Livvie sucked in a breath, certain her heart stopped beating at the sight of her guardian.

Staveley stopped dead in his tracks. He looked from Kelfield to Livvie and back again. Despite missing his glasses, it would have been impossible for him to miss the duke's unclothed state.

"Think you could knock next time, Staveley?" Kelfield drawled easily, though he never removed his eyes from Livvie.

She couldn't breathe.

A muscle twitched near Staveley's eye. "Olivia, go find Caroline and do *not* leave her side."

"But, my lord," she began, though she wasn't sure what she could possibly say to explain the situation.

Lord Staveley kept his gaze steady on the duke and barked sharply. "Now, Olivia!"

Livvie escaped as fast as she could into the hallway. She fingered the Kelfield button in her pocked and gulped. This was the worst possible thing to happen.

Two

ALEXANDER Everett pulled on his trousers, still trying to figure out why Olivia Danbury had been spying on him in his room, and wishing he'd been able to get answers from her before Staveley had barged in. "I don't suppose you'd believe that it wasn't what it looked like?" It would be exactly three seconds before his friend could find his voice to respond to that. One, two, three...

"Th-that," Staveley sputtered as he pointed to the now closed door, "was my wife's cousin."

Alex reached for his discarded shirt from the floor. "Yes, I believe we met at a dinner Caroline hosted last year." He pulled the shirt over his head and tucked it into his trousers.

Staveley pursed his lips. Alex couldn't help but find the situation just a bit humorous. After all the times he'd envisioned having Olivia Danbury in his bedroom, this particular scenario had never entered his mind. Though, honestly, he shouldn't have ever envisioned her anywhere. As the ward of his oldest friend, she was strictly off limits. Even the most ruthless rogue lived by his own code of honor.

"I'm glad you're enjoying yourself, Alex." Staveley's voice brought him back to the present. "But what in God's name do you think you're doing?"

"Nothing happened, *mon ami.*"

Staveley stared at him for the longest time, apparently assessing Alex's words. Finally he shook his head, clearly exasperated. "Oh? And assuming that's true, what would have happened if someone *else* had walked in here on the two of you like that?"

Alex shrugged. "Well, I'd hope that someone *else* would have knocked first so I could have shoved Miss Danbury back into her hiding place in my wardrobe." He found his cravat lying in a ball in the corner of the room. This one would never work. It was far too crumpled. He opened a drawer in the wardrobe to retrieve another one.

"*Her* hiding place?" Staveley's eyes were as round as billiard balls. "Damn it all, Alex. How many girls are you hiding in here?"

Alex chose not to answer that question. He turned to examine his reflection in the mirror.

Staveley advanced on him, anger flashing in his dark eyes. "Olivia Danbury came here in my care. *My care,* damn you. And now you've gone and ruined her. Her parents are in India. How am I supposed to explain that to them? Dear God! How am I supposed to explain that to my *wife?*"

"She's not ruined. Well, at least not by my hand." Much as he would enjoy such a thing, it could never happen. "So, you don't have to explain anything to anybody."

"That's not what it looked like when I walked in here." Staveley frowned. "You didn't have a stitch of clothes on and the room smells of sex."

Refocusing on himself in the mirror, Alex began to tie the fresh cravat around his neck. "I'm sure it took a few years off your life, Staveley, but on my honor I didn't touch one hair on your little cousin's head. Virginal young things aren't my usual fare."

Staveley roughly rubbed his brow, considered him, and slid into a nearby chair. "Women are such a trial. I don't think I can go through this again. I just got the last of my sisters unloaded, and now I've got *this* to deal with." He jabbed a finger in Alex's direction. "You're marrying her."

For the first time since this conversation began, Alex widened his eyes in shock. He certainly hadn't anticipated Staveley making a pronouncement like *that*—especially since he was completely innocent of any wrongdoings, at least where Olivia Danbury was concerned. "I'm doing no such thing. I'm thirty-four years old, Staveley, and women have been trying to trap me into marriage for nearly half my life. It will take more than some chit I don't even know popping out of my wardrobe to do the trick."

Staveley was quiet for a moment, and a number of different emotions cross his face. No doubt the man was concerned. If anyone had seen Miss Danbury enter his room or leave it, she'd be ruined, and all of it would lie on Staveley's head. "You have to marry sometime anyway, Alex. The state's not as bad as you make it out. Livvie's a nice girl, comes from a good family—uh—beautiful voice, and you love music."

"David," he growled in warning. Of course, he'd fanaticized about the girl, but he *never* once had marriage enter his mind. For God's sake, he didn't know the first thing about her except that whenever he saw her she made his pulse race and his cock stiffen.

"Damn it, Alex." Staveley jumped to his feet. "I've got to get this straightened out."

"Then straighten it out. But don't look in my direction."

As soon as Staveley left, Alex dropped into a chintz chair closer to the window. He was a God damned fool. As soon as he realized she would be at this house party, he should have declined the invitation. It was impossible to be near the girl without lascivious thoughts plaguing his mind. In fact, she was the reason he'd had to resort to tumbling one of The Chase's maids in the first place.

⚜

Livvie had barely turned the corner before she ran into Felicity. "*There* you are," her friend said. "I've been looking all over for you. Everyone's in the parlor. Did you get the button?"

That cursed button. How she wished she'd never agreed to this ridiculous thing. She didn't care one whit about the foolish treasure hunt anymore. Livvie she shook her head. "I've got to find Caroline."

"Oh?" Felicity asked as she gleefully linked her arm with Livvie's. "Well, she's in the parlor too. After she delivered Staveley's glasses she wanted to see what else was on the list and what we needed to win."

To win? The only thing Livvie was certain of was that *she* had lost everything. Her mind. Her reputation. Her future.

Felicity pulled her along the corridor, down the large staircase, and finally into the blue parlor—where Caroline, Viscountess Staveley, scanned the list with an appreciative grin. Then she shook her head as she handed the list to Cordie. "You girls are silly."

Phoebe pouted, her pink lips drawn up tight. "My Uncle Simon was simply horrid not to give me one of his epaulettes."

Caroline laughed. "You should ask your Aunt Madeline. She's been dying to destroy that uniform for nearly half a decade." Then she noticed Livvie standing in the doorway and smiled at her. "There you are, darling. You weren't successful at getting Kelfield to part with one of his buttons, were you?"

Livvie's lip started to tremble, but she managed to shake her head. "Caroline, I need to speak with you." If anyone could get her out of this mess it was her cousin.

"Of course." Caroline crossed the room in just a few strides. "Darling, what is wrong?" she quietly asked.

Livvie grabbed her cousin's arm and dragged her out into the hallway. "Something awful has happened—"

Before she could continue, Staveley called out to them from the other end of the corridor. "Olivia! I need a word with you."

Caroline focused on her approaching husband, and a frown formed across her brow. "What has happened, Staveley?"

He forced a smile to his face. "Nothing, my dear. I need to speak with Olivia is all."

Livvie took a staggering breath as Caroline and her husband eye each other. This was bad, getting worse by the moment, and she couldn't think of a way out of the situation. Finally, her cousin nodded and ducked back inside the blue salon, leaving Livvie alone with Staveley. Humiliated, she stared at her feet.

"Olivia, what *were* you doing in Kelfield's room?" he asked in a hushed voice.

She reached into her pocket and retrieved the gold button, presenting it to him. "We were on a treasure hunt, and I was supposed to get this."

He took the button from her and stared at it. "He didn't touch you then?"

"Heavens, no!" she responded and determinedly shook her head.

"Olivia, it is imperative that you tell me the truth."

Finally, she met his eyes. "I swear to you, Staveley, he didn't even know I was there until right before you walked in."

Staveley heaved a huge sigh, though a look of displeasure settled on his face. "I cannot express to you how very disappointed I am. As an unmarried lady, for you to go into *his* room is completely inappropriate. And now you've been compromised, Olivia."

Her worst fears were coming true, and she clutched his arm desperately. "Please, my lord. Please don't make me marry him." Tears streamed down her cheeks. "I could never be happy with a man of his character—a man so lacking. I was stupid to go in there. But please don't make me suffer the rest of my days for such a foolish—"

"Shh." Staveley brushed the tears from her cheeks. "Livvie, pull yourself together. You'll have Caroline back out here."

She took a staggering breath and tried to comply.

"You haven't told her yet, have you?" he asked softly.

Livvie shook her head. "I was just about to tell her. I know she'll find a way I don't have to marry that beast. And—"

"Not a word to *her*. Do you understand?"

No. Not at all. Livvie had always depended on Caroline to get her out of scrapes—nothing ever like this—but certainly her inventive cousin could find a way around these unfortunate circumstances. She shook her head.

Staveley pursed his lips. "My lovely wife has been trying, unsuccessfully, for more years than I can remember to marry Alex off. If she knew of this situation, she would make sure you were the Duchess of Kelfield in the blink of an eye."

Which meant that Staveley had a plan that would prevent that fate for her. She'd never felt so relieved. "Then *you* won't make me…"

He frowned and leaned in close. "Olivia, did anyone else see or hear you?"

"No." At least she hoped not. She certainly hadn't seen anyone.

"Then I'll keep my mouth shut."

Her heart leapt with joy. She would never have been able to explain the situation to Philip. He would have been crushed.

"But," Staveley continued, "if I hear the tiniest rumbling about this, or if anyone else discovers you were in his room, I'll be powerless to help you. Do you understand?"

Livvie threw her arms around Staveley's neck and hugged him tight.

"Thank you. Thank you. Thank you."

✦✦✦

"You're a damned lucky bastard," Staveley remarked as he opened Alex's door. Then the viscount knocked loudly and waited a few seconds before he stepped over the threshold. "Is it safe to enter?"

"You've acquired quite the sense of humor, Staveley." Alex motioned for his friend to shut the door and take a seat in one of the chintz chairs near the window. "Did she tell you why she was in here?"

Staveley reached into his pocket and then tossed a small, golden object at Alex. He caught the item and turned it over in his hand. One of his buttons? That didn't make one bit of sense.

"She was on a treasure hunt and needed *that* for her list."

All of this over a bloody button? Alex ran a hand through his hair. "Good God."

"My thoughts exactly," Staveley replied as he dropped into one of the chairs, pinching the bridge of his nose. "The good news for you, my friend, is that I stopped Livvie from confessing to Caroline. So you're safe. And since Livvie has no desire to marry you, and I'm the only one who witnessed anything, I'll just—"

"What do you mean since she has no desire to marry *me*?" He didn't want to be leg-shackled—and certainly not like this—but he knew that women *wanted* to marry him. The idea of being a duchess made most women giddy.

Staveley smirked. "Apparently, she finds you 'lacking'—her words, not mine, old friend."

Lacking? What the devil was that suppose to mean? Women didn't find him lacking. How dare she say such a thing! After all, she was the one in the wrong in all this. Alex hadn't brought her into his room, much as he would have liked to. And Alex hadn't asked her to spy on his intimate liaisons. She had done that all on her own.

Lacking!

His face grew taut and he abruptly stood up. "Where is she?"

Staveley reluctantly stood up as well. "I thought you'd be happy to be off the hook, you ungrateful sod."

"Where is she?" he ground out through clenched teeth.

Staveley shrugged. "Livvie is now enjoying a picnic with her friends on the west lawn."

He stormed towards the door, but was stopped by Staveley's next words. "Caroline is with them as well, Alex. I urge you watch what you say in front of my wife. If she thinks you've got an interest in her cousin, she'll plot and meddle and be an overall nuisance until you're leg-shackled to the chit."

"Point taken." Caroline Staveley could be a bane to any single man. He'd borne witness to that himself on more than one occasion. Her list of achievements in finding matches was well on its way to becoming legendary. But still, Olivia Danbury had some questions to answer, and he was going to see that she did so. Besides, he and Caroline had an agreement which prevented her from meddling in his life, though he didn't think Staveley was privy to that information.

"Oh, and, Alex," Staveley said, interrupting his thoughts, "friend or not, if I hear the slightest whisper about any of this, you *will* marry her."

He didn't really have a choice. He would never dishonor Staveley. Alex met his friend's gaze with resignation. After a curt nod, he went in search of the troublesome Olivia.

Three

ALEX spotted Miss Danbury on The Chase's soft lawn, chatting with three silly chits and, of course, Caroline. Not that he was paying the others any attention at all. He was focused solely on the blushing, auburn-haired Olivia who had just noticed his approach.

Since the night he'd first met her, he had tried not to give Caroline Staveley's little cousin any thought. He had tried to be honorable. Though now that he saw the sun reflecting off the soft red highlights in her dark hair, his resolve weakened on both fronts. She had twinkling, hazel eyes, a dimple in her left cheek that was strangely just as endearing as it was innocent, and a pair of luscious, rose-colored lips. Olivia Danbury was enchanting, and he ached to touch her, to show her in a very intimate way that he wasn't *lacking* a thing.

Alex had to remind himself, as he approached her, that the chit remained under Staveley's care. Even the most ruthless rogues had standards.

Still, it ate him up inside. What exactly did she find lacking in him? He scoffed lightly to himself when her blush deepened as he neared her.

"Miss Danbury," he began as his booted foot reached her blanket. He didn't spare a glance for anyone else—not even Caroline, which was

14

probably a mistake he'd pay for later. "I'd like a word with you."

Olivia's hazel eyes rounded in fear. Alex watched the movement of her slender throat as she swallowed nervously. And she should be nervous, if she had any idea of the images of her that were currently filtering through his mind.

"M-me?" she asked with a quiver in her voice.

The other girls all seemed to take the same deep intake of air at the same time, but Olivia bit her plump bottom lip with her teeth as she tentatively met his eyes.

Alex stared back at her with a deep intensity. "Unless you'd rather talk here in the open."

She was on her feet in the blink of an eye, and Alex reached out his arm to her. Caroline rose to her feet as well and narrowed her eyes on him. "Alex, darling, is something amiss?"

He turned a charming smile on the vivacious viscountess, a woman he had admired for years. A woman who had promised, after securing his assistance two years earlier with one of her schemes, not to interfere in his personal life anymore. "Of course not, Caro."

"But—" she began.

He leveled a hard, ducal stare on her. "Do you recall our bargain, Lady Staveley?"

Caroline's eyes widened and she looked first at Alex then to Olivia and back. "Indeed."

"Good." Alex turned his attention back to Miss Danbury, his arm still outstretched, and raised his brow expectantly. She seemed to steel herself for the interview, nodded slightly, and then placed her delicate, gloved hand on his forearm.

Desire shot through Alex straight to his loins, which should have still been sated, but strangely were not. Just as they were out of earshot of the others, Olivia turned her face up to look at him. She frowned, and her very kissable lips pursed angrily. "What are you trying to do? Ruin me?"

"I don't need to try. You've done a magnificent job of that all by yourself, sweetheart."

She snorted. "Staveley said no harm was done. So, let's just forget this little incident ever occurred. I'll go my way, and you can… Well, you can do whatever it is that you do."

Which is what he should do. But now that he had a reason to talk to her, Alex wouldn't give it up. "I don't think it will be that easy, Olivia."

Her pretty hazel eyes widened at the use of her first name, and Alex had to bite back a smile. Would her eyes widen even more the first time he thrust inside her? Because there was not a doubt in his mind that he would soon have her in his bed—Staveley be damned. And he was enjoying the idea more and more as she sputtered for an answer.

"In what way, Olivia, do you find me lacking?" he asked. "I'd very much like to dispel your thoughts on the subject."

She seemed to recover her composure and she looked away from him, out towards a copse of trees in the distance. "I don't think that will be possible, Your Grace."

Alex stopped mid-step and swung her to face him. "I think I'm owed at least an explanation, don't you?"

Olivia blushed slightly at that and then met his eyes once more. "Very well. I find you lacking *morally*, Your Grace. I doubt very seriously that you can reverse my thoughts in that regard."

Well, she had him there. He dipped his head down so that his eyes were level with hers. "Ah, but I make up for it in many different ways, sweetheart. I'm certain you'll come to appreciate those ways much more than you'll miss my lack of moral fiber."

She stared at him quietly for a long moment. Then finally, she spoke again. "I don't think I'll come to appreciate anything about you, Your Grace. Staveley said there was nothing to worry about. No one saw anything. We can both go our separate ways."

"But what if I want to go *your* way?" When her delightful pink lips pursed again, Alex could almost taste them.

"Y-you can't go my way. I'm betrothed, and my fiancé wouldn't appreciate this conversation."

Fiancé? Staveley had been remiss in mentioning that. He found himself frowning at the idea. "Who is he?" Not that it mattered overmuch. He'd still have Miss Danbury.

She swallowed again, and Alex wanted desperately to run his fingers down the base of her neck—her lovely slender neck, whose languorous movements were making his mouth go dry.

"Major Philip Moore of the 45th Foot. Now if that is all, Your Grace, I should like very much to return to my friends."

He raised her hand to his lips and pressed a kiss to the inside of her

16

wrist. "For now, sweetheart. But I don't believe I'm through with you yet." And he wasn't. He knew without a shadow of a doubt that his interactions with Miss Olivia Danbury were just beginning.

Livvie blinked up at him, uncertain what she saw simmering in his silver eyes, but it made shivers dance up her spine. Then she turned and made her way directly back to where Caroline and her friends sat watching her. She couldn't say a word to anyone about anything, as Staveley's warning still echoed in her mind.

Once she reached the picnic blanket, Livvie reclaimed her vacant spot and lifted a glass of wine to her lips so she wouldn't have to speak. They were all staring at her. Cordie, Phoebe and Felicity in awe, and Caroline with concern.

"Is everything all right, Livvie?" Caroline asked softly.

Livvie nodded her head and forced a smile to her lips. "Of course." She took a steadying breath. "Kelfield was simply informing me that he didn't wish to part with any of his buttons."

No one would believe that explanation. The longer she stayed with her friends, the harder they would press for the truth. Kelfield had vanished, as he'd probably spotted another maid in heat. Livvie handed her goblet to Cordie and rose to her feet. "It's so very hot and I think that wine went right to my head. I'm going to lie down for a while."

Before anyone could stop her, she started back for the manor house and did not stop until she reached her room. She kicked off her slippers and dropped like a heap onto her bed, still not quite sure how this whole situation had spun out of her control.

Horrid house party. Stupid treasure hunt. Insufferable duke! Until today he'd always scowled in her direction when their paths crossed, and now he seemed to relish the opportunity to make her suffer for her tiny error in judgment.

Livvie rolled to her side and opened a drawer in her bedside table. She retrieved a note which had been folded and refolded so many times she'd lost count. The edges were frayed and foolscap had yellowed. Even though she knew the words by heart, seeing Philip's handwriting made her miss him less. She rested her head on a pillow and once again opened the letter.

April 5, 1814
My dearest Olivia,

As I sit here in my tent tonight, images of you fill my mind, and I find that I miss you more dreadfully with each passing day. You are not even aware of it, my sweetest darling, but my thoughts of you are all that have kept me sane in this insane world.

Has it actually been two years since I touched you? Since I kissed you? Has it truly been that terribly long? I pray that the war will soon be over so that I may return to you.Though my duty is here, sweetest Olivia, my heart is always with you. So be patient, my love, for when I do return home I swear to never leave you again.

Yours Always,
Maj. Philip Moore

Livvie ran her fingers over his signature and sighed. War had ended, but he still hadn't returned. Along with Cordie's older brothers, Philip's regiment remained in Toulouse, keeping the city secure. Philip was doing his duty, as always, but it seemed wholly unfair that even with the war over he should still be kept from her.

Each passing day found her more anxious for his return. They'd waited so long to marry and this final duty in Toulouse didn't seem as though it would ever end. If he'd already returned, they'd be living a quiet existence in Nottinghamshire and reacquainting themselves.

A pounding on her door snapped Livvie back to the present. She carefully refolded Philip's letter and placed it back in her bedside table. "Come in," she called more brightly than she felt.

The door opened, and Cordie cautiously entered, shutting the door behind her. "Liv, tell me what's going on with His Grace."

She winced. She should have realized that Cordie would seek her out. They were close as sisters, having known each other since they were in leading strings. And though she knew she could trust Cordie with her life, she could never tell anyone of the things she witnessed today.

"Heavens! How bad is it?" Cordie dropped onto the bed beside her.

Livvie shook her head. "It's nothing, Cordie. I promise. I simply detest the man, is all. He was incredibly…ill-mannered when I tried to acquire his button." In a manner of speaking, that was the truth.

"Oh." Cordie sounded dejected.

"What do you mean by 'Oh'?"

Her friend flashed a pretty smile. "Well, the way he was looking at you made it seem as though he'd like to ravish you."

A fresh image of Kelfield and the maid popped in Livvie's mind. She sat forward, hoping Cordie wouldn't notice the blush she felt warming her cheeks. "I can assure you, His Grace does not even like me." He only wanted to torment her as a punishment for invading his space. "And the feeling is mutual. Whenever he visits Staveley, I make myself scarce as I have no intention of having to converse with the man."

"I had no idea you felt so strongly," Cordie muttered. "I've never heard you mention him before this party."

Livvie kicked her legs over the bed and walked toward her window. "Last year when cousin Caroline was playing matchmaker for the Astwicks, she hosted a dinner. For some reason she invited that lout, who arrived well after the meal began. The only seat available was the one next to me. He scowled and sulked all night, as though he couldn't believe he was at the end of the table with someone of so little import. I've never known anyone to dislike me so suddenly, even though I tried to be my most charming. He was a guest, after all. But he grunted answers to questions and made it obvious he felt I was quite beneath him."

"He does sound boorish," Cordie said from the bed. "One wouldn't imagine him to be so, considering his reputation. You should warn Phoebe and Felicity. They're both intent on setting their caps for him."

She snorted. Phoebe and Felicity had each set their caps for every single man in attendance at this fiasco of a house party. "It would be easier to convince a fish to live on land," she said, turning around to face her friend.

Cordie giggled. "You're probably right."

"Besides, I am tired of talking about the man. Tell me about your Captain Seaton instead. Did he try to kiss you?"

"Not yet," her friend admitted with a cheeky grin. "He is the perfect gentleman, but I am hopeful."

Livvie couldn't help but smile in return. Cordie always could make her feel better without even trying. If only she could help make her forget that debauched duke as easily.

Four

ALEX eyed the billiard table. His cue ball was lined up nicely to pot the red ball. As he aimed his shot, a hand clapped him on the back, which sent his stick digging into the felt and his cue ball leaping off the table.

He spun around to find Commander Simon Greywood grinning at him. "You'd have never made it anyway. Your talent has always lain in other areas."

Alex placed his cue stick on the table and sat on the edge of the table. "The same could be said about you, my friend."

Simon raised a glass of whiskey to his lips. "That was a lifetime ago." And truly it was. Life had changed so much since their days of their youthful indiscretions. He and Simon had once been inseparable, before his friend turned to the adventures offered at sea. "Anyway, I thought I should warn you."

"About what?" Alex folded his arms across his chest.

"My niece has decided she would very much like to be a duchess."

Alex laughed. "Every woman wants to be a duchess, Greywood." *All save one.*

"Yes, but she wants to be your duchess and she's trying to recruit Beth to her cause."

Alex groaned. Simon's sister was a pest. She always had been, on one front or another. Still, unless Miss Phoebe Greywood popped out of his wardrobe while he was naked, there wasn't a thing she could do that would entice him to offer for her. On second thought, he would ensure that his room remained locked at all times from now on, and he'd do a thorough search when he returned.

"Ah," James McFadyn, Earl Carteret, said from the doorway, "hiding in here, are we?"

Simon shrugged. "I was warning Alex about Beth." He then dropped into a high back leather chair beside the billiard table and kicked his long legs out in front of him. "I will never understand how you can live with my sister. Just a week spent in her presence is enough to make me rethink my retirement."

James' brow rose indignantly. "That is my wife you're talking about."

"Yes, well, she was my sister first."

James crossed the room to the sidebar and poured himself a whiskey. "Besides I'm sure Beth is doing her best to direct Phoebe in a more suitable direction."

"I'll try not to take offense to that," Alex muttered.

James laughed as he sauntered back over to the others. "It's no matter anyway, the girl is flighty. She'll be infatuated with the next fellow who crosses her path. Just wait it out." The slightest Scottish brogue could be detected in his voice if one listened for it.

"Speaking of infatuation," Simon began with a grin, "Madeline forced me to the theatre last week."

"That must have been very difficult for you," Alex drawled. After spending half of his life on board a ship, Simon was a man of action and rarely sat still for long. Alex couldn't imagine him actually suffering through an entire performance.

"You, on the contrary, are a very lucky bastard. I'd heard reports that she was beautiful, but by God, she is stunning," Simon continued.

Sarah Kane. He was obviously referring to Alex's mistress, a pretty little actress, as sweet as she was talented, both on the stage and in the bedroom. He found himself smirking back at his friends. "Indeed. Miss Kane is remarkable."

"The life you lead." Simon nodded his head. "All men should be so lucky."

Alex laughed. Though Alex had no intention of giving up his lifestyle, Simon Greywood seemed to have it all. A life filled with adventure. A happy and supportive family. And a beautiful wife of whom Alex was constantly in awe. Not many women would willingly raise her husband's bastard children, yet Madeline Greywood had done so without complaint. "I'd say you're luckier than most."

"Touché." Simon rose from his seat. "Well, gentlemen, I did promise my lovely wife a stroll in the gardens. I shall have to catch up with you later."

As soon as the commander left the room, James softly shut the door behind him. Alex's brow rose in question. James rarely sought out his opinion on serious matters. He was more likely to turn to Staveley for such things. "Something on your mind?"

His friend heaved a sigh. "I've come to you first, so you can do the right thing, Alex."

"The right thing?" This sounded ominous. Besides, Alex rarely did the right thing.

"I went to your room earlier," James began. "I started to knock, but... Well, the feminine giggles made it rather obvious you were occupied. So, when I returned half an hour later, it was to see Miss Danbury escaping your chambers. Then I later spotted you escorting the very same Miss Danbury across the Prestwick lawns."

The air rushed from Alex's lungs. "I had no idea you found me so fascinating."

"I had no idea you were quite so dissolute. I don't even want to know how long it's been going on. I don't want to have to go to Staveley..."

But he would anyway. James' moral compass was wound too tightly for him to turn his head the other direction. Even as a boy, he'd been the most noble of the bunch.

So, this was it then, wasn't it? The end to his bachelorhood. After all the debauched encounters he'd been involved in over the years—*this* was how he was finally trapped. But there was nothing to be done about it. Staveley had said that since no one had seen a thing they could all go their separate ways. *But James had seen. And James had heard*—not Olivia, but the particulars wouldn't matter. Even if he tried to explain away the incident, there would always be a part of James that would wonder at the truth.

As soon as the Scot mentioned this to Staveley, he'd find himself leg-shackled to the lovely Miss Danbury in no time at all.

Apparently that was to be his fate. And he found that the idea wasn't all that awful really. He did lust after the girl and had for a year. That was better than nothing. Still, forcing Olivia to marry him wasn't terribly complimentary to either of them—and not terribly sporting. Alex did love a good chase. If he could convince her to accept him on his own merits, perhaps they could both come out of this experience having won. An idea leapt to his mind. "James, do not inform Staveley of this, I beg you."

James' blue eyes darkened. "You know, Alex, as the father of three daughters, this puts me in a rather unenviable spot."

"Ah, but as my friend—"

"Yes, well, I'm Staveley's friend too. And what you've done with this girl—"

Alex's brow rose with the ducal hauteur he'd learned from his father, successfully preventing James from saying something that would further damage their friendship. "Would you believe me if I said I planned to marry her?" And though it was strange to hear the words escape his own mouth, Alex was amazed to discover the thought didn't frighten him, or annoy him, or seem unpleasant in any way. In fact, it seemed that this was the best idea he'd ever had, not that it was entirely his idea.

"No. I wouldn't believe you." James' frown deepened. "I *know* you. She's a very sweet girl, and I'm sure—"

"I just need time to convince her. And Staveley forcing my hand isn't really what I have in mind." Though he was going to enjoy this process immensely.

"'Ere ye serious?" James' accent was more pronounced than it had been in ages.

"I am." Alex found himself smiling. How many times over the last several years had he heard from one friend or another that it was time he settled down? How many girls had Caroline Staveley alone pushed into his path? He had a duty to his title, or so he'd been told more times than he cared to count. At some point he needed to marry, beget an heir, become a bit more respectable—but only a bit. "You know how I adore music. And Miss Danbury is quite talented." Or so he'd heard.

"Damn it all, Alex! You don't sound remotely like yourself."

"I'm sure I don't." He didn't quite feel like himself either.

Caroline Staveley paced around her room. A permanent frown had settled on her face. If there was one thing she hated, it was being kept in the dark—which was precisely what was happening at this very moment. Something was most assuredly going on, but no one had confided in her. Blast them. She knew it had something to do with Olivia and also, she theorized, Alex. It was the *what* that was driving her mad.

She turned abruptly when a soft knock sounded on her door. "Come," she nearly barked, which she immediately regretted when her sister-in-law, Lady Juliet, entered her room with her sweet, infant son in her arms. Caroline's frown instantly disappeared, replaced by a cheerful smile.

Little Benton Beckford, at nine months, was adorable, and Caroline was convinced her precious nephew would break hearts just like his father had done. "Oh, my darling, little Ben," she gushed.

"Be careful about that," Juliet warned her with a grin. "Emma confided in me that she thinks you love Ben more than her."

Caroline resisted the urge to roll her eyes. She and Staveley loved their children more than life itself, a fact that all three of them knew very well. Her youngest, Emma, was simply put out that Caroline caught her trying to hide Ben's favorite rattle because the baby was receiving more attention than she was.

With outstretched hands, Caroline scooped Ben out of his mother's arms and cradled him against her. "You," she began in a sing-song voice. "Benton Beckford, have a very silly cousin. Yes, you do."

Juliet plopped down on Caroline's bed, wiggling her fingers at her son. "Caro, be honest. How do you think my house party is going?"

Caroline cringed inwardly. Juliet had never been terribly social, and this was her first attempt at being a hostess. She didn't want to scare her sister-in-law off with critical words. Instead, it would simply be better for *her* to arrive early next time and assist Juliet with all the preparations. "I think it is going splendidly. Don't you?"

Juliet pursed her lips. "Well, I did. And though I adore Kelfield, and will never be able to repay him for his assistance with Luke a few years ago, things have changed since he's arrived."

"What things?" Caroline asked, careful not to let her raging curiosity be too obvious.

With a shrug, Juliet pushed from her place on the bed and gently ran her hand along her son's cheek. "All the girls, save Olivia—thank heavens she has her head on her shoulders—have got stars in their eyes now that Kelfield is here. They're all acting like complete ninnies."

"Well, the man does command attention wherever he goes. One can hardly blame them."

"Perhaps," Juliet sighed. "But then there's Alex himself. With all of the girls doing everything they can to attract him, he's focused himself on Olivia. I wonder, do you think it is because she's the only one *not* trying to garner his attention?"

Ben chose that moment to yank on one of Caroline's curls. Juliet yelped an apology and then pried her son's pudgy fingers from his aunt's hair. "Do you want me to take him?"

Caroline shook her head. Ben could cuff her in the eye and she wouldn't care. Not right now. *Alex had focused his attention solely on Olivia*? She had suspected that, of course. He had sought her out during luncheon and insisted on speaking to her alone. That situation had struck Caroline as very odd. She hadn't believed that Banbury tale about him refusing to relinquish a gold button either.

Well, this was simply terrible. The man truly had the worst sort of luck. Her pretty young cousin was head-over-heels in love with Philip Moore. She wouldn't give Alex the time of day. Why did he have to single out the one girl at Prestwick Chase who would rebuff his attentions?

Heartbreaking. That's what it was. If there was ever a man who needed a wife, it was Alexander Everett. She had tried forever to find a suitable match for the devil, up until their bargain of a few years ago.

Blast!

"He even asked me to seat Olivia across from him at dinner tonight."

Caroline refocused on Juliet. "Well, you're not going to do it, are you? I mean *I* may have promised not to meddle in his life, but, darling, you didn't promise that. Seat Cordelia Avery across from him. She's a much better prospect, and *not* already betrothed." Caroline had envisioned a different man for Miss Avery at the end of last season, but plans were made to be broken. Besides she didn't quite care for that naval captain who'd taken a liking to the girl.

Juliet shook her head. "I already told him I would, Caroline. I can't go back on my word. I can seat Miss Avery across from him tomorrow night."

One night.

They didn't really have a choice. She just hoped Livvie wouldn't be too charming tonight, as Alex didn't need a broken heart. The poor man had endured enough rejection from his own family over the years. She would have to figure out the right path from here on out. Caroline smiled at Juliet. "You will help me, won't you, darling?"

Five

"I WAS thinking of a game we could all play," Cordie suggested, pacing a path in Livvie's room.

"What sort of game?" Livvie asked with hesitation. She'd had her fill of games, as the last one nearly saw her lose her freedom to the most dissolute man in all of England.

"Well," Cordie began. "We'll think up three words for each other, like asp, rubbish, or...bombazine. And then we have to use those words in conversation with someone who isn't in on the game, without them realizing it or asking what it is that we're doing."

"Asp, rubbish, and bombazine?" This sounded completely far-fetched.

"Yes," Cordie spun on her heel, her green eyes twinkling gaily. "For instance, I could go up to Captain Seaton and say, 'Bombazine really is the scratchiest material known to man. I swear I'd rather face an asp than have to wear it. Every inch of it in England should be thrown in a rubbish bin.' And if he doesn't look at me as if I've lost my mind or ask what I'm talking about, then I get a point. Or three points. I don't know, what do you think?"

Livvie feared that she'd somehow be thrust in Kelfield's path saying something completely ridiculous and end up looking more foolish than she already did. She frowned her answer. "We truly are bored aren't we?"

Cordie's face fell. "Well, it's not our fault your cousin's wife has thrown such a dismal house party. Remind me to thank you again for the invitation."

Livvie laughed. "At least you're away from your mother and you did meet the captain. All things considered, you've had a much better time of it than I have."

Before Cordie could reply a knock came from the door. Livvie sat up straight. "Come."

Her cousin Caroline peeked her head in the room. "Olivia darling, might I speak with you a moment?"

She gulped. She knew Caroline would seek her out eventually. Too many things had happened in her presence for her cousin to sit idly by. "Of course," she choked out.

Cordie threw her a you-knew-it-was-bound-to-happen look. "I'll just be on my way. I've created a new game that I'm eager to share with Felicity and Phoebe."

Livvie cringed. "I am not playing that game," she called to her friend's disappearing form. An instant later the door was shut and she found herself facing Caroline alone. "Don't you look lovely," Livvie said, hoping to distract her cousin from whatever she came to say.

Caroline grinned and spun around in her gown the color of warm honey, her golden-brown curls swayed back and forth. "Do you like it?"

"Caro, you always look splendid," she replied honestly.

"You are a dear." Caroline dropped on to the corner of the bed by Livvie and grasped her hands. "I have a favor to ask, darling."

That was unusual. Generally people sought Caroline out for favors. "Of course."

Her cousin frowned a bit. "I don't mean to shock you, but I believe Kelfield has developed a tendre of sorts for you."

Livvie's mouth fell open. Of all the things she expected Caroline to say, that had never entered her mind. "I do believe you're mistaken, Caro. That degenerate does not even like me, let alone hold a soft spot in his heart for me."

Caroline frowned. "I'd hardly call him a degenerate."

Perfect! Now she'd have to listen to Caroline extol his wonderful character. Livvie fell back on the bed, staring up at her canopy. "I'd rather not hear about his finer points, few as I'm sure they are."

Caroline scoffed. "There is much more to His Grace than the wicked devil-may-care rogue he pretends to be."

"I don't think he's pretending."

"He is loyal and a true friend. He is a loving and devoted father."

Livvie snorted. "There isn't enough time in the day for him to be devoted to so many." After all, it was rumored the man had fathered dozens of children. How could he possibly be devoted to *all* of his offspring? Caroline generally was a much better judge of character.

Her cousin smacked her knee. "Olivia Danbury," she remarked reproachfully — which was saying something as Caroline was *never* reproachful. "What has gotten into you? I've never known you to be so ungenerous in nature."

Livvie rose up on her elbows and shrugged. "I'm sorry, Caroline. I suppose I'm missing Philip more and more. Being secluded in Derbyshire has made that more pronounced, I'm afraid."

Caroline squeezed Livvie's leg, and her hazel eyes seemed to understand. "I know you miss him, darling. It shouldn't be too much longer before he returns home."

Livvie bit her bottom lip and shook her head. "I don't even know if he's all right, Caroline. He hasn't written in ages."

"Darling, you know he's fine. The Averys have kept you well informed."

"But what if Russell and Tristan aren't telling them everything? What if something's happened to him? And if he does come home... What if he's not the same person anymore?"

"The same person?" Caroline echoed. "Livvie, Philip is fine. And when he returns you'll marry and everything will be as it was intended."

Livvie pushed herself off the bed and paced around the room. "But war changes people, Caroline. Henrietta's husband returned from the battlefields a completely different person and she's at a loss for what to do with him. She doesn't even know who he is." In a way it felt good to voice her concerns. She'd been holding them inside for too long.

Caroline softly snorted. "Henrietta didn't know the man a fortnight before he set off for the continent. You can't worry yourself over such a thing with Philip, darling. You've known him all your life. He may be a *bit* different, but not completely. Do try not to dwell on the situation. It'll just drive you mad."

Which was easier said than done.

"Now about that favor."

"Yes?"

"Well, I just don't want you to encourage Kelfield. I think you're precisely the sort of girl who could break his heart."

A nervous laugh escaped Livvie. "I can promise you, Caro, I have no intention of encouraging Kelfield." The last thing she needed was for Staveley to think something untoward was occurring between her and the duke. Her life would be over.

⚜

Livvie frowned as she looked directly across the table. How had she managed to end up opposite Kelfield? Blast Juliet for disbanding with etiquette and not seating the table by rank as they had every other night since her arrival. When the duke met her eyes, she could have sworn his silvery orbs twinkled at her — before they finally settled on her décolletage, where they remained for the rest of dinner.

If there hadn't been a room full of dinner guests, she would have leapt from her chair and beat him with her fists, which was really not like her at all. But Kelfield drove her to distraction. Blast him!

She had to settle for simply glaring at the man, which could not be perceived as encouraging him.

On one side of her sat the quiet Hugh St. Claire and on the other, the kind Lord Carteret, who was sending his own reproachful glances at the duke. She turned her attention to Carteret and smiled sweetly. "My lord, have you had the opportunity to visit Gosling Park recently?"

The earl inclined his head. "Actually, we have, Miss Danbury. Masten was gracious enough to host my brood for a fortnight before we set out for Prestwick Chase."

Livvie felt Kelfield's heated gaze on her, and a blush crept its way up her body. She cleared her throat and tried to give Carteret her undivided attention. "Indeed? A-and how is my cousin Robert?"

Lord Carteret's soft blue eyes twinkled warmly. "Devoted to his wife and children. I must confess I was concerned he would be unhappy that Lydia has given him another daughter. He had so wanted an heir. But I don't believe he could be any happier."

"That is good news. I believe Caroline and Staveley plan to visit them

30

later this summer. I admit I am anxious to see little Laurel myself."

"Ah." Carteret smiled. "She looks just like her mother. Blue eyes and light red hair."

Out of nowhere, a boot touched the inside of her calf. She sucked in a breath as her eyes flew across the table to land on Kelfield.

His black brows rose with feigned concern. "Are you all right, Miss Danbury?"

The rogue was daring her to say something, which she most certainly could not. Caroline was already suspicious of his interest in her. She couldn't make a scene and risk raising anyone else's notice. The very last thing she needed was for Staveley to hear something. She'd end up married to the lout.

"I'm fine. Thank you for your concern, Your—" somehow the scoundrel had been able to flick off one of her slippers— "Grace," she finished through clenched teeth.

He smiled wickedly. "Are you certain, Olivia? You seem a bit out of sorts."

She was going to kill him. Just as soon as dinner was over. Livvie glared at the duke, while her foot searched the floor for her missing slipper. "On the contrary, I. Am. Just. Fine," she clipped out.

When his foot found hers again, Livvie steeled herself against reacting, which was very difficult to do. Especially, when he began lifting the bottom of her skirt.

"So, Lord Carteret," Livvie began as she stabbed an asparagus on her plate, imagining it as Kelfield's hand, "I had the pleasure of dining with your sister before we left London."

~⚜~

How she managed to get through dinner without completely losing her mind or patience was a mystery to Livvie. She'd had to drop her ruby bracelet to the floor when it was time to depart, so that she could snatch her slipper from under the middle of the table. The look of wicked satisfaction on Kelfield's face when she emerged from the depths of the table was enough to make her silently wish him to the devil.

When the women began their escape to the drawing room so the men could enjoy their port, she had never been more relieved. Then Caroline linked her arm with Livvie's and began to escort her down the corridor. "Darling, you seemed uncomfortable at dinner tonight. Are you feeling all right?"

Livvie forced a smile to her face. "Actually, Caroline, I think something at dinner didn't agree with me." *Or someone.* "I think I'll retire for the evening."

Caroline touched her hand to Livvie's brow. "It's so unusual for you to be under the weather, darling. Is there anything I can do?"

Livvie shook her head. "I'm sure I'll feel better after a good night's rest."

Then she continued down the hallway and up the stairs towards her room. At least she could get some peace in the safety of her own chamber. However, as she rounded a corner, she stopped in her tracks. A dark figure stepped out of the shadows, staring at her.

Kelfield.

He stood tall and strong, blocking her path and Livvie narrowed her eyes on the scoundrel. He was clearly trying to intimidate her, and she had endured enough at his hands for the evening—thank you, very much. So she stalked towards him, intent on showing the powerful, handsome, maddening duke that he had absolutely no effect on her at all.

"*You* are an abysmal conversationalist," she complained and tried to slide past him in the corridor, but his strong arm stretched out in front of her and he trapped her against the wall—just like he had done earlier with his wardrobe. The duke quietly stepped closer to her and as Livvie inhaled his sandalwood scent, she had to tilt her head back to see him. He was intoxicating. Blast him!

"You were spotted," he whispered, "leaving my chambers this afternoon, sweetheart."

He was lying. If that had been true, Staveley would have pulled her aside and informed her that, no matter how much she disliked the idea, she was about to marry the brutish man who was currently holding her hostage. "How dare you?" Livvie asked, swatting at his hands which had dropped to her waist.

"As my wife," he drawled, "you'll learn I am quite daring."

Livvie glared at him. "We've been through this, Your Grace. *I* am marrying Major Moore, and—"

"Yes, but that was before Carteret accosted me while I was playing billiards and demanded to know what I was doing with you in my room earlier today. Then my old friend threatened to go to Staveley with the details."

Lord Carteret? Livvie felt the color drain from her face. Her mortification was now complete. She'd always had the utmost respect for the earl, and to know that he believed that she and the duke had... Well, for him to believe that she and the duke had done the things she witnessed earlier was quite disturbing. Heavens! She'd sat next to the man at dinner. He must believe the absolute worst about her, and her stomach roiled at just the thought.

"Then why hasn't he said something to Staveley?" she asked in a very small voice.

"He came to me first. He wanted to give me the chance to explain..."

Explain! Thank Heavens! Relief washed over Livvie. Kelfield was just toying with her. He didn't have any desire to be married to her, he didn't even like her. He was just punishing her for being in his room in the first place. Torturing her, just like he'd done at dinner. "And what did you tell him?" she asked tartly.

"I asked him to hold off on speaking to Staveley...for the time being."

"For the time being? You could have just told him the truth and then—"

"And then I wouldn't have anything to hold over you. I'm discovering that I enjoy that quite a bit." He grinned down at her with such a devilish twinkle in his silver eyes that Livvie had to take a deep breath.

The rogue! Her face heated up again and she darkened her scowl upon him. "I don't know what you're after, but I'll go to Staveley myself and tell him, and—"

"And?" the wicked duke prompted with a raised brow. "He made it quite clear to me, and I'm sure to you as well, that if *anyone* had seen anything I'd be leg-shackled to you in the blink of an eye."

"What a charming term!"

He lowered his head and his grin grew more rakish. "Indeed. I am currently envisioning shackling *your* legs to my bed and ravishing you."

Livvie sucked in a surprised breath. Then she stared at him in complete bewilderment. After all, what did a proper young lady say to such a ribald statement made by such a debauched man? Then there was a tiny little part of her that was titillated by the suggestion—not that she

33

would ever admit that to another living soul, as long as she lived. "You are reprehensible."

"Don't worry, sweetheart, you'll get used to me after twenty or so years of marriage."

She couldn't image a worse fate. "I-I'm not marrying you. No matter what Staveley says, or anyone else for that matter."

"No?" he asked with a feigned innocence.

"No." Livvie started to feel a bit more in control, and she pushed at his chest.

A serious look settled on his face. "Maybe we can come to some sort of agreement then."

Agreement? What sort of agreement? Livvie thought she'd agree to just about anything if it meant she wouldn't have to marry this wicked, wicked man. "What do you want from me?"

"I'm sure I can convince Carteret to keep his mouth closed, if—"

"Oh! Thank you, Your Grace!" she gushed, hoping that he had at least one gentlemanly bone in his body.

But, of course, he didn't.

"On two conditions."

Livvie gulped. *Two* conditions? She wasn't certain she could live with *one* condition he would come up with.

"The first, sweetheart, is my name. You will always call me Alex—not Your Grace, not Kelfield, *not* something derogatory—"

Was he mad? To do so would completely ruin her, and she shook her head. "Absolutely not!"

"But Alex, no matter what and no matter who you are talking to. If you refer to me by any other name or term, and I learn of it, I will tell Staveley what Carteret witnessed myself."

Livvie's mouth fell open. Never in her twenty years had she dealt with such an arrogant, heavy-handed, controlling man.

When she simply stared at him, Kelfield continued, "And second, after everyone has retired for the evening, you will leave your room and join me in mine. You do still remember its location, I'm sure."

Suddenly calling the scoundrel 'Alex' didn't seem so difficult anymore—much better than meeting him for an assignation. She stared at him in complete, astounded wonder. How could he even think of asking such a thing of her? "I'll talk to Lord Carteret myself and explain what happened, and — "

He started to laugh, which was most frustrating. "And who do you think he'll believe, Olivia? The man's known me for longer than you've been alive. Besides there's my reputation to consider. An innocent young miss would *never* leave my chambers untouched — everyone knows that, most especially Carteret."

"Oh?" she asked with indignation. "I will not give you my virtue and be ruined in reality."

"I've not asked for your virtue, Olivia. Only your company."

She stamped her foot in anger. "Why are you doing this? Why are you so intent on punishing me?"

He leaned forward and brushed a gentle kiss across her brow, which didn't fit with the man she thought him to be at all, and she couldn't help but shiver.

"I'm simply playing the hand I was dealt, sweetheart," he whispered. "You're the one who snuck into my room to steal from me and then neglected to reveal yourself when you should have. *You* landed us in this mess. And nothing is free. If you want to be rid of me you'll have to pay my price. You can come to my room, or Staveley can force you to marry me. I win either way."

"Are you mad?" she hissed. "I'm in this trouble for being in your room to begin with. If anyone were to see me I'd be ruined for sure."

Kelfield's silver eyes twinkled. "Then you'd best be careful."

⚜

The look of surprise on Olivia's face made Alex smile. Her pretty hazel eyes widened and her mouth dropped open. That luscious mouth. He had plans for that mouth.

And soon, very soon, he would have that mouth on him... Just not tonight.

The first step was getting Olivia in his room, to have her make that decision, to have her cross his threshold. After that first step, everything else would fall into place. Tonight he intended to learn all about her. Seducing her would come later, when he had more time and had won her over. Until then he would have to be a very patient man.

Olivia glared at him. Then without a word, she tipped her nose in the air and brushed past him down the darkened hallway. The girl was spirited, which Alex liked a great deal. Conquering her would be both challenging and rewarding.

With a little swagger to his step, he started towards his chamber in the other wing of the house. He'd have to find something to occupy his time until Miss Danbury arrived.

LIVVIE paced back and forth across the floor of her room. What was she supposed to do now? She couldn't go to Caroline—not after Staveley's warning. She couldn't go to Staveley either—not if she didn't want to find herself thrust into the unhappy role of the Duchess of Kelfield. And she certainly couldn't go to Lord Carteret. She didn't think she'd ever be able to look the earl in the face again—not knowing what he must think of her. How completely humiliating.

She would have liked to be able to discuss the situation with Cordie, but her friend was rather busy entertaining Captain Seaton at the moment, or so she imagined. Besides, what could Cordie really do other than commiserate with her? And as comforting as that would be, it wouldn't help her find a way out of this mess she'd gotten herself into.

No, in this she was all alone.

Why was His Grace suddenly so intent on enjoying her company? Just last night he was scowling at her from the other end of the dining room table, for heaven's sake. What had changed in the last day?

She felt herself blush as answers to *that* question began to flood her mind. What had changed? Well, for one she couldn't erase Kelfield's magnificent, very naked, image from her mind, which was quite infuriating. As was her reaction to seeing him in such a state. For another, she'd seen more from peeking out of the duke's wardrobe than she had ever imagined on her own. Those images would stick with her forever. And then there was Kelfield. He had changed, hadn't he? He didn't seem to be quite the same man — especially when he whispered in her ear or when he gently kissed her forehead. He was still arrogant. That hadn't changed at all, but... Oh, it was all so confusing.

And now she was supposed to go to his room!

She stopped her pacing and stared at her reflection in the cheval mirror in the corner of the room. What did one wear to such a meeting? After all, she'd told Caroline she wasn't feeling well. If she was spotted in the same gown she'd worn at dinner, suspicions would be raised. And she couldn't wear a nightrail and robe to visit the wicked duke. The last thing she needed was to appear in such an ensemble in front of him.

After several different clothing scenarios filtered through her mind, Livvie finally decided to wear her robe over her elegant evening gown. If anyone saw her in the hallway, she could say she'd gone in search of the library and a book to fall asleep to. Then once she was in Kelfield's room she would be properly garbed in something much more appropriate than a nightrail.

She sat on pins and needles for what seemed several hours, though it couldn't really have been that long, until she felt certain that everyone else had retired. Finally, she snuffed out the candle in her room, took a steadying breath, and then stealthily began the path that led to Kelfield's door.

Livvie looked over her shoulder as she turned down the final corridor, making sure that no one saw her. When she came to Kelfield's room, she glanced around one last time then pushed open his door and snuck inside, her heart pounding viciously in her chest.

The duke, who was reclining on his bed with a book and a pair of spectacles, quirked one black eyebrow upwards at her entrance. "I take it the coast is clear."

"Oh, shush," she hissed, undoing her robe and throwing it at his head.

He caught the silk wrapper and laughed, a rich sound that sent shivers down Livvie's spine. She wished her heart would return to its normal pace and that he wasn't quite so handsome in his shirt sleeves and form-fitting trousers. The image brought back to mind his splendid, naked form she had admired earlier in the day, stinging her cheeks with a blush. "You're the one who forced me to come here in the first place."

He removed his wire-rimmed glasses, stood up, and made his way to a small sideboard, where he poured a healthy amount of wine into a goblet. Then he lazily crossed the room, offering the cup to her. "Here, sweetheart."

Was it poisoned? Ridiculous as that seemed, she didn't trust him at all. Livvie shook her head. "No, thank you."

The duke pushed the goblet into her hands with a rakish grin. "Go on, Olivia. It will help calm your nerves."

No, it wasn't poisoned. He wouldn't kill her. He planned to disgrace her instead, she was certain. Hating him, she took a long sip of the wine and glared at him over the goblet.

"Not all in one gulp, sweetheart."

Her glare darkened.

She had abided by his requests... Well, she hadn't yet called him Alex. But she had come to his room. He hadn't demanded any more of her than that. Livvie lowered the goblet and shook her head. "I will *not* share your bed."

His handsome face broke out into a wide grin. "Good God, Olivia. Still worried about your virtue? I swear to you, I've never had to force a woman into my bed."

Well, what did he want with her then? Why blackmail her into coming to his room in the first place? They could *talk* somewhere else. In the middle of the day, with witnesses about. "Indeed?" she asked skeptically.

"On my honor," he answered as he gestured to one of the room's two chintz chairs. "Every one of them has come willingly."

On his honor? Was he serious? She knew all about him, and there wasn't an honorable bone in his body. He had the unfortunate habit of seducing other men's wives, and had even installed the wife of a vicar in his Mayfair home for some time. Nearly a decade earlier, he had started a very scandalous Hell-Fire Club, leaving the better half of Town in an uproar. He haunted the theatre and had taken several different actresses as his mistresses at one time or another. And he had fathered dozens of children out of wedlock—everyone knew that. She didn't trust his honor. Not as far as she could throw him.

"Please—" he gestured again— "sit down, Olivia."

She heaved a sigh and sat, then sipped her wine, staring at him over the rim. After flashing her a seductive smile, Kelfield took the spot opposite her, his silver eyes twinkling. Then he cocked his head to one side, studying her. "Now, tell me, Olivia, who are you?"

She nearly choked on her wine. It was certainly not what she expected him to say. "W-who am I?"

"Hmm." He nodded. "I admit you are a mystery to me."

She was a mystery to him? He thought about her? She would have never believed that. It was flattering in a strange sort of way. "There's not much to tell...Alex."

At the use of his name, his smile widened. "My dear, you can't tell me that. You've captivated my interest since we first met. I simply don't believe that there is nothing to tell."

A gurgled laugh escaped her throat. "Captivated you? Honestly, Your Gr...Alex, you are unkind to toy with me. I know very well that you dislike me. You haven't made much of a secret of it."

He frowned at her and his eyes darkened to a deep gray. "You think I *dislike* you?"

Livvie chewed her bottom lip. He didn't seem terribly happy anymore. She nodded once.

"I don't know what gave you that idea, but I do like you. Far better than I should."

"You do?"

His brow rose and his sinful smile returned to his lips. "Today, when you were hiding in here, the things you saw... Did your temperature rise? Did you imagine that it was *you* I was kissing? *You* I was touching?"

She couldn't believe he asked her that! Of all the inappropriate things to say! But most disturbingly—how did he know? She shook her head, admitting nothing. "Of course not!"

With a chuckle, he shrugged. "Pity. Because it was you *I* was imagining, Olivia."

Her mouth fell open and she blinked at him, unsure if she'd heard him correctly.

"Since we first met, I have wanted to touch you. Taste you. But you were the forbidden fruit—under Staveley's care. Off limits for me."

"Oh," was all she could manage. Her temperature was certainly starting to rise now. She stared at him, looking so devastatingly handsome, like a Greek God, and her breath rushed out of her.

After a moment, he leaned back in his chair, though his seductive smile remained firmly in place. "So, humor me, sweetheart. Who are you?"

Livvie took another sip of wine, grateful now that he'd forced the drink on her. When she lowered the goblet, his eyes were still on her. "I...um... Well, I am from Papplewick," she nervously blurted out, as if it was supposed to mean something. She sounded like a fool, she was certain.

"Nottinghamshire?"

No one ever knew where Papplewick was, and Livvie smiled. "Yes. You've not been there?" She would have heard if the wicked Duke of Kelfield had entered the village. The news would have been on everyone's tongues.

"No," he admitted. "I simply know my geography. It's required of all dukes, you know."

Another laugh escaped Livvie and she shook her head. "No, I had no idea it was a requirement. I do hope Prinny doesn't discover that the young Duke of Prestwick couldn't find Papplewick on a map."

A charming smile lit up his face, and Livvie's heart beat faster. It was such a shame the man was so handsome, so wicked, and so arrogant. And it was a dreadful shame that merely sitting across from him made Livvie's belly feel all fluttery.

"Poor Prestwick. I promise not to reveal his secret. Though he is just a boy. I'm certain Prinny wouldn't strip the child of his title. Not yet anyway."

"I'm relieved to hear it."

"So, you're from Papplewick? Small village."

Livvie grinned, starting to feel more at ease in his presence. "Indeed. However, there were plenty of amusements to keep my interest."

"Such as?" he asked with a raised brow.

"Sherwood Forest for one." Livvie sighed as memories from her childhood rushed into her mind. "Cordie and I would take turns playing Maid Marion, while Philip, Russell, Tristan, and Gregory would act out the roles of Robin Hood, The Sheriff, Prince John and Little John. We'd play for hours."

"Philip?" the duke asked, his smile having vanished. "Your Major Moore?"

Livvie immediately sobered up and nodded. "Yes. I've known Philip all my life."

Kelfield seemed to make note of that and then he edged forward in his chair. "And Cordie? Do you mean Miss Avery?"

Livvie's smile returned to her face. "The Averys were our closest neighbors. Cordelia and I have grown up together. We went off to girls' school together, and we enjoyed our come out seasons together." Then she laughed, thinking about all their wonderful times. It was a good thing they were such good friends, since their parents always forced them together. Life would have been very different if they'd not gotten along. "Cordie is the youngest of five, and I'm an only child. But I never lacked for sibling interactions. Her brothers Gregory, Russell, and Tristan always treated me as if I was another little sister. Do you have any siblings, Alex?"

⚜

Probably. Just none that he knew of. Besides, Alex didn't want to think about his familial relations, let alone speak of them. He shook his head. "No."

In the reflection of the candlelight, Olivia's eyes danced as she spoke of her childhood. Games that she, the Avery children, and that damned Philip Moore had played together. She was enchanting. There was a little lilt to her voice as she spoke about her past, and the dimple in her left cheek was more pronounced.

Alex longed to brush his hand across her cheek, taste that dimple with his tongue. The longer he sat with her, the more certain he was that she would make him a splendid duchess in so many ways.

This wasn't the path he'd ever supposed he would take, forced into marriage, but since circumstances had conspired against him, he was very fortunate Olivia had been the one hiding in his wardrobe and not one of her silly friends. Life with any of the others would have been unbearable, but with Olivia...well, with her he was looking forward to their future.

As she relaxed and opened up, time flew by. He learned all sorts of things about his future bride. She enjoyed the pianoforte, but was abysmal with watercolors—or so her childhood governess had informed her. She did reasonably well with history, but was not terribly proficient with a needle and thread. "All thumbs," she'd said. She loved horses, but was afraid of dogs. "I was simply terrified," she confessed. "If Philip hadn't been there, I'm certain the hound would have torn me to shreds—"

A look of devotion crossed her face as she spoke of Philip Moore, and Alex felt a stab of jealousy. Damn the man for knowing her as a child. It wasn't fair to the rest of the population as a whole or to him individually.

"The thing was rabid," she went on to explain, "and it had to be put down. And I know it's silly, but I've never conquered my fear of dogs since. It is the one thing that makes life at Staveley House difficult."

That's right. Staveley's son had a small beagle. Whenever Alex would visit, the blasted dog would try to make a snack of his boots. "Nelson?" he asked.

She nodded her head. "I know he's just a little fellow, and it is silly. I know it is. But that dog absolutely terrifies me."

Alex made a note to keep every hound he owned locked securely in his kennels. In his home, she'd fear nothing and he'd always keep her safe. Major Moore's services were *not* needed.

Olivia covered a yawn with her delicate hand. "Alex, it is very late. May I please return to my room?"

He rose and offered her his hand. When she touched him, desire shot straight to his groin. He was even more enchanted with Olivia Danbury than he had been when the evening began. "Indeed. It is late."

He led her towards the door and then stopped. He'd meant only to learn about her this evening, but now he needed a kiss. Just one, to make his dreams bearable. Alex, slid his arm around Olivia's waist and anchored her to him, holding her lithe body pressed against his. "Has the esteemed Major Moore ever kissed you, sweetheart?" he whispered.

Surprise reflected in her hazel eyes, then she shook her head, pushing gently at his chest. "That's not really your concern, Alex."

"Has he?"

Olivia met his eyes and then nodded. "Of course."

"And was it good?" he asked softly, though he knew she could hear him clearly.

"I-I," she stammered, swallowing nervously.

"Did his kiss make your toes curl, Olivia? Did it make you ache for his touch? Or was it a very chaste kiss from a very chaste man?"

Even in the darkened room, Alex could see a blush creep up her lovely neck. "I think," he whispered across her lips, "that before you marry Moore or anyone else, you should be properly kissed at least once."

Then he slowly pressed his lips to hers. She trembled in his arms, and Alex silently celebrated when a soft moan escaped her throat. He nibbled at her bottom lip, coaxing her to open for him. When she did, his tongue slid inside the heaven of her mouth, flicking against her tongue.

She tasted better than he'd imagined, like sweet wine and innocence. Her soft lilac scent tickled at his nose, and he was lost to her.

When she moaned a little louder, more urgently, her hands slid up his chest, searing him until they settled on his shoulders. Alex deepened his kiss, hoping to assuage the need she stoked in him, wanting to breathe her in and never let her go. He splayed his hand across her back, molding her against him, and when her tongue softly touched his bottom lip, he thought his cock would burst right out of his trousers.

Olivia twirled the hair at the base of his neck around her finger, panting as Alex delved back inside her mouth. He could take her now, make her his in every way. But he'd told her that her virtue would be safe, at least for tonight. However, she'd be a lot easier to walk away from if her tongue didn't dance so seductively with his.

Alex moved his hands to her shoulders and eased her away from him. Her eyes flickered open and she stared at him in complete shock, which did quite a nice thing for his confidence. He smiled and caressed her bottom lip with the pad of his finger. "I don't think I can let you marry Major Moore, sweetheart."

She stumbled backwards and shook her head. "This...I...i-it was a mistake."

But it didn't feel like a mistake, not to either of them—he could see it in her eyes. Alex took a step towards her, but she backed away, shaking her head. "Stay where you are." Then she edged towards the door, turned the knob, and bolted.

It was for the best. For now, anyway. He was going to marry the girl. Despite her eager kiss, it was obvious that she was innocent. Alex planned to keep her that way until their wedding night. He could only go so far until then, or at least until she agreed to marry him—his resolve was only so strong where she was concerned.

He turned back to his bed and smiled. There on his pillow was her discarded, frilly pink robe that she'd thrown at him. Alex brought the soft silk wrapper up to his nose and inhaled. Lilacs. He closed his eyes and smiled to himself.

⚜

When Livvie made it back to her room, her heart was nearly pounding out of her chest. She had no idea what in the world had come over her. Never in her life had she pressed herself against a man like a wanton. Not once. Not even with Philip, whose soft kisses had never affected her the way Alex's heated one had.

As soon as his lips touched hers, a frisson of desire race through Livvie, finally settling low in her belly, pooling inside her. Just thinking about it had the same effect on her now.

He was addictive. That was the only explanation. He must have that effect on most women, if even half the tales about him were true—which she now believed wholeheartedly. The man knew how to kiss and touch and turn her brain to complete mush.

There was only one thing to do. She needed to stay as far away from him as possible. She couldn't trust herself around him. That was abundantly clear. So she needed to keep the temptation of him at a safe distance. Australia seemed a fair distance. And she needed to get him off her mind or she'd never get to sleep. She began to recite old nursery rhymes over and over to keep him from planting himself in her thoughts.

Olivia threw off her dress and slipped under her bed linens. But when she closed her eyes, she could feel him holding her captive in his strong arms, inhaling his breath.

Then out of nowhere the memory of the maid popped into her mind and she squirmed unconsciously. Alex had kissed the woman's bare breast, but he'd thought of her. She desperately wanted to know if having his mouth on her would feel as heavenly as she imagined.

She recited more nursery rhymes, and prayed that slumber would somehow find her.

Seven

ALEX rose early. After another uncomfortable slumber filled with nightmares of his past, he was eager to start the day and wipe them from his mind. The dreams hadn't come to him in years, but ever since he'd arrived at Prestwick Chase they had returned full-force to torment him. Perhaps it was because the estate reminded him of Everett Place. Not that the reason mattered. They'd stay with him until they left again, his dark memories haunting him in the dead of night. His midnight conversation with Olivia had been his only respite.

After a bath and his morning ablutions, he opened his wardrobe and his eyes fell to his midnight blue waistcoat—the one missing a gold button—and he smiled to himself. He ought to make Olivia return to his room to sew the button back on. Then he remembered her saying she was all thumbs when it came to needles and thread. There was no point in destroying a perfectly good waistcoat. He'd just have to think of something else.

He quickly dressed in a pair of buff doeskin breeches, a crisp white linen shirt, and a chocolate brown jacket. Then he strode to the breakfast room. Once there, he found Staveley and Caroline just finishing their meal. The sight of this particular duo put a bit of damper on his exuberance. He would have to be careful how he went about in front of them. "Good morning," he drawled.

Staveley dabbed his lips with his napkin, then smiled. "Alex, I was just on my way to the library."

Not that this was a surprise. The man practically lived in his own library in Curzon Street. "A new set of old tomes awaits your perusal?" he asked as he filled a plate at the sideboard.

"Indeed." Staveley nodded as he rose from his seat. Then he dropped a kiss on his wife's head and squeezed her shoulder. "Do try not to get into any trouble, my love."

Caroline grinned up at him, her hazel eyes sparkling. "Staveley, you make me sound like a child. I do *not* get into trouble."

Alex snorted at that and slid into a spot opposite the troublesome viscountess, who shot him a murderous look.

"Oh, that is priceless coming from you, darling," she replied with an affronted brow.

"Touché," he answered with a wink. He truly did adore Caroline. She was the exact opposite of Staveley and had kept the man on his toes for more than a dozen years. In Alex's opinion, Caroline's zest for life kept Staveley young, despite his reclusive leanings. The man would be a hermit if not for his meddlesome wife.

As Staveley started his retreat to the door, Caroline called out to him, "Darling, promise me you won't hole yourself up in there for the rest of the day. Your son was hoping you'd play chess with him this afternoon."

Staveley nodded. "Yes, my love. Adam and I have an appointment set for after luncheon." Then he escaped into the hallway.

Caroline turned her calculating eyes on Alex. "Darling, have you acquainted yourself with Miss Avery? She is quite accomplished. Her watercolors are simply inspired and she is such a sweet girl. I'm certain if—"

"You're interfering again," Alex remarked as he sliced up a sausage on his plate.

Caroline pursed her lips and drummed her fingers on the table. "Shouldn't there be some moratorium to our agreement? After all, it's been two years, Alex, and I haven't plagued you even once."

At that moment, Lady Juliet slid through the door, a smile alighting her pretty face. "Good morning."

"Morning," Alex answered with a wink, then turned his attention back to Caroline. "And the lovely Juliet has enjoyed two happy years of marriage. When *she* ceases being happy, we can reconsider our agreement."

Juliet slumped down in a chair next to Alex, glaring at her sister-in-law. "Caroline, certainly you're not trying to renegotiate?"

With a look of feigned innocence, the viscountess shrugged. "It was worth a try. The man needs someone's help, and who better than me?"

Juliet slid Alex a look of commiseration. "It's only because she cares so much about you. And truly, her matches seem made in heaven."

Caroline nodded fervently. "And Miss Avery is—"

"I am not the least bit interested in Miss Avery." Other than what the girl could tell him about Olivia, since they'd grown up together.

Caroline furrowed her brow. "Well, then Miss Greywood is quite a charming girl, and—"

Alex leveled her with a stare. "I will handle my own affairs, Caroline. That was the agreement we made, and I am holding you to it."

"B-but," she sputtered, "darling, it *can't* be Cousin Olivia."

His eyes narrowed on her. Apparently he hadn't been careful enough with his attentions. "I haven't a clue what you're talking about, Caroline."

Exasperated she pushed back her chair and paced in front of him. "Oh, for Heaven's sake, Alex. I'm not blind, you know."

"I'm well aware of that." In fact, she saw much more than he was comfortable with. She always had. Caroline was more perceptive than any woman of his acquaintance, tender hearted and always willing to play the role of confidante—which was a lethal combination.

In his younger days, Alex had unwisely confided some of the darker secrets of his past to her before he'd even realized she'd extracted the information from him. He'd been more on guard ever since. Still, she was a dangerous woman to spend an inordinate amount of time with.

Caroline glanced at him with a look of sympathy, which was unnerving. No one ever looked at him like that. "Darling, you know how much I adore you. I just don't want you to set your heart on Olivia. She's betrothed to her childhood sweetheart and is just awaiting his return from the continent so they can marry. Much as I want you to find happiness with someone, and I applaud your excellent taste as always, Olivia isn't that woman."

The situation was not up for debate, and certainly not with her.

Caroline had promised not to interfere, and he would see that she kept her word in that regard. He steeled his features and raised his brow. "I've been keeping my own council for nearly three decades, Caro, and I will continue to do so. I appreciate your concern, but I'm a grown man, and I am capable of taking care of myself. Thank you."

Most women would be miffed with his curt tone and dismissive words, but not Caroline. She simply sighed and shook her head. "Since there is nothing I can say that will make you see reason, just proceed with caution."

With nothing left to say, Alex agreed with a stiff nod.

He sat for an excruciating period of time, hoping that Olivia would come down for breakfast, but she didn't arrive. After listening to incessant giggling from her three rather silly friends, he finally left the breakfast room. Moments later he crossed paths with James, dressed for riding.

"Hunting?" his friend asked, lifting his crop in the air.

"Hunting?" Alex shook his head. "I think not. My prey of choice doesn't live in the woods."

With a look of chagrin, James chuckled. "Miss Danbury, I suppose?"

"Hmm." Alex turned the corner towards the library, where he was sure Staveley was happily thumbing his way through the Prestwick tomes. Then he stopped and turned to look at James with assessing eyes. He could actually use his friend's council. "What is your opinion of the girl?"

"Does it matter? The die is cast, is it not?"

"Humor me."

"In that case, I think she's a bit young for you. She's closer to Liam's age than yours."

So, James wasn't going to give him a real answer. Well, damn him! There were plenty of men of their acquaintance who had married women with a much more significant age difference than there was between him and Olivia. Besides, women closer to his age were already married or old maids—for a reason. "I'm afraid your son will just have to find his own bride."

"Isn't…wasn't she betrothed to someone else, Alex?" James asked warily.

Minor details. "He left her to seek glory on the battlefield and I wish him the best of luck in that regard. But if Moore had any real desire to marry her, he should have done so before he left for the continent. Olivia is fair game, as far as I'm concerned."

James furrowed his brow and hastened his pace to keep up with Alex. "Are you sure you know what you're doing? She's a lovely girl, but a bit innocent for you. Chrissakes, Alex, she's a lot innocent for you."

Well, of course she was. That was one of her endearing qualities. He had never been tempted to settle down with any of the harlots or tarts he normally associated with. There was a certain sort of woman one dallied with, and another sort one married. Olivia was definitely the latter, and if last night was any indication of how they would go on, Alex looked forward to slowly continuing to instruct her on how exactly to lose that innocence and become his perfect duchess.

However at the moment, he was starting to get annoyed that he'd even asked James' opinion. Apparently his old, hypocritical friend had a very selective memory. "I believe the same could have been said about you, Carteret, when you finally met Bethany at the altar."

Finally, James smirked. "That was a long time ago."

"You were just as debauched as either Simon or myself, and Beth was as pure as freshly fallen snow."

James chuckled and slapped Alex's back. "Fine, *mon ami.* I'll just wish you the best of luck… I'll refrain from mentioning that you could already be married to the girl, if you'd let Staveley force your hand."

So much for not mentioning it. Alex merely shrugged. "I don't want her to have to marry me, James. I want her to want to."

⁂

Livvie blinked her eyes open as sunlight filtered in through her window. She thought she'd heard something. Ah, there it was. She turned her head towards the sound and realized that someone was knocking on her door. "Come in," she called, though it sounded as if a frog had croaked it.

Her door opened and Cordie bounded inside, a brilliant smile across her face. "Heavens, Livvie, are you going to sleep the day away?"

She struggled to sit up and shook her head. "What time is it?"

"Almost time for lunch. And I have so much to tell you."

"You do?" Livvie asked as she rubbed the sleep from her eyes, then threw off the counterpane.

Cordie was nearly bouncing on her toes. "He kissed me."

Last night's kiss in Kelfield's room flashed in Livvie's mind and her heart raced. "Who?" she asked.

Cordie threw her arms around Livvie's waist, beaming with joy. "Gabriel, of course."

Had she been sleeping more than one day? Livvie had no idea who Gabriel was, and she shook her head. "Who?" she asked again.

"Captain Seaton. Gabriel."

Livvie had no idea that was the captain's Christian name. But she should have realized it. She must still be half asleep.

Then Cordie dropped into one of Livvie's chairs and stared up at the ceiling. "Oh, Livvie, he takes my breath away. I've been dying to tell you all morning long. But Lady Staveley said you needed your rest, that you must still not be feeling well." She lifted her head and stared at Livvie. "You look all right to me. How are you feeling?"

That was certainly the question of the day. Sleep had eluded her most of the night. Whenever she closed her eyes, she could feel Alex's lips on hers again and she wished she hadn't fled his room. What must the man think of her? Most likely that she was a foolish child. It was better not to think of the duke. It was better to focus on other things.

"I'm fine." She plastered a smiled to her lips and moved to the chair opposite Cordie. "So the captain kissed you?"

Cordie sat forward and clasped Livvie's hands. "Oh! It was heavenly. Truly," she gushed. "Last night after you retired, Phoebe played the harp, I sang, and Felicity played the pianoforte—not as well as you would have—"

Livvie smiled at Cordie's blind loyalty. She'd heard Felicity play once or twice since they'd arrived and she was perfectly fine.

"But since Kelfield never made an appearance, by the way, I think I have come to agree with you. The man is simply rude beyond compare. He must have known that everyone wanted to impress him with their talents, and he stayed away intentionally. And then at breakfast this morning, he looked at the three of us as if we were some hideous species he wasn't familiar with. The man is quite disconcerting. Now having met him, I am not quite certain what all the fuss is about. I think—"

Livvie knew exactly what all the fuss was about. If he kissed every woman like he did her, it was no wonder they all fell at his feet. "Cordie, you were telling me about Captain Seaton."

Her friend blushed and her soft green eyes sparkled. "Yes, well, after Phoebe and Felicity retired, as the duke wasn't around to entertain, I found myself alone. And since it was such a perfect night I thought I'd go for a short walk in the garden. There wasn't a cloud in the sky and all of the stars twinkled like diamonds. And when I tilted my head back to see the stars above me, Gabriel came up from behind me and slid his arm around my waist."

"That sounds very romantic."

"Oh, but that's not even the best part, Livvie. He whispered in my ear how beautiful I was and that he would carry my image with him when he went back to sea." Cordie sighed and then flashed another brilliant smile at Livvie. "And then he kissed me. I felt certain I was floating in the clouds."

Cordie certainly had the look of a girl in love, and Livvie squeezed her friend's hand affectionately. "I am so happy for you."

"Did you feel like this? With Philip?"

She couldn't remember ever feeling like she was floating in the clouds and she didn't remember her toes ever curling. Philip must have been away for far too long. Shouldn't she remember those things? What if she'd never felt them? Was that possible? Livvie forced a smile to her face and nodded, thinking of Alex's heated kiss instead. "Yes, of course."

Cordie frowned at her. "You don't have to pretend with me, you know. I am awful and insensitive. I didn't mean to make you miss Philip."

Livvie shook her head and then embraced her dearest friend. "Cordelia Avery, you're not awful. And I'm very happy for you. Let me dress and we'll celebrate... Isn't Captain Seaton waiting for you now?"

"No. The men have gone hunting this morning."

Thank heavens. She wouldn't have to face Alex. At least not yet. It would be quite a difficult thing to do after last night.

⚜

"Ah, I didn't realize the room was occupied," Captain Seaton remarked as he entered the yellow parlor.

Alex dropped *The Times* to his lap. The naval office was a bit stuffy for his taste. Still, the man was better company than the young women milling about the hallways. He gestured to an overstuffed chair opposite him. "I thought you went hunting with the others."

The captain nodded. "Aye. Foolish of me. I have sea legs, not a seat for riding." He crossed the floor and sat across from Alex, his back straight as a board. "Anything of note?" he asked, pointing at the paper.

Alex tossed *The Times* to the captain. "Prinny met with more than ten thousand returned troops in Hyde Park." But apparently Olivia's Major was not among them, or he'd be here now. No, Philip Moore was still somewhere on the continent, where Alex hoped he would stay for a very long time.

"Hmm." Seaton began to scan the paper. "And foreign dignitaries as well?"

"Will you retire, with the war over?" Honestly, the man seemed too stiff for civilian life.

"No." The man frowned at him. "Just because Napoleon is on Alba does not mean England's shores should be left unprotected."

Which wasn't what Alex had suggested. Before he could respond, he was distracted by soft feminine laughter coming from the hallway. He looked towards the open door, and caught sight of Olivia walking down the corridor, arm-in-arm with Cordelia Avery. The captain, however, missed it as he was still glaring at Alex.

Completely distracted, Alex rose from his seat and started for the door.

"Kelfield?" the captain called after him.

But he paid the man no attention and quit the room.

Olivia was just rounding a corner in front of him. She wore a soft yellow dress that flowed gently about her slender legs and tempting bottom. He could still catch her, if he quickened his pace — which he did. Then he stopped in the middle of the corridor and assumed a carefree position. "Miss Danbury?"

Her spine straightened at the sound of his voice, and Alex couldn't help but smirk. It was good that he was already affecting her, and he looked forward to their next encounter.

She and Miss Avery turned around to face him.

"Olivia," he drawled softly, watching a pretty pink blush stain her cheeks.

"Yes?" she whispered.

He closed the gap between them and reached for her hand, which she tentatively placed in his. Alex gazed into her hazel eyes as he pressed his lips to her gloved fingers. "Go riding with me today."

Miss Avery sucked in a surprised breath, not that Alex or Olivia paid her a bit of attention. Their eyes were only for each other—his searching hers for some depth or acknowledgement of their connection, and hers begging him not to do this in front of her friend. He reluctantly released her hand and nodded. "Please go riding with me today," he amended.

She swallowed and then shook her head. "I'm sorry. I'm afraid I have plans."

"Change them."

Olivia turned her attention to her companion. "Cordie, I'll meet you in the music room directly."

"Livvie!" her friend uttered in shock.

"I'll be along shortly."

It was quite obvious that Miss Avery did not want to leave her friend alone with Alex, and she kept her eyes level on him. When Olivia whispered something in her ear, Cordelia Avery sighed unhappily, but then left them alone in the corridor.

As soon as she was out of eyesight, Olivia grabbed Alex's arm and towed him into the closest empty room. "What are you doing?"

He closed the door behind them, then turned to face her. She was lovely, and he was dying to have her back in his arms, to have her lips back on his. "Go riding with me, Olivia, and I'll answer all of your questions."

She shook her head and folded her arms across her middle. "I can't go riding with you. I shouldn't even be alone with you, Alex."

"Why not?" he pressed, taking one of her hands in his.

"B-because," she stammered, and waved her free arm between the small space that separated them.

"Because of the connection that's between us? Sweetheart, that's exactly why you *should* go riding with me."

"Do you ever take no for an answer?"

"Never," he responded. "Not when it's important."

Olivia chewed her bottom lip and wrung her hands. "Important?"

"Give me today, Olivia. I'm just trying to catch up. Moore has known you all his life, and I'm just trying to even the playing field, so to speak."

"Alex! I am marrying Philip and last night I met all of your conditions. Please don't make this difficult for me."

It was difficult for her. Perfect. He couldn't help but smile. If she didn't feel something for him, if she wasn't drawn to him, it would be easy to reject him. Difficult was good. "I can't let you marry Moore, sweetheart, just because *he* had the good fortune to grow up outside Papplewick."

"What are you saying?" she whispered.

"I'm going to change your mind, Olivia. I'm going to make you my duchess. Go riding with me today."

She was staring at him, wide eyed, and Alex gently caressed her cheek.

"Just riding?" she asked quietly.

Triumphant, he nodded. "Riding *and* lunch. You haven't eaten yet today, if I'm not mistaken."

Eight

ATOP a spirited mare, Livvie followed Alex's lead into the woods and across a wildflower-sprinkled meadow. He was a powerful man, and he handled his hunter like a master horseman. His sculpted legs hugged the animal's back and his black hair whipped in the wind. He was magnificent. Strong. Intoxicating.

And he wanted to marry her.

Never in Livvie's wildest imaginations would she have conjured up such a situation. Most girls, probably every girl she knew in fact, would leap at the chance of being this man's duchess. The offer was more than tempting, especially when memories of the night before washed over her. She wanted to feel that way again, to have him hold her again, to feel him all around her.

But she couldn't let that happen. She was engaged and she adored Philip.

Unable to watch Alex's splendid backside any longer, she urged her mare forward, and overtook him, sprinting towards another copse of trees.

The chase was on, and he was a shadow right behind her. They traded the lead back and forth under the shade of the woods and the brilliant sun of the open meadows and overgrown moors, until he finally burst past her on a straight away and pulled up at the edge of some ruins. Breathing heavily, Livvie pulled up beside him just as he was dismounting.

"Where, did you learn to ride like that?" he asked with an appreciative smile.

"Philip," escaped her lips before she could stop herself.

Alex easily lifted her from the sidesaddle. Then he lowered her body, brushing it against his, until her boots were firmly on the ground. "Can you ride, astride?" he asked with a devilish twinkle to his silver eyes.

Livvie shook her head as the warmth from his gaze heated her skin.

"Then I'll have to teach you," he promised and gently brushed his knuckles across her cheek.

She took a step away from him to compose herself. What had she been thinking when she agreed to this ride in the first place? That was just it. She wasn't thinking. Being in his presence, she seemed to lose all rational thought.

This was most certainly a foolish an idea. She would just have to regain control of the situation somehow and put some sort of distance between them.

Livvie started towards a slope overlooking the medieval ruins. A crumbling foundation littered the moor that appeared to have been two or three different buildings at one time. A single wall of ivy-covered limestone arches stood as a backdrop against the countryside. Wild orchids of varying colors, cowslips, and bluebells carpeted the floors of what she imagined had once been majestic rooms.

Alex's arm snaked around her waist and she sucked in a breath as he pressed himself against her back. "Running from me so soon, Olivia?"

She turned in his arms and her heart leapt when she realized his silver eyes were dancing with merriment.

"Hardly." She pushed away from him and started down a stony path towards the ruins. Then she glanced over her shoulder, smiling coyly at him. "*Now*, I'm running from you." With a giggle, she lifted the skirt of her riding habit and quickened her pace.

But he didn't follow her.

Instead he stood at the top of the slope, with his arms folded across his muscled chest, watching her with an amused look. "I'll bring lunch down there. I'm certain you're famished. God knows I am." Then he disappeared from view.

Livvie reached the arches and ran her fingers along the vines. What was left of the ruins appeared to have once been an abbey. It was probably destroyed during the Reformation. But before then, it must have been thriving. She lost herself in creating a past for the place. Kind monks. Brave knights. Pretty maidens. The make-believe games she had played with Philip and the Averys as children flooded her memory.

"Olivia," Alex's low voice rumbled in her ear and she nearly jumped a mile in the air, since she hadn't heard his approach at all.

Then he chuckled, and placed a calming hand on her shoulder. "Lunch is ready, sweetheart."

She turned to face him, smiled softly, and allowed him to lead her to where he'd set up a heavy blanket on the ground near a patch of brilliant yellow cowslips.

"Where did you grow up, Alex?" she asked, looking back to the arches.

"Who says I have?" he replied as he opened a knapsack and retrieved their repast: some pheasant, brown bread, apples, currants, and dates. Then he handed her one of two flasks. "Cold well water," he informed her.

"Thank you." Though she was hungry, she was much more interested in the duke who sat next her. He had promised to answer her questions if she came with him. "Where were you raised?"

"Here and there," he answered around a bit of pheasant.

Odd that he was dancing around her rather simple question. Her curiosity was piqued. "You and Staveley met at Harrow?" she asked, taking a bite of bread.

"Hmm," he agreed, "along with Carteret and Greywood."

She waited for him to say more, but he didn't. He finished his pheasant, dropped a currant into his mouth, and stared out towards the ruins.

Livvie turned her attention to the pretty wildflowers at the corner of their blanket. "Cowslips. It's rare to see them in June."

He blinked at her. "I beg your pardon."

"Cowslips—the flowers," she explained, pointing at the patch of bright yellow just a few inches away from his hand. "They usually bloom in April, or at the latest May."

Apparently flowering schedules where not high on the duke's list of interests, because he looked at her as if she had uttered something completely nonsensical. "Do you garden, Olivia?"

She smiled at him and shook her head. "No. But there's a legend about cowslips. Would you like to hear it?"

"A legend about a flower?" He quirked a grin at her. "I can hardly contain myself."

Livvie giggled, but continued anyway, "Legend has it that Saint Peter dropped the keys to the gates of Heaven, and when they fell to earth they became cowslips."

Alex chuckled, pulling a stem of the yellow flowers from the ground. "I imagine they might resemble keys if one was deeply foxed."

"Speaking from experience, are you?"

He winked at her, and Livvie's heart flipped. She reached for her flask in an attempt to compose herself.

As she took a sip, Alex asked, "Do you suppose God sacked him?"

She nearly choked on her water.

"I mean how hard is it to hold on to a silly set of keys?" he continued. "Saint or not, old Peter should be sacked. And why is there a *set* of keys. How many locks are there? Shouldn't one key suffice? "

"I've never thought about it." She laughed, thoroughly relaxed. It seemed like forever since she'd enjoyed herself so much, and he did seem more at ease.

"Wherever did you hear such a ridiculous story?" he asked, his silver eyes dancing.

"I don't know," she confessed with a shrug. He brushed the soft flower petals against her neck sending a shiver of anticipation racing along her skin.

"Well," he began and dropped the stem to his lap, "I don't think Saint Peter will let me in on my own accord. Do you suppose if I hold on to these I'll be able to unlock the gates myself?"

"I suppose in *your* case, it couldn't hurt, lacking in morals as you are. I would imagine you could use all the help you can get."

⋆⸎⋆

Alex threw back his head and laughed. Not many women would dare say such a thing to him. Some might think it. But none would say it.

He was even more enthralled with her, and was very glad that she had agreed to this excursion with him. It was good to have her away from Prestwick Chase and all the prying eyes there. Good to have her all to himself.

He leaned back on his elbows, stretching his legs out in front of him and appreciating how the sunlight hit Olivia's cheeks, giving her a warm glow. He should take her some place warm on their wedding trip. Italy perhaps. Or maybe the Azores. "Have you traveled extensively?"

Olivia looked at him quizzically. "Have I traveled extensively?" she echoed.

He nodded.

"I suppose that's subjective. I've been as far north as Yorkshire and as far south as the Dorset coast."

There were so many things he was going to introduce her to then. "Where would you like to go? If you could go anywhere?"

She giggled and shook her head. "You told me that if I went riding with you that you'd answer all of *my* questions."

"Where would you go?"

"You'll think I'm silly."

He thought she was enchanting. "Olivia," he pressed.

"Papplewick. Now, don't you think it's my turn to ask the questions?"

Alex couldn't help but smile. Of all the places in the world she could go, Olivia wanted to go to her childhood home. She was very different, this future bride of his. Almost his exact opposite. Moral. Naïve. Innocent.

And now she was blushing under his stare. No one would have ever believed that *he* would have a blushing bride. He hardly believed it himself. What a fortuitous turn of events.

"Alex!" Olivia pursed her lips.

"Yes, sweetheart?"

"That's hardly fair. I've answered all of your questions."

"Life is rarely fair," he responded with a wink.

She narrowed her pretty, hazel eyes on him and then cocked her head to one side. "I suppose it doesn't really matter, since I know *all* about you anyway," she saucily bated him.

"Do you indeed?" he asked, unable to keep the amusement from his voice.

"Yes," she replied matter-of-factly. "To start, I know that you have dozens of children."

He'd heard the same thing, of course, for years. But there was only Poppy. The light of his life. The only person whose love he never questioned. "Dozens?" He raised his brow. "I'm afraid the number is a few less than that. Is that the best you can do, sweetheart?"

Olivia gaped at him, but then again she did deserve it. Young women shouldn't go around asking wicked dukes about their by-blows. He stifled a grin.

"No. I also know that you stole a vicar's wife from him and installed her in your Mayfair home."

"Ah. Aunt Mary," he replied evenly, knowing full well that he was driving her mad and enjoying every moment of it. Then he lay back on the blanket, using his arm as a pillow, staring up at the cloudy sky. "That one there." He pointed at a large puffy cloud above them. "Don't you think that looks like a sailing ship?"

Olivia playfully smacked his arm. "What do you mean 'Aunt Mary'?"

With a wolfish grin, he tugged at the hem of her habit. "Kiss me, Olivia, and I'll tell you all about my dear old Aunt Mary."

"You are impossible." She folded her arms across her middle, making her delectable breasts rise, even in the confining habit. They must be uncomfortable in such an outfit, and Alex began to fanaticize about freeing them, making his mouth water in the process.

He needed to taste her again, especially with the memory of last night's kiss so fresh in his mind.

In one swift move, Alex hauled her on top of him. Her nose touched his, and her hazel eyes were wide with astonishment. Then just as quickly, he rolled her beneath him, pinning her to the ground, and lowered his lips to the delicate skin at the base of her neck. She tasted like the sweetest honey, and he wanted to devour her, every inch.

"A-Alex!" she panted, squirming beneath him in an innocently seductive way. "What are you doing?"

He dragged his lips from her heated skin and stared down at her, caressing her cheek with his hand. "Changing your mind."

Then he lowered his head again, this time claiming her mouth.

⚜

Hot and cold danced along Livvie's skin, leaving a delicious tingling sensation in its wake. A delicious desire raced through her, like fingers of lightning warming her from the inside out. She couldn't think. She couldn't protest. She could only breathe in the scent of leather and heat that filled her senses and hope that he never stopped kissing her.

His tongue mingled with hers and stole her breath. Heat flashed along her legs his knee slide between her thighs and left her panting with need. Then his talented fingers trailed along her body, softly brushed against the side of her breasts, and reluctantly settled at her waist.

Livvie was in heaven. A heaven she didn't know existed until now.

His lips were soft but firm as they teased and melded with hers.

"I can make you want me, Olivia," he whispered across her lips.

She arched against his knee unconsciously. She already wanted him. If he did anything else, she'd lose her mind entirely.

He chuckled against her mouth. "Eager, are you?" Then he rose up on his elbows, just gazing into her eyes. "How about if we play a little game?"

"I'm certain your games are dangerous" she whispered.

"Ah," he responded with a wink. "That's the glory of this particular game. You'll be in complete control, Olivia."

"Complete control?" she asked skeptically. After all, he'd taken control of everything, ever since he'd found her in his wardrobe.

Balancing on one arm, Alex trailed one hand up her belly then let it hover right above her breast. "Whatever you ask of me, I will do it. And if you don't ask, I won't continue."

Feverish and out of breath, she shook her head. His silver eyes twinkled as she arched her back, wanting his touch, but not wanting to ask for it.

"Say, 'Touch me, Alex.'"

This was not a good idea. She had lost her mind to even consider doing what he asked. "Touch me, Alex," the words were barely audible.

A seductive smile spread across his face as he lowered his wicked fingers to her breast. The contact was exhilarating, like nothing she'd ever experienced before.

He stroked her, rubbing his fingers across her swollen nipple, making her wish that riding habits were made of a far thinner material.

After a while, he stilled his hand and gazed into her eyes. "Would you like more, sweetheart?"

She nodded her head.

"Or would you like to try something different?"

When she stared at him quizzically, he laughed, rose up on his knees, and placed his hands on her jacket buttons. "Because you see, I would like to taste you, Olivia. But the decision is all yours. You're in control. You can stop now, or have me simply touch you as I was before, or you can ask for my mouth."

Her eyes must be wide as saucers and she hated feeling like a silly child. Livvie swallowed and closed her eyes, remembering when she saw him take the maid's nipple into his mouth. Even then she'd wanted to know what that felt like. "Taste me, Alex," she whispered again.

"My pleasure."

By the time she'd opened her eyes, he'd unbuttoned her riding jacket and was tugging the bodice of her blouse and chemise to free one breast from its confines. She sucked in a surprised breath when he dipped his head and took her peaked nipple into his wet, warm mouth.

Instinctively, she ran her fingers through his hair, relishing in the amazing intimacy. He did more than just taste her. He suckled her. He licked her. He nipped at her very tip. Livvie thought she would come completely unraveled from his ministrations. Then she moaned when his knee inched higher between her legs, causing a maddening pressure to build inside her. Alex simply chuckled against her breast.

A rumble sounded in the distance, but Livvie paid it no attention until the first drop of rain hit her cheek. Her eyes flew open, and Alex raised his head, a self-satisfied smile curved his lips.

He quickly pulled her blouse back into place. "Sweetheart, much as I would love to fondle you all afternoon, we'd best start back or risk being washed away."

Disappointment crashed over her, even though she knew he was right. She breathed heavily, staring up at the darkening sky above them and wished that they had met in a different life. It would be incredibly easy to fall for Alexander Everett.

Nine

FROM where she was strolling the Prestwick Chase gardens on Captain Gabriel Seaton's very powerful arm, Cordelia Avery noticed dark clouds off in the distance. A feeling of foreboding washed over her and she shivered.

Gabriel noticed her reaction and stopped, his warm, brown eyes focused on her. "What is the matter, my dear Cordelia?"

She smiled up at him, wondering how she had been so lucky to have discovered him — or rather that he had discovered her — at this tedious affair that pretended to be a House Party. "Nothing," she lied, and they quietly walked on, listening to the nearby skylarks.

She couldn't tell him. She couldn't tell *anyone*. However, she was terribly worried about Livvie and the approaching storm echoed that concern in her soul. Not even a fool could have missed the heat radiating between Olivia and Kelfield that morning. The air nearly crackled when they were together. In all her twenty years, Cordie had never known Livvie to look at anyone that way.

Not even Philip.

He'd been gone too long, leaving Livvie alone. That was the problem. She silently cursed the entire city of Toulouse to the devil. Philip, along with her brothers, Russell and Tristan, should be home already. Many others had returned from the continent's battlefields. It was unfair that they were still in France.

Unfair and now dangerous, or at least the duke was dangerous.

Kelfield was an imposing man—sinfully handsome, charming when he wanted to be, and extremely powerful in every sense of the word. It only seemed natural that Livvie would be swept up by his attention. Cordie was certain she would have felt the same if the duke was demanding *her* company, and if she hadn't started to lose her heart to Gabriel.

The man's reputation, which had at one time been titillating, was now a pressing concern. Not that she didn't trust Livvie's judgment—she did, or she normally would have. Again the image of the two of them in the hallway that morning, gazing only at each other, flashed through Cordie's mind and she cringed. Kelfield was only concerned about himself. Everyone knew that. And she didn't want to see her dearest friend get caught up in something that was certain to hurt her.

Riding? Why had he insisted they go riding? To get Livvie alone without the watchful eyes of those who cared about her. Obviously. What if Livvie was in some sort of trouble?

"My darling." Gabriel stopped again, tipping her chin up until she looked at him. "You look distressed."

She forced another smile to her face and shook free from his hold. "Truly, sir, I am fine. I was just thinking I might like to go for a ride. Would you go with me?"

He frowned, looking out at the darkening horizon. "Not with a storm brewing. I'll take you riding tomorrow, if you want."

Tomorrow would be too late. She scrunched up her nose. "Then might we go to the stables at least?"

"Are you very fond of horses, my dear?"

Hardly. She'd been kicked by one of her father's hunters when she was as a child after Russell had startled the thing. Ever since, she'd been careful not to ever be behind one. Though she handled herself fine in the saddle, she generally preferred other amusements. "Of course. Isn't everyone?"

He rubbed his chin. "If you were unable to ride, say for months at a time, would it make you unhappy?"

What a bizarre question. "Why should I be unable to ride?" she asked, tugging him towards the path leading to the Prestwick stables. If they hurried, perhaps she could find out from the groom how long Livvie and Kelfield had been gone. Perhaps she could find out if he knew in which direction her friend had ridden. Then perhaps she could start out on her own to find them. Better her than someone else.

Gabriel stumbled after her, but steadied himself. "I don't know," he replied. "What if you were away...say, at sea for months on end?"

Cordie's feet stopped working and Gabriel slammed into her back. She turned her head and blinked at him. "What if I was a sea for months on end?" she echoed, not certain she'd heard him correctly.

A smile flashed across his handsome face. "I'd like to talk to your brother once we're back in London—"

"M-my brother?" She must sound daft, repeating everything he said, but she couldn't seem to help herself.

Gabriel caressed her cheek with his callused thumb. "Only if you want me to. Life as a seaman's wife isn't always easy. Just ask Mrs. Greywood. But... Well, some captains and commanders have their wives with them, and..." His brow furrowed instantly as he looked over Cordie's shoulder. "Sweet Neptune," he muttered in astonishment.

Cordie turned and saw what had captured Gabriel's interest. Livvie was racing towards the house with Kelfield fast on her heels, holding a yellow flower of some sort against his chest. A peal of laughter escaped Livvie as Kelfield reached for her, but he missed. Then the two of them rounded the side of the house, disappearing from Cordie's view.

Good heavens! It was worse than she thought.

⁂

The back French doors were open and Livvie was almost there. Just as she was about to dart inside, Alex grabbed her waist and hauled her backwards into the wall of his chest. He was panting against her ear, and Livvie felt lightheaded in his embrace. "Alex," she giggled, "someone will see."

"Nonsense," he growled and kissed the side of her neck. "No one's around." Then he spun her to face him and presented the cowslip he'd picked during their lunch. "For you."

She smiled coyly and shook her head. "That's your one chance at heaven. I won't take it from you."

"Sweetheart—" he dipped his head down— "you're all the heaven I want."

Then he kissed her very softly.

Livvie was certain that her toes curled.

Once inside Prestwick Chase, Alex left her with the flower and a self-satisfied smile, promising to find her later. She lifted the cowslip to her nose and inhaled the light scent.

Honestly, she would have been happy to spend the rest of the day with him. Riding. Laughing. Chasing. Kissing. The man knew how to kiss and how to touch her. She grinned, remembering how glorious he had made her feel all afternoon. How strange it all was. Just a few days ago, she couldn't abide him at all.

She began to climb the stairs, lost in her thoughts, until—

"Livvie!" Caroline's voice brought her out of her reverie. Her cousin's eyes widened as she descended the steps towards her. "Heaven's, Livvie, you'll catch the ague if we don't get you out of those clothes."

She hadn't even realized she was wet from the ride. Funny what spending time with Alex did to her.

Then Caroline proceeded to drag her up to her room, demanding she bathe and change into something dry.

After she slipped into a simple, pink day dress, Caroline returned to her threshold wearing a slight frown. "Am I to understand that you went riding with Kelfield today?"

"Yes, we had a delightful time." Livvie chewed her bottom lip and then picked up the cowslip from her bedside table. She brought the flower to her nose. The fragrance was still light and sweet.

"Indeed?" her cousin asked with a raised brow. "So much for not encouraging him," she grumbled.

Livvie twirled the cowslip with her fingers, avoiding Caroline's scrutinizing gaze. It wouldn't do for her cousin to start asking her questions she didn't know how to answer. But after her ride with Alex, she had so many unanswered questions of her own. "Do you remember when you said that he was a devoted father?"

"Of course."

The flower twirled faster. "H-how many children does he have?" She should at least know what she was getting herself into.

"Olivia," Caroline began, her voice a mere whisper. "You are playing with fire."

She heaved a sigh and met her cousin's concerned eyes. "I know."

Caroline rubbed her brow as if to stave off a headache.

Livvie pressed forward, hoping that she could learn something about the man. "But I'm certain that everything I have ever heard about him is false. I just can't reconcile the evil Duke of Kelfield with Alex. He doesn't seem like the same man at all." Well, except for the wickedly wanton feelings he stirred in her, but other than that…

"Alex?" Caroline asked with a frown.

Livvie shrugged. "He asked me to call him that." Demanded was more like it, but now she couldn't imagine calling him as anything else. "Please, Caroline, are the ugly rumors true?"

"Some of the things said about him are utterly false, some are exaggerations, but some, Olivia, are unfortunately true. Adore Kelfield as I do, he is a dangerous man."

That was an understatement, but Livvie wasn't about to be deterred. She was certain her cousin knew the answers to many of her questions, and she was determined to have at least some of them answered. "How many children *does* he have, Caroline?"

With a look of resignation, Caroline dropped onto the bed. "I shouldn't even be discussing this with you."

"I know, and I thank you for it."

"He has a daughter — Poppy. She lives with her mother in Bloomsbury, but he sees her regularly and adores her."

Livvie nodded and then steeled herself to hear about the rest of his children, the dozens he was supposedly devoted to. But Caroline said nothing else. "Go on," she urged.

"She's a sweet little girl. I believe she's four now. Pretty thing. She has his eyes and dark hair, but I've only seen her once."

Livvie blinked. "Only *one* little girl? What about the others? The hordes they attribute him with?"

Caroline shrugged. "I suppose it is possible that he has more. I'm not privy to all of his liaisons. However, if he has more than Poppy, I don't believe *he* knows about them. He has always made certain that she is well cared for, and I don't see why he wouldn't do the same for any other."

How very interesting. That was certainly not what she expected. What else had she been wrong about in regards to this man? Livvie dropped onto the bed, next to Caroline. "Poppy's mother — who is she?"

"For heaven's sake, Livvie!"

"Please, Caroline. Please tell me."

"Do you know what you're getting yourself into?"

"No," Livvie answered honestly. "But you'll tell me anyway, won't you?"

"Ellen Fairchild," Caroline finally divulged with a furrowed brow.

"The actress?" The wind rushed out of Livvie. She had seen Ellen Fairchild on the stage more than once. She was very talented. She was also very pretty.

Caroline nodded.

Livvie sighed, feeling a bit self conscious and gangly all of a sudden. Ellen Fairchild for heaven's sake! The woman was a raving beauty. *She* would come up terribly short in a comparison with that particular woman.

"Olivia, darling," Caroline's voice interrupted her thoughts, "would you care to tell me where you were last night?"

"Where I was?" she asked, her heart suddenly in her throat.

"I came to check on you, since you weren't feeling well, but you weren't in your room."

Heavens! She hated lying to Caroline. For one thing she always tried to be honest, and for another, she felt certain that her cousin could see right through her anyway. "Oh…well…I couldn't sleep and thought I might find a book in the library." There. She hadn't said she'd *gone* to the library. It wasn't technically a lie.

"Oh," Caroline replied, still studying her. Then she smiled brightly and took Livvie's hand in hers. "Well, darling, I have another favor to ask of you."

"You do?"

Caroline nodded and her golden brown curls bobbed up and down. "Tonight at Juliet's ball, I'd like for you to keep Lord Clayworth company."

"Lord Clayworth?" Livvie hadn't known *Lord Adonis* would be in attendance. That wouldn't make Cordie happy at all. Perhaps she'd be so engaged with her captain she wouldn't notice.

"Hmm," Caroline continued. "His ancestral seat, Bayhurst Court, is not far from here. I thought it would be good for him to bring his sister, Lady Rosamund. The poor girl is painfully shy and a bit awkward, I'm afraid. But since she should be debuting next season, Juliet and I believe she could benefit from this little event, get a bit of experience with these sorts of things."

Then one would think that Caroline would want her to spend time with Lady Rosamund, befriending her, making her feel comfortable. "You want me to keep *Lord Clayworth* entertained?"

"Do you remember the ball I held in March?"

Most balls, soirees, and fetes tended to blur together — but Caroline's events always stood out for one reason or another. The particular ball she was referring to had caused quite a fuss. All of the hired servants had been painted silver and dressed as scantily clad Greek sculptures — an idea she claimed was Juliet's, though Livvie had a hard time believing that. And the musicians had played more waltzes than was considered fashionable. But mostly the March ball stuck in Livvie's mind because Lord and Lady Laude had gotten into a horrible fight in the middle of the room, with him complaining about her cavorting with the Maruqess of Haversham. The Staveley Ball was talked about for weeks. "Yes, of course."

"Well, Clayworth was supposed to be in attendance, but the obstinate man failed to arrive. I've yet to forgive him for the slight."

"Did he *mean* to slight you?" It always seemed to Livvie that the earl was quite fond of Caroline.

Her cousin flashed a grin. "Somehow he has gotten it into his mind that I've turned my matchmaking machinations on him."

It all made sense now. "Which, of course, you have."

"Which, of course, I have," she agreed with a grin. "But that doesn't mean I want him to be certain of the fact. It will make the next season that much more difficult for me. Tonight he'll expect me to try to pair him up with one of the young ladies in attendance, which means that is the very last thing I will do. Instead, I'd like to lull him into a false sense of security."

Livvie couldn't help but laugh. For years she'd heard men bemoan Caroline's abilities in this arena. They spoke of her as though she were an all-knowing deity bent on stealing their freedom. She imagined *this* conversation would make Lord Clayworth shudder in fear. "You want me to keep him entertained?"

Caroline winked at her. "Livvie darling, *you* are happily betrothed.

That makes you the only safe girl I can thrust in Clayworth's path."

"Actually, Caroline, I know that Phoebe Greywood had her eye on the earl. Perhaps—"

Her cousin fell out in a burst of giggles. "Goodness, Livvie, Brendan would decimate the poor girl." When Livvie stared blankly at Caroline, her cousin smiled and continued. "Miss Greywood is young and silly. She wants a man to fawn all over her, to shower her with attention. That man is *not* Brendan Reese."

When Livvie frowned, Caroline explained, "He is one of Robert's closest friends, you know. And he is unfortunately very similar to my brother in many regards. Stubborn. Rigid. Set in his ways. He'll need a strong woman who can handle him. I would have thought Cordelia was a good match for him, but she seems so taken with Captain Seaton. But no matter, I'll find the right lady next season. And that means I need him to fall into a false sense of security."

"Very well." Livvie beamed at Caroline. "I will keep Lord Clayworth company."

Ten

ALEX was in hell.

And he was fairly certain that Caroline Staveley was responsible for his current predicament—her wink and wiggling of fingers from the other end of the dinner table were all he needed to convict her of the offense. Tonight he found himself in the unenviable spot directly across from the giggly Miss Greywood and in between the bubble-headed Lady Felicity and the level-headed Miss Avery, who continually sent him disapproving glances.

Meanwhile, Olivia was across the room, at another table entirely, smiling and chatting with Brendan Reese, the Earl of Clayworth—a brooding, pretty boy with dark, blue eyes and sandy blond hair. Of course with Olivia's laughing eyes focused on the earl, Clayworth seemed perfectly happy this evening. Lucky bastard!

Alex inwardly cringed before turning a charming smile on Miss Avery. If he couldn't converse with Olivia, at least he could gather information from her dearest friend. "You hail from Papplewick, do you not?"

"Just outside," she answered with a frown.

"I hear it is a lovely village."

He could see Miss Avery's internal struggle. She didn't want to encourage him, but the ghost of a smile tugged at her lips. "I've always

72

thought so, Your Grace."

Apparently, Miss Greywood felt his question had opened the door for her to blather on and on about the Greywood estate in Norfolk — as if he hadn't seen the place a million times, himself. The girl seemed incapable of shutting her mouth.

Though he had a reputation of being rather charming, one he generally lived up to in the presence of attractive females, he was barely able to contain his irritation by the end of the excruciating meal. He had honestly never heard so much incessant prattling in all his days. The ordeal reminded him of the Greek myth of Echo. Hera had punished the loquacious young nymph by taking her voice away, and Alex wished the Queen of the Gods had saved her wrath for Phoebe Greywood. Whoever married the girl would have to either be deaf or resort to Odysseus' remedy of blocking out unwanted sounds by pouring melted wax in his ears.

When everyone began to adjourn to the ballroom, Alex escorted Miss Avery from the table, as she was the only one of the three that didn't drive him stark raving mad. "How are you enjoying your stay in Derbyshire?"

Cordelia Avery rolled her eyes. "Is that the best you can do, Your Grace?"

He nearly choked at her brusqueness. "I beg your pardon."

She shook her head. "You spent all dinner sulking, staring across the room at Livvie. You obviously know that we grew up together, since you specifically mentioned Papplewick. And while either Felicity Pierce or Phoebe Greywood would have been ecstatic if you had offered your arm to one of them, you chose me. So what exactly do you want to ask me about Olivia?"

Alex had to swallow a smile. He did like Miss Avery's spirit. It was no wonder she and Olivia were such good friends. "You are certainly bold, are you not, Miss Avery?"

"She loves him, you know? And she misses him. You shouldn't toy with her emotions."

He heaved a sigh. He didn't believe for one second that Olivia had confided their *activities* to her friend. She wouldn't risk anyone discovering what they were about when no one else was around — which meant Miss Avery was simply concerned for Olivia's sake. That was actually admirable, and Alex's respect grew for the pretty brunette. "Your loyalty commends you, my dear. But your suspicions are off the mark. I do not mean your friend any ill will."

As they stepped over the threshold into the ballroom, Miss Avery scowled when her eyes landed on the Earl of Clayworth, speaking with Olivia and a pretty blond girl. "I suspect even you would be a more welcome companion than *him*."

A laugh escaped Alex's throat. Miss Avery didn't like the supercilious Clayworth either? He liked the girl more and more. "My dear, what could *Lord Adonis* have possibly done to incur the wrath of such a beautiful lady?"

"He's a fraud," she replied, staring at the object of her disdain. "Cold hearted and cruel."

"You know the earl well?" The animosity he detected was deeply seated. Odd. He'd never known Clayworth to dally with young ladies. He generally avoided them like the plague, preferring gaming tables of one sort or another to the company of women.

"I know enough, Your Grace."

"Miss Avery," came the smooth voice of Captain Seaton from behind them. "I do believe this first dance belongs to me."

Alex relinquished the starry-eyed Miss Avery into the captain's anxious keeping. As the pair made their way to the middle of the room where sets were forming, his gaze flicked across the room to where Olivia was still charming Lord Clayworth.

She must have felt his stare, because she met his eyes over the sea of people, and a pretty blush stained her cheeks. Alex winked at her, and couldn't help but grin when her blush deepened. He was just about to walk across the room to rescue her from Clayworth when someone clapped him on the back.

"I've never seen you moon over a girl before," Simon remarked in sotto voce. "It was always the other way around."

Alex growled at his friend. "Don't you have a wife to entertain?"

"Do you know what you're doing?"

He dragged his eyes from Olivia and looked over his shoulder at Simon. "I always do. Excuse me, will you?"

With an amused expression, Simon bowed with mock grandeur. "As you wish, Your Grace."

After scowling at his irritating friend, Alex strolled around the perimeter of the ballroom. Clayworth had monopolized Olivia's attention long enough.

⸙⸙⸙

Livvie tried not to blush from the seductive smiles and subtle winks that Alex sent her way. Which was a difficult thing to do. However, there was a room full of witnesses, and she really shouldn't encourage him. So, she turned her attention to Lord Clayworth — Lord Adonis to the *ton* — and his rather unusual sister.

She had actually enjoyed Lord Clayworth's conversation for most of the night. The man could be charming if he wanted to, he just didn't want it very often. Caroline had been right about the earl — he had been relieved to have her company over dinner, and he was a bit more personable than normal.

She was surprised about Lady Rosamund Reese, however — having never met the girl before. Caroline had warned her that the young lady was painfully shy, but something else seemed off with the girl. Though she possessed her brother's striking features and was physically quite lovely, there was a vacant expression behind her dark blue eyes and she didn't appear to understand much of what was going on around them. She seemed slow, for lack of a better word. This girl would be eaten alive by the *ton*, and this evening alone couldn't possibly prepare her for a season in London.

"Lady Rosamund," Livvie smiled, trying yet again to engage the poor girl, "that is such a lovely gown."

Lady Rosamund furrowed her brow, but didn't say a word.

"Rose, say 'thank you,'" Lord Clayworth patiently directed his sister.

"Th-thank you," Lady Rosamund muttered quietly.

Livvie was, therefore, relieved when Alex appeared at her side just as the first chords to a waltz began. Ever since they'd arrived back from their ride — their eye-opening, delicious ride — she had wanted to be alone with him, as foolish as she knew that was. He made her knees weak and her pulse race. And he was mysterious, leaving her with many unanswered questions.

As he reached out his hand to her, his sinful silver eyes twinkled as if he knew her every desire — and she had a sneaking suspicion that he just might. "Dance with me."

Without a moment's hesitation, she placed her hand in his and couldn't hide her smile. Tingles raced up her arm from his touch and her eyes locked with his.

Alex nodded a farewell to the earl. "Clayworth."

Then he led her to the middle of the ballroom where other couples prepared for the dance. When he bowed, excitement washed over Livvie and she had to catch her breath. He was such a magnificent specimen, and she swallowed nervously. Then she clumsily dipped a curtsey before he pulled her into his arms and led her into their first turn.

"Miss me?" he asked with a devilish smirk.

Livvie almost stumbled, but he pulled her more securely against him. He took her breath away and she blinked up at him. "Don't you think you're holding me a bit close?" she whispered.

His smile deepened, and she felt it all the way to her bones. "Not as close as I'd like to," he answered and pulled her even closer.

Livvie shook her head. "Alex! People are watching us. *Caroline* is watching us."

In response, he tugged her even closer until her breasts rested against the wall of his chest, anchoring her to him with his hand splayed across the small of her back. "I've never let that dictate to me in the past, and I'm not about to start now."

"Still trying to ruin me?" she asked coyly.

He shook his head, his silver eyes twinkling. "No. I'm changing your mind, or have you forgotten already?"

About Philip. She nearly stumbled again—which was most unlike her. She was generally quite graceful on the dance floor. She hadn't thought about Philip since she'd returned from her ride with Alex. How could she have forgotten him? Even for a moment? Her brave war hero, still in Toulouse? The man she had loved since he was a boy?

She *was* playing with fire.

"I can't, Alex," the words rushed out of her mouth before she could hold them back. "I won't change my mind." She shook her head when he frowned in response. "Perhaps if I'd met you sooner, or...I don't know."

He sighed and flexed his hand across her back. "I can't give up on you, sweetheart. Not when you're destined to be my duchess."

Destined to be his duchess.

If only she wasn't so weak willed where Alex was concerned. Until now she'd always thought of herself as someone with great fortitude. But Alexander Everett was intoxicating, and when he touched her, when he looked at her, all her resolve seemed to vanish away.

Now he was staring wolfishly at her décolletage, which flooded her with memories of him touching and tasting her by the ruins that afternoon. Livvie's nipples tightened, rubbing exquisitely against her silk chemise and gown.

"I'm afraid I've been neglectful."

"Neglectful?" she giggled.

"Hmm," he said softly, sending ripples of desire along her skin. "I was only able to lavish one breast with attention. I shall have to remedy that tonight."

She swallowed. Hard. His suggestion nearly made her melt in his arms. But, truly, she could not let this progress any farther, much as she wished it could. It had already gone too far. "Please, Alex, don't say such things to me."

"Sweetheart, I promise that when you return to my room this evening, I won't *say* a word."

Despite herself, Livvie laughed. "You are incorrigible."

The song ended and Alex offered her his arm, which she gladly took. Heavens, the man was strong. She could feel his power though his jacket and shirt. Livvie sighed, wishing she could take what he offered, but in her heart she knew it was a ruinous path. "You'd best return me to Clayworth's side."

Alex stopped in his tracks. "What the devil is going on with Clayworth? You can't seem to get enough of his company, yet Miss Avery can't abide it."

Livvie shrugged, there was no harm in telling him. "The Averys were close with the earl's late wife, a friend of Cordie's older sister. I met the countess a time or two, but I don't remember much about her, except that she was very pretty. Anyway, Cordie doesn't think the earl treated Lady Clayworth particularly well."

"And your association?"

"Oh, well, I'm simply doing Caroline's bidding. She has focused her matchmaking sights on him."

She'd expected him to laugh, since he knew what Caroline was about, but a deep frown had settled on his face instead. "She means to pair him up with *you*?"

A gurgled laugh escaped Livvie's throat. "Heavens, no, Alex!" Then she feigned a look of seriousness, like a foot soldier repeating his orders. "I am to lull him into a false sense of security—being happily engaged and not the least bit interested in him—so she can blindside him next spring. She says any other girl would make him suspicious."

"Are you?"

"Making him suspicious? I don't think so. He seems more relaxed than he does in London."

"Happily engaged?" he ground out.

Why was she not able to keep her mouth closed about Philip? But perhaps that was for the best. Perhaps if she spoke of him continuously, Alex would stop tempting her with his seductive looks and wicked words. "Of course," she answered with a false smile.

He nodded curtly, and then returned her to Clayworth's side. Without a word to anyone else, he quit the room. Livvie was certain a part of her heart had gone with him and she cringed.

⋘⋙

"Well, that was quite a performance out there," James remarked as he planted himself in an over-stuffed chair across from Alex in the blue parlor.

Until the Scot had tracked him down, Alex had been alone with only his thoughts and a smooth glass of whiskey for company. This course he was on didn't quite make sense anymore. What if Olivia never accepted the only path that was open to them now? What if she hated him for forcing this on her? What if she never forgave him for allowing her to believe she had a choice in the matter?

He frowned at his friend. "Performance?"

James chuckled and kicked out his long legs in front of him. "Aye. Are congratulations in order?"

"What are you blathering about, you bloody Scot?" How much whiskey had he had? James usually made some sort of sense.

James grinned at him. "Well, your impending nuptials, of course. With the way you were holding Miss Danbury, it looked as if you'd already married the girl. I take it convincing her has gone smoothly."

Alex picked at an imaginary piece of lint on his jacket, not at all comfortable about discussing his failures with Olivia. He did have a reputation to uphold, after all. "Things are going well." Or they would be, if he could find a way to erase Philip Moore from her mind completely. Damn the major.

"I am glad to hear it," James replied. "The entire situation has made me uneasy from the onset."

"God forbid you be uneasy, Carteret." Alex downed the rest of his whiskey in one gulp.

"When will you make the announcement?"

There was only one way he knew of to keep James from asking any more questions about Olivia. He adored his children. That was his major weakness. "How is Liam enjoying Harrow?"

James smiled. "Better than my first year. It helps that his cousin Alasdair started the term with him."

"He's a very bright boy. He'll do well."

James sat forward in his seat and ran his hand through his dark blond hair. "Aye. I hadn't been back since we were boys. It hasn't changed at all. I remember thinking at the time that it was among the most grand of places."

Alex snorted. "Strangely enough, I remember you saying something of the sort." When James had first arrived at school, Alex had already spent two years inside those hallowed halls, since his father had shipped him off at the age of ten. "Of course, back then your brogue was so thick no one could understand a bloody word you said."

James smirked. "*You* were merciless. Hounded me day and night until I sounded as English as you."

A laugh escaped Alex. "You still don't sound as English as me."

"Jamie," Bethany, Countess Carteret, called from the doorway, "why are you hiding in here?"

The earl leapt to his feet like a boy who had been caught doing something he wasn't supposed to. "Kelfield and I are talking, love."

She heaved a sigh. "You and Kelfield should be in the ballroom. There aren't enough men to go around, and there are some poor girls who haven't danced all night."

He chuckled, crossing the room to his wife. He raised her hand to his lips and kissed her fingers. "Have I deserted you, darling? Have you not danced?"

"James McFadyn, it is not me I am speaking about. But our poor niece is nearly beside herself from lack of attention."

"Well, I doubt that dancing with one of her uncles will make Phoebe feel any better, Beth."

Alex cringed. He couldn't imagine having to dance with Phoebe Greywood. They'd have to lock him up in Bedlam afterwards. It was best to keep quiet, so Beth wouldn't volunteer him for the chore. Perhaps she'd even forget about him entirely. He held his breath.

"Nevertheless, Jamie, do dance with the girl. Her spirits are so low."

Bethany started to drag James from the parlor, but he threw back a look over his shoulder to Alex. "Kelfield, if I have to go, so do you."

"Where is that decreed?" Alex protested, annoyed that Beth was now looking in his direction.

"The law of friendship. Besides, I'm sure Miss Danbury misses your company."

That Alex wasn't certain of, but he followed the Carterets anyway.

Music filtered down the corridor and it grew louder as they approached the imposing doors of the Prestwick ballroom. As soon as he stepped inside, he caught sight of Olivia. She was dancing the quadrille with some young fellow, a joyful smile alighting her face.

He *had* to convince her to marry him before it was too late. Before she realized she didn't have a choice.

His time was running out.

Eleven

ALEX stalked into his room. The evening had been tedious to say the least. How everyone else could dance and chat about inanities all evening, he had no idea. Despite his title, he just wasn't meant to spend too much time in polite society — doing so always left him irritable. The only bright spot of the night was when he'd held Olivia in his arms. Her smile could light up an entire room. Just being in her presence made him feel like a young buck again, until some reference to Major Moore popped up and his sun came crashing down.

He tore off his cravat and dropped it to the floor at his feet, then he shrugged out of his jacket. When he opened his wardrobe, a bit of pink silk at the bottom caught his eye. Olivia's wrapper. It was still where he tossed it earlier this morning, so that the maid assigned to his room wouldn't notice it and get all the servants' tongues wagging in speculation about who the evil duke's midnight guest might have been.

Alex sank down to his haunches and lifted the soft silk to his nose. It still smelled like lilacs. He smiled, remembering the look of fire in her eyes when she'd thrown it at him the night before. He did enjoy her spirit.

It was too bad he hadn't been able to convince her to return to his room this evening. After all, she wasn't immune to his touch, and he would rather enjoy trying again to convince her to marry him without the watchful eyes of the other guests.

She probably should have her wrapper back. It was ungentlemanly of him to keep it. In fact, he probably should return right it now. This very moment.

A wicked smile spread across his face.

⚜

Livvie sailed into her room and nearly collapsed onto one of the chairs. The last several hours had been quite tiring. When she wasn't dancing, she was keeping Clayworth company—but the rest of the evening she'd been haunted by the look on Alex's face when he'd quit the ballroom. It said a million different things and yet nothing, all at once. Though he eventually returned, he seemed agitated and hadn't approached her again. Perhaps Caroline had been right. Perhaps she had the power to break his heart. The idea was like a dagger to her own.

She removed the pins from her hair, lost in her thoughts about the predicament she was in. It was all so confusing, and she wasn't sure at all how it had even happened. She loved Philip, she always had—but Alex made her feel exquisite things she'd never experienced, never knew existed. It was a shame they weren't two sides of the same man. Of course, such a man couldn't possibly exist except in novels.

A soft knock on her door caused her to sit up straight. That was odd. She'd already said goodnight to her friends and to Caroline. Livvie rose, shaking the remaining pins from her hair, and crossed the room. When she pulled the door open, her breath caught in her throat.

Alex.

Looking more devilishly handsome than any man had a right to, he stared straight into her soul. His evening jacket was gone, as well as his cravat, but he wore a sinful smile that turned her legs to jelly.

She couldn't let anyone find him standing in the hallway outside her room, so she grabbed his waistcoat and quickly tugged him inside. "What are you doing here?" she hissed after closing the door as softly as she could.

He didn't answer, just pulled her into his arms and claimed her mouth with his demanding lips. Livvie was breathless and would have staggered, if he hadn't anchored her to him. She closed her eyes, relishing the experience. Heat emanated from Alex, and wanton desire pooled deep in her belly. She wanted him. Wanted him to touch her like he had earlier. To taste her. To never stop.

She couldn't help but moan when he tilted her head back further and surged inside her mouth. Her hands slid up his very strong chest, feeling his muscle and sinew beneath his crisp shirt. His hands began to move up from her waist, until he cupped her breasts, making her pant and want more. Alex backed her against the closed door, sending tingles racing down her spine. His weight against her, pushing her into the hard door, was exhilarating.

There was also something else. Something that was becoming increasingly more obvious. She'd seen him naked. But she still wasn't prepared for how it felt to have his rather large manhood, hard and firm, pressing against her belly.

She blinked her eyes open. "Changing my mind?"

Alex quirked a grin at her. "Returning your wrapper." Then he reached inside his waistcoat, revealing her pink silk robe folded against his body. "But I like your suggestion better." He tossed the wrapper over his shoulder and scooped Livvie up in his arms.

She gasped and stared at him in awe as he crossed the room to her bed. "Alex!"

"Why don't we continue the game we started this afternoon, sweetheart. You're still in control. I'll stop or leave whenever you ask."

She was somehow on her feet again, and his long fingers were already pushing her buttons through their holes, while his lips brushed against the side of her neck. Fire scorched her skin wherever his lips and fingers touched. Livvie couldn't think straight, she was lost to the feel of his bare hands on her shoulders, her arms, her back—slipping her dress down her body, until it pooled at her feet.

She looked up into his silver eyes and nearly lost her breath. He was staring at her with such desire she thought it quite possible she might swoon.

Alex dipped his head, gazing deeply into her eyes. "You remember the rules, don't you, Olivia?" he whispered across her lips.

She dumbly nodded her head.

"Say, 'Kiss me, Alex,'" he prompted with a gravelly voice, pushing a lock of her hair behind her ear.

"Kiss me, Alex."

He cupped her jaw and pressed his lips to hers, soft and sensual.

Floating in the clouds was an apt description.

Before Livvie knew it, she was on her back, with him hovered over her, his knee once again between her legs. She arched against him, not even meaning too; and he deepened his kiss, running his hands through her mane of hair.

"I want you, Olivia," he growled low in her ear.

Heavens, she wanted him too — wanted to feel his hands on her, his lips on her, his weight on her. She ran her hands up the length of his body and sighed.

"Say, 'Touch me, Alex,'" he said against the hollow of her neck.

"Please touch me, Alex."

She expected him to put his hand on her breast like he had at the ruins, but instead he slid his hand down her leg. Livvie thought she would fly off the bed at his touch, so gentle and warm, but completely unexpected.

"A-Alex," she panted.

But he was still kissing her, and his hand reached the hem of her chemise. "Hmm?"

She swallowed. Hard. "W-what are you doing?"

He lifted his head, grinning rakishly at her. "Touching you, sweetheart. Just like you asked. You didn't say where." He squeezed her thigh, and his wicked hand inched higher. "But if you want me to stop, you just have to say the word," he reminded her and then nipped at her neck.

She felt certain she would perish if he stopped. Glorious spirals of wanton desire raced over her, and she wanted to feel more. His smile deepened as he cupped her through her drawers and she arched against his hand.

Livvie could only blink as he lifted her chemise up to her belly and untied her drawers. Somewhere in the back of her mind, a little voice was warning her that this was wrong, but it was drowned out by the rest of her screaming *yes*.

Alex slid the drawers from her body then tossed them over his shoulder. When the cool air hit her, Livvie tried to pull her legs closed, the first set of panic settling, but he leaned down and kissed her belly. "It's all right, sweetheart."

His hand caressed her leg in a soothing, circular motion, comforting her. Then he slowly moved one long finger through the springy hair at the apex of her thighs. The circular motion continued through her feminine folds, and Livvie thought her heart would stop. She let out a breath she didn't know she'd been holding, and then sucked it back in when his finger slid deep inside her.

Shocked and yet invigorated, Livvie almost sat bolt upright, but Alex's steady gaze stilled her. His movements were slow but extraordinary, as he stroked her in and out, over and over. Then he took a spot on the bed next to her, never missing a beat with his talented fingers, and cradled her against him.

He smelled deliciously of sandalwood and expensive whiskey, and Livvie relished his embrace, the strength of him surrounding her. She felt heady and wild and safe all at once.

Then Alex stilled his finger inside her, while his thumb searched her until he found a sensitive nub. He lightly grazed it, sending sparks straight to her core.

"Oh!" she almost screamed.

Alex chuckled. "That's just the beginning, Olivia. Relax," he whispered. Then he tilted her head back and claimed her mouth while he continued his exquisite torture with his thumb.

Pressure was building within Livvie, and her breathing became rapid, as if she couldn't take a full breath of air. Alex's slick finger slid back and forth inside her, and Livvie writhed helplessly in his arms. "Oh, Alex!" she whispered.

And then...then the world stopped spinning.

Livvie wasn't just floating in the clouds, she hovered high above them, feeling as if she was alive for the first time in her life, soaring through the sky. She slowly drifted back to reality, and chanced a glance at her duke. Dangerous didn't even start to describe the man. He was so much more than that. Livvie wanted all that he offered, all he could teach her. Everything.

She kissed his chest, where his shirt had come undone. Soft hair tickled her nose.

His muscled arms encircled her, holding her close. "Marry me, Olivia." His voice was raspy.

Livvie closed her eyes and took a deep breath, inhaling his scent. Boneless and sated, she didn't want to think about the future, or about what this all meant. She just wanted to stay in the safety of his arms. "I-I need time, Alex."

He kissed her forehead and caressed her back. "Just don't take too long, sweetheart."

~~❦~~

Livvie woke with a start, blinking into the darkness. *What was that?* Then she noticed the large body next to her, which was quite a surprising thing. Where was she?

Then it all came rushing back. Alex and the things he'd done to her. Good heavens, he was still here!

He was thrashing around in his sleep, mumbling something. "No!" he yelled.

Dear Lord, someone would hear him! Panic raced through Livvie and she scrambled atop him. "Shh!" She put her hand over his mouth, hoping he'd wake. "Alex, please."

His body was cold and clammy beneath her, and his agitated tossing and turning continued. Livvie struggled to calm him. "Please wake up."

Finally Alex stilled and Livvie could tell he was awake. His breathing was no longer labored, but steady and even.

"Alex," she whispered, sliding to his side. "Are you all right?"

He grunted an unintelligible answer.

Livvie breathed a sigh of relief. It had been a bit frightening. She rested her head on his chest and listened to his heart pounding rapidly. "You were having a nightmare."

He sat up abruptly, almost knocking Livvie to the ground. "I was not!" he growled.

Still a bit shaken and confused by his tone, Livvie sat up next to him, softly touching his shoulder. "Are you all right?"

He turned his head, scowling at her. "I don't need to be coddled, Olivia."

She instantly removed her hand from him and slid away. Really, he needn't be so gruff. She was only trying to help. "Well, then, I suggest you remove yourself to your own room."

His face softened. "I didn't mean it the way it sounded."

"You shouldn't be here anyway," she pointed out with a sniff. Then she hopped off the bed to give him all the room he needed and sunk into one of her chairs.

He rubbed his whiskered jaw, staring at her. "Sweetheart, we really should talk."

Of course they should. Heavens! The things he'd done to her. Just the memories heated her skin all over. Livvie shook her head. "I don't think this is the proper time or place."

He stood, snatched his abandoned waistcoat from the floor, and kissed the top of her head. "You can't put it off forever, Olivia." Then he stole away into the darkened hallway.

⚜

As Alex headed for his room, he roughly rubbed his face, trying to wipe the haunting images from his mind. Another one of those damned dreams! Though he'd been plagued with them on and off nearly all his life, he'd never grown accustomed to them. They always left him winded and feeling like a vulnerable ten-year-old boy again. God, he hated that Olivia had seen him like that.

Once they were married, separate chambers would be a necessity. He couldn't ever allow himself to fall asleep in her bed again. He shouldn't have done so this time. It had just *happened*. She had been so soft and peaceful in his arms, he didn't want to leave her. Still, he shouldn't have fallen asleep. What a foolish mistake. In the future he'd have to be much more vigilant.

He rounded a corner and ran smack into Staveley of all people. Damnation! All he needed was to be questioned by the viscount. Alex forced a bored expression on his face. "Evening, Staveley."

"Alex?" Staveley's brown eyes widened. "What are you doing up?"

"I could ask you the same question."

His friend shrugged. "Ah, well, my little Emma's been having bad dreams. The child has such a vivid imagination and it takes over at night. Caroline asked me to check on her."

Poor Emma. Alex could commiserate. "How very domestic of you," he drawled.

Staveley frowned. "Yes, well, some of us are. What are *you* doing up?"

"Can't sleep."

The viscount smirked. "I know where Luke Beckford hides the good whiskey. You want a draught? It might help."

"Lead on, my friend."

Twelve

BREAKFAST was a lonely affair. With only an irritable Phoebe Greywood to keep him company, Alex offered a curt goodbye and went in search of some sort of entertainment. As if on cue, Staveley found him moments later in the corridor.

"Morning, my friend," the viscount began with a grin.

"You're awfully chipper."

Simon shrugged and looked at him quizzically. "Well, why not? Anyway, I was just on my way out to the lawn. Beckford has set up croquet course for later in the day, and I thought to scope it out."

"Croquet?" Alex asked with amusement. As far as entertainments went, that was rather tame for the adventurous commander.

Simon chuckled. "Any opportunity to beat Staveley at anything puts me in a good mood."

They were soon on the lawn, where Simon spotted his sister and wife near the gardens watching their respective broods laughing and chasing one another. The commander smiled when his eyes landed on his wife. "Excuse me a moment, will you, Kelfield?"

He didn't wait for an answer, just bounded across the lawn, slid his arms around Madeline Greywood's waist and planted a kiss on her cheek. Even after their many years of marriage, the pair was still very much in love.

Alex watched the interaction with a twinge of pain in his heart, wishing that Olivia had accepted his proposal last night. She hadn't said no, which was a step in the right direction, but she hadn't said yes either. He walked towards the Greywoods and Bethany Carteret.

When Beth's blue eyes landed on him, they grew wide with barely contained excitement. "Alex! How wonderful to see you," she gushed.

The woman was fond of him, but this seemed a little over the top, even for her. "Thanks, Beth," he said dryly.

"Do you have news?" she asked, reminding him of an eager child, nearly bouncing on her toes.

"News?" He frowned.

"Oh, never mind," she replied evenly, though she continued to look at him as if she knew all of his secrets.

"Why are you looking at me like that?" He narrowed his eyes on the countess.

"No reason," she answered too quickly.

No reason, indeed. The little tug of her rosy lips made it obvious that she knew something. Or thought she did.

"Beth," Simon called from behind him, "don't hound Kelfield."

Alex spun around on his heels, and was surprised to see Simon wore the same knowing look Beth did. They were both driving him mad. "What is it that the two of you think you know?" he demanded of his friends.

Simon's lips quirked up in a grin. "Well, my old friend, the word is..."

"Simon, don't you dare!" Beth squeaked and rushed towards her brother. "You'll spoil everything."

Spoil everything? He normally thought of Bethany Carteret as a level-headed woman. Had she completely lost her mind? "Spoil what?" he growled.

The siblings exchanged a look, and then Simon shrugged. "Apparently my sister and my wife have gotten it into their heads that you have an attachment for Miss Danbury—"

Alex fought to keep his expression neutral. He wasn't quite ready to entertain questions about Olivia. It was imperative that he secure her affections first.

"They are convinced that you plan to offer for the girl. I've told them how ridiculous that is, but neither one of them pays me any bit of attention."

He snorted and shook his head. "Well, *apparently* your sister and your wife have too much time on their hands and they are inventing things to keep themselves entertained."

Beth pouted. "But James said…" Then she sucked in a breath, covered her mouth, and turned a bright crimson.

James? The same tight-lipped James who never revealed any secrets? The very same James who had promised to give him time to deal with Olivia? *That* bloody James? He was going to slowly kill the Scottish bastard. What exactly had he told his wife?

This sort of thing was precisely why he preferred not to spend time within polite society. And though he didn't care one whit what anyone thought about him, protecting Olivia's reputation was important to him. She was going to be his wife and he wouldn't see her name sullied, not even by his friends.

"What *did* James say?" Staveley asked from the top of the lawn.

Alex hadn't even realized the viscount was in the vicinity, and he felt his face drain of its color. Damn Bethany Carteret and her big mouth. All he needed was for Staveley to be suspicious.

Bethany smiled sweetly and rushed towards Staveley. "Nothing much, Staveley. He just hinted that Alex would be marrying soon."

Staveley's eyes flashed to Alex's, then they narrowed to little slits. "How interesting. Who is the lucky lady, Kelfield?"

Alex fought to keep his composure and he shrugged, which was quite difficult with all eyes on him. With a bored expression, he drawled, "How should I know?"

Staveley glared at him, mumbled some words to Bethany and then started back across The Chase's lawn. If Alex was a betting man, he'd wager the viscount was in search of Carteret, who, if asked directly, would tell Staveley everything. His last moments of freedom were ticking away.

One of Carteret's daughters squealed with delight, and Alex glanced at the children, chasing each other at the entrance of the gardens. Visions of Poppy entered his mind, and he wondered how best to handle the current situation.

Madeline Greywood watched the children as well. Adoration filled her pretty, sea blue eyes. She was just the person he could get good, solid, unemotional advice from. Alex strode towards the slight blond, his hands clasped behind his back. "Life is so innocent at that age."

"Indeed." She smiled up at him.

"Maddie, may I ask you a rather personal question?"

Obviously curious, she raised her brow and nodded. "Of course, Alex. You know that."

He cleared his throat, never having broached this subject with even Simon before. "How did you react when Simon first told you about Kurt and Kitty?"

Madeline's blue eyes twinkled. "So, it's true? You *do* have your heart set on Caroline's young cousin. I didn't quite believe Bethany when she told me."

Alex scowled. "Apparently James can't keep his blasted mouth shut."

With a charming laugh, Madeline tapped his chest. "Don't be upset. You know he can't keep secrets from *Beth*. And she can't keep them from me. It's all part of being a Greywood."

"Loose lips?"

"I'm afraid so." Then she lost her smile and focused on him, cocking her head to one side. "Isn't the lovely Miss Danbury already betrothed?"

Alex shrugged, and looked out towards the gardens. "Inconsequential."

"Inconsequential?" Madeline echoed. "To you or to her?"

He gazed down at his best friend's wife. Madeline Greywood was unlike most women of his acquaintance. One didn't have to sugarcoat information for her or dance around any particular subject. As an American, she looked at life differently. She was a strong woman with a level head—and she'd actually tamed Simon, which was quite an accomplishment by anyone's standards. "To us both, I imagine, by the time Staveley finds James."

Madeline's pretty eyes widened, and she looked off towards the manor where Staveley had recently disappeared. "I see. And you're concerned about Miss Danbury's reaction to Poppy?"

She was perceptive too. Alex nodded. "She thinks I've got dozens of children."

Madeline giggled. "Oh, heavens. I suppose she also believes you keep women tied up in your home?"

That happened *one* time, nearly a decade ago. Besides it was Simon that had done the tying up, and the women involved had enjoyed the entire thing. Predictably, rumors had spread across Town that the Duke of Kelfield kept hordes of naked women bound up for his amusement. "That particular question didn't come up, and I'll thank you not to bring it to her attention."

Her smile faded. "Sorry. What is it you wanted to know, Alex?"

"Well, how did *you* react when Simon told you about the twins?" *Bastard twins.* Those words weren't necessary. Madeline would know what he was really asking.

She sighed. "It's not quite the same situation, dear."

Not understanding what she meant, he frowned in response.

"In the first place, Kurt and Kitty's mother died in childbirth. I never had to see her or hear about her. But Ellen is very much alive. She's beautiful, talented, and famous, Alex. Miss Danbury will hear her name on a regular basis. It might be a bit disconcerting for her. I think it would be for me."

"But there's nothing between Ellen and me," he said.

"Not now. But there was at one time, or Poppy wouldn't be here," Madeline pointed out. "Miss Danbury will have to come to terms with that. But, Alex, you're hardly the first nobleman to have an illegitimate issue. And since Poppy lives with her mother, it's not necessary for Miss Danbury to spend time with her, or to even know her. You may not want to address the situation at all. At least not at first, in any event."

That idea hit Alex hard in the chest. He wanted Olivia to care for him enough that she could love Poppy, just as Madeline did Kurtis and Kitty Greywood. "How did Simon tell you?"

She smiled at him, a warm, sincere smile that was uniquely hers. "Very poorly, I'm afraid. He didn't mention Kurt and Kitty until we were on English soil."

"He didn't?" The two had met and married in the Caribbean. It wasn't until months later that the pair, along with his crew, had arrived in England. They'd spent many weeks aboard his ship. But Simon never mentioned his children? Not once?

She shook her head, a look of annoyance settled on her pretty face.

"He didn't think it was important."

"And yet, *you* don't think it's important for me to tell Miss Danbury?"

"Your situation is different, Alex. You aren't asking Miss Danbury to raise Poppy. And she already believes you've fathered dozens. I just wouldn't go into the details at first. This I have finally learned after years of marriage, but feel free to ask Beth or Caroline for their opinions. However, I know for a fact there is a lot they don't bring up in front of James and Staveley—Caroline in particular, as it keeps disharmony from creeping up. But I am also equally certain that Simon, James, and Staveley don't tell us everything either."

He smiled at her honesty, one of her most endearing qualities. "I thought you said James couldn't keep secrets from Beth."

"There are secrets and then there are *secrets*."

Simon came up behind them and clapped a hand to Alex's back. "I've never seen Staveley glare, not even at his degenerate brother-in-law. What *did* you do?"

Madeline brushed her hand along Simon's arm and smiled. "I'll leave him to you, my love."

Simon draped his arm across Alex's shoulders. "That bad, is it?"

Funny, Simon was his best friend, the one he was the most similar to, the one who knew most of his secrets; but he was the only one of his friend's that didn't have a clue about what was going on with Olivia. Since his impending nuptials were now a foregone conclusion, he told Simon everything about Olivia, the wardrobe, and Staveley's discovery.

"Staveley's reasonable. I'm certain marriage isn't necessary, especially since she's already engaged. We can all keep our mouths shut."

Alex scowled at him. "Yes, your sister has done a magnificent job of that so far." He shook his head as the two of them started down a winding path. "Besides, I've been trying to convince Olivia to accept my suit ever since it became apparent that marriage was our only recourse, and if she hadn't been compromised before, she certainly has been now."

"So you're to find yourself a married man then?" Simon swallowed a laugh. "I never thought to see *you* in such a situation."

"Neither did I," he growled miserably.

"Oh, come now, Kelfield. You're not indifferent to the girl. I've watched you drool over her since the day you arrived."

Alex shot Simon a murderous look.

"And marriage? Well, some of us find the state much to our liking."

Alex shook his head. "Yes, those of you who had the opportunity to pick your own wives. Not all marriages are as—" he struggled to find the right word, " —happy as yours, James', or Staveley's."

"Staveley's marriage was arranged."

Alex snorted. "By Staveley. You were gone then. He spotted Lady Caroline Beckford, vivacious and full of life, at some ball. He found out who she was, and the next day agreed on said *arrangement* with her brother, Masten, never having worked up the courage to dance with or even speak to the girl. But he still got to do the picking."

"Do you find Miss Danbury's character or intellect lacking?"

On the contrary, Olivia was charming in every way. She was perfect. He only wished she felt the same about him, that he'd had more time to convince her to accept him before she didn't have a choice in the matter. "She's enchanting. Unfortunately, she loves her fiancé. And I've tried, Simon, truly I have, to win her over—to get her to accept me before this thing was forced on both of us. But I've run out of time."

You know, even if most marriages aren't as happy as ours, most are not as unharmonious as your parents'."

Unharmonious? That was a euphemism. Dreadful. Ghastly. Cruel. Those were more apt. "This has nothing to do with them."

Simon's gaze bored into him. "Liar. I've known you forever, Alex. How many years did we share a room? You never allowed yourself to expect anything from anyone, lest you become disappointed. You never rushed to get the post. Never once believed that anyone had sent you a letter or package—"

"And no one ever did," he reminded his friend. Except for once, his first year at Harrow when he'd received word from his father's solicitor that his mother had *died*.

"You never went home, convinced the duke didn't want you there."

Alex didn't want to rehash those terrible years or think about that bastard. Not ever. "I think it is fairly obvious he didn't want me there, Simon. The man never wrote, visited, or sent for me. And as much as I'm enjoying this trip down memory lane, none of it has anything to do with my situation with Olivia."

"The point I'm trying to make, my old friend, is that you judge everyone by your father's measuring stick. Since he was an incredible bastard, you never expect anything from anyone. You're always convinced that people will disappoint you."

"An expectation they generally live up to."

"I suggest you give Miss Danbury the benefit of the doubt. I've been watching her, Alex, and she's not indifferent to you either."

No, she filled his arms nicely, and he rather imagined that she liked being there, especially if last night was any indication. It wasn't her passion he was concerned about. It was her heart, and all the unanswered questions that went along with it.

Moments later, he was summoned by a footman. Lord Staveley requested a word with him in Mr. Beckford's study.

Thirteen

SOMETHING had happened, but Livvie didn't know what exactly. It was rather obvious, however, that it wasn't good. She sat on an uncomfortable settee while Caroline paced a path in front of her. She'd been summoned from her room by Lord Staveley and told under no circumstances was she to leave the blue salon. That had been a full hour ago.

"Please, can't you tell me what's going on?" Livvie asked for what seemed like the hundredth time. Until now, Caroline had quickened her pace when she asked, or frowned, or simply shaken her head—all of which were rare reactions for her loquacious cousin.

Finally Caroline stopped walking and dropped onto the seat next to her. "Darling, why didn't you tell me? Haven't I always been there for you?"

"Tell you what?" Livvie's heart pounded viciously. Had someone seen Alex enter or leave her room last night? Or was she simply anxious and this all had to do with something else entirely?

Caroline frowned. "There's no point in hiding it anymore, Olivia. Lord Carteret has told Staveley everything. Your mother will have my head."

She felt the color drain from her face. "Everything?"

Caroline clasped Livvie's hands and nodded. "He's meeting with Kelfield as we speak. There's no time to waste. And we are very fortunate that Staveley has connections to the archbishop. You can't imagine how many times that's come in handy."

"The archbishop?" she echoed, feeling her freedom slip away, making all of this much more real.

"You don't have time for the banns to be read, Olivia. Too many people already know that *something* has gone on. And he *is* Kelfield. None of us want to see your reputation tarnished. Besides, anyone would believe that if Alex found the woman he wanted to marry, he wouldn't wait for banns. He's very impatient in that way. He'd marry by special license in any event. That does work in your favor."

"B-but Philip—"

Caroline sighed, squeezing Livvie's hand. "There's no Philip, Olivia. Not anymore. I am very sorry... But I am certain that Alex will take care of you. He'll have to answer to me if he doesn't." She tried to smile, but it didn't quite reach her eyes.

Just then, the door swung open, and Alex stepped over the threshold. His grey eyes looked angry and his jaw was set tight. Unsure how any of this had even transpired, Livvie swallowed uncomfortably, barely meeting his gaze. What she saw there chilled her to her bones.

"Lady Staveley," he began, though his eyes never left Livvie, "I'd like a private word with my betrothed."

"Alex—" Caroline started.

"Thank you for keeping her company, Caroline, but that will be all."

No one ever dismissed Caroline in such a fashion. Livvie was surprised when her cousin quietly left the room with a submissive nod. Then Alex stood before her and offered his hand. Livvie took it, staring up at him. Even angry, he was the most handsome man she'd ever known.

He lifted her from her seat slipped his arms around her waist, holding her close. "I didn't want it to happen like this, sweetheart." Then he dropped a gentle kiss on her brow.

She didn't know what to say. She didn't think she could speak without her voice cracking. Livvie simply nodded.

He stepped away from her and dipped a short bow. "I'll see you in

Town."

And then he was gone.

※

Prestwick Chase was fairly subdued after Alex departed. Everyone knew that the duke was destined for Lambeth Palace to obtain a special license, and Livvie felt as if her indiscretions had been bared for all the other guests. Though Juliet, Lady Carteret, and Mrs. Greywood smiled sympathetically whenever they saw her, not everyone else was as kind. Mrs. St. Claire, and some of the other matrons, avoided looking at her altogether. That hurt a bit, as she had always tried to be kind Mrs. St. Claire, who had been a fairly insecure merchant's daughter before her marriage. However, Livvie preferred being ignored by Mrs. St. Claire and the others like her to the looks of caustic derision that Captain Seaton seemed to reserve just for her.

Livvie's friends remained her strongest supporters, and one or more of them always surrounded her, giving her strength. However their constant hovering was also unsettling, as she didn't know how to answer most of their questions.

"Did he kiss you?" Felicity asked, in hushed tones while they played silver loo in the blue salon.

Phoebe dropped her cards to the table, leveling the young girl with an annoyed look. "Heavens, Felicity, he had to have done much more than that for Livvie to have to marry him."

Livvie's cheeks burned and she would have left the table altogether, if Cordie hadn't placed a staying hand on hers. "Nonsense. They're simply in love and His Grace can't wait to marry her."

In love? If only that were true. Unfortunately, it was nothing more than a Banbury tale.

"So then, he did kiss you," Felicity pressed.

Livvie nodded her head, but said nothing else. She didn't know what to say.

"Of course he did," Cordie assured them, as if she had all the answers. "He kissed her when she accepted his proposal. Livvie is very fortunate to have such a man in love with her."

She was grateful for Cordie's defense, though Livvie was ashamed that her friend's words were entirely false.

"I think it's more than that," Phoebe insisted. "My Uncle James said we'd all have to pack up and go to London for the wedding and show our support, to keep talk down. Why should there be talk unless something more than a kiss transpired?"

Cordie heaved a sigh as if she was dealing with the most simple of simpletons. "I'm certain that is exactly what Lord Carteret is afraid of. Kelfield doesn't want to wait for the banns — that's what Lady Staveley told me. He is very anxious to marry Livvie. Therefore, some people will think it is more than that, which is why we'll all go to London for the wedding. Show our support. Keep people from saying things that aren't true."

Livvie stared at Cordie. If she didn't know the truth herself, she'd easily believe her friend's version. Cordie was very convincing.

The entire party set off for London the next morning — a full day after Alex had departed Prestwick Chase. While her young cousins and their governess filled one of Staveley's coaches, Livvie, Cordie, Caroline, and Staveley occupied the other. The tension in the air was so thick, it was hard to breathe. There was very little talking, and Livvie tried to remain stoic, refusing to let herself cry.

She didn't know what she would have done without Cordie, who always seemed to know when she was at her weakest and would smile or squeeze her hand.

Finally, after hours of silence, Staveley turned to his wife. "You'll need to take care of dealing with St. Georges."

"Yes, darling."

"And get invitations sent post haste."

"Of course."

Cordie broke in with a smile. "My mother and I will help in whatever way you need us, Lady Staveley."

It wasn't until that night at an inn that Livvie finally relaxed a bit. It was a great comfort that she and Cordie would share a room, though it was most certainly the last time they would ever do so. She was to be married in just a matter of days to a man she barely knew, while Cordie continued down a different path alone.

Livvie collapsed on the lumpy inn bed, staring up at the cracked ceiling above her. "Why did you say all those things to Phoebe and Felicity last night?"

Cordie quietly sat next to her and leaned her head against the wall.

"Because they needed to hear them, and I won't let anyone ever think ill of you."

Cordelia Avery really was the most loyal of friends.

"Even if the unflattering things they're thinking about me are correct?"

With a shake of her head, Cordie smiled sadly. "Do you love him?" she finally asked.

Livvie turned on her side, staring into her friend's concerned, green eyes. "I-I don't know," she answered honestly. He made her heart race, but it wasn't necessarily the same thing.

The particulars behind her hasty marriage had not been discussed, though Livvie was certain Cordie had her own theories about the situation. She really was the dearest friend not to pressure her in any way, but to simply offer her support. She hadn't even asked about Philip, which Livvie was very thankful for. She didn't know what she could possibly say, and she didn't think she could ever repay Cordie's fierce loyalty.

After a moment, Cordie sat forward, taking Livvie's hands in hers. "He is very handsome, and he does seem enchanted with you."

She was enchanted with him. The way she felt when she was with him. The naughty things he whispered to her. His eyes that seemed to stare right into her soul. But still…he couldn't be particularly happy with this turn of events. Never mind the fact that he had proposed and told her more than once she would marry him, he didn't seem at all like himself the day he left Prestwick Chase. The hardened look on his face still had her stomach tied up in knots, and she wasn't certain they would ever come untangled.

"He must love you very much," Cordie offered.

He said he wanted her. He never said he loved her. And truly, she hadn't expected it. They barely knew one another, after all. She tried to smile at her friend, though her lips started to quiver.

"What's wrong, Livvie?" Cordie's comforting green eyes searched hers for an answer. "You can tell me anything, you know?"

She blinked back tears and squeezed her dearest friend's hand. "It's just nerves."

Cordie wrapped her arms around Livvie and held her tight. They had been through so much together, since they were tiny children. She couldn't remember a day in her life they hadn't seen each other.

Cordie started to laugh. "Just think. In a matter of days you'll be a duchess. I shall have to call you 'Your Grace', and — "

"Don't you dare!" Livvie choked on a combination of a laugh and a sob.

"It'll all be fine, Livvie. It'll all work out. You'll see."

◦◦◦

Just as Alex reached the front step of Kelfield House, his special license in hand, the door was wrenched open before him. His butler, Gibson, a normally pleasant young man in his twenties stood on the threshold, looking quite harassed. "Your Grace! Thank God you've returned."

It was unusual for a man so young to oversee a ducal household, but Alex's reputation had kept older, more qualified candidates from seeking the position. For the most part, he'd been happy with Gibson's work and didn't consider the fellow's age a hindrance. Though at the moment, the butler looked almost possessed and Alex was a bit flummoxed by his appearance. An older butler would have had years of practice of maintaining his composure, despite whatever problem waited inside Kelfield House.

And whatever the problem was, it would have to wait. He had enough on his plate at the moment.

"Gibson." Alex brushed past his butler into the main entryway. As soon as he stepped inside his home, he was assaulted by a childish squeal. Then a pair of tiny arms threw themselves around his legs.

"Papa!"

Startled, Alex smiled down at Poppy, his energetic five-year-old daughter. He ruffled her ebony hair and sunk down to embrace her. He wasn't quite sure why Poppy was here instead of with her mother, but at the moment he was just glad to see her. His daughter never failed to put a smile on his face, and he desperately needed just that at the moment.

"What are you doing here, my little angel?"

Fingers smeared with pudding of some sort grabbed at his neck cloth as Poppy kissed his cheek. "Ellen said I was to live with you from now on."

Completely thrown, Alex stood up and frowned at his daughter. He always hated the fact that Ellen made the child call her by her given

101

name. Though at the moment, he was much more concerned with the rest of her statement. *Live with him from now on*? She couldn't live with him. He was marrying Olivia in three days' time.

Why would Ellen say such a thing? They had an agreement that had worked fairly well up until now — Poppy lived in a little house with Ellen, and Alex paid for whatever they required and then some. He saw Poppy every fortnight or so, lavishing her with gifts and magical stories, but she'd never before come to Kelfield House. Suddenly the harassed look of his butler started to make sense.

"Where is Ellen?" he asked his daughter.

She grimaced and looked down at her feet. "Italy."

"Italy!" Alex nearly roared, then he looked up at Gibson. "What exactly has happened in my absence?"

The butler lost a bit of his color and grimaced. "Well, Your Grace, the Contessa de Vatoni arrived shortly after you left for Derbyshire — "

Who the devil was that? "Contessa de Vatoni?" He furrowed his brow in agitation.

The butler scrambled to the hallway table and retrieved an envelope, pushing it into Alex's hand. Irritated, he ripped the letter open and began to read. Had the world turned on its side since he was last in Town?

> *Kelfield,*
> *I'm off to Italy with my new husband. I'm leaving you Poppy.*
> *Hope you understand that she cannot remain with me in my new*
> *role. Best of luck to you both.*
> *Fondest wishes,*
> *Ellen de Vatoni*

Alex read the words over and over, as if consecutive readings would change the meaning of the letter. It wasn't even a letter. It was a note, and a rather unfeeling one at that. Ellen had married, then abandoned Poppy to him with a few scribbled sentences? He chanced a glance at his daughter, who was nervously biting her bottom lip.

What was he supposed to do with the child? He didn't have the first clue of how to proceed. Oh, he was fabulous at spoiling her and telling her outlandish tales, and he loved her dearly. But to raise her? He was completely out of his element. If Ellen valued her life, she'd never leave Italy.

"You won't send me away, will you, Papa?" Poppy asked quietly.

Alex's head snapped back to his daughter. He couldn't possibly have heard her correctly. "Why would I send you away?"

Poppy's shoulder's hung balefully. "Ellen said you might send me away. She said you wouldn't want me."

Before he knew it, Alex had snatched Poppy up into his arms and held her tightly. How could Ellen do this to their child? And how dare she say such awful things to Poppy? Memories of his childhood flashed in his mind. The hatred in his father's icy blue eyes when he informed Alex he was sending him off to school. It was the last time he'd seen the man. Alex had only been ten. The loneliness that engulfed him as a boy was suffocating. That Ellen would even suggest he would do the same thing to his own child, his own precious Poppy, was preposterous! On second thought, Italy might not be far enough away to keep Ellen safe from him.

"I've always wanted you, angel. And you're not going anywhere." Though what he was going to do with her, he had no clue. But no matter what, he wouldn't send her away, not like his father had done.

Poppy started to giggle. "Let go, Papa. I can't breathe."

"Sorry, my love." He brushed a kiss to her forehead and then put her back on the ground, sinking down on his haunches to be on eye level with his child. "Where's Mrs. Seeber?"

Certainly, her stuffy nurse would have an idea of how to go on. But Poppy shook her head, her raven curls swaying back and forth. "She quit."

Quit? Quit! "Why?" It seemed as though the room started to spin and his head began to throb.

Poppy scrunched up her little face, as if trying to get the words right. "She said something about a den of 'niquity? I don't know what it means."

Alex knew what it meant. The stodgy Mrs. Seeber had been more than happy to take his blunt for years, caring for his bastard daughter on the other side of Town, but God forbid she step one foot in the devil's den. Well, good riddance! The problem was he couldn't even maintain a proper butler. How was he to raise a child if no suitable nurses or governesses would step over his threshold?

And then there was Olivia on top of everything else.

He was at a complete loss. He tousled Poppy's hair one last time and then started down the corridor towards his study. He needed time to think and come up with some plan, but his daughter was quick on his heels.

"Where are you going, Papa?"

"Just to my study, sweetheart."

"Oh. Where've you been for so long?"

"Derbyshire."

Derbyshire.

Olivia.

What would she think about his situation? If he couldn't even keep an overpaid nurse in his employ, what business did he have raising Poppy or taking Olivia as his wife?

How was he ever going to explain this to Olivia? Any respectable, well-bred lady would balk at raising her husband's illegitimate child. Madeline Greywood's words echoed once again in his mind. She'd warned him that Olivia would have a hard time dealing with the whole Ellen scenario. But Ellen was in Italy. Did that change things?

"Are you all right, Papa?" Poppy tugged on his jacket.

Hardly. He feigned a smile for the child and tapped her nose. "Of course, angel. But I need to go out for a while." To figure out what the hell he was supposed to do now.

"You're leaving again?" She pouted.

Gibson groaned behind them, and Alex shot a reproachful look at his butler. Then he turned back to Poppy. "Just for a little while. Why don't you go find Mrs. Parker?" The housekeeper should be able to keep her entertained until he returned.

Gibson cleared his throat behind him. "Your Grace let Mrs. Parker go on holiday to visit her sister in Cornwall."

Hmm. Alex frowned. That was the last holiday he would approve. Maybe ever. Before he could continue, he heard Poppy's little voice, "Mr. Gibson, do you want to play with my dolls again?"

Alex suppressed a laugh when his butler winced. Apparently, he'd have to raise the man's pay considerably, but it was worth it to see Poppy smile.

Fourteen

UNDER the circumstances, going to visit Sarah Kane wouldn't make sense to many, but Alex greatly appreciated her council. She was more than his mistress—she was his friend. But most importantly, she was a woman, and a kind one at that. Her insight into this situation would be most appreciated.

He hurried across Town to a quaint little home on Bedford Place. The home he'd purchased for Sarah was always warm and inviting, just like she was. He breathed a sigh of relief as he stepped over the threshold. This was one place he'd always been comfortable, where the problems of the world didn't exist.

Alex found Sarah seated in her small drawing room reading a script. She was so immersed in the activity that she hadn't heard him enter the house, or even clear his throat in the doorway. He smiled, watching her mouth move as she silently read the lines to herself. He'd seen her engrossed like this many times before. Finally, he stepped further into the room. "Sarah?"

Her pretty green eyes sparkled when she saw him and she leapt from her chaise, dropping the stack of papers in her vacated spot. "Alex! How wonderful to see you." She crossed the small room and stood on tiptoes to brush a kiss to his lips. "How was Derbyshire? I didn't expect to see you for at least another sennight."

Alex tossed his cane and hat to a small chair in the corner of the room and fell onto a settee with an exasperated sigh. "Did you know Ellen left England?"

Sarah acknowledged this with a slight incline of her pretty little head. "It was a whirlwind. The Conte saw her performance and fell instantly for her. They married days later and left for Italy." She gestured to the stack of papers she had been reading. "She was to play Lady MacBeth, but now Henry's given it to me."

Despite his anxiety for his own life, he was happy for Sarah. She had waited so long for a starring role. "Congratulations, sweetheart. You definitely deserve it. Though I think the role of heartless bitch is more suited for her."

She grinned at him and sunk back onto her settee. "That's why it's called acting. But thank you, I think." The she frowned, studying him. "You don't look like yourself, Alex."

He didn't feel like himself, and he wasn't sure if he ever would again. "My life has certainly been turned upside down. Ellen left Poppy. I'm getting married in just a few days, and I don't have a clue how to proceed."

Several emotions flashed across Sarah's pretty face. "Good heavens, you've been busy. Is Poppy all right?"

"Other than Ellen telling her that I wouldn't want her, and most likely I'd send her away—I suppose she's doing well. I cannot believe that Ellen just abandoned her. I'd like to get my hands around her neck."

Sarah smiled sweetly, compassionately, as was her nature. "It could be worse, Alex."

It couldn't possibly be worse, and he glowered his response.

"She could have taken Poppy with her," Sarah explained. "You might not ever have seen her again. I know how much you love her. You wouldn't want that."

His face fell. He hadn't even considered that as a possibility. What if he'd returned from Derbyshire and Poppy was gone forever? He couldn't even imagine what that would have done to him. "I suppose you're right, Sarah."

"You'll manage with Poppy. I don't have any doubts... Did you say you're getting *married*?"

He sighed deeply. "In just a few days. But Poppy—Sarah, I don't know how to tell my bride—how to explain—"

Sarah reached for his hand. "There is nothing to explain. Poppy is your daughter and you love her. Your bride will have to understand. Truly, Alex, she must be an amazing lady to have captured your heart, and so quickly."

"It's not a love match."

She cocked her head to one side, again studying him, and frowned. "I see."

"All the same," he threw in quickly, "I don't think she would understand about us."

Sarah's green eyes twinkled. "Of course she wouldn't."

He hated that she could see through him. "It's *not* a love match, Sarah."

"Yes, you said that."

He chose to ignore her insolence. "Anyway, I want to make certain that you are taken care of."

Sarah shook her head. "Alex, you have been more than generous in the past. I will have my choice of protectors. So, there is nothing for you to worry about where I'm concerned."

The year before he'd had the house put in her name, just in case anything should happen to him. Still, she was a wonderful woman and he would never forgive himself if any harm came to her. "Even still, should you ever need anything, Sarah, you need only ask."

She brushed a singled tear from her cheek, smiling at him. "I will be fine. I know how to play this game, Alex. I've been doing it all my life."

"But you're crying."

A stream now trickled down her cheek. "I'm just surprised is all. It's nothing for you to worry about. I think you've got enough to focus on at the moment."

"Sarah—"

She raised her hand so silence him. "Don't. I will always be grateful to you for finding me at Madam Palmer's and opening doors for me that would have otherwise been closed. You don't owe me an explanation or anything else."

In most men's eyes she would have been correct, but Alex held himself a little higher than that. "Sarah, I want you to promise me that if you are ever in trouble, you'll come to me."

She wiped away the last of her tears and shook her head. "I'm certain that would not make your bride happy."

A self deprecating laugh escaped him. "I'm certain my bride is not happy to be saddled with me. Whether or not you need my help at some unknown date will be inconsequential to her, I assure you."

Sarah studied him again, then finally inclined her head. "Only if you promise the same. If you need an ear or a shoulder, you know where to find me."

"Center stage, before your adoring fans."

Poppy Everett woke up in her new room, the happiest she'd ever been. It was so wonderful living with her papa, and she would get to see him every day from now on, which was what she had always wanted.

After spending her first week at Kelfield House waiting for him to come home, he had completely worn her out upon his return. Yesterday they had gone to the Strand, where she ate an Italian ice, and then they had gone to Astley's Amphitheater, where she watched the most amazing show with horses and wildly dressed entertainers. Then she'd stayed up late while he told her a bedtime story about a princess with magical powers who fought dragons and played with unicorns. It was delightful.

After tucking her into bed, he promised that he'd get her a new nurse with a heartier constitution than Mrs. Seeber possessed. Poppy didn't know what that meant, and she didn't care. Now that she was with her papa, she didn't need or want anything else.

At first she had hoped that Papa would let her keep the room that connected to his, because then she could see him all the time. But he'd shook his head and said *that* room belonged to someone else. Poppy couldn't figure out who that someone else was though. There were only a handful of servants and none of them slept in that room.

Mr. Gibson told her that it was the duchesses' chambers, but there wasn't a duchess. So Poppy didn't see why she couldn't have it, but she didn't want to make Papa angry, so she stopped asking.

Life was going to be different here. Life was going to be better. She didn't have to sit quietly for hours while Ellen read to herself. She could have tea parties on the floor, bang Cook's pots and pans together, or traipse through the attic looking for treasures of one sort or another. She could sing loudly and dance through all the rooms, and not get yelled at by Mrs. Seeber. Life with Papa was wonderful.

After sleeping late, Poppy slid out of bed and fumbled around in the chest that Ellen left for her and found her favorite blue dress with lots of lace. She quickly threw it on, overlooking the rip on the hem, because she always felt like a princess in this dress. She decided against stockings or slippers because papa wouldn't mind. Then she bounded down the stairs, ready for a new set of adventures with her father.

Mr. Gibson frowned when he saw her. "Miss Poppy," he whispered, "His Grace would like for you to wait for him in your chambers."

It was Poppy's turn to frown. "Where is my papa?"

The butler sighed and bent down towards her. "He's meeting with Lord and Lady Staveley at the moment, miss. Now be a good girl and do as you're told."

Poppy turned around and started to stomp up the stairs, but when Mr. Gibson returned to his post near the door, she tiptoed back down the steps. She was certain if Papa *saw* her he wouldn't make her wait in her room.

She quietly sped down the hallway toward her father's office, but stopped when she heard soft music coming from one of the rooms. That was strange. She hadn't heard music the whole week she was here. Poppy crept towards the sound and poked her head inside. A very pretty woman with dark hair sat at the pianoforte, humming as she played.

With her eyes closed, Livvie's fingers sailed over the keys. The wistful music of Vivaldi was a balm for her soul, as it kept her mind off the conversation that was taking place down the hallway. After the trip from Derbyshire and spending most of the previous evening addressing wedding invitations that had gone out this morning, she had hoped to at least lay eyes on Alex. But when she arrived with Caroline and Staveley, the rather young butler had asked her to wait in the parlor. She'd been waiting for what seemed like forever, and she figured if she was going to live here, it wouldn't hurt to familiarize herself with the layout.

That was when she spotted the music room, her favorite retreat in any house. The pianoforte seemed to be calling out to her. Livvie sat on the cushioned bench.

The rich music washed over her, and Livvie lost herself to the sound, completely unaware of her surroundings.

"Are you my new nurse?" a tiny voice asked from the hallway.

Livvie's eyes flew open and she turned her head and discovered a beautiful little girl with raven hair and large silver eyes sporting a fairly shabby blue dress. One look at the child and Livvie did not have a doubt as to her identity. She was the feminine version of Alexander Everett in every way.

"Nurse?" she echoed.

The little girl nodded, taking a few steps forward. "Papa said he would get me a new nurse. Mrs. Seeber didn't want to live in a den of niquity."

Livvie nodded, understanding completely. She wasn't sure she wanted to live in a den of iniquity either. "I'm Olivia," she said with a smile and shifted on the cushioned piano bench, making room for the child.

"Oh, that is a pretty name," the little girl responded with a toothy grin. Then she climbed up on the bench, planting herself next to Livvie. "I'm Poppy."

Which, of course, Livvie had already deduced. "It's very nice to meet you, Poppy," she replied with a smile. And it was. Alex was so enigmatic, she'd felt certain she would never get the chance to meet his daughter. It was encouraging that he didn't intend to keep that part of his life separate from her, not after Caroline had explained how dearly he loved the child. A bit of hope sprung up in her heart. Though this marriage wasn't what she'd planned, it was inevitable now, and the fact that his life was opening up for her went a long way towards making their union successful.

"Do you want to have a tea party with me?" Poppy asked, interrupting Livvie's thoughts.

Little Poppy really was very charming. It would be difficult not to like her. Livvie found herself smiling at her soon-to-be step-daughter. "That would be lovely."

Poppy clapped her hands together. "Papa likes honey in his tea, but I like sugar. What do you like?"

Livvie made her way to the bell pull and gave it a slight tug. "Oh, I like sugar too. And milk."

"Do you know my papa?"

Livvie nodded and started back for the piano bench. "I do." Not as well as she'd like, but that would change very soon.

Moments later the door opened and the harried looking young butler entered. "Yes, Miss Danbury?"

"Miss Poppy and I would like some tea, Gibson."

Apparently Gibson hadn't noticed Poppy, because when his eyes landed on the little girl, they grew enormous. "Miss Poppy!" he hissed and his face turned slightly purple.

The child sucked in a breath. "Mr. Gibson, I just wanted to see Papa."

"I've already told you, miss. His Grace is in a meeting. And you are supposed to be in your room."

Poppy had a room at Kelfield House? That was a bit surprising to Livvie. Though not as surprising as actually seeing the child in the flesh. Hadn't Caroline said the girl lived with her mother in Bloomsbury?

With her most charming smile, she said to the butler, "Actually, Gibson, Miss Poppy is keeping me company." And she was grateful for it. Waiting for Staveley and Caroline to finish their conversation with Alex and his solicitor was nearly killing her.

"Very well," the butler responded with a frown before removing himself from the music room.

"Mr. Gibson plays dolls with me," Poppy informed her.

That image made Livvie giggle. Gibson was fairly young for a butler, but she still couldn't imagine the man playing with a little girl's toys. "Do you have lots of dolls, Poppy?"

The girl nodded her head. "Oh, yes. Do you want to see them?"

Livvie smiled at the child. "Should we invite them to have tea with us?"

Poppy beamed. "That would be fun." Then she raced from the room as quickly as she could.

Livvie stared after her, trying to sort out the situation. How often was Poppy at Kelfield House? And in the coming years would she have to see Ellen Fairchild on a regular basis? Livvie frowned at the thought. Alex was going to be her husband, and she didn't relish the idea of spending an inordinate amount of time with his ex-lover. In fact, she didn't like to think about him spending time in anyone else's bed either — past, present, or future.

It was fairly uncharitable of her. And while she would never begrudge Alex time with his daughter, she'd really rather not be forced to spend time with Ellen Fairchild. Hopefully, he wouldn't ask it of her. Then again, she didn't really want Alex to see the stunning actress without her either.

"Why do you look so troubled?" Alex asked from the doorway. He raked a hand though his black hair and stood before her, so handsome and virile that he took her breath away.

She didn't realize until this very moment how much she had missed him, and she leapt off the seat, wiping her hands nervously on her skirt. "Alex."

"Are you quite all right, Olivia?" He stepped into the room, a look of concern upon his face.

"I-I," she stuttered. "Of course." She sounded like a fool, just gaping at him. Then she dipped a belated curtsey. "Your Grace."

He frowned at her. "We've long ago moved beyond formalities, sweetheart."

Just then, Poppy barreled into the room, her arms overflowing with little dolls of all shapes and sizes. "Pardon me, Papa," she said and then flounced on the floor in front of the piano bench, scattering her dolls all over the rug. "Here they are, Olivia."

❧

Alex's eyes widened. What the devil was going on? He hadn't even gotten the chance to explain to Olivia. And...did his daughter just call her by her first name? He swallowed. Hard. "Poppy," he barked. "What are you doing in here?"

"Showing my dolls to Olivia," she answered as if it was the most logical explanation in the world.

Olivia stepped towards him, chewing her plump bottom lip. "I asked Poppy to have tea with me. I hope that was all right."

He wasn't quite sure what to say to that. Why did the most unexpected things happen when Olivia was around? Popping out of his wardrobe? Asking Poppy for tea? What was in store for him over the next several years?

Gibson entered the room with tea service, and Olivia graced him with one of her stunning smiles. It occurred to Alex that it was the first time in the longest while that he'd seen that charming dimple of hers. Blast his butler for being the recipient!

"Gibson, I expressly asked you to have Poppy wait for me in her room."

The butler blanched. "Yes, Your Grace. I—"

"Poppy," he began, looking at his daughter. "You will go to your room and stay there until I come for you."

Poppy's face fell. "All right, Papa." Then she slinked from the room, the butler close behind her.

Then Alex refocused on Olivia, only to discover that her smile had vanished as well. He stepped towards her. "I was going to tell you about Poppy."

"She's precious," Olivia replied. "I think it would be nice if she was at the wedding."

He nearly fell over. That was certainly not what he'd expected to hear from her. "You do?" he asked in amazement.

Olivia nodded, closed the gap between them, and tentatively touched his chest. "That is, if it's all right with her mother."

Her touch sent warm shivers to his soul, and he ached for her affection. Wished she'd come to him willingly. It would make the rest of this much easier. But she hadn't, and if he was wise he would remember that. "Olivia," he began, stepping away from her reach, "about Poppy...I returned from Derbyshire to find her here. Her mother...well, her mother has moved on to greener pastures, and Poppy will be with us."

Olivia's hazel eyes widened in surprise, which was a harsh reminder that she'd never wanted a life with him, let alone Poppy. "With us?" she asked with a whisper.

Alex nodded. "I know that none of this is what you'd planned. I don't have any illusions, Olivia, that if given the choice you wouldn't marry me, but that's not really in our control anymore. It is what it is. All I ask of you is that you try to come to terms with our situation and make the best of it."

She frowned at him. "Where is Caroline?"

"She and Staveley are in the gold parlor, where you were supposed to be waiting. Apparently, none of my females can do what is asked of them."

Her back visibly stiffened at the comment, and she folded her arms across her chest. "*I* am not one of your females."

Alex raised his brow challengingly. "I just finished signing documents claiming otherwise, Olivia."

She tipped her head high in the air. "Thank you for reminding me what a perfect beast you are. I'd nearly forgotten." Then she stomped out of the music room.

He stared at the pile of dolls in the middle of the floor and rubbed his brow. That certainly could have gone better. He could have been conciliatory. He could have made an attempt at being charming. He could have dropped at her feet and begged her to care about him.

But he hadn't. And he wouldn't. This was, as he'd explained to Sarah, not a love match. It would be wise if he didn't forget that. If it took raising Olivia's hackles a bit, so be it.

Alex scooped up Poppy's dolls and started off for her room. He probably should have told her about Olivia yesterday, before she stumbled upon her in the music room. It was foolish that he hadn't.

He found Poppy lying on her bed, her rosebud lips thrust out in childish pout. Alex sat next to her, depositing her dolls on the pillows. "Poppy," he began with a sigh. "Did you like Miss Danbury?"

"Miss Danbury, Papa?"

"You just met her. Olivia."

Poppy's smile returned. "Oh. I wanted to show her my dolls. And we were going to have tea."

He smiled at his daughter. "There'll be plenty of other days to show her your dolls and have tea."

"She is my new nurse?" Poppy asked excitedly.

"No, angel." Alex placed her on his lap and kissed the top of her head. "Olivia is going to be my wife."

Her head fell back to look at him, big silver eyes were wide with surprise. "Wife?"

"Tomorrow, angel. And she'd like for you to be at the wedding. Do you think you'd like that?"

Poppy nodded her head. "Yes, Papa. But Ellen said you wouldn't ever get married."

"Ellen has been wrong about a great many things, my little love."

Fifteen

LIVVIE looked around her room at Staveley House. How strange that it was her last night here. She never would have believed that a fortnight spent in Derbyshire would have such permanent repercussions on the rest of her life. Tomorrow she would be married—not to Philip as she'd always thought—but to the mysterious and wicked Duke of Kelfield.

The man was maddening, to say the very least. He had relentlessly pursued her for nearly a week. He had opened her eyes and introduced her to delicious thoughts and feelings she'd never experienced before. He was arrogant and yet charming at the same time. He made her want him, like she'd never wanted anyone. But he hadn't seemed the same man when he left Prestwick Chase—subdued and morose. And he hadn't seemed the same man today—infuriating and closed off. She wasn't sure what to think about him.

There were also the bizarre circumstances of his child. Poppy did seem like a sweet little girl, and Livvie had quite liked her. But she didn't know what to think about this situation. Good heavens! She was going to be a step-mother. And what exactly did 'greener pastures' mean anyway? Was Ellen Fairchild gone for good? And if not, how soon before she made an appearance? He really should have been clearer.

Then there was the state of Kelfield House. Caroline had informed her after they returned that only a skeletal staff was in residence, and that she would have to quickly hire a nurse for Poppy, several maids, and footmen. Luckily her own lady's maid, Molly, who had enjoyed the last fortnight off, would be joining her at Kelfield House. That was one friendly and familiar face she could count on. But there was so much to do, and she'd never planned on this. She had no idea about running a ducal —

A soft knock on the door interrupted her thoughts. "Come in," she muttered, miserably.

Caroline peered inside, concern etched across her brow. "How are you holding up, darling?"

"I'm feeling like a Christian about to be sacrificed to the lions."

Caroline suppressed a smile. "I'm certain Kelfield would prefer to be referred to as a wolf." Then she sat next to Livvie on the bed and took her hands. "And I do believe he cares a great deal for you."

Livvie snorted. "You couldn't tell it with the way he behaved towards me today."

"Well, he once told me that it could be quite frightening for a fellow who spent all of his time skirt chasing to settle on only one woman. It could just simply be nerves on his part — though I'm certain he'd never admit to that."

Was that all it was? Livvie wanted to believe that, but there was something different in his eyes — a pain of some sort.

"Anyway, Olivia, since your mother is not here to give you guidance, I hope you'll allow me."

Here it was. *The Talk.* The one every girl had with her mother or female relative the night before her wedding. Her friend Henrietta's mother had terrified the poor girl so badly with The Talk, Hen nearly jumped out of her skin when her new husband touched her hand at the altar. At the time, Livvie and Cordie had thought the entire affair quite amusing. How different things looked now.

Just because Livvie knew The Talk was coming didn't make it any more welcome. Though honestly, it was probably better coming from Cousin Caroline than it would have been from her very prim mother.

"As you know, I married Staveley when I was barely sixteen. The night before my wedding, your mother attended me and I was simply terrified. Can you imagine being afraid of Staveley of all people?" Caroline asked with a self deprecating laugh. "I was terribly young. Livvie, I'm going to try to give you better advice than she gave me—just promise me you won't tell her I said that."

Well, that did sound promising. Much more so than whatever Henrietta's mother had told her. Livvie nodded her head.

"It is said quite often that women should simply endure their husband's amorous activities dutifully. Grin and bear it. I've heard that countless times, Livvie, and in my opinion it is worthless drivel. The marriage bed can be one of the greatest joys of your life, not something you barely tolerate. In fact, I would image that if one's husband is Kelfield, this aspect of married life will be quite satisfactory—if even half the stories about him are true."

"Caroline!" Livvie felt her cheeks flush.

"It's the eve of your wedding, Livvie, and the man will be your husband tomorrow. Time for being missish is over." Caroline squeezed her hand. "There's nothing to be afraid of. Intimacy between men and women, husbands and wives, is a completely natural occurrence. Instinct will take over to some extent. If you trust your husband, Livvie, and keep an open mind, he'll bring you all sorts of pleasures you'd never envisioned."

Heavens! She already experienced more pleasure than she'd ever known at his hands. How much more was there? And what should she be doing? "What about him, Caroline? How do I bring him pleasure?"

"That," Caroline sighed, "is hard to say. One man is different from the next, or so I've heard, but I am confident that Alex will direct you. Follow his lead, Livvie."

There was something that was both exhilarating and terrifying about that idea.

"I want you to have love and passion and acceptance in your marriage. I'm confident he's capable of providing all of that for you. Make sure you offer it in return as well."

⚜

Sleep eluded Livvie most of the night. When she rolled out of bed the next morning, the morning of her wedding, she felt more trepidation than she ever had in her life. Molly entered the room with a bright smile and cheerful disposition. She eagerly dressed Livvie in a new silver gown with a gauzy white over dress, commissioned a month earlier, but not worn until now. She certainly hadn't imagined she'd wear this ensemble to her own wedding. Then Molly dressed her hair up, intertwined with white lilies and tiny rosebuds, gushing over her appearance with nearly every breath.

When Livvie stared at her reflection in her room's floor-length mirror, she was surprised at her transformation. She was indeed a bride. Just not how she'd ever imagined it.

She didn't quite remember the drive to St. George's, though once she arrived the sheer number of guests and well-wishers when she stepped out of the coach was astounding. Weddings were not typically characterized as a crush, but there wasn't a better way to describe hers. It was staggering.

She and Caroline peeked inside the chapel, staring in disbelief at the throng. Nearly every person Livvie had ever met was in attendance, as well as several dissolute noblemen she'd heard about and seen but never met before. The Marquess of Haversham, for goodness sake! He was possibly the only man whose reputation was worse than Kelfield's. Depending on the day.

"They don't actually believe I'm leaving their ranks," a voice whispered in her ear.

Livvie spun around to find Alex standing there, looking sinfully handsome, as always, a blinding white cravat with a sparkling ruby pin set apart from his black coat and trousers. "Alex! It's bad luck to see me before the wedding."

He quirked a grin at her, his silver eyes twinkling. "Sweetheart, you'll be a duchess in a matter of minutes. Luck is for the lower classes."

Then Alex looked down and smiled at his raven-haired daughter, who appeared at his side holding a little doll. He lifted the child up in his arms and handed her to Caroline. "You'll stay with Lady Staveley today, Poppy."

Caroline tapped the girl's nose affectionately and smiled. "You'll even get to come home with me afterwards, Poppy. I have a daughter, Emma, a little older than you. I'm certain you'll have a splendid time with her." Then Caroline winked at Livvie. "You'll be all right. And you," she said to Alex, "need to be down front."

He nodded his agreement and gently touched Livvie's chin. "Keep this up, sweetheart." Then he started down the aisle amid a sea of soft gasps and hushed whispers.

Livvie looked at the little girl in Caroline's arms. Poppy wore a cheerful yellow dress, with a wide blue ribbon and a bashful smile. "Hello again, Poppy. I am glad you're here."

Poppy's face lit up. "Do you still want to have a tea party? I brought one of my dolls."

Livvie nodded. "We shall have one every day, if you like."

"But not today, darling," Caroline interrupted. "You'll be too busy playing with Emma and the others. And for now, we need to take our seats." Then she carried the child to the front of the church and claimed her spot beside Staveley.

Livvie closed her eyes and took a calming breath. She'd never been more nervous in all her life. Not even when she'd faced down that ferocious dog when she was just a girl.

⚜

The murmuring voices of the crowd faded away, as Alex focused solely on his bride walking towards him. She was breathtaking in shimmery silver and white, like an ethereal princess. Though she smiled when she faced him and held his hands before the altar, he knew Olivia was nervous, and he wished he could spirit her off to some place where he could ease her worries away.

The clergyman began and then droned on, as they were apt to do, and Alex caressed Olivia's hands with his thumbs, losing himself in her pretty hazel eyes and blocking out everyone but her.

"I do," he heard her say, and he snapped back to the present.

"And do you, Alexander Everett—"

"I do," he hastily replied, to which there was a smattering of chuckles throughout the cavernous room. He didn't care about how anxious or smitten he appeared to the crowd in general. Besides, it would only add credence to the story they'd sent out about his impatience to have the girl, the banns to be damned.

Olivia blushed prettily, making Alex want her even more.

"Well, then, Your Grace," the clergyman cleared his throat, "you may kiss your bride."

Alex wasted no time in doing so. He pulled Olivia against him and pressed his lips to her soft ones. It was fairly tame as far as his kisses

119

went. However when she sighed against his mouth, he couldn't help but raise his head with a self-satisfied smile, looking out at their throng of guests, some cheering, some gaping.

"Her Grace and I are thrilled all of you were able to attend our wedding," he called out to the crowd, immediately silencing them. "Please join my dear friend, Lord Carteret, who is hosting a wedding breakfast in our honor this morning. I do hope you enjoy yourselves immensely." Then he scooped Olivia up in his arms. Ignoring her startled gasp, he continued, "Alas, I plan to enjoy my wife, so I'll have to receive your felicitations another time."

"Alex!" Olivia whispered against his chest as he carried her, sauntering towards the open doors in the back of the church. "You can't do *this* in front of everyone."

With a wicked smile, he replied, "Sweetheart, I'm Kelfield. I do whatever I please."

Then he strode outside to his awaiting coach, nodded to his coachman, Coleman, and helped his wife inside. Almost immediately, they rambled down Hanover Square with Olivia watching him from across the coach.

Wide-eyed, she shook her head. "Have you quite lost your mind? We can't forgo our own wedding breakfast. What will everyone think?"

Alex slid forward in his seat and ran his hand gently across one of her perfect thighs. "Well, my young and innocent wife, they all think that very soon I will have my cock deep inside you. And they'll be correct."

"Alex," she whispered in shock.

He leaned back against the squabs and grinned unrepentantly at his bride. "You did have The Talk with Caroline, did you not?"

She gaped at him, and her mouth dropped open. It was a look he much enjoyed on her. "The Talk?"

"Yes. Didn't she explain to you what to expect in our marriage bed?"

Olivia shook her head in bewilderment. "You know about The Talk?"

He couldn't help but chuckle. "Of course, sweetheart. All men know. I'm just relieved you got Caroline and not Bethany Carteret."

"Why?" she asked innocently.

"Because Staveley has always been a well-pleasured man. One can see it in his countenance. I believe that is why he gives her free rein to cause all sorts of trouble, without ever lifting a finger to stop her."

"Because he's well-pleasured?"

Alex winked at her. "Don't underestimate what a man will allow his wife if she takes care of all his needs. Bethany on the other hand controls James' behavior with access to her bed. If he displeases her, she punishes him by refusing his husbandly rights. She leads him around by his prick, like a besotted fool. You should know, Olivia, I won't be controlled in that way. You're my wife and you won't shut your chamber door to me."

She swallowed. Her hazel eyes grew large as she listened to him. "Do you all sit around and discuss these things? About Caroline and Lady Carteret and Mrs. Greywood?"

Alex grinned widely. "They never discuss their wives in that way, Olivia, and I'll never speak so of you."

"But then—"

"I am a man with eyes. It is not difficult to determine if you know what to look for."

"And you do?"

"I always have." And as he looked at his wife across the coach from him, he knew he was the luckiest of men. He had tasted her passion and knew what awaited him when they arrived at Kelfield House. From the first moment he'd laid eyes on her, he'd wanted her in his bed. Philip Moore might still own her heart, but Alex was determined to erase the major from Olivia's mind. Now that she was his wife, he had all the time in the world to accomplish the goal.

The coach rolled to a stop. A moment later the door opened and Coleman lowered the steps. Alex smiled at Olivia. "We have arrived, Your Grace."

Sixteen

TAKING Alex's hand, Livvie looked up at her new home. Kelfield House loomed above, impressive and formidable, like its owner. Alex led her up the front steps, then once again scooped her up in his strong arms and crossed the threshold. "Gibson," her husband said, as he walked past the butler and down a hallway towards a steep staircase that he began to climb.

Livvie's heart was in her throat. He couldn't be doing this. Not this soon. She wasn't ready. It was still light out, for heaven's sake. Her fear must have shown on her face, because he slowed his pace and looked at her. "Do you remember at Prestwick Chase, that last night in your room?"

As if she could ever forget it. The memories had come to her every night since, making her want him with every fiber of her being. Livvie nodded and he smiled in response, sending tendrils of desire straight through her.

"This will be better, sweetheart. Trust me." Then he quickened his steps and made his way to a large mahogany door, nudging it open with his shoulder.

The duchess' chambers. *Her chambers.* There was no mistaking the grand room with a large four-poster bed, adorned in swaths of light blue silk, cream bows and golden cords. Alex returned her to her feet with a devilish grin. "I have wanted you since that first night at Staveley's a year ago."

"You scowled at me all night. I couldn't imagine why you disliked me."

"It annoyed me," he began with a chuckle, "that I desperately wanted to ravage you and knew it could never be." Then he kissed her hand and then placed it on the large bulge in his trousers. "From the very first, you've done this to me."

Livvie stared at him, surprised to see desire flicker in his eyes as she tentatively squeezed him with her hand. She would never have imagined doing such a thing, but Caroline did say she was to follow his lead.

She bit her lower lip, starting to feel a bit more comfortable with this role of being his wife, and raised her hand to rest on his chest. "Alex," she whispered, "what do you want of me?"

"Everything," he answered huskily, moving his hands up her sides. "So now, my wife, you will remove your clothes. Lovely as they are, I'd like to see you without them."

Livvie swallowed. Hard. "M-my maid. The buttons..." She turned so that he could see the intricate row at the back of her gown. She'd never be able to undo it herself.

Alex hugged her to him and began the chore of unbuttoning the over dress and the silver gown beneath. Livvie could only breathe him in. Sandalwood. Desire. Intoxicating duke. Her delicious, unrepentant husband.

In no time, the gown pooled at her feet, leaving her in only her chemise and drawers. Alex shrugged out of his jacket and pulled at his cravat, tossing each article across the room in a heap. He pulled his shirt over his head, and then stopped, staring at her with one black eyebrow raised. "Olivia, I am waiting for you to remove the rest of your clothes."

She blinked her eyes wide, not realizing that she'd been admiring his very masculine form. The rippled muscles across his chest and arms. His lean waist and taught belly. Then there was his magnificent bottom — though it was still clothed, she remembered it well from her hiding place in his wardrobe.

Alex dropped onto the bed, folded his arms across his chest, and kicked his legs out in front of him. "Drop to your knees, Olivia."

Remembering similar words once spoken to the maid, Olivia flushed, staring at the bulge that was straining the seams of his trousers. He quirked a rakish grin and then chuckled. "My boots, sweetheart. Remove them, will you?"

She must be blushing, and she dropped to her knees more to avoid his stare than because he'd asked for her to do so. Livvie took a steadying breath and began to pull off his black Hessians.

As the first boot slipped off, Livvie looked up and found him gazing at her with amusement, which she didn't quite appreciate since she'd never removed a man's boot before. She was doing her best, as well as trying to forget what she thought he'd asked of her. "Yes?" she asked with her own raised brow.

He wiggled his other foot for her attention. "Did you think I was going to ask you something else, Olivia?"

She tugged at his second boot, evading his silver gaze. "Of course not," she lied, now trying to sound cheerful.

When the boot sprang free, he took her hands in his and pulled her atop him on the bed. His arousal pressed against her belly and desire once again raced through her. Alex kissed the hollow of her neck and slid his hands down her back until they cupped her bottom, nearly sending her to ecstasy.

"If I had asked something else of you," he began, slowly inching his mouth towards one of her aching nipples, "as my wife, I assume you would comply."

Livvie caught her breath as he suckled one breast and touched the other through her chemise, certain she would expire of the sensual torture. He grazed her with his teeth and warm tongue, wetting the silk and driving her mad.

Then he stopped, rolled her beneath him and hovered over her. "Would you do whatever I asked of you, Olivia?"

She closed her eyes, reveling in the feel of his masculine form pressing her into the bed, feeling her damp chemise lightly abrading her nipples. She nodded her head, Caroline's advice ringing in her ears. "Yes, Alex. I'll do whatever you ask of me."

"Good," he growled wolfishly. Then he slid one large hand down her body and pulled her chemise up to her belly. "Take this off. All of it." He ran his finger along the edge of her drawers. "I want to see all of my wife."

Livvie shimmied out of both articles of clothing, keeping her eyes on her husband, until she was completely bare beneath his stare. His silver gaze heated her skin wherever it lingered and made her ache for his touch. Alex momentarily left the bed to remove his trousers, freeing his erection. He stroked himself, while his eyes bored into her.

His shaft grow even larger in his hands and she shivered, wanting something that she didn't quite understand. Alex knelt on the bed and nudged her legs wide with his knees.

"You are stunning, Olivia."

Then he ran his fingers along her thighs until they reached her dark, springy curls. With his thumbs he parted her folds, and Livvie arched against his hands. He lightly pressed the tip of his manhood against her opening. She gasped at the contact as hot fire raced through her veins. "Oh, Alex."

He looked at her in awe. "God, Olivia, I thought I'd need to prepare you, but you're practically dripping."

She wasn't quite sure what that meant, but he did look pleased. She smiled tentatively at him. With a ragged breath, Alex pushed himself slightly deeper inside her, stretching her. Livvie's eyes grew wide and she gasped.

He let his weight push her deeper into the mattress. Livvie panted, relishing the feel of him around her and inside her.

Alex stared into his wife's eyes, so innocent and yet filled with desire. She was so damned tight, he thought it quite possible he'd explode before piercing her maidenhead. He grasped handfuls of bedclothes and tried to keep control on his mounting lust.

Olivia writhed beneath him, and it was nearly his undoing, drawing him further inside her.

"God, Olivia, don't do that!" he rasped.

She stilled and looked up at him apologetically.

Alex smiled tightly. "You're fine, sweetheart, I just don't want to hurt you."

Her throat constricted as she swallowed, and he closed his eyes to the erotic sight. She was the most sensual woman with absolutely no idea what she did to him.

And she was his.

Alex dipped his head to her breast and took one taut nipple in his mouth, sucking it hard. She tasted like the sweetest wine and was just as intoxicating. His cock twitched to sink further into her as she moaned. Then he stopped at the evidence of her innocence and smiled at her.

"You're mine, Olivia." Then he claimed her mouth as he thrust fully inside her.

She didn't scream as some virgins were wont to do. Instead she moaned louder, clutching him to her. Dear God, she was incredible. Alex anchored her hands beneath his as he pumped into her over and over.

Livvie was certain she was going to come undone. With each thrust inside her, an amazing pressure built in her core and her mind ceased functioning. The only thought in her head was of Alex, of the delicious precipice he was leading her towards. Each touch, each thrust, each ragged breath drove her closer to the edge.

And then she fell over.

Once again floating high above the clouds. "Alex!" she cried, unable to stop herself from convulsing around him.

He clutched her ferociously in his embrace and called out as his own release took him. Livvie could feel his life's blood rush into her and she fell limp in his arms. He collapsed beside her and drew her into his embrace, burying his head in the crook of her neck.

They lay there for what seemed forever, struggling for breath and holding on to each other. When her pulse began to steady, Livvie opened her eyes, studying this husband of hers. It was certainly a strange path to this juncture, one she never would have imagined—but one she was thoroughly pleased with. "You are amazing," she whispered and tenderly ran her hand along her husband's jaw.

Alex opened his eyes at the touch and smiled rakishly. "Flattery will get you everywhere, sweetheart." Then he rolled her beneath him. "Shall I ravish you again?"

The suggestion was thrilling and Livvie nodded, enjoying the lust-hued twinkle in his eyes.

After being "properly ravished" most of the day and enjoying a quiet dinner together, Livvie was surprised that Alex left her that evening, retiring to his own suite of rooms. Wrapped in a long, flowing robe, she stared at the door that connected their rooms with a frown.

It had been such a glorious day, and she really shouldn't complain, but...well, it *had* been such a glorious day. She'd never felt more connected to another living soul. Alex had caressed her and made love to her, and...well, she just didn't see why he wouldn't stay with her all night. For heaven's sake, the man had spent the night in her room at Prestwick Chase before they married.

It was probably just her silly romantic notions. Her parents shared a room, as did Caroline and Staveley – she'd just assumed she would too. And after the day they'd had, after all they'd shared...well, it just didn't seem right.

⚜

An anguished yell woke Livvie from her peaceful sleep. She sat bolt upright, staring into the darkness of her room. Her eyes flew to the connecting door that led to Alex's chamber. There was movement inside, and then the flicker of lamp light illuminated the doorframe.

She swung her legs out of bed and started for the door, but stopped when the memory of their last night in Derbyshire flashed in her mind. Alex had suffered from an awful nightmare at Prestwick Chase. Had he just experienced another one?

He hadn't wanted her to *coddle* him then. Was that different now that they were married? She reached for the handle and started to push it open, but stopped when she heard him mutter, "Goddamn bastard."

Apparently he was fine, if a little agitated. She wrapped her arms around her belly and slipped back into her bed. Perhaps Caroline could give her some direction of how to go on. No one had more experience in dealing with difficult men.

Seventeen

CAROLINE arrived early at Kelfield House, with precocious little Poppy in tow. If she didn't adore Alexander Everett so much and believe that he was simply besotted with Livvie, she would be quite put out with him. That little display at St. George's the day before had done nothing to help Livvie's tarnished reputation. Though she was working on a solution to that.

Gibson opened the door wide, and Caroline was glad to note the fellow seemed more stoic than he had when she and Staveley called earlier in the week, which was an improvement. However there was still work to be done with him. The man needed to appear more like a ducal butler and less like an exalted footman.

"Gibson," she began, "are the duke and duchess receiving?"

The duchess is in the music room. His Grace has gone out."

Poppy let go of her hand and raced down the corridor. With a shake of her head, Caroline sighed. The child would need to be reigned in a bit as well, no matter how adorable and charming she was, or how badly she wanted to check on her dolls' welfare.

Livvie had certainly found herself in a bizarre household, and Caroline was certain that she could use all the help she could get. It was a good thing she came prepared. "Lead the way, Gibson."

Vivaldi. Caroline could hear it from the hallway. That meant that Livvie was worried. She always played Vivaldi when she was worried. Haydn when she was happy and Bach when she was sad. It made it easy to determine her moods if one knew her well.

Caroline waved the butler off and continued down the corridor alone. Whatever was bothering Livvie didn't need to be overheard by the staff. She stood in the doorway of the music room and watched her pretty young cousin, eyes closed while her fingers danced across the keys in deep contemplation.

Caroline plastered a large smile across her face, determined to be of whatever help Livvie needed. With feigned cheerfulness, she strode inside. "Olivia darling!" she gushed and dropped a kiss on her cousin's cheek. "How wonderful to see you."

Livvie's dimple blinked at Caroline as she pushed off the piano bench. Then she threw her arms around her neck. "Caro, I'm so glad to see you."

Caroline squeezed her cousin tight and then stepped away, admiring the girl. "Well, you're all in one piece, I see."

Immediately, Livvie looked bashfully at the ground.

"Heavens, Livvie, I'm teasing you." Caroline linked her arm with her cousin's. "Now, darling, invite me into the parlor for tea."

Always the good soldier, Livvie grinned. "Caro, would you like to join me for tea in the parlor?"

"Spoken just like a good duchess."

⚜

Livvie was quite relieved to have her cousin by her side, as Caroline was constantly a pillar of strength. That was something she had always admired about her. Growing up without a mother and with two older brothers, Caroline had learned early on how to manipulate and manage the males of the species, nearly perfecting the ability to an art form.

If anyone could help her figure out how to extract Alex's secrets, it was Caroline.

As they walked arm in arm to the parlor, she looked at her cousin. "Isn't Poppy with you?" she asked, suddenly remembering that she now had a step-daughter.

"The little imp ran off to check on her dolls as soon as we arrived. She fretted about them all evening, I'm afraid. Luckily, Rachel still had some of hers stored away in a trunk. By the way, at thirteen, Rachel feels she is too old for such frivolities and has gladly offered to give them up to Poppy, if you'd like."

It was so odd to suddenly be in the role of a step-mother. It was completely foreign to Livvie. Even growing up with the Averys, she and Cordie were the youngest, and she'd never had to take care of anyone before except herself. Recently she hadn't even done a good job of that. "I shall ask Alex if it's all right."

Caroline stopped walking and shook her head. "You'll do no such thing. The man is besotted with you. Don't give up what little power you have, Olivia. You'll never get it back if you do. Make your own decisions and consult him only if necessary. Accepting secondhand children's toys is something you can decide all on your own."

"I've just never done," she explained, waving her arm in an all-encompassing gesture, "this before."

Caroline smiled brightly. "I have all the confidence in the world that you will manage splendidly, darling."

Livvie wished she had half of Caroline's faith in herself. After last night, she couldn't seem to erase the images of her husband thrashing in his sleep or the echoes of his anguished cry that had awoken her from a rather peaceful sleep. She didn't want to take the wrong step where he was concerned. She grasped Caroline's elbow and pulled her into the closest parlor.

"I desperately need your advice," she admitted in a hushed whisper.

Caroline's brow furrowed, but she nodded. "Of course, Livvie. What has you so troubled?"

"Alex."

"Did yesterday go badly?"

An immediate blush stained her cheeks. "No."

Apparently more at ease, Caroline grinned. "On the contrary, it appears to have gone particularly well. Good for you, Olivia."

Livvie shook her head. "Not *that*, Caroline... That was amazing," she added with a sigh. "But I'm rather concerned about something else. I think Alex suffers from terrible nightmares."

Caroline led Livvie to a chaise and they both sat. "Everyone has nightmares from time to time. It was only one night, Livvie. I agree, however, one's wedding night it not the perfect time for such a thing. But I'm certain it's nothing to get yourself worked up about."

"But it's not just once. There was the night at Prest..." She hadn't intended to tell Caroline about that night, but she'd already said too much. Nothing to do now but get on with it. Besides she was *already* married to the man. "There was a night at Prestwick Chase as well. That's two nights, Caroline, and awful nightmares, both of them."

Caroline sat back in her spot, a deep frown etched across her brow. Finally she focused on Livvie. "Did you ask him about them?"

Livvie shook her head. "When I tried to comfort him in Derbyshire, he barked at me. And last night...well, last night he insisted on separate chambers. But I heard him in the dead of night, Caroline, and the sound was heart-wrenching. He was already gone this morning when I awoke, and Gibson doesn't know where he is."

Caroline folded her arms across her chest. "Something must be done about the state of this home, Livvie. Gibson should always know where his master is. To that end, I took the liberty of personally visiting a service yesterday. I looked at their books and have set up interviews for you this afternoon. Candidates for the positions of maid, footman, but most importantly nursemaid for Poppy will start arriving around one o'clock."

Livvie shook her head, completely frustrated. Important as all that was, it was not her most pressing concern. "Caroline, that wasn't where I was going with this conversation. I am well aware that changes need to be made here, but I am most troubled about Alex at the moment."

With a worried smile, Caroline took her hands. "I know you are, darling. Which is why I think that you're exactly what he's always needed. How fortuitous your blunder in his wardrobe has turned out to be." Then she sighed deeply. "Listen, I've known Alex more than a dozen years. He's always kept part of himself hidden from even his dearest friends, unless you're lucky enough to slide beneath his defenses undetected. He didn't have the happiest of childhoods, and while I don't know if that is what haunts him now, I wouldn't be surprised if it is related."

Livvie leaned closer to her cousin as curiosity took control of her. "*You* know what haunts him." It wasn't a question. The answer on plain on Caroline's face.

Her cousin shook her head. "He needs to tell you himself, Olivia. His secrets aren't for me to disclose, though I don't think I know them all anyway. You're his wife—"

"Which is precisely why you *should* tell me," she interrupted, annoyed beyond belief that Caroline wouldn't give her the information she sought. What good was it having a cousin with the ability to extract information from anyone if she wasn't willing to share what she'd learned?

"Be worthy of his trust, Livvie. Let him know that he can unburden himself with you, that it's safe to do so. If I tell you something out of turn, it will only cause problems for both of you. And that is the very last thing I want."

Livvie didn't want that either, but she'd like *some* direction. "I don't even know where to begin."

"I think you do. Support him, show him—"

"Good morning, ladies," Alex's voice interrupted them from the doorway.

Livvie leapt to her feet, blushing when he quirked at grin at her. "Alex." She smiled back.

⚜

He would never tire of that dimple. Alex crossed the floor, kissed his wife's soft cheek, and inhaled the light lilac scent that always encompassed her. "Olivia," he whispered huskily in her ear, wishing they were alone. Then he stepped away from her and kissed Caroline's outstretched hand. "Lady Staveley."

Caroline tilted her head to one side, as if assessing him. "*Cousin* Alex. I am certain formalities don't rule at Kelfield House."

Cousin Alex? He hadn't actually thought about the ramifications of being Caroline Staveley's relation when he'd decided to marry Olivia. Though looking at his seductive wife, Alex couldn't imagine giving her up if even to distance himself from the vexing viscountess. He smirked at his new cousin. "I imagine a great many things will change at Kelfield House now that Olivia is here to rule over the place." He drew his wife to his side and then sat next to her on an old, brocade settee, lazily draping his arm over her shoulders.

"Yes, a great many things, indeed," Caroline responded, still assessing him—which was unnerving. He hated it when she focused those all-knowing eyes of hers on him. Then she brightened with a smile. "I have decided to throw a ball."

"You have?" his wife asked gleefully.

Alex cringed. He really disliked those sorts of societal affairs. One would think now that he was married he could avoid such things from here on out. Not that he had regularly attended balls or soirees before he was married either, but he wasn't about to start now. He shook his head. "You know very well I don't attend such affairs, *Cousin* Caroline."

Her hazel eyes turned dangerously dark. "Well, you'll attend mine. After that little performance yesterday at St. George's, Livvie will be lucky to be received anywhere. For a man who was supposed to be protecting her reputation, you've done an abysmal job thus far."

Alex hated that Olivia's face turned white at her cousin's proclamation. It couldn't really be all that bad. He'd certainly weathered worse. Besides they *were* married. What else did those societal harridans want from him? "You're exaggerating."

"Yes, because I'm so prone to that," Caroline shot back tartly. She very rarely spoke tartly to him. Perhaps it *was* worse than he thought.

Alex reached for Olivia's hand. "Don't worry, sweetheart."

At that moment there was a scratch at the door, and Alex was glad for the disruption. He'd never been so happy to see his butler. "Come."

Gibson opened the door and stepped inside with a letter on a silver salver. He nodded at Olivia. "Your Grace, this has just arrived via messenger."

Alex waved the man closer so Olivia could retrieve her letter without leaving his side. She smiled as she picked up the heavy vellum. "It's from Cordie."

The butler cleared his throat. "Your Grace, the messenger awaits your reply."

"Oh," Livvie responded. Then she tore open the envelope and quickly scanned the note. "She wants to go shopping tomorrow, like we always do."

"That sounds like a wonderful idea," Alex remarked, enjoying the radiant glow she suddenly had about her. "Feel free to buy whatever you like, sweetheart." *Preferably something sheer.*

Olivia hopped up and smiled at him and Caroline. "Let me jot off a reply, and I'll be right back."

"Take your time," Caroline offered with an indulgent wink.

As Olivia quit the room, Caroline's smile vanished and she pinned Alex with an irritated glare. "You are very fortunate that I adore you."

He sat forward in his seat, leveling the viscountess with a stern look of his own. "Out with it, whatever it is, Caro."

"I don't know why you even agreed to marry her, if you were just going to turn around and ruin her seconds after your vows."

"Oh, for God's sake! Melodrama does not become you."

Caroline's glower darkened. "Alexander Everett, while you and Livvie were holed up here, I was out there." She pointed vaguely toward one of the room's windows. "And I am telling you, her reputation is in tatters. As she is *your* duchess, I'm expecting you to do everything in your power to correct that."

Damn! He certainly hadn't intended that. He roughly rubbed his brow. "Dear God."

"Your actions no longer reflect only on you, Alex."

"I am well aware of that, Caroline," he growled in frustration.

"One wouldn't know it by your reckless behavior."

"You're very fortunate I adore *you*, Caro, or I'd throw you out on your ear."

She took a deep breath, and then spoke very calmly, "You *will* attend my ball, Alex. I'm dragging Masten back from Dorset for it, as well as Clayworth from Derbyshire. And every other stodgy fellow in England I can dig up will be there and no one will dare cut her. Not in my home."

The idea that anyone would cut her made Alex clench his teeth. He would strangle anyone who did so. "We'll be there, naturally."

Olivia swept back into the room, smiling sweetly, and Alex motioned for her to retrieve the spot beside him. "Sweetheart, I was just telling our cousin we'd be thrilled to attend her ball."

"Truly?" she asked, her pretty hazel eyes twinkling.

"And the theatre," Caroline offered with a smile. "Astwick has offered me his box at Drury Lane tomorrow."

Drury Lane! Did it have to be bloody Drury Lane? Alex winced.

"Macbeth is Staveley's favorite," Caroline continued, apparently unaware of the uncomfortable spot she'd just put him in. "It's a bit morose for my taste, but the more somber the entertainment, the more respectable one appears."

Livvie was surprised at how easy it was to staff a ducal residence. Of course Caroline had, most likely, weeded out all the unacceptable prospects before they'd gotten to her. But all in all it was a very successful day. In the end, the most difficult position to fill was that of Poppy's nurse. Never having been a parent before, she wasn't quite certain what qualities were most important, and she barely remembered her own nurse.

She'd met stern women, loud women, old women, and shy women of all shapes and sizes. But when Mrs. Bickle entered her parlor, Livvie knew she'd found the right woman for the position. The nursemaid was older, with streaks of grey in her otherwise black hair. She was plump with rosy cheeks and kind brown eyes that put Livvie at ease.

During the interview, Poppy burst through the door and stopped in her tracks when her eyes fell on the older woman.

"Poppy," Livvie said with a smile, "would you like to meet Mrs. Bickle?"

Her step-daughter nodded, and her pretty raven curls bobbed up and down. "But, Olivia, we haven't had our tea party."

Livvie felt awful. She had told the child they could have one every day if she wanted, yet she'd been so busy with hiring staff, she hadn't spent any time with Poppy. She really should get to know the girl. "Of course, sweetheart. We'll have it now."

When Poppy smiled, her whole face lit up. "Do you want some too?" she asked the old woman.

"I would enjoy that, miss," the nurse answered with a smile.

Eighteen

AFTER another amazing evening with her husband, Livvie once again drifted off to sleep alone. Though it shouldn't have surprised her when Alex's tortured cry from his chamber awoke her, it was still just as unnerving as it had been the previous night. She needed to find a way to help him and wished Caroline had given her some clue as to what was so troubling to Alex.

During the short ride to the Avery townhouse, Livvie's mind focused on the problem at hand. How could she show him she was trustworthy? How could she get him to confide in her? He rarely gave a straight answer to any of her questions about his past.

The coach halted, and Livvie waited patiently for Coleman to lower the steps in front of the Avery townhouse. She nodded to the coachman and then climbed the steps to the Avery's door, her mind still on Alex. Before she could even knock, Sanders, the Averys' butler who Livvie had known practically all her life, opened the door and looked down his long nose at her, disdain etched across his ancient brow. "I'm sorry, Your Grace, but Miss Avery is not in."

Livvie blinked up at the tall, slender butler, knowing full well that Cordie most certainly was at home. They were supposed to go shopping, and Cordie would never forget. The stern look on Sanders' face and the clipped way in which he spoke to her could only mean one thing.

She was not welcome at Avery House.

Not anymore.

"I see" she replied, trying to keep her voice from cracking. "Well, please tell Cordelia that I called."

"Of course, Your Grace." Then Sanders shut the door firmly in her face.

Stunned, Livvie descended the Avery steps in a daze and walked back to her awaiting coach, the Kelfield coat of arms emblazoned on the side. She had thought that some people might shun her for her exploits with Alex, especially after Caroline's dire words from the day before. *But the Averys?* She'd known them forever. Her whole life. They were like her second family.

Coleman stood before her, concern in his coal black eyes. "Are you not staying, Your Grace?"

Livvie pushed back the tears that were threatening to fall, and she shook her head. "No, Coleman, I'm not staying. Could you please take me home, instead?"

The coachman frowned, but nodded. "Of course, Your Grace."

The short ride back to Kelfield House was terribly uncomfortable. She'd never known a day when Cordie wasn't part of her life. It was so hard to imagine that she wasn't allowed to see her dearest friend.

Gibson opened the door and Livvie made her way to the nursery where she found Poppy and Mrs. Bickle looking over some books. Poppy's childish giggle brought a smile to Livvie's face, but she left the pair to go about their day. Alex was out, though she didn't know where. Even in a house now fully staffed, for all practical purposes, Livvie was in the den of iniquity all alone. Not quite sure what to do with herself, she made her way to the music room and sat down at the pianoforte.

She was unaware how long she sat playing Bach's Air on String of G, when Gibson interrupted her by clearing his throat. Livvie stood up from the bench, staring at the butler. "Yes?"

He stepped towards her and offered a note on a silver salver. "This just arrived for Your Grace, and the messenger is awaiting your reply."

Livvie could tell by the handwriting the note was from Cordie, and her heart swelled. She broke the seal and scanned the letter quickly.

Dear Olivia,

I do not even know how to begin. I am so dreadfully sorry about today, and I have been on the outs with Mama ever since she banned you. Unfortunately Kelfield's overzealous actions at your wedding have convinced Mama that I will be tainted if our friendship continues.

My heart aches that I cannot see you, my dearest friend. Please tell me that you are doing well, as I miss you terribly and worry about you constantly. We shall have to find a way to meet without Mama's knowledge.

Your devoted friend,
Cordelia Avery

Livvie had never considered that her hasty marriage would have repercussions on Cordie, and she was furious with herself for not considering her friend's future. She quickly went to her small study and dashed off a response to her most loyal of friends.

My Dearest Cordelia,

Please do not worry about me. I understand fully that Lady Avery simply does not wish for my indiscretions to tarnish your name, and truly I do not wish for that either. I am sorry I did not consider that before my visit today. I am certain the scandal of my marriage will soon die down and all will go back as it was before. At least I pray it will. We will just have to be patient.

Yours always,
Olivia Everett

The two of them kept a messenger darting back and forth between the Averys' and Kelfield House all afternoon.

Olivia!

Have you quite taken leave of your senses? How can you possibly agree with my mother on anything? Keeping us from visiting is unconscionable. You are my dearest friend in the world, and I hate that I cannot see you. Please say you and the duke are attending the Staveley Ball. I am certain we will be able to find a way to speak there.

Anxious to see you,
Cordie

Dear Cordelia,

I never thought I would agree with your mother either, but surely you do not wish for your association with me to reflect poorly on you. Upon further recollection, I seem to recall that even your Captain Seaton was standoffish towards you after my relationship with Kelfield was discovered. I do not want to be responsible for your heartbreak, my dearest friend.

Love always,
Olivia

Liv,

Please do not concern yourself about Captain Seaton at all. In hindsight, I have quite decided that I do not care one whit for that supercilious seaman. Besides, I could never be content with a man who thought he could dictate who my friends should be. I am certain your Kelfield would never do such a thing. Please tell me that he treats you well.

Your curious friend,
Cordie

Cordie,

I am sorry to hear about Captain Seaton, though I understand your concerns completely. You may rest at ease about Kelfield. His Grace treats me exceedingly well, and despite not being able to see you, I am quite happy. Kelfield and I will indeed be at Cousin Caroline's ball. I so look forward to seeing you there. I will ask my cousin to have gaming set up as well, since I know Lady Avery loves the tables. Hopefully, we will have the opportunity to speak freely.

Always yours,
Livvie

When Alex returned from an afternoon spent at his club, trying his damndest to look respectable for all the world, he was surprised to find Olivia solemnly flipping pages of a book in their yellow parlor. She didn't appear to be reading, just staring blankly at the pages. He couldn't imagine what could possibly have upset her, and he frowned stepping into the room. "How are you, sweetheart?"

She smiled softly and dropped the book to her lap. "Hello."

It was a forced smile. He didn't know everything there was to know about his wife, but he knew a feigned smiled when he saw it. No dimple. That was the secret. He crossed the room and took the spot beside his wife, tucking her under his arm. "How was your shopping excursion? Tell me you ordered something sheer to wear just for me."

Olivia blinked at him. "Pardon?" she asked.

He dipped his head and inhaled the lilac scent of her hair. "I'm attempting to seduce you, Olivia. A little assistance on your end would be most welcome."

She laughed and slid out of his hold, a genuine, playful smile lit her face. "Absolutely not. Your seductions last for hours, and we are to meet Caroline and Staveley for dinner and then attend Macbeth."

Alex pulled her back to him and buried his head in the crook of her neck, nipping at a particularly tender spot. "We'd have much more fun staying here. Alone," h

She giggled as his hand traveled up her side and he cupped her breast. She was delightful, and after spending most of the previous day in her bed, he was quite anxious to repeat their performance. There was something completely right about being in Olivia's arms, something he'd rather not spend too much time contemplating.

"You are incorrigible," she answered, brushing her lips lightly against his, making his cock ache to be back inside her. "But we promised we'd attend. And we're supposed to be respectable."

"I was respectable all day," he complained. "You have no idea how awful it is, having to discuss the merits of high shirt collar points all afternoon with feather-brained dandies."

Olivia kissed his chin. "Poor Kelfield," she cooed. "Did you have to pretend to be a proper gentleman all afternoon?"

Dear God, her kisses were going to undo him. "It was a testament to my devotion to you, my adoring wife. Now you'd best reward me." He tugged at her bodice.

"I'll reward you later," she promised, scrambling out of his grasp. When he frowned at her, she looked pleadingly at him. "Please. Caroline thinks this will help begin to repair my standing."

The situation couldn't be all that bad. Despite the fact that he'd like nothing more than to sink into his wife, he also wanted, very badly, to avoid Macbeth altogether. How awkward it would be to watch Sarah on stage while he sat next to Olivia. The entire thing had a very bad feel to it. Besides, no man should be required to do such a thing. "Sweetheart, I think Caroline is simply worried about you, and that is very kind of her. But it can't be that dire. She's exaggerating the situation, not intentionally though, I'm sure."

"I've been banned from the Averys', Alex." Olivia's plump bottom lip trembled with the admission. "Cordie's not allowed to see me anymore."

When a single tear trailed down her cheek, Alex's heart constricted in his chest. He hated seeing her in pain. "All right," he gave in, rubbing his temples, hoping he could get through the night. "We'd best get ready then."

Olivia smiled, stepped towards him and brushed a soft kiss to his lips. "Thank you."

"Of course," he replied, tucking a stray curl behind her ear. "Whatever makes you happy, sweetheart." And part of him believed that sentiment was much more true than he would have ever thought possible.

⚜

It was setting up to be a most uncomfortable night. In front of Staveley and Caroline, Alex and Olivia sat in Astwick's awful box overlooking the sea of theatergoers and the stage. If one had come for the entertainment, their position was awkward being on the far left side of the theatre. Unfortunately, it would be only too easy for Sarah to spot him. And while things had ended well with her, Alex had no desire to hurt her any more than he feared he already had.

Of course they hadn't come to see Macbeth — they'd come to be seen. Which they were. Other peers — most respectable, some not — were much more curious about the happenings in Astwick's rotten box than they were the stage. Well, they could look all they wanted. Alex wasn't going to give them anything to wag their tongues about. He didn't even drape his arm around Olivia's chair, though he wanted nothing more than to do that very thing.

What had happened to him? Days ago he'd been a devil-may-care rogue, and now he was sitting stoically in an unfortunately placed theatre box, putting on a respectable face to the world because his wife had had tears in her eyes. He was a goddamned fool. He just wasn't sure when the transformation had taken place.

Olivia looked over at him and smiled. His heart leapt at the sight, proving what a pathetic mooncalf he'd become.

Sounds of thunder echoed throughout the room, silencing the crowd. Then the curtains rose, revealing three old witches on the stage. "When shall we three meet again? In thunder, lightning, or in rain?" the first one asked in a screechy voice.

Olivia grabbed his leg, and he nearly shot out of his seat from her touch. But he forced himself to remain steady, placing his hand over hers, squeezing lightly.

Surprisingly, the first act went fairly smoothly. Even when he caught Sarah's eye, she hadn't reacted to seeing him. In fact, she was amazing, a wonderful Lady Macbeth. Alex was happy that her dreams were coming true.

When intermission came, Caroline tapped Olivia's shoulder. "Livvie, Sally Jersey is just over there. Come with me, we'll go say hello."

Alex rose as well, shaking his head. "Sally Jersey hates me. You should choose someone else to make a stand with."

Caroline winked at him, linking her arms with Olivia's. "That's precisely why we should seek her out, Alex. If Livvie could charm her, it would go a long way to restoring her name. Besides, Sally adores me."

The two ladies slipped out through the drapes at the back of the box, and Alex turned his attention to Staveley. "You're damned lucky things have gone well. Drury Lane, for Chrissakes, Staveley?"

The viscount shrugged. "I hadn't thought about Miss Kane. Besides, this was all Caroline's doing."

"One would think you could exert some control over your wife."

Staveley simply chuckled. "You got yourself into *this* mess."

"It *is* you," came an amused deep voice from behind them.

Alex turned to see Marcus Gray, the Marquess of Haversham, standing before him, arms folded across his chest, a smug look plastered across his face. "A wholesome evening with the duchess?" he inquired.

With a chuckle, Alex reached out his hand to his old debauched friend. "How are you, Marc?"

"Staveley." Marc nodded in acknowledgement. Then he slid into Olivia's vacant seat, his icy blue eyes filled with mirth. "What the devil has happened to you?"

Alex shrugged. "I've gotten married, perhaps you've heard."

"Everyone's heard." Marc's brow rose with amusement. "I was there, in case you don't remember."

"I remember. I just don't recall inviting you."

Marc's smirk grew larger. "You old devil. What happened? Did you get caught dipping you prick in her inkwell?"

It took all the strength Alex had not to throw the malevolent marquess over ledge. "That is my wife you're impugning. I'll thank you not to ever do it again," he growled.

Marc shook his head, unaffected by Alex's temper. "Relax, Kelfield. I had one of those, too. I didn't mean anything by it." After studying Alex a moment, the marquess leaned back in his seat. "I've heard rumor that you've given up Miss Kane. Is married life truly that delicious? Or are you just taking a holiday from the lovely Sarah until you tire of your wife?"

Sarah could do so much better than Haversham, which was really what he was asking. Breaking Alex's balls was just an added benefit. He shook his head. "Miss Kane is free to do whatever she chooses."

"Perfect. I think I'll take her off your hands then."

There was a slight gasp from behind them, and Alex turned in his seat to see Olivia's wide hazel eyes leveled on him. He couldn't quite read the look on her face, but he was certain it did not bode well for him.

Nineteen

LIVVIE watched her husband scramble to his feet, a guilty look plastered across his handsome face. That was certainly telling, wasn't it? She had always known he was the furthest thing from a proper gentleman. But were he and the lecherous marquess actually discussing women as if they were items to be shared or exchanged?

Philip would never do such a thing. She pushed the thought from her mind. Philip wasn't her husband, Alex was…and now he was stepping towards her.

"Olivia," he said softly.

She forced a smile to her face, though her back was as straight as an arrow. "Am I interrupting something, Alex?"

"Of course not, sweetheart. How was Lady Jersey?" He reached for her hand, and she allowed him to put it on his arm.

"We haven't been introduced," the wicked marquess remarked, bowing in her direction.

Alex cursed under his breath, glaring at the other man. "Marc, this is my wife, the Duchess of Kelfield." Then he smiled down at her. "Olivia sweetheart, this is the Marquess of Haversham, an old friend."

Which, of course, she knew. *Everyone* knew who he was. After all, the marquess was just as notorious as her husband. "My lord," she replied politely.

Haversham had the audacity to wink at her as a roguish smile tugged at his lips. "Marc. Please. All beautiful women call me Marc, or at least I like for them to."

Alex's jaw tightened and his eyes shot silver daggers at the marquess. "I'm sure *someone* must be missing your scintillating company, Haversham. Perhaps you could go find them."

"Subtle, Kelfield." Then the marquess threw back his head and laughed. "My dear," he said to Livvie, "it was very nice meeting you."

After Haversham escaped their box, Livvie stared up at her husband. "Well, I seriously doubt *he'll* help my standing in society."

"Do you want to go home?" he asked quietly, once they resumed their seats.

Livvie glared at him out of the corner of her eye. "Heavens, no. I'd hate for you to forsake the rest of Miss Kane's performance," she hissed back.

He frowned at her, but Livvie refused to look at him, keeping her eyes level on the crowd below them.

"This is exactly why I didn't want to come here tonight," he growled in her ear.

"Then you should have said something," she muttered between clenched teeth.

"I did."

Livvie finally turned to glare full-force upon him. She wasn't sure what she was most angry about: the fact that he and the marquess had spoken so disparagingly about the pretty actress. or that she'd spent the last hour unknowingly watching a woman with whom Alex had obviously shared a bed. Both were disturbing thoughts. "Not loud enough."

"I found it hard to refuse my wife when she had tears in her eyes."

Livvie turned her attention back to the stage, trying her best to appear like a respectable wife before the hordes of patrons who seemed inordinately interested in their box. After all, it was easier to face the crowd than her husband.

At that moment, Caroline slid back into the box, took her seat and whispered to her husband, "Was Haversham here?"

"I'm afraid so," Staveley muttered.

Before Caroline could say another word, Alex turned his head and glared at her. "Don't even think about starting in on me."

⋘⋙

Livvie was glad the coach was dark as they rambled home after the play. She didn't want to feel the heat of Alex's silver glare. In fact, she didn't want to see Alex at all. The lecherous rogue.

Thankfully, he hadn't uttered another word to her, and in kind she hadn't spoken to him either. That was fine. She didn't know what she would say anyway, and she'd just like to forget the entire night had even occurred.

When the coach rolled to a stop, she hopped out as soon as Coleman lowered the steps. Then she bounded into Kelfield House, leaving her husband in her wake before quickly retiring to her room.

Molly appeared a moment later and started to undress Livvie. Normally the maid was quite loquacious, but she must have sensed that something was amiss because she said very little, only glancing at Livvie with concern filled eyes. Then without warning, the door that connected Alex's chamber to hers flew open.

Livvie sucked in a surprised breath and Molly dropped her brush.

"Out!" Alex barked at the maid.

Molly stood frozen like a statue until Livvie touched her arm. "It's all right, Molly. I'll see you in the morning."

When the maid left through the door, Livvie picked up the fallen brush and started towards her mirror to prepare her hair for bed. It was much easier to do than facing her angry husband.

"Would you care to tell me," he began in a chillingly calm voice, "just why you are behaving like a spoiled child?"

A spoiled child? She suppressed the urge to hurl her brush at his head, as that would only seem to prove his point. Instead Livvie sat down at her mirror and removed the pins from her chignon, staring at her reflection. "I am tired, Alex. It has been a long day. Perhaps we can discuss your penchant for bedding actresses in the morning."

She unwound her hair, letting it fall about her shoulders, soundly ignoring her husband until his hand squeezed her shoulder. Then her eyes flew to the mirror when she saw him looming dangerously behind her, leveling her with an icy stare. Alex dipped his head until his lips touched her ear. All the while his eyes never left hers in the reflection. "The only woman I want to take to bed is you."

"Until you tire of me? And then what? Will you retrieve Miss Kane from your friend, Haversham?" She regretted the words almost the instant they left her mouth.

His eyes flashed angrily in the mirror, and Livvie swallowed nervously.

"I'll do whatever pleases me, Olivia. And to that end," he rasped, plucking at the strap to her chemise, "I'd like you to remove this."

"Go to the devil." She scrambled from his grasp and glared at him.

Alex stalked towards her like a lion, and her breath caught in her throat. "I've already told you, Olivia, that you'll not keep me from your bed."

Livvie tipped her nose in the air and sprinted for her door. "Enjoy it the entire night for all I care." Then she bolted from the room, escaping into the hallway and slammed the door firmly behind her.

⚮

Alex stared at the closed door in complete shock. Women didn't walk out on him. *His wife* certainly wouldn't walk out on him. And for God's sake, the woman was only wearing her chemise. She couldn't go traipsing about the house in nothing more than some flimsy, nearly transparent silk.

He snatched up her pink wrapper, still lying on the bed, and stalked off after his wife. Damn her! He didn't chase after women.

As he opened the door, he found a befuddled Gibson drenched from head to toe, smelling of whiskey. The butler blinked at him in shock. "Her Grace," was all the man could manage in explanation. Then he dropped to the floor, retrieving an upturned beveled glass from the runner.

"Where?" he barked.

"Headed for the stairs, sir." Gibson replied, now dabbing at a spot on the rug.

Alex stormed off down the stairs and rounded the corner. He nearly slipped on a vase lying on the floor, and belatedly noticed water and lilies littered all about. Well, she was certainly making it easy for him to find her. Olivia had left all sorts of carnage in her path to escape him.

He'd expected her to seek refuge in the music room as she often tended to be there, pounding out her feelings of the moment. But the corridor was silent. He stalked inside one parlor after another and then stopped when he noticed the library door was closed. As he got closer, muffled sobs filtered into the corridor. *Olivia was crying.*

His heart stopped.

Alex's anger instantly evaporated, and he slowly opened the door. The library was mostly dark, except for where the moonlight filtered in though the undrawn windows. Olivia was huddled on the damask chaise, her knees pulled up to her chin. With each sob, he felt more helpless and was rooted to the floor.

Though he must've made some sound, because her head snapped up and she tried to wipe away her tears. "Go away."

He probably should. The sight of her curled up and crying reminded him of another time. Another woman. His mother. And he tried never to think of *her*. But if he left Olivia, her image would haunt him the rest of the night. He didn't need any more demons.

Alex stepped inside, quietly closing the door behind him. Then he crossed the room and knelt at his wife's side.

She glowered at him and swiped at her tear-stained cheeks. "I said, 'Go away'."

Gently brushing away her tears with the pad of his thumbs, Alex flashed her a roguish smile. "Yes, but I'm Kelfield and I do as I please."

"Don't." She choked on a laugh and hugged her knees tighter to her chest. "Don't be charming. I'm angry with you and am determined to stay that way."

"Are you also determined to stay cold?" he asked and then draped her pink wrapper over her shoulders. "Sweetheart, you really should have a care. As much as *I* enjoy seeing you in only your chemise, the house is fully staffed now, and I'd hate to have to sack all the new footmen for falling in love you."

A gurgled laugh escaped her. "Please go away. You're being charming."

"Well, I can't help it," he replied, taking one of her delicate hands in his, softly kneading it with his thumb. "It's a curse."

She laughed again and Alex's spirits lifted with the sound. "I do wish you'd stop. You're making it very difficult for me to remain furious with you."

It was now or never. Better to get all the cards on the table. Alex sighed, staring deeply into his wife's shadowed face. "Olivia, why exactly are you furious with me?"

She sobered instantly, and began to tick off the reasons with her fingers. He soon wished he hadn't asked at all. "Well, first of all, you were a perfect beast just now in my room—bellowing at Molly and acting like a selfish lout. But before that I was angry because you let me sit in that box without telling me what was going on. I had to hear about Miss Kane from that lecherous wastrel Haversham, when *you* should have told me. All night I sat and watched Miss Kane, without having any idea who she was to you. Do you know how foolish that makes me feel? Then I looked around at the other boxes. Everyone was looking at us, and I realized they were all looking for my reaction to the situation."

"I doubt everyone was. Women don't really know those sorts of details, sweetheart. Caroline didn't, and she's generally well-informed."

"That does *not* make it better, Alex. If you'd told me, we wouldn't have gone tonight. Do you think I want to look at a woman all evening and know my husband has shared her bed?"

Then she'd need to go around Town with a blindfold on to avoid them all. "Olivia," he started cautiously, "I'm not going to give you a list of every woman I've bedded."

"Not enough foolscap?" she asked tartly.

"Not appropriate," he answered.

She scowled at him. "And then there was the charming conversation between you and the marquess about that actress. You just gave her to him, like—"

"I most certainly did not. Sarah makes her own choices. Though she can do better than Haversham, she can have him if that's what she wants."

"She makes her *own* choices? Well, isn't that novel for a woman?"

All of Alex's muscles tensed at her less than subtle reference to her own lack of choice in marrying him. "I didn't make society's rules, Olivia, and I rarely live by them. So don't blame me for your predicament. You were the one to sneak into my room, after all."

"That wasn't what I was saying."

"Wasn't it?" he asked challengingly, as his face heated up.

"I've just never considered that sort of woman had more freedom than those who lived respectable lives."

He shouldn't have taken offense at her words. They were the truth by society's standards. But he didn't seem able to help himself. "Respectability is subjective, which you should well know with the way people have treated you since we've married. Sarah Kane is a kind soul, her choice of profession notwithstanding. Don't ever disparage her."

Olivia's mouth dropped open and she blinked at him in astonishment. "You love her."

Alex shook his head. There was no way to explain it. She was too unworldly to understand. "Not in the way you mean. Sarah is—was—a very good friend, and I wish her the best of luck." He gently touched her tear-stained cheeks. They were red and puffy. The sight tore at his soul. He'd never wanted to hurt her, never wanted to bring tears to her eyes. "Listen, sweetheart, I'm sorry about tonight. I suppose I could have told you the reason I didn't want to attend the theatre, but..." He sighed. "Well, I didn't know how to tell you. It's not something a man can easily say to his wife."

"She's not your m-mistress anymore, is she?" Olivia sniffed and wiped at her eyes.

He shook his head. "I don't need a mistress. I have a very pretty wife that makes me lust after her all the time."

Alex expected her to blush, but instead she buried her head against the back of the chaise and fresh tears started to fall. The sight was almost too much for him to bear. He leaned forward and scooped her into his arms, then settled himself on the chaise with her on his lap. "Olivia," he began, cradling her against him. "What's the matter now?"

She shook her head and burrowed closer into his warmth. "You'll think I'm silly."

"I won't," he promised, gently smoothing her hair with his hand.

Quietly, Olivia played with one of the buttons on his shirt, staring at his chest. He thought she wouldn't speak at all, but then she said in a very tiny voice, "I don't like to think about you with other women. I know you've been with them. Everyone knows. But I don't like to think about it."

Alex's heart swelled with hope. Was it possible she had feelings for him that extended outside of the bedroom? He'd hoped that someday she could grow to care for him, despite not having had a choice in their marriage. It seemed too good to be true. "Watch what you say, Olivia," he said with a self-deprecating laugh, "or you'll have me believing you'd actually choose to be my wife."

"Alex, I…" She placed her hand on his heart and stared into his eyes. "I love being your wife."

He couldn't help but chuckle with disbelief. "Despite the fact that you're raising my daughter and that you're not allowed to see your best friend?"

She nodded. "I adore Poppy, though I'm not so sure about my mothering skills. And Cordie…well, talk will eventually die down. Someone else will do something that will capture the *ton*'s interest. I'm sure Lady Avery will come around in the end." Then she rested her head against his chest, touching him softly through his shirt, making his heart pound rapidly. "But you, Alex…surely, you know what you do to me. The intimacies. The way you make me feel."

His naïve wife. Not that he was surprised. Olivia didn't realize that men and women pleasured each other all the time. Love didn't have anything to do with sex. Her feelings were simply confused. If they'd not married and Philip Moore was in London, she would have chosen the Major. He didn't have any doubts about that. Still, the idea that she loved being his wife was an intoxicating one. Alex sighed. "Oh, sweetheart. What am I to do with you?"

Olivia hid her face in his shirt, avoiding his gaze. "I knew you'd think I was silly."

He tilted her head back to look at him. "I don't think you're silly. I think you're delightful."

Then he kissed her.

Twenty

IT WAS a tender kiss. One that, like so many of his, made her toes curl. When Livvie opened her mouth, a moan escaped her. Alex chuckled against her lips and then swept his warm tongue inside her mouth to tangle with hers. She slid her hands up his chest, all muscle and sinew, to settle on his strong shoulders.

"Olivia," he rasped, moving his hands along her curves until he plucked at one nipple.

Spirals of desire raced through Livvie and she pressed herself closer to her husband, reveling in the feel of his aroused manhood under her bottom. She wanted to feel him all around her, inside her, pushing her slowly to the edge of insanity.

Livvie shifted on his lap, causing a groan to escape his lips. Then she ran her hands through his inky hair, twirling her fingers through the short curls at his neck. "Make love to me, Alex."

He grunted his answer, sliding her chemise up over her hips. Alex squeezed her thigh, sending a shiver of anticipation straight to her core. Livvie's head fell against his chest, and one of his clever fingers parted the springy hair at the apex of her thighs. When he touched her sensitive nub, she thought she would completely unravel.

Slowly, methodically, he stroked her in and out, over and over. His touch, his ministrations, drove her wild. "Please, Alex," she begged him for more, which he freely gave.

Just as Livvie was certain she would expire, he chuckled, soundly kissed her, and opened his trousers. "Get on top of me, sweetheart."

"On top?"

He stroked her cheek and even in the dim light she could see his grin. "It's just like riding astride."

Livvie looked down as his engorged manhood and swallowed. "You haven't taught me how to do that yet."

"Consider this your first lesson," Alex rasped, reaching for her. "Straddle me. Put your knees on either side of my legs."

She did as he asked but felt strange doing so. None of their other couplings had been like this. "You're certain?"

He nodded, slid his hands back under her chemise, and grasped her hips with his long fingers. Then he lowered her to him, slowly impaling her on his staff. "Dear God, Olivia," he whispered appreciatively.

He stretched her and filled her and made Livvie see stars when she closed her eyes. "Oh, Alex."

"Now move on me, Olivia. Ride me up and down."

The suggestion sent delicious shivers across her body. She leaned forward, holding on to his shoulders and moved over him. It was enthralling and she slid back and forth, watching his face as he neared his pinnacle.

The scent of rich sandalwood teased her and sent her spiraling to her own edge. Alex's hands tightened on her hips as he thrust upward over and over. Then he lowered one hand between her legs and again very lightly grazed her throbbing, sensitive nub.

Livvie lost all consciousnesses and was only vaguely aware of him spilling himself inside her with a primitive growl. She collapsed atop him, panting, tying to catch her breath.

Alex wrapped his arms around her, holding her close for what felt like forever. Then he finally kissed her brow. "We'd best go back upstairs, sweetheart."

"Must we?" she whined. She was so comfortable, so sated, she hated to move.

"You don't want poor Gibson to find us like this. Besides, this chaise is not comfortable enough to spend the entire night. You can trust me on that."

When she frowned in response, Alex chuckled. "Be a good girl, Olivia, and I promise we can christen all the other rooms later."

Good heavens! He was brash. She loved that about him. He was so unrepentant and confident. Arrogant, that's what she used to call it. But she no longer minded that quality in him. In fact it was intoxicating.

Livvie rolled off him, staring blankly at the darkened library. She would blush whenever she entered this room in the future.

Alex quickly righted himself and then scooped her up in his arms. She'd never felt so safe, so protected, so cared for. He carried Livvie back up the stairs to her chambers, her sated body limp against his. He placed her on the counterpane, apparently prepared to tuck her in for the night, but she held on to his neck, forcing him to fall on the bed beside her.

"Sweetheart, let me put you in bed," he whispered across her lips.

Livvie frowned in response. "No, because then you'll leave me. Please, Alex," she begged, holding tighter to him, "stay with me tonight."

He paused a moment, looking into her eyes and Livvie thought he'd agree, but then he shook his head. "You wouldn't want me to stay all night."

"But I do," she tried to assure him.

Alex kissed her softly and traced her jaw with his fingers. "Olivia, it's late. Get your sleep."

He pulled back the counterpane and slid her under the covers. Livvie pouted when he started to leave her. She hated being separated from him and longed to spend the night in his arms, feeling his strength, this warmth, his love.

His love? He'd never said those words.

"Goodnight, sweetheart," he whispered as he opened the door that led to his room.

When he was gone, Livvie blinked up at the canopy above her. His love? Did he love her? At times she thought he did. The look he often had in his eyes when they were alone. The way he touched her, filling her with desire. The way he whispered her name during their lovemaking.

She knew for certain that she loved him. Her heartbeat quickened when he was near. Her breath would catch whenever he met her eyes. When he wasn't around, her thoughts were only of him. She didn't doubt that she'd loved Philip—she probably always would—but those sweet feelings paled in comparison to for what she felt for Alex. The intensity of her feelings for her husband were so strong, there wasn't another word for it but love.

And she hated being cut off from him at night.

≺∙ᵉᵗᵗᵗ∙≻

Livvie awoke with a smile on her face. The memories of Alex's seductive touch were fresh on her mind. She knocked on their adjoining door but received no answer. So, she pushed it open only to find the room empty and already cleaned. She heaved a sigh, wishing she'd caught him before he'd left for the day. He'd had another bad dream the night before. She had been sorely tempted to go to him, but she hadn't the courage to do so.

After Livvie's bath and morning ablutions, Molly dressed her for the day in a fashionable robin's egg blue dress with tiny, white rosebuds. She quickly broke her fast and started for the music room. Haydn was racing through her veins.

Then she stopped in her tracks.

She could play the piano and lose herself in the music...but it suddenly seemed a much better idea to spend the day with Poppy. They'd enjoyed a daily tea party ever since that first day, but she should spend more time with the child. Her decision made, Livvie turned towards the stairs and made her way to the nursery. Mrs. Bickle was patiently listening to an outlandish story, while Poppy waived her arms wildly. "And then the princess rode the unicorn up to the castle, and..."

The child stopped talking when she noticed Livvie in the doorway. "Don't stop on my account, Poppy."

But her step-daughter paid her request no notice and rushed towards her. "Do you want to have a tea party?"

Livvie shook her head, taking in the tattered blue dress that the girl always seemed to wear. An idea hit her. She couldn't go shopping with Cordie, but she could certainly go with Poppy. "Is this your favorite dress?"

The girl nodded her head. "Papa says I look like a princess in it."

"Ah," Livvie replied, understanding completely now. "Would you like to go shopping with me today, Poppy? We can order you some new dresses."

Poppy frowned. "But Papa likes this one."

Livvie tapped her nose and smiled. "I'm certain that we can pick out some new ones that he'd like just as well. The blue is pretty on you, but I think pink might be even prettier. Oh, and green will make your eyes sparkle."

"Really?" her step-daughter asked, her silver eyes wide.

"Absolutely. We can look at fashion plates and pretty silks and muslins."

"Oh, yes, let's!" Poppy gushed, her raven curls bouncing up and down.

Livvie smiled at the child then turned her attention to the nursemaid. "Mrs. Bickle, will you see to it that Poppy is ready to leave in half an hour?"

"Of course, Your Grace."

⚜

Madam Fournier's small shop in Bruton Street was both exclusive and high priced. The tiny French modiste's talents were well sought after, and while an appointment would normally have been necessary, Livvie was warmly welcomed for two reasons. The first was that Caroline had been a patron of Madam's for many years and had helped the woman build her clientele. But the second reason was that Livvie was now a very wealthy duchess and regardless of the *ton*'s view of her, shopkeepers would welcome her with open arms.

"Your Grace!" the small dressmaker gushed when Livvie and Poppy entered her shop. "You do me such a compliment coming here."

Livvie smiled in response. "Thank you, Madam. This is my step-daughter Poppy, and we would like to look at some fashion plates."

The modiste's smile faltered. "For the child?"

"Yes, and for me, of course, as well. Lady Staveley is hosting a large ball next week, and I know it is short notice, but I would like something new."

"Something that speaks to your new—what is the word—exalted station?"

Well, that was one way of putting it. Livvie nodded. "Yes."

"Then you shall have it, Your Grace."

156

In no time, Livvie and Poppy sipped tea and flipped through Madam's fashion plates. Poppy was measured, poked and prodded, but she giggled nearly the entire time, thoroughly enjoying herself and the attention. One would think that after living with her actress mother, Poppy would have been accustomed to costumes, gowns, and fabrics, but the child was mesmerized by the entire event.

It was surprisingly enjoyable to experience mundane activities through the eyes of a cheerful five-year-old. Livvie's heart swelled as the girl flipped through swatches of fabric and asked the modiste all sorts of questions, which the dressmaker and her assistants happily answered in a rapid, French-English mix.

"She is adorable, no?" the seamstress, Amelie, asked of the others.

"*Oui*," Madam answered with an indulgent smile. "*Elle est délicieuse.*" Then she turned her attention to Livvie and rubbed her chin. "Now I am thinking of your dress, Your Grace."

"Have you an idea?"

After squinting her eyes and tapping her lips, Madam shouted, "Copper!" from across the room.

Livvie nearly jumped out of her skin. "I beg your pardon."

"Copper," the Frenchwoman repeated. "That is your color, Your Grace. Your eyes, your hair. Copper for the gown for Staveleys'."

She didn't think she'd ever worn that color before. But since it wasn't scarlet or something equally daring, Livvie smiled at the modiste. "Cousin Caroline raves about your genius, Madam. I willingly put myself in your capable hands."

The Frenchwoman's light eyes twinkled. "*Vous serez radiante.*"

"Thank you," Livvie replied. Then she motioned to Poppy, gingerly running her fingers over the designs, and she crossed the room to the modiste. "For my daughter, I'd like something suitable for church on Sunday. Do you think that is possible?"

Madam Fournier laughed. "For the right price, Your Grace, anything is possible, yes? She likes this ragged dress she wears?"

"It's her favorite," Livvie confided quietly.

"Ah." Madam nodded. "Something for church and something for fun then. I will have them delivered in the morning."

"So soon?" That was quite shocking. Madam was known for her abilities, not her speed.

The Frenchwoman glanced at her assistants hovering over the pretty little girl. "For *la petit ange*? Look at them. They won't go home until they've finished her dresses. But not for you, your gown will take longer. I must think how to make it most *spectaculaire*."

"As long as it arrives before Staveley's ball, you may have all the time in the world." Livvie then slid closer to the modiste and whispered, "Madam, my husband has been hinting that he'd like me to order..." It really was hard to say and her face heated up.

Luckily, Madam took pity on her. "Actually, Your Grace, the duke was here *ce matin*. I do know what he'd like."

Livvie blinked at the woman. "He was here?"

Madam explained, "He assumed since Lady Staveley is my client you were as well, and thought I might have your measurements."

Oh, well that did make sense. Livvie smiled with relief. What a strange feeling, however. No man had ever ordered clothing for her before. Who knew what Alex had picked out? She'd best not think about that, or she'd be wearing a permanent blush the rest of the day.

"Just *feignez* surprise when he presents them. I am thinking I would not like to anger this man, your husband."

Livvie and Poppy eventually left the shop, and by the time they arrived back at Kelfield House, their carriage was weighted down with slippers, bonnets, gloves and ribbons. Apparently Poppy loved ribbons, for when she'd seen them in the store, her eyes lit up and she twirled them about her body.

As they stepped out of the Kelfield coach, Livvie was surprised to see Lady Carteret and Mrs. Greywood departing her home. When they spotted her, the two women smiled brightly, rushing toward them.

"Oh, my dear," Lady Carteret gushed, "we were so worried we'd missed you."

Twenty-One

TAKEN aback by the approaching women, Livvie plastered a smile on her face. "Oh. Lovely to see you. Poppy and I have been shopping. Would you like to stay for a visit?" Though she didn't know either woman well, it was nice not to be a pariah to *everyone*. Their husbands were Alex's oldest friends, and it was probably time she got to know them better anyway.

"Thank you," Mrs. Greywood replied with a smile, her sea-blue eyes twinkling when they landed on Poppy.

Gibson opened the door, and all four of them filed inside. Livvie ordered tea and scones and then directed her guests to the gold parlor, but Poppy held back and tugged on her dress.

"Yes, sweeting?" Livvie asked.

"I think Mrs. Bickle is lonely. May I go back to the nursery?" Which was probably for the best anyway. Who knew what these women had come to say to her?

Livvie smiled and pushed one of the child's black curls behind her ear. "Of course, Poppy. I'll visit you once Lady Carteret and Mrs. Greywood have left."

Poppy threw her arms around Livvie's middle and held her tight.

"Thank you, Olivia. Shopping was grand."

It had been most enjoyable. Livvie caressed Poppy's back and then pressed a kiss to her forehead. Spending time with her step-daughter was more delightful than she would have thought. They would have to make a habit out of such excursions. Awash in new maternal feelings, Livvie grinned at Poppy. "I think so, too. And just wait until your new dresses arrive."

How lovely it would be to have more children, Livvie thought as she neared the gold parlor. *Children?* She supposed she would have to give Alex an heir at some point. The idea brought a smile to her face.

She stepped inside the parlor, and found both ladies' eyes fixed on her, seated in white damask chairs. "Lady Carteret, Mrs. Greywood, how nice of you both to call," she replied and took a spot on a gold brocade settee across from them.

Mrs. Greywood shook her head, her pretty blue eyes sparkling. "There's no point in being formal," she informed her with a charming American accent. "You're part of the club now. She's Bethany and I'm Madeline — most people call me Maddie."

She was part of a club? Well, it was certainly better than not being included. "Which club am I now a member of?"

The two women giggled. Bethany finally answered, "Marriage to those four. I would have invited Caro to join us, but I know she is working tirelessly on preparations for her ball. Besides, you know her just as well or better than we do, and this will give us a chance to better acquaint ourselves."

"We would have come earlier," Maddie explained, "but we wanted to give you time to settle in. Especially after we learned Poppy was living here."

Olivia felt at once protective of her step-daughter and sat up straighter. They weren't going to cast judgment on that situation, were they?

Maddie smiled sweetly. "Olivia, relax. You are among friends. When I married Simon I found myself in a similar situation. I know it isn't always the easiest going."

Bethany sighed. "My brother is very similar to Alex. I'm not sure which of them was the worst influence on the other."

"I'm not sure if that is a compliment or not, Beth," Alex remarked from the open doorway, though his eyes were on Livvie. "Sweetheart, remember not to take *any* advice from her."

The comment brought a blush to Livvie's cheeks as she remembered Alex's relief that the countess had not been the one to have The Talk with her before their wedding.

"On the contrary," Bethany playfully shot back. "My dear Olivia, I have known this rogue since I was in leading strings. I'm certain my insight on him could be most useful for you."

Like perhaps what sorts of terrible things haunted him in his sleep? Livvie was instantly intrigued.

Alex stepped into the room and then claimed the spot next to his wife. "Beth was always a pest. Following Simon and me everywhere we went. It was impossible to shake her."

"Forgetful in your old age, Kelfield?" Beth asked sweetly. "I couldn't have cared less what wickedness the two of you were up to."

Maddie giggled across the room. "You'll have to forgive them, Olivia. Alex is an honorary Greywood, and I'm afraid when they're all together, they behave like siblings."

Like she and the Averys used to.

A twinge of sadness washed over Livvie just as Gibson entered with tea. She was glad for the interruption and began pouring for her guests. Bethany took hers with two sugars and milk, and Maddie took hers straight. When she offered Alex a cup sweetened with sugar, she apologized. "If I'd known you were going to be here, I'd have asked Gibson for honey."

Alex's silver eyes twinkled as his fingers brushed hers under the saucer. "How did you know I liked honey?"

"Poppy told me."

"Alex," Maddie gushed, "she is precious. Truly an adorable child."

He responded with only a wink.

Livvie reclaimed her spot beside Alex and smiled when he lazily draped his arm around her, barely touching her shoulder and sending frissons of desire coursing through her veins. Despite the losses she'd suffered from their union, she wouldn't want to give up life as his wife. She had never felt so complete, so at one with the world, than when she was with him.

"You do know, Alex," Bethany began, "Maddie and I came to visit

Olivia, not you."

Livvie's eyes flew to her husband. She expected him to be furious, or in the very least annoyed, but he was grinning from ear to ear. "You do realize, Beth, that you're still a pest."

Maddie shook her head with a laugh. "Honestly, Olivia, you should see them at Christmas when they're all together — Maxwell, Simon, Alex, Benedict, Bethany, and Charles. Grown up children, each of them. I'm not sure how my mother-in-law handled such an unruly lot."

"Is that an invitation?" Alex asked. "For Christmas, I mean."

A beautiful smile lit up Maddie's face. "You're always welcome, Alex. You know that."

Bethany sat forward in her chair. "Yes, of course. You know mother loves having you. But don't you think that it's time you opened up Everett Place?"

Alex tensed at Livvie's side before a patronizing smile settled on his lips. "No, I don't." Then he turned his attention to Maddie. "How much longer are you and Simon in Town?"

Where was Everett Place? And why did he dismiss it so easily? As Livvie took a sip of tea, she glanced at Alex out of the corner of her eye. Though she was his wife, there was still so much she didn't know about him.

"It's your family home, Alex. It shouldn't be neglected for so long." Bethany frowned at him.

Alex narrowed his eyes on the irritating countess. "Indeed? And the last time James set foot in Briarstrath was...?" he asked, though it seemed as if he already knew the answer to that. "From what I understand, it's crumbling to the ground. Glass houses and all that, Beth."

"Simon and I will return to Norfolk after Caroline's ball," Maddie informed them in an obvious attempt to break up the tension in the room.

"I do hope you'll be on your best behavior, Alex," Bethany remarked then raised her teacup to her lips.

"When I want your advice, Beth, I'll ask for it. Until then, James is the only one you should be pestering."

❦

Caroline sat in her small study sorting through her correspondence, conflicting emotions ravaging her. There was a letter from her sister-in-law Lydia, a thank you note from her friend Hannah Astwick, and an invitation to a garden party from Louisa Ridgemont. All the usual sorts of things she found in her post, but at the corner of her desk sat a cannon ball waiting to explode.

She cast an annoyed glance at the unwanted missive. *Damn him!* Livvie had been waiting for months to hear from Philip Moore. Why did the major have to write her now? It was a most inopportune time.

She could hide the letter. Throw it away. Pretend as if it never arrived at Staveley House. Though that was simply delaying the inevitable. He'd only write again.

Or she could take the letter to Kelfield House and give it to Livvie. That was the moral thing to do. Livvie could make her own decision about the letter. She could read it if she wanted. Or she could toss it in a grate. But that was putting her dear cousin in a terrible spot. One she didn't need to be in at the moment.

If Caroline wasn't mistaken, Livvie truly cared about Alex, and it was no secret that Alex was enamored with Livvie. He'd made that quite clear at their wedding. Which was the crux of the problem. They were married, and hopefully on a path toward happiness. Nothing Philip Moore had written would help them. It could only hurt.

She'd been deceptive in the past. Come up with all sorts of manipulative plans of one fashion or another, but she'd never discarded someone else's personal correspondence. That seemed beyond the pale.

Could she wait a few days? Maybe a week? Give Livvie and Alex's blooming relationship time to congeal. It wasn't the best plan she'd ever come up with, but it was the best she could think of at the moment.

Caroline opened her top desk drawer and dropped the letter inside.

"Where is Everett Place?" Livvie asked Alex over dinner.

His fork stopped midway to his mouth, and then he dropped it to his plate. "Didn't I tell you not to pay attention to anything Bethany Carteret had to say?"

"No," Livvie answered honestly. "You said not to listen to any of her advice. Is Everett Place your ancestral seat?"

"Then I'm amending my statement. Don't pay attention to anything Beth has to say." Alex retrieved his fork and took a bite of carrots.

Even over the soft candlelight, his face appeared taught, his jaw firmly set. She couldn't understand why this was troubling for him. It was really a rather simple, unemotional question. She wasn't asking to visit Everett Place, just inquiring as to its location. Why did he keep so much of himself hidden? It was quite worrisome.

Alex looked across the table at her and frowned. "You haven't eaten anything, Olivia."

She shook her head, her appetite long gone. "I'm not hungry."

"Damn her."

"I beg your pardon."

"Beth doesn't seem able to keep her mouth closed about anything." He took a deep breath. "Everett Place is my ancestral home. It is near Brockenhurst in Hampshire. I haven't seen it in nearly two decades, and I don't have any plans to remedy that in the future — near or otherwise. Now, eat."

Livvie picked up her fork and speared a small floret of cauliflower. Her appetite wasn't any better, but he was waiting at the other end of the table, staring at her. She popped the vegetable into her mouth and chewed, though her stomach protested the action. "There. Are you happy?"

He inclined his head and returned to his own meal.

Livvie watched him and moved the food around her own plate, hoping he wouldn't notice that she wasn't eating anything else. The room was deafeningly quiet, which was torturous. "Poppy and I went shopping today."

Alex looked across the table at her, one black eyebrow raised in question. "Indeed?"

"Yes. We went to Madam Fournier's and had a lovely time."

A smile crossed his face, and Livvie thought about the order he placed earlier in the day with the modiste. "I understand she is very talented. Did you commission something?"

So he wasn't going to tell her he'd been there himself. Not that she was surprised. The man seemed to hold more secrets than anyone she'd ever known. "Yes, and Madam and all her assistants were enchanted with Poppy. She had a grand time and left the shop with her weight in ribbons."

"Thank you," he began, a serious look upon his face, "for accepting the situation as gracefully as you have. I know Poppy must have been a surprise for you. I do want to assure you that there aren't any others. You won't have to raise a houseful of my children."

"But I want to raise a houseful of your children," Livvie said, without thinking. At his stunned expression, she continued, "I mean, you'll need an heir."

"Yes, I suppose I will," he said, his eyes sweeping across her form with a lascivious twinkle.

Once dinner was over, Alex escorted Livvie to the music room. He insisted she play something for him on the pianoforte, and she happily began to entertain him with Haydn's Surprise Symphony. She had barely gotten through the tranquil opening before his breath warmed her cheek.

"I believe there was a little matter of christening every room in the house, wasn't there, sweetheart?" he whispered in her ear.

The chords and melodies were soon forgotten as Alex stripped her down in the middle of the music room and laid her across the piano bench, making passionate love to her.

Sated and breathless, she rested in Alex's arms as he once again carried her to her room. He gently tucked her into bed, ignored her request for him to stay with her through the night, kissed her lips, and left for his room, as always.

Hours later, like every other night since their marriage, Livvie awoke when her husband's screams broke the silence. But unlike every other night, she decided not to ignore them this time. She slid out of bed, wrapped her pink wrapper around herself, and crossed the floor to the door that connected her chamber to her husband's.

Taking a breath for courage, she pushed the door open and rushed into his room.

Twenty-Two

ALEX roughly rubbed his face, trying to wipe the awful images from his mind. Then he heard something creak, and he blinked his eyes open. Even in his darkened room, he could make out his wife's silhouette. Alex quickly sat up in his bed. "Olivia!" he barked. "Go back to your room."

Willful woman that she was, Olivia rushed from the doorway and knelt at his side. "Alex, what is wrong?"

She gently touched his arm, making him recoil. Bloody hell, he hated that she saw him like this again. But it was dark..."I will be obeyed, Olivia. Go back to your room."

Olivia tipped her chin stubbornly in the air. "*I* am the Duchess of Kelfield, and I'll do what I please. Now tell me what is wrong?"

For a moment he gaped at her. Then Alex fell back on his pillows and laughed. He couldn't help it. How many times had he said the same thing to her?

His reaction must have frightened her, because she looked at once panicked. "Are you all right, my love?"

He rolled to his side, facing her, barely keeping himself from touching her. "I never thought to have those words thrown back in my face, sweetheart."

She grinned at him. "Yes, well, what's good for the goose and all that."

Alex tucked one of her curls behind her ear, and smiled sadly. "You should go back to your room. You don't need to see me like this."

Stubbornly she shook her head. "Yes, I do. I'm your wife." Then she traced his jaw with her finger. "What haunts you, Alex? I hear you every night and it tears at my heart. Please tell me."

Every night?

Horror washed over him, and Alex blanched, sliding away from her. "You've heard me? Why didn't you say something?"

Livvie furrowed her brow. "I... Well, after the night at Prestwick Chase, you... Well, I didn't know what to say. But we can't go on like *this*, Alex."

He agreed with a firm nod and sat up. "No, I should say not. I'll have you moved in the morning. I had no idea, Olivia. I'm very sorry." What must she have thought all those nights? Poor girl.

She stood up, hands on her hips, glowering at him. "You'll do no such thing, unless you plan to move me into this room. I will never leave your side, so don't even think about it."

What could he possibly say to that? Besides, she was here, looking delectable. Alex lifted his counterpane as an invitation for her to join him in his bed. With a look of surprise, Livvie quickly slid beneath the covers before he could change his mind. He held her back against the wall of his chest and pressed a kiss to her neck. "My stubborn wife."

It was overwhelmingly comfortable to have her share his bed. Alex sighed and splayed his hand possessively across her taught belly. This was how he'd wanted it all along, but it just wasn't wise. Damn her for taking advantage of him in this vulnerable state.

"Alex," she finally whispered, "what haunts you?"

"Olivia, go to sleep." Letting her stay was one thing. Telling her was something else.

"I only want to help you."

If only she could. Alex laughed sadly. "Sweetheart, you can't help. I've been having those dreams on and off since before you were born."

She took a moment, apparently to absorb that before stating, "Talking about them can help. It has for me in the past."

"Talking about it won't help."

"How do you know? Have you talked to someone else?"

"Sweetheart, you're making it impossible for me to go back to sleep."

Olivia turned in his arms. Her beautiful face, so filled with concern, touched his soul. "Good. I don't want you to go back to sleep. I want you to tell me what wakes you at night."

Apparently, she wouldn't stop until he told her something. He heaved a giant sigh. "My mother, Olivia. Are you happy now?" He hadn't spoken of her in years. How strange it was to say those words.

"What about your mother?" she asked softly.

He hugged her against him and kissed her brow, feeling more peace than he had in the longest while. "You are most obstinate. Very well. If I tell you, will you promise to go back to sleep?"

"Yes, of course."

"When I was told my mother died, I was convinced that I was responsible for her death." The images were always of her mangled body and his father's bloodied hands. Even though in the light of day he knew the dreams were false, when he was dreaming, the rational part of his mind didn't function properly. The visions were so awful, so real, he always woke up. Panting. Sweating. Cursing himself a fool for falling victim to it again.

Olivia placed her delicate hand on his chest. "What happened, my darling?" she asked in the most soothing voice.

He had no intention of telling her. She didn't need to know. But he found himself saying, "It was my mother's birthday. She was always skittish, as if she was constantly about to jump out of her skin, especially around my father — which was understandable. No one liked to spend an inordinate amount of time with the man. Perhaps his well-paid paramours, but no one else." Then with a self-deprecating laugh he added, "I know. Like father like son."

"I wasn't thinking that," Olivia protested and snuggled closer to him, her lithe body molding so perfectly against his.

He stroked her back, relishing the feel of her connected to him. "It's all right if you were. I've thought it enough times myself."

"Why do you think her death was your fault?"

"I don't anymore," he confessed. *After all, one couldn't be responsible for the death of a woman who was still alive.* "But I did then. I'd gone to her chamber to surprise her with flowers. I heard screaming. The door was bolted, and I peeked through keyhole to see her maid attacking her, or so I thought, and I ran to for my father for help. He was just down the hall." His body tensed with the telling, and Olivia held him closer. "Father rushed to her room and broke open the door..." He choked at the memory. Not an attack, an intimate encounter. One he'd been too innocent to understand at the time.

"And?" Livvie prompted.

"The maid wasn't attacking her."

"But she was screaming? What was the maid doing?"

"Pleasuring her. They were screams of ecstasy." He snorted at the memory. "Apparently the only thing my father, mother, and I have had in common is we all preferred women in our beds."

Olivia sucked in a breath.

"Father was furious. He beat the maid senseless and then started on Mother." He'd never seen the man in such a fit before. He still couldn't get his father's bloodied hands out of his memory.

"And she died?" Olivia asked horrified.

"No, but a week later father sent me off to Harrow, two years earlier than anyone else. I never saw either of my parents again." That was mostly true. He'd seen his mother once more, years later, though he preferred never to think about that meeting.

"Well, Alex, I don't see how you'd be responsible then."

"You didn't see her before I left. She was barely recognizable and she blamed me." She still did. "So when I got a letter from my father's solicitor later that year saying that my mother had died, I felt certain that it was at my father's hands. Because of what he'd seen, what I'd brought him there to see. Sleeping with another man was one thing, but a woman... Well, that he wouldn't tolerate."

"He killed her?"

"I'd always believed so. I knew her blood was on my hands. After that, I spent every holiday from school those first few years with her sister, my Aunt Mary — the one who was married to a country vicar. You remember the rumors about the vicar's wife I installed here."

"She really was your aunt?"

He chuckled, running his hand along her back, finding comfort. "She really was. After I met Simon and the others though, I spent time with their families, and didn't go back to Aunt Mary's. Father didn't want me home, and I didn't want to be there."

"You *never* saw him again?"

"Never. Though I did hear things about him, naturally. I wasn't the first wicked Duke of Kelfield. My father had quite the reputation before me. I've simply picked up the torch."

"I can't imagine what you saw. My poor Alex."

He kissed the top of her head. His dear, sweet wife. "I'm hardly poor."

"Have you had the awful dreams for twenty-four years?"

They'd stopped for a while after he found out she was still alive, only to start up again at the most inopportune times. "When I was a boy, almost every night. As I got older, I would go through periods of having them and then they'd go away again."

"How long has this set been going on?"

"They started my first night at Prestwick Chase."

"How long do they last? When was the time before that?"

"Shh, sweetheart. I've told you what happened. It's late. Go back to sleep."

⚜

Livvie awoke to the most wonderful feeling — Alex holding her in his arms and kissing her neck. Then he rose above her and smiled rakishly. "Ah, sleeping beauty awakes."

"What time is it?" Honestly, it seemed dreadfully early.

He answered by opening her wrapper and laving one aching nipple. "I do think I could get used to you sleeping in my bed."

Livvie couldn't hide her smile. "Finally! I've been asking you for that since our wedding."

"My little minx," he replied before returning his lips to her skin, and one hand found her damp opening between springy curls.

Livvie closed her eyes, breathing in sandalwood and savoring the feel of him all around her. Then he stopped moving and chuckled. She opened her eyes, to find him grinning wickedly.

"I've been thinking," he began, once again stroking the damp curls between her legs, nearly making her come undone. "This awful ball Caroline is making us attend. I truly detest such events. To make it bearable for me, don't wear any drawers to Staveley's that night."

Her eyes grew round with surprise and she gasped. What a most improper suggestion. Even from him! "Alex!"'

He nuzzled against her neck. "Be a good girl, Olivia, and do as I request."

"I could *never* do such a thing," she sputtered, but gasped again as his finger found her entrance.

"Oh, I think you could," he said smoothly. "We won't be able to escape for long, and I want to have instant access to you, sweetheart." His finger delved deeper, just as his thumb found her sensitive little nub. Livvie thought she would expire on the spot. When she groaned from the pleasure he stoked in her, Alex whispered in her ear, "Say it, Olivia. Say, 'Yes, Alex. I won't wear drawers to the ball.'"

She wished she could resist him, but as she tried to shake her head the intensity of his fingers increased. "Y-yes, Alex. I won't wear drawers to the ball, damn you."

He chuckled against the soft skin of her neck before he nipped her there. "Good girl. Now let me reward you."

⚜

Lying sated and boneless in Alex's arms, Livvie smiled against his chest. Her husband was simply amazing. She could stay lying with him like this forever.

Without any warning, the bedroom door flew open and Poppy raced inside. "Olivia, I've been looking all over for you."

"Poppy!" her father barked, jerking up from his spot. "Out! You can't come barging in here like this."

Her bottom lip thrust outward to an immediate pout. "But, Papa, my new dresses are here."

Pulling the counterpane up to her neck, Livvie sat up in the bed. "Poppy dear, go to Mrs. Bickle and I'll be along shortly."

She did as she was bid, skipping out of the room without a care in the world.' Alex fell onto his back with a thud. "Dear God, I think she just took five years off my life."

Livvie snuggled against him, kissing his chest. "I'm just glad she didn't come in five minutes earlier."

Alex groaned at the thought. "I'm going to have to bolt the door with crossbars."

Livvie slid out of bed, wrapping her robe tightly around her. "As long as it's not bolted against me."

He grinned at her. "You've become quite the little wanton, Olivia. Didn't I tell you long ago that I'd make you want me?"

"Arrogant man," she replied with an answering grin. Then she started for the connecting door. "Before you leave for the day, do come and see Poppy's new dresses. She is very excited about them, obviously. And she's been wearing that tattered blue dress over and over since you apparently told her she looks like a princess in it."

"I'm amazed the dresses are here. Madam Fournier is not the quickest modiste in London."

Livvie quirked a grin at him, she couldn't help herself. "Oh? Have you ordered something from Madam?"

His silver eyes narrowed to little shards. "What do you know?"

"Nothing," she said brightly, feigning innocence. "*Is* there something to know?"

He climbed out of bed in naked splendor and stalked towards her. "You do know. She told you."

Livvie shook her head. "Only because I was going to order something myself, and she saved me the embarrassment. I do not know what you've ordered. I blush every time I think about it."

"I like it when you blush." Alex pinned her against the door, kissing her neck and caressing her curves, the evidence of his desire pressing against her belly.

"Alexander Everett," she panted, playfully pushing against his muscled chest, "your daughter is waiting for me."

"She can wait a bit longer," he growled, scooping Livvie back in his arms. Then he returned her to his bed and made love to her all over again.

Twenty-Three

"I HAVE seen neither hide nor hair of you since Macbeth," came the lazy drawl of Marcus Gray over the murmur of the other members of White's.

The club was traditionally too mainstream for Alex, but he was trying his best to play the role of respectable husband. Olivia hadn't mentioned her estrangement from Miss Avery since that first day, but he knew it still bothered her.

"What does that tell you, Marc?" Seated in an over-stuffed leather chair, Alex didn't even bother to look up from his perusal of *The Times*. That should have been rude enough to make any decent person leave him in peace.

Of course, Marc wasn't decent. "Well, you can't be avoiding *me*. So I can only assume you're keeping that pretty little wife of yours tied up at Kelfield House. Has she asked about me?" The marquess flopped down on a settee across from him and smirked.

Alex could see the smirk right over the edge of his paper and he scowled in response. "Only to berate me for my poor choice of friends."

"Browbeaten already, are you?" Marc asked cheerfully.

Alex folded his paper in half, narrowing his eyes on his old debauched friend. "I'm certain you know me better than that,

Haversham. Now what do you want?"

"To curse you for leaving Miss Kane so well positioned."

"Turned you down flat, did she?" Good for Sarah.

"Bastard," he answered with an incline of his head. "She's attached herself to Haywood. Can you believe that?"

The penniless Lord Haywood was a bit of a surprise. Though he was young, closer to Sarah's age than either himself or Haversham. The whelp had better treat her well. He shrugged his answer. "I told you, Sarah is free to make her own choices."

"I still can't account for you just giving her up. Doesn't seem like you at all."

"Well, times change."

"Ah, Kelfield, there you are," came Simon's deep voice from behind them. "Ready for tonight?"

"What's tonight?" Marc asked, rising from his seat to shake Simon's hand.

"Nothing," Alex answered, though he was drowned out by Simon's reply.

"Caroline Staveley's ball, of course."

Marc fell back on the settee with a laugh. "You? A ball?"

"It's for Olivia," Alex growled.

Marc's laughter echoed of the walls of the club. "God, Kelfield! You've turned soft. Married a fortnight and she's already wrapped you around her little finger. What's next, Lady Astwick's soiree? Or perhaps tea with Sally Jersey?"

"I suspect," Simon remarked with a wolfish grin, "that Kelfield likes being wrapped around his pretty young wife. It's always easy to spot a well-pleasured man. Which reminds me, how goes your pursuit of Miss Kane?"

Marc's smile vanished instantly. "You can go straight to hell, Greywood."

"That well?" Simon's blue eyes danced wickedly. "Forget I asked." Then he turned his attention to Alex. "Anyway, Maddie and I have been charged with escorting you and Olivia to Staveley's, and it's about time to leave, my friend."

"Caroline has so little faith I'll show up?"

Simon quirked one eyebrow upwards. "You are sitting here and not at home preparing for the event."

But that didn't mean he intended to forgo the blasted thing. "Very well. Lead on, Commander."

～✦✦✦～

Livvie gazed at her reflection in the floor-length mirror. Madam's copper gown was extraordinary. Pearls adorned the scooped neck bodice and mesh sleeves. The silk lovingly hugged her curves, and she was surprised at the transformation. She had never worn drab gowns in the past, but this one was spectacular. She didn't even look like the same girl. Of course, she wasn't the same girl. Livvie Danbury was gone, replaced by Olivia Everett, the Duchess of Kelfield.

"Mmm," grunted Alex from their connecting door. Then he stalked towards her, raking his lingering gaze across her. "You are breathtaking."

"Please, Alex," she said modestly.

He grinned wolfishly. "I can hardly wait to peel it off you. Say we can stay here instead of going."

"You," she giggled, "will do anything to avoid this ball. But Caroline would just march over here and drag us both kicking and screaming. That would not do to help repair my image."

"I think your image is perfect." Alex ran his hands lightly along her arms.

"Well, of course *you* do. You're the wicked Duke of Kelfield, who does whatever he pleases." Then she placed her hand on his chest, staring up into his silver eyes. "Besides, Cordie will be there tonight, and I haven't been able to speak to her since before our wedding. I miss her dreadfully."

"All right, sweetheart." He pulled her close and kissed her brow. "I'll go, and I'll even try to appear respectable. But you must promise to follow me if we get the chance to be alone."

"We can be alone *here*, when we return."

"It's not the same thing. Sneaking about adds an air of excitement to the whole mix. Like when you visited my room in Prestwick Chase."

He'd kissed her for the first time in that room. She'd never been the same since that visit. But he was right—it was exciting. "Whatever my husband wishes."

～✦✦✦～

Caroline smiled as Alex and Livvie entered her ballroom along with Simon and Madeline Greywood. Something told her that the decision to have the four of them arrive together was a good one.

Next to Caroline, her brother Robert Beckford, Earl of Masten cursed under his breath. "I detest Kelfield," he complained, not for the first time that evening.

Caroline resisted the urge to grind her teeth together, as doing so would negatively affect the serene look she had mastered for the evening. Besides tonight she needed to maintain her temper. She plastered a bright smile on her face. "Yes, Robert, you've made that abundantly clear. But as he's family now, I'll thank you to hold your tongue. At least for tonight. Livvie needs our support."

Robert scowled, looking again across the room at Olivia. "None of this would have happened if Aunt Jane had sent her to stay with Lydia and me—"

"She would have been miserable," Caroline interrupted him. "Her friends are here. Her life is here. And I, for one, don't appreciate your implications, Robert. Livvie has been with us for over a year, and until now nothing untoward—"

"Until now, indeed."

Caroline glowered at her brother. "I've heard all I intend to, Robert. Now, I want you to stay near Livvie. And when Clayworth gets here he can help you stand sentry."

"What has Clayworth done to be in your debt?"

Caroline flashed him a cheeky grin, "Nothing. But both of you are the two stuffiest men in all of England. I want her to appear as respectable as possible."

━━◆◆◆━━

Alex resisted the urge to cringe as the stuffy Earl of Masten approached him and Olivia. He had never gotten along with the man, and that was even before Alex had tried to seduce Masten's wife. It was possible the earl had forgotten. Possible, not probable.

"Masten," he drawled in greeting.

The earl barely flicked a glance at him. Instead, he focused his attention on Olivia. "My dear sweet girl, how are you holding up?"

Before Olivia could respond, Alex interrupted her. "You make it sound as if she's caught something deadly. In most cases, becoming a duchess is applauded."

"Yes, but this isn't most cases," Masten replied with an icy glare.

"Robert," Olivia began, smiling sweetly, her seductive dimple making an appearance, "I am very happy. Please be so for me. And now, tell me, how are Lydia and the children?"

Masten's stony face broke out into a grin, making the man look like a happy schoolboy. "They are wonderful, Livvie. Melody chatters all day long and Laurel has just started rolling over. And Lydia," he flashed a quick glance at Alex, "couldn't be happier."

Well, that answered that. Masten definitely remembered. Alex possessively slid his hand along his wife's waist. "Do send her our best."

Masten's scowl returned.

Olivia sucked in an elated breath, and both men turned their attention to her. "Cordie *did* come. Excuse me, will you? And do try not to antagonize each other."

Livvie started toward the terrace doors where she and Cordie had planned to meet. She watched as Lady Avery vanished into the card room, hopefully for the entire evening. Then with a sly grin, Cordie crossed the room to her side.

Immediately, the two embraced. "Livvie!" Cordie gushed as she held onto her. "I feel like it's been forever. How are you? Is Kelfield treating you well?"

Livvie blushed at the question, but nodded. "I couldn't be happier, Cordie. Truly. Alex is..."

"Alex is what?" Alex asked as he came up behind them, resting his hand on Livvie's shoulder. His sinful, grey eyes twinkled as they landed on her.

Livvie beamed up at him, linking her arm with his. "Alex is perfect, of course."

He chuckled and leaned towards her, a rakish grin on his face. "Sweetheart, don't tell *everyone*. I've a reputation to protect, you know."

"Alex," Livvie began softly, "aren't you supposed to be keeping my cousin Robert company?"

"We nearly came to blows when you walked away. Hello, Miss Avery. You look well this evening."

"Thank you, Your Grace."

Livvie couldn't help but smile at her husband. It really was very sweet that he was so attentive. Still, she'd like to be alone with Cordie, if just for a while. "We never get any time together. Do you think could manage conversing with Lord Caretert or Commander Greywood without it coming to fisticuffs?"

He squeezed her hand, stepped away, and winked at her. "Whatever you wish, sweetheart." Then he smiled at Cordie. "I'm only leaving her in *your* care. Don't let any other blackguards or scoundrels near her."

Livvie giggled. "Go on with you. I only have a fondness for *my* scoundrel, as you well know."

After Alex disappeared into the crowd, Livvie turned her attention back to Cordie. "I am so glad to see you. Are you sure it's all right? Won't your mother be furious if she learns you've been associating with *that scandalous duchess?*"

"Of course she will," Cordie answered honestly. "So we'd best make it worth our while."

Just then Livvie looked across the room and frowned. "Oh bother!" she whispered with a frown. "Don't look now, but Lord Brookfield is headed our way, and his eyes are on you, as usual."

Cordie groaned, which was completely understandable. Viscount Brookfield was an unrepentant fortune hunter, nearly twice their age, and he always smelled awful. Unfortunately, he'd set his sights on Cordie and her large dowry at the end of last season.

"My darling girls!" came Caroline's voice from behind them. "I am so happy you found each other."

"Caro," Livvie whispered behind her fan, "you must get rid of Lord Brookfield. He'll try to monopolize Cordelia."

Caroline frowned at the approaching viscount. "I don't even recall inviting him. No matter, I'll take care of it."

As the man reached them, Caroline smiled beatifically. "My darling Brookfield," she gushed. "Lady Astwick, the dowager that is, was just asking me about you."

"Indeed?" Brookfield gulped.

Livvie suppressed a laugh. No one ever wanted to deal with the dowager Lady Astwick. In fact, Livvie avoided the old dragon whenever possible. Only Caroline ever seemed to get along with her.

"Oh, yes!" Caroline assured him. "In fact, my lord, I promised her ladyship that I would send you right over to her as soon as I saw you."

"You did?" he squeaked.

"I did. She is there in the corner." Caroline gestured to the other side of the room where many widows lined the wall. "Do you see her?"

Brookfield's face turned white. He'd most assuredly seen the widowed marchioness, and he nodded sullenly. "Indeed, I do."

"Splendid!" Caroline happily clapped her hands together. "Do go on, my lord, I would hate to keep her ladyship waiting."

Brookfield spun on his heels and started across the room, his head hung low, like a man headed to the gallows.

Triumphantly, Caroline turned back to Livvie and Cordie. "Well, that's over. Now then—" she looked Cordie up and down— "no Brookfield for you, darling. I shall endeavor to find you a handsome gentleman by the end of the evening."

A laugh escaped Cordie's throat. "Lady Staveley, that is not necessary in the—"

"Caroline." The rich, baritone voice of Lord Clayworth floated over Livvie's shoulder.

Livvie turned and smiled at the handsome earl. It was so nice that he chose to attend this evening. As he was seen as a paragon of honor in the eyes of the *ton,* his support would go a long way in helping to repair her reputation.

"Brendan!" Caroline's smile grew wide as her eyes fell on Clayworth. "Darling, I am so glad you found time to attend my little ball."

Clayworth raised one golden brow mockingly. "You didn't really give me much choice."

Livvie winced. It wasn't terribly flattering that he would openly admit to Caroline's browbeating him to attend.

Her cousin laughed charmingly and tucked her hand around Clayworth's arm. "Darling, you know my cousin, the duchess, of course. But have you met Miss Cordelia Avery?"

"No. I don't believe I've had the pleasure." Clayworth sounded less than pleased, though he did manage to smile pleasantly at Cordie.

No doubt the man thought Caroline was attempting to pair him up with her friend. Livvie grinned at the thought. While many women would swoon in the presence of Lord Adonis, Cordelia Avery would never be one of them.

"Then allow me the honors," Caroline continued. "Lord Clayworth, Miss Cordelia Avery of Nottinghamshire."

"I am pleased to make your acquaintance, Miss Avery."

"The pleasure is all mine," Cordie replied with a feigned sweetness. Livvie bit back a laugh. It wouldn't do for the earl to know that the tone in Cordie's voice was actually a dangerous one.

Caroline then tapped Clayworth's chest with her fan. "Darling, you never dance. Might I persuade you to take to the floor this evening?"

The earl glared momentarily at her then the look of irritation vanished, as if it had never been there. "Yes, of course, Caroline." His eyes swept across Livvie before landing on Cordie. "Miss Avery, may I see your dance card?"

Stunned, Cordie raised her wrist for the earl, where her dance card and small pencil dangled. Then he scribbled his name for the next song.

Poor Clayworth. He apparently had awful luck. Any other lady in the room would have been pleased to dance with him. But he had to pick the one who disliked him deeply.

The first chords of a waltz began, and Clayworth offered his arm to Cordie. Livvie watched as her friend was practically dragged to the middle of the dance floor, but she didn't have much time to contemplate Cordie's predicament. Alex came up behind Livvie at that moment and slid his arm around her waist.

"I need you," he whispered in her ear, and a frisson of anticipation raced up Livvie's spine.

Twenty-Four

LIVVIE looked over her shoulder. Alex's silver eyes, dark with desire, focused on her. "Now?" she whispered, glancing around at the throng of Caroline's guests.

"Now," he growled, making her knees almost buckle. Then he grasped her elbow and led her out of the ballroom. "Where was your room?"

"Upstairs in the family wing."

"Lead on."

"But Cordie—" she started to protest.

"Is well occupied with that self-important earl. If you hurry, we can be back before anyone realizes we're missing."

The idea was exciting. Livvie tugged Alex down the corridor and then up the flight of stairs that led to the family's sleeping rooms. She threw open the door to her old chambers and quickly pulled him inside.

Alex lit a candle near the bed and turned to face her with one wicked black eyebrow arched. "Well, raise your skirt for me, Olivia."

She blushed to her roots, shaking her head. She'd expected a quick tumble, not some sort of exhibition.

"Now," Alex commanded as he sat on the edge of the bed and

gestured an upward motion with his hands.

Livvie couldn't believe she was obeying him. He was truly wicked, but her fingers tugged her copper skirt upwards to her knees and cool air swirled about her thighs. Alex grinned devilishly and again gestured higher. "I'll tell you when you can stop, sweetheart."

She stared into his silvery grey eyes, swallowed, and complied with his wishes until the hem of her dress was above her waist.

"Enough," his gravelly voice reverberated throughout her. Livvie turned her head away, unable to look at him, knowing that he was seeing her displayed nearly naked since she'd obeyed his earlier request and hadn't worn any drawers.

"Look at me, Olivia." His seductive voice enveloped her.

Her heart pounding wildly in her chest, she met his eyes. Desire laced through the look he sent her, and Olivia thought her legs might buckle beneath her—especially when Alex stood up and sauntered over to her, his wicked fingers taking the bunched up copper dress from her hands. "You're so quiet, sweetheart," he replied and ran his free hand along her bare belly and hip. Then he kissed the hollow of her neck. "Say, 'Touch me, Alex,'" he said against her skin.

"T-touch me, Alex."

"With pleasure." His clever fingers parted her curls and found her sensitive nub that quivered when he touched it. "Is that better, sweetheart?"

Olivia nodded and her head fell against his shoulder as he worked her into a frenzied state.

Alex toyed with her folds, and his fingers become slick with her wetness. "Say, 'Enter me, Alex."

On a sob, Olivia whispered, "Please enter me, Alex."

One long, slender finger delved inside her soft opening, and she shuddered. With a languorous motion, he stroked her in and out, over and over, until she was writhing in his arms—begging him to take her.

❧✦❧

Alex undid his trousers and pressed her against the wall. Then he lifted her in his arms and sunk into her. Olivia's legs wrapped around his hips, sending him straight to heaven. It didn't take long for him to find the release he'd needed ever since he'd first seen her wearing the mesmerizing dress.

Though he would like nothing better than to throw Olivia over his shoulder, take her back to Kelfield House, and enjoy her over and over again, a ballroom full of people were probably just now wondering where they were. Alex lowered her to the ground and kissed her. "God, you're amazing," he whispered across her lips.

With a charming giggle, Olivia straightened her skirts. "How am I supposed to go back downstairs and pretend *that* didn't just happen?" she asked.

"We could go home," he offered hopefully.

She playfully swatted at his chest. "This is important for me. I don't ask much of you, Alex."

"And Miss Avery is downstairs. I know. Perhaps I'll go to the card room so I won't be tempted to toss up your skirts again."

"No!" Olivia almost squealed. Then she bit her lip. "Lady Avery is in the card room. I don't think that's the best idea... Commander Greywood goes back to Norfolk tomorrow. Perhaps you could just talk to him, say your goodbyes, and we'll leave as soon as Cordie and I have talked."

It was as good a plan as anything else. Alex pulled open the door so they could return, only to hear his wife's earth shattering scream. Before he knew what was happening, Staveley's beagle, Nelson, burst into the room, barking and growling. Olivia scrambled atop the bed, shaking in terror.

Alex lunged for the dog, but Nelson darted under the bed. The rumble of the dog's growl grew louder. "Come on, sweetheart. We'll shut him in here."

Olivia shook her head back and forth. "No. I can't."

Damned bloody beagle!

With an irritated sigh, Alex got down on his hands and knees, lifting the edge of the counterpane. Nelson's teeth were bared and he barked. "Oh for God's sake, dog! You've chewed my bloody boots more times than I can count." He slid under the bed, thinking momentarily that if anyone saw him like this, he'd be the laughingstock of London. The beagle started to nip at him, and Alex glared at the dog. "On my life, Nelson, if you bite me I'll see you thrown in the Thames."

Then Alex scooped Nelson up in his arms and looked into the dog's black eyes with a frown. "You are a menace."

Nelson licked his face.

Alex crawled out from under the bed holding the little devil by the scruff of his neck. Olivia was pale and still frightened. He nodded to her and quit the room. The corridor was quiet, and he wished he knew where the beagle was supposed to be kept. He poked his head inside a darkened bedroom. It seemed to be empty, so he deposited the little beast inside, firmly shutting the door behind him.

As he started back for Olivia's old room, he could hear muffled barking and then a child's squeal. Good God! None of this had been his plan. He rushed back into Olivia's room, to find her still quivering, still standing on the bed—as if the beagle could have made the impossible jump.

"Are you all right, sweetheart?"

She took a deep breath and nodded. "Thank you."

"We need to go. I have to find Staveley. The little beast woke one of the children." He picked her up and placed her back on the floor.

"Which room?" she asked, catching her breath.

"The one next to us, on the right."

"Emma. Let's hurry."

Once in the hallway, more giggles escaped the child's room. "Emma's not afraid of the dog?"

"No, she adores him. They all do." Olivia grabbed tightly to his arm. "I am sorry, Alex. I know I shouldn't be afraid of the creature—"

He pulled his wife into his embrace and kissed her. "You have nothing to apologize for. I'm just so sorry you had to go through that." Then he quickly escorted her down the staircase.

As soon as they reached the ballroom, they found Caroline standing near the doorway, a grave expression on her face. "And just *where* have you been?"

"That beast Nelson was on the loose, Caroline," Alex explained rapidly. If he kept talking, she couldn't ask questions. "I figured you wouldn't want the thing making an appearance down here, so I tossed him in one of the bedrooms. But I think I woke Emma in the process."

She glared at him and started down the corridor. "Don't think for one minute that I'm through with you, Alexander Everett," Caroline threw over her shoulder as she disappeared around a corner.

As if he had ever considered it would be *that* easy to get rid of

Caroline. He smiled down at his wife, who was still looking a little pale after the encounter with the dog. "Are you sure you're all right?"

"My hero." She grinned in response.

He liked the sound of that, and her charming dimple made him stiff all over again. This night couldn't end soon enough. "Go finish up with Miss Avery so I can have you all to myself again."

Olivia giggled at that and then set off through the crowd to find her friend. Alex watched her departing form, the sensual swing of her hips, and sighed. Marriage was good. His friends had been right. Thank God he'd caught *her* hiding in his wardrobe and not someone else.

A hand clapped him on the back, and he turned to find Staveley smiling at him. "You do seem happy, Alex."

"I suppose I am. Olivia is truly delightful. I get to spend time with Poppy every day. Who knew domesticity could be so enjoyable?"

"I believe I'd been telling you for years."

Alex laughed. "Yes, but I rarely listen to you, Staveley."

"You rarely listen to anyone," his friend grumbled. Then Staveley blinked across the room. "What is *he* doing here?"

Alex followed the direction of Staveley's stare and his own eyes grew wide. Haversham stood in the entrance, surveying the crowd. When he caught the marquess' eye, Marc started towards them.

"Beckford has certainly gotten priggish since he's married," the marquess said in greeting.

Staveley chuckled. "Something my wife thanks God for every night."

Marc looked Alex up and down. "And where is your lovely duchess?"

"Talking with a friend of hers," he drawled.

Marc stared out at the sea of people. "Ah, there she is. *Who* is that delightful creature she's talking to?" he asked, with an appreciative grunt.

"Miss Avery," Alex answered. "But she's not your sort."

A rakish smile curved the marquess' lips. "Funny. She looks exactly like my sort."

"Then I suggest you stop looking. Lady Avery is a high stickler and won't appreciate your attentions towards her daughter. She hasn't even let the poor girl talk to Olivia since our wedding."

"They're talking now," Marc replied, his eyes fixed on the pretty Miss

Avery.

⚜

"You are truly happy?" Cordie asked for at least the tenth time.

Livvie smiled. She'd never been happier than when she was with her husband. "You know that old adage about reformed rakes making the best husbands? Very true."

"Is he truly reformed?"

"Mostly." He spent his days at White's and his afternoons playing with Poppy. But his nights were spent with her in wild abandon—most definitely not the actions of a reformed rake. "But enough about me, Cordie. Tell me what you've been doing."

"I've taken to walking Rotten Row with mother on a daily basis." She rolled her eyes heavenward. "Then she drags me along to all sorts of charitable teas and luncheons, and lectures me nearly non-stop about my comportment."

"All because of me?" Livvie asked quietly, as the first chords of a waltz began.

"All because I refused Captain Seaton. Honestly, Livvie, I so envy you. Kelfield would never dream of dictating who you could visit, who your friends were. I was glad to know that about the captain before I accepted him. What a dreadful life that would have been. And in watching you and Kelfield, I think I know exactly what sort of man might suit me."

"What sort?" Livvie asked, almost afraid of the answer.

The sort who won't restrict me. The sort who will give me free reign. Someone like your Kelfield."

A shadow fell over them, and Livvie looked up into the dancing blue eyes of the Marquess of Haversham. Good heavens! *Why had Caroline invited him?* "My lord," she said coolly.

A roughish smile lit his face. "My darling duchess, I have already asked you to call me Marc."

Livvie shook her head, a false smile plastered on her face. "But that would imply we are intimates, Lord Haversham, and we are not."

"My loss," he replied with a wink. Then he focused his light blue eyes on Cordie. "We have not had the pleasure."

Livvie straightened her back and pursed her lips. "If you're looking for a proper introduction, then I suggest you find Miss Avery's mother."

An anguished squeak escaped Cordie's lips. Livvie turned to look at her friend and was disheartened to find her gazing at the wicked marquess in wonderment. *Someone like your Kelfield,* echoed in her ears. Livvie nearly groaned.

Haversham smiled at Cordie. "I'm rarely proper. So I think I'll forgo speaking to Lady Avery, as I'm sure she'd only tell me no, and I have no desire to be turned away from you, my dear."

Cordie sighed. "That's not the least bit conventional, my lord."

He took her hand in his, raising it to his lips. "Conventional is boring. Might I entice you to stand up with me?"

"Cordie," Livvie whispered, "your mother will have an apoplexy."

"Let her," Cordie whispered back. Then she accepted the marquess' arm and allowed him to lead her onto the dance floor.

What was Cordie thinking? Haversham? Livvie stood, dumbstruck, staring at the two of them. A month ago Cordelia would never have taken off with the disreputable marquess. Until this very moment, she'd never noticed a rebellious streak in her friend. Her heart pounded with worry.

A pair of familiar hands planted themselves on her waist and Livvie turned her head, frowning at her husband. "I think she's lost all sense."

"The damned blackguard. I told him to stay away from her. I turned my back for two minutes, offering my farewell to Simon."

Suddenly there was a shrill scream from the game room doorway. Then a bobbing purple ostrich feather appeared to rush through the crowd. Livvie didn't need to see who it was. Only Lady Avery could make the scene any worse. She couldn't watch the altercation, and she buried her face against Alex's chest. "May we go home now?"

Twenty-Five

NEARLY a fortnight later, Caroline was still annoyed with the Marquess of Haversham. Her ball had been the talk of the *ton* ever since it ended, but not in the way she'd hoped. Though Livvie hadn't suffered from the wicked marquess' blatant disregard for propriety, the situation hadn't helped her any either. And who knew when anyone would see Miss Avery again. Her mother had caused quite the scene, ripping the girl out of Haversham's arms and marching her out the front door.

As she sat in her white parlor, contemplating what was to be done about the situation, her decrepit butler, Merton, entered the room and announced, "Her Grace, the Duchess of Kelfield."

"For heaven's sake, Merton," Livvie said from behind him. "Such pomp and circumstance is not needed. I lived here, you might remember." Then she slid into the room with a smile.

"Olivia darling!" Caroline stood and crossed the room, enveloping her cousin in a warm embrace. "So good to see you."

"You, as well, Caroline. I hope it's all right, I brought Poppy and she's gone up to play with Emma."

"Of course! Sit, sit," she directed, leading Livvie to a white damask chaise and taking the spot next to her. "How are you doing?"

Livvie's smile vanished. "Not well, I'm afraid. I've been feeling awful. I think all this anxiety is making me ill."

"Oh, darling, don't fret. Everything will be all right."

Livvie shook her head. "I haven't heard from Cordie since your ball. I sent a dozen messengers with notes for her, but Lady Avery has sent them all away, returning each letter unread."

"They left Town," Caroline informed her. "I still can't imagine what she was thinking to stand up with Haversham."

"She was looking for someone like Alex, and Haversham appeared before her at the wrong time."

Caroline couldn't help but gape. "Looking for someone like *Alex?* Good heavens, that's a dangerous road to travel. I hope she didn't inform Gladys of her plans. Who knows what that harpy is capable of?"

Just then the door opened and Staveley stepped inside. "Oh, Olivia, I didn't know you were here. How are you, my dear?"

"Wonderful, thank you, Staveley."

He winked at her and then turned his attention to his wife. "Dear, I've run out of quills. Do you happen to have any?"

"Yes, of course. The top drawer in my desk."

"Thank you," Staveley replied and left them alone.

Caroline was still reeling from Olivia's comment about her friend. "Doesn't she realize what a dangerous sort of man he is? You were terribly lucky with Kelfield. Though he was a rogue to be sure, he's always had a kind heart. I'm not sure the same can be said for the marquess. Of course, I remember when he abducted that girl who jilted him years ago. Her family covered it up and she hastily married another fellow, but he's certainly not the sort I would trust within an inch of my life."

Livvie's eyes grew wide. "He abducted a girl? Honestly, I had no idea, Caroline."

"It was a long time ago, even before his marriage. The good news, I suppose, is that if you can't get a letter through to her, Haversham can't find her either. I'm sure she's relatively safe from the blackguard."

"Perhaps. But Lady Avery's over-protectiveness is what drove her into the marquess' arms in the first place. She doesn't want to be dictated to. She thinks someone like Alex or Haversham will give her more freedom than Captain Seaton would have."

Caroline rubbed her brow. She did not envy Gladys Avery in the least, and she sent up a silent prayer that neither of her own daughters would ever throw themselves in the path of notorious scoundrels.

"Olivia," came Staveley's voice from the doorway. "This was with today's post," he said, waving a letter in his hands. "How fortunate you came to visit."

Caroline's heart sank as she met her husband's eyes. She'd gone through the post herself today and nothing had come for Livvie. But in the top desk drawer where she'd sent Staveley to get quills, Major Moore's letter had been accumulating dust. She'd never found the right time to give it to Olivia.

Blast it!

She obviously hadn't been thinking clearly, or she never would have sent him there in the first place. Staveley was too honorable for his own good.

⚜

Who would send her a letter here? Everyone knew she lived at Kelfield House. Then it came to her in a flash.

Her mother.

In India, it would take months for her parents to learn of her marriage. Livvie anxiously snatched the letter from Staveley. It had been forever since she'd had word from her parents. And then her heart stopped as she turned the foolscap over in her hands.

Philip's handwriting.

She felt sick all over again. And then everything went black…

"Dear God! Olivia darling!" Caroline's words sounded far away, as though she was in a tunnel of some sort. "What were you thinking giving her that letter?"

"Olivia?" Staveley asked.

Livvie managed to blink open her eyes, and she found herself staring into both Caroline and Staveley's concerned faces. "Wh-what happened?"

"You fainted," Staveley explained. "I'll get water."

Caroline helped her back to her feet and over to the chaise. "Darling, take a deep breath. Are you all right?"

Livvie nodded her head. "I just hadn't expected to hear from Philip. Oh, Caroline, I feel like such a fool." She waved her arm in the general area where she'd collapsed.

"It's completely understandable. Just take another breath." After Livvie complied, Caroline continued. "You don't have to read the letter, darling. Especially, if it's too difficult."

Except that she *did* need to read it. She owed at least that much to Philip. How incredibly disrespectful not to do so. The letter in her hand shook with a tremor and she clutched it to her heart.

Staveley rushed back with a goblet of water. "Here, Livvie, drink this."

Alex rolled over, missing Olivia's warmth. He blindly reached across the bed, hoping to pull his wife back into his arms, but she wasn't there. His eyes flew open and his mind whirled. She hadn't seemed herself all day. Distracted was an apt description. Even though they now shared his bed, it was the first night since they'd married they hadn't made love.

The soothing smell of lilacs invaded his senses when he squeezed the pillow next to his. Where was

When there was no answer, he threw on his robe and went in search of his wife. He didn't have to look far. A warm glow of candlelight spilled into his room from under their connecting door.

Livvie sat on her bed, staring at Philip's letter for what felt like forever. Every time she started to open it, she stopped herself. It didn't matter what he'd written — not really. She was married to Alex and nothing would ever change that. She didn't want it to ever change. Still, Philip had been such a large part of her life, long before she'd ever met Alex.

And she *did* love Philip. She always would. Not the deep, all-encompassing love she felt for her husband, but it was love. She could never think about her childhood without remembering Philip as well. He was a part of her, always had been. Philip was honorable and brave. Sweet and loving. He was everything she'd ever wanted — until Alex blazed his way into her life, and she realized she wanted someone, something completely different than she could have ever imagined.

It was painful to know she would hurt him — her dear, sweet Philip, who deserved much more than she'd given him. It was inevitable. The letter taunted her from her lap, and she swiped at her tears.

She was acting a coward.

Finally, Livvie took a deep breath and opened the letter.

June 8, 1814

My dearest Olivia,

I received the most wonderful news today, my love. In just a few days, I will begin my journey home and to you. I had begun to think this time would never come, that I would remain in France for the rest of my days. Now as my departure approaches, I find myself more anxious than ever to see you, to hold you, to finally give you my name. I promise to never leave you again, as our separation has been very difficult for me, as I am sure it has been for you. For that I am very sorry.

I love you with all my heart, Olivia, and I thank God every night for keeping me whole and hale and able to return to you.

I wish you could have seen Russell's face when he got the news. He was...

"Olivia?" Alex asked from the doorway.

She dropped the letter, as if it had burned her, and tried to wipe the trail of tears from her face.

"I didn't mean to wake you," she offered lamely.

"You're crying," he said and quickly crossed the room to her side.

Livvie stood and tried to shuffle the letter under the bed. "I'm fine. I just—"

"What is this?" Alex asked, scooping the letter off the ground.

Livvie wished the floor would open her up and swallow her whole. Why did Alex have to wake up? Why did he have to find the letter? "It's nothing. Really," she pleaded.

"It's not nothing. It's a letter." He gently touched her cheek. "Has something happened to upset you, sweetheart?"

"No," she answered quietly, hoping he'd hand the letter back to her. She'd done nothing wrong, but she wasn't certain he'd see it that way.

"Olivia, I'm not a fool," he said softly. "You're awake in the middle of the night, crying, reading a letter, and then hiding..." Alex's silver eyes narrowed to angry shards of steel, as he apparently worked out the mystery on his own. "Philip Moore," he growled.

He thrust the letter at her, as if the pages suddenly scalded him. Livvie watched them scatter about the floor. She swallowed nervously as his murderous gaze settled on her. "Alex, it's not what you think," she hastened to explain.

But her husband paid her no attention. Without another word, he stalked across the floor to his chambers, slamming the door closed with such a force the floor quake beneath her feet.

Livvie stared at the closed door for the longest time. She'd never seen him lose his temper. Not like that. Not with her. The sound of a key turning in the lock of their connecting door hit Livvie's ears, and her heart sank. An emptiness settled deep in her belly and she felt sick. Livvie dropped onto her bed, her body wracked with tears.

~~~

Alex paced around his room, cursing himself for a fool. He'd always known she loved Moore. It had never been a secret. Yet, he'd still foolishly allowed himself to believe that she'd come to care about him anyway, that she *loved* him. Ridiculous. Fatuous. Delusional. All born from his love for her.

A lump formed in his throat as he overheard her, next door, sobbing her eyes out. Alex winced at the sounds she made. It was unbearable, listening to her pain, knowing that despite everything she still loved Philip Moore.

Another rejection from a woman he loved was too much for him to face. Alex threw on the clothes he'd worn earlier in the day. He couldn't stay here tonight, knowing that his marriage slowly crumbled away with each sob she uttered. That was of course if he pretended that they'd had a marriage of note in the first place. Olivia had never chosen him— would never have chosen him.

The last several weeks were false. He'd known it all along, but he'd allowed himself to believe the lie. He wouldn't continue to do so.

Alex hurried from his house and easily hailed a hack. "Bedford Place," he barked at the driver. Then he sank back against the old squabs and closed his eyes. One name, a balm for his soul – *Sarah.*

Twenty-Six

AS THE hack rolled to a stop in front of Sarah's quaint home, Alex looked out the window. He didn't even need the full moon to make out the house, as warm candles glowed in her front room. Thank heavens! He wouldn't want to wake her. Then male laughter from within halted Alex in his tracks, and his heart sank even more.

William Haywood must be with Sarah. Her new paramour. His successor.

He squeezed his eyes tightly, willing all his pain away. He couldn't intrude on Sarah, not even after the promise she made him give her. They'd both moved on. He just hoped she had found the happiness that eluded him.

Alex opened the door and yelled back up to the driver. "Change in plans. St. James instead, please." He could drink himself to oblivion at his club, which was much preferable to hearing his wife cry over the only man she'd ever loved.

⋘⋙

Under the hazy full moon, Major Philip Moore could make out the chalky cliffs of Dover. England! Home! Thank God! There were times in the last few years when he didn't think this day would ever come.

In another day he'd be in London, with Livvie back in his arms where she belonged. Then he'd never let her go. He'd seen enough of war and death in his twenty-five years to last a lifetime. A quiet, peaceful life awaited him in Papplewick, and he could hardly wait to start it.

A hand clapped his back and he turned, grinning into the green eyes of Captain Russell Avery. "Nearly home."

"Indeed," Russell smiled in return. I've been dreaming the last little while about a hero's welcome in the arms of a sweet-smelling English girl. Tristan and I have plans to go straight to Madam Palmers once we arrive in London."

Philip chuckled and shook his head. "Your mother won't let you out of her sight."

"Well, that's where you come in, my friend. You can distract her with your tales of valor while Tristan and I escape out the back."

Again Philip laughed. "Sorry, Russell. Once we get settled, I'm heading over to Lord Staveley's. It's been forever since I've seen Olivia. You don't think she's forgotten me do you?"

"Livvie?" Russell asked, shaking his head. "She worships you. Always has."

The words brought a smile to his face. He worshiped her too, ever since they were children. "How soon do you think I can marry her? I don't want to wait three weeks."

"Lord Staveley has connections to the Archbishop. I'm sure you won't have to."

◆◆◆

Philip was elated to finally be back on English soil. He'd sat in a carriage all the way from Dover, across from his two dearest friends, Captain Russell Avery and the captain's younger brother, Lieutenant Tristan Avery. Now as they rambled towards South Audley Street, he could hardly believe the journey was coming to an end. They had all grown up together, but after experiencing the hells of war by each other's sides, the three of them were closer than most brothers.

Still one didn't want to intrude. "Are you sure your mother won't mind putting me up for a while?" he asked his compatriots. He could find a lodging house for a day or two, just long enough to see Olivia and obtain a special license, before they returned to his land in Nottinghamshire. God, how he missed Olivia Danbury! The memory of her smile and charming dimple had gotten him through most of the war. Her ethereal beauty and kind heart. There was no other woman like her in the world. And she was his.

He couldn't wait to see her again!

Russell snorted. "For God's sake, Moore, you saved Tris' arse more than once. You'll have a damn near impossible time getting mother to let you *leave*."

"Too true," Tristan added with a weary smile. "Besides you're family in every way that counts. I do hope Cordie doesn't drag us off to balls and such. I never much cared for those sorts of affairs."

"Ah, but think of it," Russell began with a mischievous twinkle in his green eyes, "we're returning heroes. Girls will be throwing themselves in our path."

"I'd rather be left alone," Tristan grumbled.

When their coach came to an abrupt stop, Russell threw open the door and anxiously jumped out of the conveyance.

Philip followed him out but bumped into his strangely immobile friend. "Out of the way, Avery."

Russell stepped aside and shook his head in astonishment. "Tris," he hissed, momentarily glancing back over his shoulder at his brother. "I know it's been forever, but isn't that the Marquess of Haversham?"

All three men strained their necks to see a well-dressed gentleman ambling down the street. Philip had never met the marquess, but the brothers Avery had once been patrons of a fashionable bawdy house which the infamous Haversham frequented on a regular basis.

"It looks like him," Tristan confirmed.

"I thought so," Russell said morosely. "He just left our home."

"Our home?" Tristan echoed. "What would a man like that be doing at Avery House?"

The answer hit all three of them at the same time. "Dear God," Russell muttered. "If he touches one hair on Cordelia's head, I'll shoot him."

"Only if you get to him before I do." Tristan replied, scowling after the nobleman's now disappearing form.

Philip sighed deeply. He didn't envy his friends in the least. Cordelia Avery had always had a bit of a stubborn streak, but he'd thought she would have outgrown that by now. How fortunate he was that Livvie was so level-headed.

The coachmen threw their bags down from the top of the rig and the three officers ascended the steps to the Averys' fashionable townhouse. The door was wrenched open, and they were assaulted by the disembodied shrill screams of Lady Avery. "Do you think I want you following in Olivia's scandalous footsteps, young lady?"

Olivia's scandalous footsteps? The three officers quickly piled inside the entryway and Sanders shut the door behind them.

"Livvie is happy, Mama!" Cordelia Avery's irate voice echoed off the walls. "And a duchess! A *duchess* for heaven's sake! They're not generally denigrated, you know."

"They don't generally behave in such ill fashion either."

"You should want as much for me. And Haversham is a marquess! Loads better than a puffed up naval captain."

"Captain Seaton was a decent man." Lady Avery's voice rose even louder as the three men looked at each other horrified expressions.

Philip was certain they'd missed something. Olivia wasn't a duchess. At least *his* Olivia wasn't. Although he would like to know what exactly they were shouting about.

"Gabriel Seaton was a dictatorial prig and I'm glad he's gone."

Russell turned to Sanders, standing stoically by the door. "You'd best announce us before it gets any worse."

The butler nodded and slinked down the hallway.

Tristan frowned at Philip. "Did she say Olivia was a *duchess*?"

Philip shook his head. It must be someone else. "We must have misheard."

"I only heard *Haversham*." Russell remarked, stalking after the butler, quickly followed by the other two. A moment later, a squeal of joy came from one of the rooms. Then the door flew open, and Lady Avery and Cordie rushed out into the hallway. Russell embraced their mother while Tristan was nearly knocked to the floor by their sister, then they switched partners.

Philip watched the excitement, smiling widely. It was good to be home.

"Philip Moore!" Lady Avery rushed towards him, arms outstretched. "My dear boy, I can never thank you enough for keeping Tristan alive."

Tristan groaned nearby. "Mother, I wish you wouldn't say it like that."

"Into the parlor, all of you," the baroness demanded, directing the group inside the nearest room. "And, Sanders, tea, if you will. Who knows when these boys have had decent fare. You're all too thin, the lot of you."

Philip soon found himself, sitting on an uncomfortable settee in a light blue parlor, lined from wall to wall with knick-knacks of various sizes and colors. A frilly room to be sure. It reminded him instantly of the Averys' estate outside Papplewick.

As the Averys gushed over each other, he watched the scene with an overflowing heart, though his mind was still trying sort through the strange argument had greeted them on their arrival. It had sounded like Cordie said Olivia was a duchess.

He was relieved when Cordie, who he'd known her entire life, took the seat next to him. "It is good to see you, Philip. We have been so worried about all of you."

"Indeed we have!" Lady Avery seconded, then her eyes filled with tears as she looked at her youngest son. "Tristan, my heart stopped when we got the news you'd been injured."

"Mother, it was nothing," the lieutenant protested.

"Don't listen to him, mother," Russell interrupted. Then he began to tell the Avery women how Philip had knocked Tristan to the ground seconds before a ball would have lodged itself inside his chest. The lieutenant had suffered from a broken arm, but otherwise he was whole and hale.

Philip knew the story and he paid no attention to the retelling. His mind was echoing, 'Livvie is happy and a duchess!' over and over. When he couldn't take it anymore he touched Cordie's hand. "I didn't mean to eavesdrop, but you were yelling when we arrived."

Cordelia Avery blanched and the room fell to silence.

Philip pressed on. "Were you talking about *my* Olivia?"

"See here," Russell cut in, apparently just now remembering the argument they had interrupted. "I'll not have my sister falling prey to Marcus Gray. What was he doing here?"

"I'll put a ball in his skull if he returns," Tristan threatened.

"And a blade in his chest," Russell added.

"Charming!" Cordie remarked mordantly. "It's so wonderful to see that the two of you are still so civilized after your stay in the army."

Russell shook his head at his sister. "You can't bait us like that, Cordie. Have you gone and lost your mind? I mean Haversham for God's sake? Do you have any idea of his reputation?"

"I know that he'd grant me the freedom to do as I pleased. He wouldn't dictate who my friends could be. Or what I could say. Or what I could do. And he cares about me, Russell. So both of you—" she paused, gesturing wildly to her brothers— "had better keep your pistols and swords to yourselves, or I'll never forgive you."

Lady Avery smiled wistfully at her sons. "It is good to have you home. Perhaps you can talk some sense into her. Ever since Olivia..."

Philip's eyes flew to the baroness'. "Pray continue, my lady. Ever since Olivia what?"

She looked away from him, so he turned his attention to Cordie at his side.

"Ever since Olivia what? Please tell me."

Cordie's green eyes dropped to the floor. "I-I suppose that means you don't know."

"Know what?" he demanded, pulse racing through his veins.

Cordie glanced up at him, an apologetic smile on her face. "I don't think she meant for it to happen, Philip. It just did."

"What happened?" he nearly bellowed.

She took a deep breath. "Well, you see, we'd gone to a house party in Derbyshire at the home of the Duke of Prestwick—"

Livvie is happy and a duchess! "She married the Duke of Prestwick?" He didn't know the duke and shook his head, thoroughly confused.

"No," Cordie quickly replied, "His Grace of Prestwick is just a boy, but *his* sister is married to Livvie's cousin, Lucas Beckford. It was the worst house party I've ever been to. There were no entertainments to speak of, and surly naval captains abounded, and we were dreadfully bored."

Philip was beyond frustration and he rubbed his forehead. "For the love of God, Cordelia, pray get to the point."

When it appeared she would not, Lady Avery cleared her throat and explained. "The Duke of Kelfield was in attendance as well, Philip." Her frown was most disconcerting, making his heart constrict in his chest. "The girls returned early from the country and two days later Olivia was

Kelfield's duchess. I'm unsure of what all transpired as Cordelia had gone alone to keep Olivia company. I entrusted Cordie would be safe in Lord and Lady Staveley's care—a mistake I won't make in the future."

Cordie leapt off the settee. "I've done nothing wrong, Mama. And yet you insist on keeping me locked up here like some villain."

Philip stopped listening for the most part, though he could still make out bits and pieces of the argument. His broken heart stopped beating and he sank back against the settee. His hopes and dreams gone, without his knowledge, without a fight from him. Everything he'd ever wanted had been stolen from him. His dear, loving Olivia. It was too awful to accept.

The Duke of Kelfield? There wasn't a more depraved soul in all of England. How could this have happened? What had the man done to his poor, sweet girl? Had he forced his attentions on Livvie? Compromised her in some way? Of course he had! Livvie was honest and honorable. She would never go willingly to Kelfield or anyone else.

The wind rushed out of him. Numb, he couldn't think or feel. "Dear God," he finally muttered under his breath. Then he leapt to his feet. "I'll kill him!"

As he started for the door, Cordie wailed behind him. "Philip, no! Please stop! Listen to reason."

But there was no *reason* to what had happened to him. He'd left England, an adoring fiancée, and a promising future, only to return to find it all had been stolen from him in the most indecent of ways. He had to kill Kelfield. He didn't have a choice. Someone had to free Olivia from the bastard.

They could send him to the gallows for all he cared. As long as Olivia was safe, it would be worth it.

Philip rushed outside and hailed a hack. "Kelfield House," he barked, hoping the driver knew the location since he did not.

Twenty-Seven

WARM light suddenly poured into Livvie's room. She groaned, rolled over, and tried to block the assaulting brightness from her eyes. She never wanted to get out of bed, and she wanted to stay like this until the end of time.

"Come on, Your Grace, it is very late," Molly said from somewhere near the drapes.

Then she vaguely heard Poppy's little voice ask, "Is she sick?"

"Oh, little dear, it's just the natural way of things. Her Grace will probably sleep in late most days in the coming months," the maid explained.

Livvie managed to sit up. Her eyes were still sore from having cried herself to sleep and her bones and muscles were drained and weary. When she opened her eyes, Poppy stood beside her, smiling widely.

"You are a slug-a-bed. You're late for our tea party."

Late for tea? It couldn't be past four. "What time is it?" she asked Molly.

"Quarter of five, Your Grace."

Quarter of five? "Can't be." She'd never slept so late in all her life. Livvie threw off the counterpane and swung her feet over the side. Then the room began to spin and she closed her eyes again.

Molly touched a hand to her brow. "Miss Poppy, why don't you wait for the duchess in the gold parlor? I'll have her down shortly."

Livvie heard the patter of Poppy's feet race from the room, then she blinked her eyes open to find Molly's concerned expression hanging over her. "I'll be fine, Molly. I just had a bad night." The images of Alex's hardened jaw and cold eyes washed over her. Livvie almost shivered. She needed to set the situation to rights. "Will you ask the duke to attend me?"

Molly pursed her lips. "His Grace left in the dead of night and he hasn't returned."

A new wave of illness washed over Livvie. He was still furious with her or he would be home at quarter of five. He always enjoyed his afternoons with Poppy. Livvie groaned and wiped at a tear that was stinging one of her swollen eyes. She'd never felt so awful in her entire life. "Does Gibson know where he is?" she asked hopefully.

The maid shook her head. "I'm sure he'll come home, but not until he's good and ready. Men like the duke do things in their own time and not before. In the meanwhile, Your Grace, you need to concern yourself with your own health."

Her Grace will probably sleep in late most days in the coming months. Livvie frowned. "Molly, why did you tell Poppy I'd start to sleep late?"

Molly took a deep breath. "You might not. My mother did with each of her babes. But every woman's different."

Livvie's eyes widened in surprise. "Babes? But, Molly, I'm not..." And then she started thinking back. She and Alex had been married for six weeks. She hadn't had her courses in eight. Everything had been so hectic since they'd met, she hadn't noticed that her time hadn't come.

It was probably nerves. It wouldn't be the first time. She's gone three months without her courses after Philip had left for the continent. But once her anxiety had settled, her body had returned to normal. She had certainly been living with as much anxiety now as she was then. Still, it would be best to be sure one way or the other. "Please arrange for Doctor Watts to pay me a visit."

"Yes, of course."

After Molly helped her into a peach day dress adorned in white ribbons, Livvie made her way down the stairs. Her empty stomach grumbled and she looked forward to tea and scones with Poppy. Anything that was part of her normal routine would be good.

As she turned down the corridor towards the gold parlor, Alex's familiar chuckle halted her. She almost wept, she was so relieved. Livvie stepped inside the room, thrilled to see Poppy sitting on Alex's lap enchanting him with one of her unicorn stories.

"Your imagination is intoxicating, my love," he said to his daughter, kissing the top of her head.

Livvie cleared her throat and stepped towards the pair, only to see Alex's smile vanish. Her heart ached to see his stubborn jaw was still tight with anger. His steely eyes pierced her soul and she nervously searched for something to say. "Molly said you hadn't returned."

"Well, apparently, Molly was wrong." His icy voice washed over her, leaving her cold and miserable. Then he shifted Poppy from his lap and ran his hand along her curls. "Be a good girl for me."

Poppy nodded her head. "How long will you be gone, Papa?"

"I don't know, angel."

"You're leaving?" Livvie asked, dismayed.

His cold eyes flashed to hers. "I have business to attend to, Olivia." Then he rose from his seat and lifted Poppy in the air, planting a large, smacking kiss on her cheek. "Go back to Mrs. Bickle for just a little while."

As Poppy slinked from the room, Livvie refocused on her husband, whose angry eyes found hers. The uncomfortable distance between them was killing her. She had to explain. "Alex, please don't leave. I know you're furious with me, but I was only reading a letter."

He scoffed. Loudly. "You were reading a letter from the man you love. A letter that you purposefully kept hidden from me. And you were reading the letter in the middle of the night, when I'm sure you felt it was safe to do so without my knowledge. Don't pretend otherwise."

Livvie stepped towards him. "*You* are the man I love, Alex. I was reading the letter, but..."

"And how many others were there, Olivia? How many other nights that I know nothing about?"

"It's not like that. And it was only last night—"

"Of course," he said mockingly. "How unfortunate that I caught you the *one* night you were disloyal to me."

"Disloyal?" she squeaked. Then she shook her head, "Alex, it was only a letter. I only received it yesterday, and I didn't think you'd understand. I wonder, where would I get an idea like that?"

"Sarcasm does not become you."

"And acting a tyrant does not become you."

He simply glared at her, and Olivia moved closer to him, confident that if she could just touch him, he would lose his anger. "Please, let us speak calmly. I do not want us to suffer through another night as we just did."

"Olivia," he replied icily, stepping away from her, "you have no say on how I spend my nights. And I'll thank you to remember that."

What did he mean by that? Livvie frowned. "Alexander Everett, as your wife—"

He laughed derisively. "Do not mistake me for a dolt, Olivia. You are only my wife because you were caught in my room, and not for any other reason."

"Alex! How can you say that?" How could he think that after the nights they'd spent together? After the sweet words whispered in her ear? Livvie gaped at him.

"It's the truth, sweetheart. Had James McFadyn not seen you exit my room, you would be waiting for Philip Moore's return this very moment. I'm sorry that didn't work out for you."

"I'm not!" Livvie stomped her foot to emphasize the point.

⊰ ⊱

Alex couldn't stand there any longer, looking at her, knowing that she would never truly be his. That though she was his wife and he loved her more than life itself, her heart would always belong to Major Moore, damn his eyes. Alex turned his back on her and started for the door.

"Where are you going?" she demanded, chasing after him into the corridor.

"Wherever the bloody hell I want to," he snarled in return.

Olivia grabbed his arm and he snatched it back from her, stalking purposefully towards the main entryway. When Gibson saw the determined look on his face, the butler quickly opened the front door.

Standing there on the front porch was an army major. Tall, with dark, scathing eyes, and a set chin. Alex stopped in his tracks.

"Kelfield!" the man spat at him.

Olivia gasp behind him, and as he turned to look at her, the officer's fist met with Alex's eye and he fell to the ground.

"Philip!" Olivia wailed as she dropped to her knees beside Alex.

Philip? Dear God! Alex pushed Olivia away from him and scrambled back to his feet. His eye was burning miserably, but he wouldn't give Philip Moore the pleasure of seeing him in pain. "You're the noble major that my wife adores? Hitting a man unaware? Not very sporting of you, Moore."

"I've come to demand satisfaction from you, Kelfield," the major hissed with a murderous look in his dark eyes.

"Philip, no!" Olivia cried from behind them. "Don't do this. Please."

Alex looked back at her, his wife whom he loved but who loved another. "Worried he'll make you a widow, Olivia?

Panic flashed in her hazel eyes and she threw her arms around his middle. "Please, Alex."

"Don't worry, sweetheart," he whispered. "I'm sure he's a better shot than I am. Then your hopes and dreams can be returned to you."

"*You* are my hopes and dreams, you stubborn man."

Alex pulled out of her grasp and faced Moore again. "I accept your challenge, Major."

Olivia whimpered behind him, but Alex focused his attention on the officer.

Weapon?" Moore asked.

Alex reassessed the major's murderous glare. One shot from a pistol from a man who was proficient with the weapon was suicide, and not terribly sporting. If Moore was intent on killing him, Alex was going to make him work for it. "Swords."

The response did not affect the major in the least. "Name your second."

"The Marquess of Haversham. Yours?"

A strange look crossed the major's face, but it was soon gone. "Captain Russell Avery."

Alex couldn't help but chuckle. "I'll send Haversham over to Avery House to work out the details, if that bitch Gladys Avery will let him in her house." Then he pushed past the major, descended the steps, and stalked off down Park Lane.

⚜

Olivia gaped after Alex's departing form and the room started to spin again. Before she fell to the floor, Philip caught her in his arms. "Dear God, Livvie, how did this happen to you?"

He deserved answers, but Livvie couldn't give him any at the moment. Her own life was in too much disarray. She pulled out of his arms and tears streamed down her face. "Philip, please," she begged. "Withdraw your challenge."

"I cannot," he stated firmly, frowning at her. "The man has dishonored you. I will not let that go unanswered."

"He has not," she said, swiping at her tears. Her cheeks ached, red and stinging from all her crying last night and this morning. "Philip, he is my husband. Do not do this in my name, I beg you."

"Olivia, you cannot care for that man." The incredulous tone in his voice sobered Livvie.

She tipped her chin in the air. "Of course I do. He's my husband." When he winced at her words, she softened her voice, "I am so very sorry for hurting you. That was never my intent. I pray you believe me."

"You would never hurt anyone willingly."

"But I have done so, and for that I am truly sorry. I know it must be difficult to come to terms with, but I am the Duchess of Kelfield and I do love my husband. So if you ever loved me, Philip, please withdraw your challenge."

Philip stared at her for the longest time. In his proud frame, Livvie could see the silly boy she grew up with, the young man who had fascinated her, the stoic soldier who was a hero, the man she always knew she would marry. Part of her would always love Philip, but he was her past. Her future was Alex. Her entire heart belonged to her arrogant duke, who didn't even seem to believe her love was real.

Finally, Philip shook his head. "He took you from me. He took my life. I got through the war, through each battle, because I knew I was coming home to you — my love, my heart, my soul. I will not give him my honor as well. It's all I have left."

Twenty-Eight

"YOUR Grace," Doctor Watts began, sitting at Livvie's bedside, "you are with child."

Livvie's mouth fell open, a flood of emotions swamping her. Surprise that it was true. Elation that she was to be a mother. Terror that her husband could soon foolishly die on the field of *honor*. Happiness that she could give Alex an heir. Fear of the unknown.

She didn't know whether to laugh or cry.

"It is early in your term," the doctor continued, "but I am unhappy with what I see, Your Grace. You look as if you've been through quite the ordeal. I would never presume to guess at what goes on in another's home, but I am concerned about your health. You have dark circles under your eyes, your maid says you haven't eaten at all today, and I've never heard a heartbeat as rapid as yours on a healthy woman."

Livvie shook her head. It was just the tension of the day. Alex's anger! Philip's return! A duel, for heaven's sakes! "Doctor, this child is most important to me, more so than my own life. Tell me what you want me to do."

"Stay in bed. Eat. Don't get yourself all worked up. Remain calm."

Easier said than done. But she would do it for the child. Livvie nodded her head. "Of course, Doctor Watts. Thank you."

⋘❦⋙

Ever since Cordie had gotten wind of the duel, she was determined to fix the problem. Men were so ridiculous with these sorts of things. Having endured three brothers her entire life, she was well aware of that fact. Women, by far, had cooler heads. So it was up to her to make things right.

She found Russell sitting in the library, reading and drinking some brandy. Perfect. Her middle brother was always the easiest to manipulate when he was drinking. She flopped down in an over-stuffed leather chair across from Russell.

He looked up at her and raised his brow. "You want something."

"I do not." She feigned innocence.

Russell grinned at her. "I've not been gone all that long, Cordelia. When you want something, your nose scrunches up just a bit."

Blast her brother for knowing her as well as she knew him. Not that she was going to let that deter her. "Russ, about—"

He roared with laughter. "Russ? You only call me that if you've exhausted all other options. What is it, Cordie?"

"Very well," she said, sitting forward in her chair, dispensing all pretense and cutting to the chase. "This duel between Kelfield and Philip. It's to be swords?"

"How do you know that?" he asked, narrowing his green eyes on her.

"Tristan."

Russell sat back in his chair with a, "Humpf."

"So it's to be swords. Will it be first blood or to the death?"

"Haversham hasn't shown up to discuss the terms. And," he said, pinning her with his gaze, "no, you won't see him while he's here."

"Oh for heaven's sake, Russell, the marquess is the last thing on my mind at the moment." She sighed, shaking her head. "Olivia loves her husband. You would only have to see them together to know that. Please make it First Blood. It would destroy Livvie if Kelfield died. Injured, she could live with."

"This is not something that concerns women, Cordie."

She frowned at her brother. "Spoken like a pompous man."

He chuckled. "Tristan should be shot for even telling you in the first place."

208

"Well, I suppose since you're all intent on killing each other, he can be next on the list." Then she touched her brother's leg. "Please. Livvie is my dearest friend, Russell. I don't want to see her hurt. If either of them died, she would be devastated. You grew up with her, same as me. I know you don't want that."

Russell sighed. "I'll agree to it if Haversham will. But if you tell anyone that you talked me into this, I'll deny it and put snakes in your bed again."

Cordie's mouth fell open. "That was *you*?" Then she smacked him. "Russell Avery! On more than one occasion you and Gregory both told me that Tristan was the culprit. I threw a rock at his head."

He threw back his head and laughed. "You always had awful aim."

He could laugh at her if he wanted to. One down, one to go. She kissed Russell's cheek, then excused herself and made a beeline to the front parlor so she had a good view of South Audley Street. The Marquess of Haversham wouldn't get past her.

Luckily, she didn't have to wait long. Only one man walked with the strong, purposeful gait of Marcus Gray. Cordie's heart flipped in her chest. She raced out of the parlor and reached the door before Sanders could do so. The butler eyed her with displeasure.

Cordie tipped her nose haughtily. "Sanders, I know it was you who pilfered Lord Avery's best whiskey." She'd held that information forever, knowing it would come in handy at some point.

The old man's face went white at the revelation. "Miss Cordelia!"

"I'll never say a word, Sanders, if you turn your back for five minutes." There she doubted Caroline Staveley could have done it any better herself.

"Five minutes, miss." Then Sanders ducked around the corner.

She could have kissed him. Instead, she wrenched the door open and smiled at Haversham. "My lord, we meet again."

A seductive grin spread across his handsome face. "Butler duties? What other talents are you hiding, Miss Avery?"

She grabbed his arm and pulled him inside. Haversham stumbled and pulled her against his strong body. "Not here," she whispered, pulling out of his grasp and tugging him towards the front parlor.

Once inside, Haversham shut the door behind them and pulled her back into his arms. His warm, sensuous mouth covered hers and Cordie had to struggle to maintain her senses. She pushed at his muscled chest and staggered backwards. "My lord, I need to speak with you."

"I much prefer what we were just doing," he replied, barely touching the side of her neck, sending shivers across her skin.

Her cheeks heated up and she shook her head. "Please, I don't have much time."

"What are you concerned about, angel?" he asked smoothly, kissing her fingers.

"This duel—"

"You know about that?" He dropped her hand.

Men and their silly rules. She didn't have time for explanations. Sanders would be back any minute. "Please make it just to first blood drawn, my lord."

He shook his head. "Kelfield made it quite clear he wanted it to the death."

Blast the duke for being so proud! Cordie frowned at him. "But as seconds, you and my brother set the stipulations."

"You do realize that neither gentleman would be happy with your interference?"

Probably not. Definitely not. Though she didn't have time to worry about that at the moment. Either man could die, and it would be a travesty. She stepped closer to the marquess and placed her hand on his chest. "Please."

His pulse quickened at her touch and he pulled her closer to him. "I suppose I could be convinced to see things your way," his low voice rumbled across her.

She tipped her head back to see him and began to toy with one of the buttons on his waistcoat. "What would it take, my lord?"

His grin widened. "What are you offering?"

Cordie had bargained with her older brothers most of her life, and she was fairly proficient at it. She smiled coyly. "A kiss."

Haversham stroked her neck and dipped his head toward hers. She was certain he would kiss her again, but instead he whispered in her ear. "You've already kissed me, Cordelia. I want something else."

"A kiss is all I can offer," she replied softly, inhaling the heady scent of his citric shaving lotion.

"But you'll kiss me again. Right now if I wish it, because you enjoy my kiss. That's not a bargaining chip, my beautiful temptress."

Cordie sucked in a breath. Were all men so arrogant? "I do enjoy your kiss, but I can go forever without having it again," she taunted him.

He stared at her, his light blue eyes raking her from top to bottom, warming her skin as he did so. She thought he wouldn't say anything and then a scratching came at the door. Good heavens, Sanders already! Cordie nearly groaned. "One moment, Sanders."

Haversham ran his finger along her lower lip. "A kiss, then," he said and grinned wickedly. "But I choose where."

"As long as it's not out in the open for anyone else to see." After all, she hoped to marry the man, not be publicly ruined by him.

His eyes danced with merriment. "My gorgeous girl, you can rest assured that no one but I will see where I plan to kiss you."

Where could he possibly plan to take her that was so mysterious? His coach? Vauxhall? Not that she had time to contemplate the situation, as the scratch at the door came again, more insistent this time. "Coming, Sanders."

⚜

Livvie sat in her bed, flipping through the pages of *La Belle Assemblée*, hoping to get the day's events off her mind. It was futile, but she didn't have a choice. Alex had not returned home. Neither had she heard any word from him. It was enough to drive her mad. But she tried to remain calm as Doctor Watts had been very clear about that, and he didn't want her out of bed until his next visit.

There was a soft knock at her door. "Come," she said hastily, hoping someone had brought her news.

Caroline stepped inside and smiled at her. "Darling, how are you?"

"Worried sick," Livvie admitted.

Her cousin sat in a chair at her side. "Men are foolish. They have to get these sorts of things out of their system."

"Caroline! One of them could be killed. Alex could be killed. Why did he pick Haversham? Why not Carteret or Staveley? Someone who could talk some sense into him?"

"Darling, don't get yourself worked up. I talked to Doctor Watts myself. I know that he wants you to avoid hysterics." Then Caroline clasped Livvie's hand. "I should have thought it was a possibility that you'd conceived when you fainted yesterday. I'm sorry I did not."

Livvie smiled wistfully. "Lots of things make sense now. I was feeling ill and kept thinking it was all the anxiety from the last few weeks. It never occurred to me that I was with child."

"It is wonderful news, Olivia," Caroline gushed.

"Alex doesn't know."

Caroline nodded. "It's better that way for now. The news would only distract him."

"But what if…" *What if he dies*? Livvie couldn't bring herself to utter the words. "Doesn't he have a right to know?"

Caroline knew what she was asking and she shook her head. "Don't worry, Olivia. I received a note today from your friend, Cordelia."

"She sent *you* a note?"

"She said she would have sent it to you, but she's certain her correspondence is being monitored. Anyway, that's not what I'm trying to tell you. Apparently, Miss Avery is quite adept at persuasion. She somehow managed to get both Captain Avery and Haversham to agree the duel will end with the first blood drawn. Unless Alex is very unlucky, he'll be alive on the morrow. Injured, I could not say. So take that worry off your mind. Focus on your child."

Livvie took the first calming breath of the very long, awful day. *First blood drawn*. It was something. She chose not to think about the possibility of infection or how deeply the first thrust of a sword could plunge into a man, especially when his opponent was Philip Moore, a swordsman with excellent skills. *First blood drawn*. It was better than nothing.

After Caroline left, promising to return in the morning, Livvie tossed her magazine to the floor. Fashion was the last thing on her mind. She lay down on her side, clutching a pillow in her hands, wishing it was her husband. Livvie closed her eyes, praying for all she was worth that Alex would be safe.

Then her bedroom door opened.

Twenty-Nine

"OLIVIA?" came Poppy's little voice from the doorway.

Yes, Poppy?" Livvie sat back up. "What is it?"

Her step-daughter swiped at a tear and shuffled towards the bed. "Papa always tells me a bedtime story."

"Oh. Do you want me to tell you a story?"

Poppy shook her head. "Your stories aren't as good."

The honesty of a child. Livvie held in a laugh, the first one of the day. Bless Poppy for giving it to her. "Would you like to tell me one then?"

Poppy climbed up on the bed next to Livvie and rested her raven curls on one of the pillows, her silver eyes sad. "Olivia, can I stay here with you?"

"You mean sleep here?"

Poppy took a deep breath. "I don't want to be alone. I wish Papa didn't go away."

"Me too," Livvie confided, feeling the bond with her step-daughter strengthen. No one loved Alex like the two of them, and no one would miss him like they would. "You may stay if you'd like, Poppy."

The little girl snuggled against her, and Livvie held the child close. She closed her eyes, thinking about Poppy, Alex, and the child she carried. Livvie sent up a silent prayer that her little family would go unscathed the next day.

⚜

In the wee hours of the morning, fog slowly lifted from Hyde Park. The sun was on the very edge of the horizon, but the waning full moon could still be seen in the sky. Alex glanced across the clearing to where Major Moore was surrounded by two other regimented army officers. From the looks of them they were Averys. Haversham came up behind him and clapped Alex's back. "Just waiting on the doctor and Clayworth."

Alex grimaced, his eyes still on Philip Moore. "Tell me again, Marc. Why isn't this to the death?"

"I had no idea you were so bloodthirsty, Kelfield. If you don't like the way I manage things, you should pick someone else as your second next time. My management assures you will most likely *get* a next time."

"Thank you for your confidence in my abilities," he replied drolly.

Marc laughed. "I don't doubt your abilities, you savage beast." Then he sobered up a bit. "Assuming you were to run the whelp through, would you have been prepared to leave your wife and Poppy? Live in exile on the continent? It's better my way."

"I've already left Olivia. Whether I'm abroad or in England matters very little."

Marc's eyes grew round in surprise. "You've left your wife?"

Alex shrugged. Everyone else would know very soon anyway. "She prefers Moore, and I prefer not to be reminded of the fact."

Marc glanced at the major with a frown. "I suppose I should have let you run him through then. Sorry, Kelfield, I didn't know. That's what I get for listening to females."

"What does that mean?" Alex glowered at his friend.

Marc raked a hand through his dark hair. "Miss Avery was—"

Incredible! Alex rubbed his brow. "Did you seriously betray me for an opportunity to toss up the girl's skirts?"

"They are very nice skirts," Marc replied in defense of himself.

"Bastard."

"And she was quite convincing."

"I'll just bet she was. Philip Moore is a family friend, Marc. She wouldn't want to see him hurt any more than my wife would." His irritation grew and he looked out across the park. "Where the devil are Watts and Clayworth?"

As if on cue, Staveley's coach rambled out of the fog into view. It plodded forward, finally stopping a few feet from the awaiting men. The door opened and Doctor Watts climbed out of the equipage, followed closely by Staveley and Clayworth, who had somehow been roped into officiating the event.

Immediately, Staveley made a beeline for Alex and Haversham.

The marquess grinned at him. "You *do* leave your library on occasion, Staveley. Good to know."

The viscount ignored the jab, focusing on Alex. "How are you?"

Aching. Miserable. Barely sober. "Fine," he answered.

You smell like whiskey," Staveley complained.

"Gentlemen," Clayworth called out, "it is time."

Alex shrugged out of his coat and removed his waistcoat and shirt. Then he retrieved his rapier from its scabbard and strode purposefully to his mark. Just a few feet away, Philip Moore did the same.

They circled each other, and Alex sized his opponent up. Moore was fit and furious, but his glare didn't worry Alex in the least. He'd been fencing ever since he was big enough to hold a sword.

Moore's dark eyes narrowed. "She's too good for you." He lunged forward. Alex's rapier met the metal with a clank as he parried safely to his left.

"But she's mine nonetheless," Alex taunted him, circling around the major. Then with the flick of his wrist, he aimed his sword at Moore's chest, missing his mark when the major leaned away from the blade.

They parried and jabbed at each other, back and forth, learning the other's strengths and weaknesses while their witnesses waited with bated breath.

Moore's rapier came quickly to Alex's middle, but he was able to force the sword away with his own, almost knocking his opponent to the ground. But the major steadied himself and came back at Alex. Their swords clanked together and Moore forced Alex backwards. The major was forceful—more so than Alex had expected. The officer lunged again, with fire in his eyes, and plunged his rapier into Alex's left shoulder. "Agh!" he cried out in surprised agony. Pain shot down his arm and across his chest, and he dropped his sword to the ground as he fell to his knees.

"Halt," Clayworth called out.

Then he was quickly surrounded by Staveley, Haversham, and Doctor Watts.

"Lay him down," he heard the doctor say through the pain-induced haze. The physician applied some ointment to Alex's shoulder and pressed a cloth to the wound.

"How bad is it?" Staveley asked.

"He's going to be in pain for a while, but he'll survive if we can keep infection down." Then the doctor leveled Alex with a glare. "Your Grace, this is precisely the sort of thing your wife doesn't need."

His wife. Alex closed his eyes, imaging her pretty smile, pretending she loved him. An icy chill washed over him. "I only require you opinion on my shoulder, doctor."

The physician returned his attention to the wound, wrapping it tightly in cloth. Then he glanced up at Haversham. "Get him back to Kelfield House."

"No! Don't you dare take me there," Alex barked, staggering back to his feet. "My shirt, if you will, Marc."

As Haversham retrieved his discarded clothing, Staveley stepped forward. "Alex, you've lost a lot of blood. You should go home to your wife."

"I need your opinion less than Watts'."

"But there are things you don't know," Staveley persisted.

Alex shook his head. "Stay out of my affairs, Staveley. I married the girl because of my friendship for you. I don't owe you anything else."

"Stubborn bastard," Staveley muttered.

Marc returned with his shirt and jacket.

"Thank you. Play my valet, will you. Help me slip this over my arm."

New pain rushed through Alex when Haversham slid his arm through the fine lawn sleeve of his shirt, and he winced. Then he turned his attention to Philip Moore. "You are apparently the better man."

"That was never in question," Moore replied acidly.

"No, I suppose not." Alex smiled half-heartedly. "I'm sorry these fine gentlemen have deprived you the opportunity to see me dead." He took his jacket and draped it over his arm.

Then he started off towards the Park Lane entrance, leaving the assembled men staring at him in shock.

"Kelfield," the doctor called after him. "That shoulder needs to be attended to."

He raised his good arm, indicating he'd heard the man, but continued on his way, never slowing his gait.

⋞⋞⋐⋗⋗

Livvie sat in her bed, staring out the window, praying Alex would be unharmed. She wasn't certain how she could possibly reduce the anxiety of her life, and yet knew she needed to find a way. Poppy moved in her sleep and Livvie smoothed the girl's raven hair off her face. She had to find a way to make everything right for her family.

"Olivia?" Caroline called through the door, "Are you awake?"

"Yes, come in, please," she answered, unable to hide the anxiousness from her voice.

The door pushed open and Caroline slipped inside. She smiled widely when her eyes fell on Poppy. "She doesn't know about this mess, does she?"

Livvie shook her head. "Alex told her he was going away for a while. She was lonely last night and wanted to stay with me."

"I see." Caroline sat in the chair next to Livvie's bed.

Her cousin seemed very enigmatic, and Livvie couldn't read her expression, which was maddening. "Is it over?" she asked, keeping her voice low to avoid waking Poppy.

Caroline nodded. "By all accounts, Alex is fine, though he lost the duel."

Livvie's heart ached and she started to rise, but Caroline gently pushed her back against the pillows. "Doctor's orders, darling. And as I said, Alex is fine, a minor shoulder injury is all."

His shoulder? *Merciful God! Please keep infection from him.* "Is he here?"

Caroline pursed her lips and then shook her head. Of course he wasn't here. He would have come to her if he was, which meant he was still angry with her.

"Staveley doesn't know where he is. He stalked off once the match was decided."

"He stalked off? But he was *injured*! Didn't someone stop him?"

"No one stops Kelfield from doing what he wants."

She knew that better than anyone. "But his shoulder, Caroline—"

"The man is thirty-four years old. He knows what needs to be done. And you are not supposed to be worrying. I'm only telling you what I know because I know that not knowing will make you even more anxious. Alex will be fine. And he will come home."

᭬

But Alex didn't come home.

A fortnight later, Livvie was still waiting for his return. She knew he wasn't dying from infection, because he was in the gossip columns every morning, tearing at another piece of her heart.

She filled her breakfast plate from the sideboard and sat down to read her smuggled *Mayfair Society Paper*. When Caroline learned she was perusing the gossip columns, she had ordered Molly to ban them from her mistress. Luckily, Livvie was able to persuade one of the scullery maids to buy them for her and leave them in her seat at the breakfast table.

Livvie didn't consider that going against the doctor's wishes. Even though Alex's exploits broke her heart morning after morning, she would be much more anxious *not* knowing what Alex was up to.

She sat down at the table and lifted a bit of baked egg to her mouth, as she opened the rag and scanned it for mention of her husband. Predictably, there it was…

A leopard cannot change his spots. Neither can the wicked Duke of W. reform his roguish ways. Despite His Grace's recent effort to persuade society that he is a changed man, the truth always wins out. A ruse can only be perpetuated so long. If His Grace isn't visiting houses of ill repute, he's ogling pretty actresses, drinking himself into a stupor, or going through his fortune at hazard tables from one end of town to the other. And speaking of lost fortunes, the Earl of G. has reputedly…

Livvie stopped reading the society rag and dropped it to the table. She didn't care what the Earl of G. had done. Only the lines about her husband held her interest. Some papers went as far as to name the bawdy houses he patronized, or the gaming hells he frequented. She didn't need to know the names of the actresses, always assuming it was Sarah Kane who kept him occupied at night.

The idea haunted her and tore at her soul. She'd begun to realize that Alex was never coming home and tried to make peace with that, but found it was impossible to do. No matter how badly he despised her, she couldn't stop loving him any easier than the aforementioned leopard could change his spots.

She lifted a piece of toast to her lips. When the breakfast room doors flew open and Poppy rushed inside, Livvie choked on her toast from surprise. She quickly swallowed some tea and shook her head at her step-daughter. "Poppy Everett, how many times have I told you not to go running into rooms?"

"Sorry, Olivia." Poppy looked at once bashful, staring at her feet. "But Lady Staveley has come with Lady Carteret. They're waiting in the gold parlor."

"Oh?" Livvie frowned. "Well, they should just come in here."

Poppy shook her head. "Lady Staveley says you need your breakfast. But I thought you'd want to know."

Livvie smiled at the child. Whenever she looked into Poppy's pretty, silver eyes, she thought of Alex—just as unrepentant as his daughter. "Thank you, sweetheart. I'll be along shortly."

She forced herself to eat her eggs, some ham and blueberries, wondering the whole while about what would have forced Caroline and Bethany to her doorstep so early in the morning. As soon as she was certain she'd eaten enough to make Doctor Watts happy, Livvie pushed her plate aside and quickly made her way to the gold parlor.

"Darling," Caroline gushed at her entrance, "I am glad that you're looking well. Doctor Watts will be so pleased."

"Thank you, Caro." Livvie took a seat in on her chaise opposite her two guests in large wingback chairs. "Bethany, it's nice to see you."

"You are a dear," the countess replied with a smile. "I don't know that I would be so graceful, in your position."

Livvie sighed. "You mean married to a leopard who can't change his spots?"

Caroline narrowed her eyes. "Where did you get a copy of today's column?"

"If my husband can do whatever he wants, I should certainly be allowed the same latitude."

"Caroline," Bethany added with a frown, "of course she's reads the columns. If it was James I'd do exactly the same thing, and so would you if it were Staveley."

All three women burst into giggles at the thought of mild mannered Staveley being accused of even one of Kelfield's sins. Although it was completely inappropriate, the laughter did help to raise Livvie's spirits, if only momentarily.

"Actually, Livvie," Caroline said, the merriment gone from her voice, "Beth and I put our heads together, and we think we've come up with a solution to your problems."

Thirty

LIVVIE blinked at Caroline and Bethany. They had a solution to her problems? She couldn't even fathom what they meant by that. "You do?" she asked in bewilderment.

"Indeed," Bethany gushed. "You must take Poppy and go Everett Place."

Livvie felt certain she hadn't heard her correctly. Which problem did they think this was a solution to? "I fail to see how removing myself from Town will bring my husband home. Unless you think he won't return here with me in residence. And if that is the case, then that does not solve my problem in the least."

"Darling, just listen," Caroline began softly. "I like to give credit where credit is due, and Beth has come up with a wonderful plan. You see—"

"Well, you know how dictatorial Alex is," Bethany cut in. "I mean you must know, you're married to the man. And you must trust me, it would drive him stark-raving mad if you were to pick up and leave—without his permission—especially if you were to go to Everett Place. I'm not sure why he has such an aversion to his ancestral home, but it works to your advantage that he does."

Before Livvie could find words to respond, Caroline added, "Besides, country air would be most beneficial for you at the moment."

That was what this was really about. Caroline just wanted to get her out of London and away from all the gossip. Livvie shook her head, annoyed that they had fabricated this *plan* to manipulate her into the country. Well, it wasn't going to work. "I'm not going anywhere."

"Now, Livvie, see reason," Caroline said in her sweetest voice, the one that wasn't supposed to seem patronizing even though it was.

"You can save your breath, Caroline. I'm not leaving."

Bethany pouted. "Are you certain? I was convinced it would grab his attention and sober him up."

There was something in Bethany's voice that caught Livvie's attention. "Have you seen him?"

Beth shook her head. "No, but James has. Once. Barely recognized him."

If she only knew where he was staying, she'd go to him herself, somehow convince him to come home. It was one of the things she scoured the society rags looking for, though it was all a complete waste of time. "Do you know where I can find him? Does James know?"

"I wish we did. James said he'd never seen him so foxed, and that is saying something."

Caroline scowled at the countess. "She is supposed to remain calm, Beth. You're not helping."

"Sorry," Bethany replied with a frown, and then she moved on to what she must have thought were safer topics. "Poppy is such a darling girl. You should bring her to Carteret House, so she can play with my Fiona. They're of an age."

"Thank you."

"But do tell her to be wary of my sons. Morgan has entered his pirate stage, and Liam has just started fencing lessons."

"Beth!" Caroline barked.

"Oh. Sorry." The countess blushed. "I don't seem to be able to say anything right today."

"No, you're fine," Livvie said, but she was drowned out by Caroline.

"Actually, Beth, why don't you take the coach and go shopping on your own. I'd like to stay with Olivia for a while. You and I can talk later."

Bethany seemed happy to leave, and Livvie was soon left in only Caroline's care. Her cousin sat forward in her seat, studying her.

"I'm not a side-show event at a carnival, Caro."

"Of course not." Caroline sighed. "You think I'm trying to coerce you into the country."

"I'm not going."

"Yes, you've said that. But, darling, Beth is right. It might be the one thing that wakes him up. I couldn't say this in front of her, but I do know why Alex hates Everett Place."

"Because of his parents." Livvie knew the answer, but didn't believe that his aversion to his childhood home would bring him around. There wasn't a more stubborn man than Alexander Everett.

"Good, he's told you. I didn't want to break his confidence, but I would have done so, for your sake."

"Caroline, what happened there was forever ago. I'm certain the place still haunts him, though his nightmares have diminished some since he told me about his mother's death. But I honestly don't see how my leaving London would do anything other than put even more distance between us."

"Death?" Caroline asked in shock. "When did this happen?"

Livvie was thoroughly confused. Weren't they talking about why Alex avoided Everett Place? "When he was a child."

Caroline took a deep breath, relief evident on her face. "Darling, your mother-in-law is not dead — she was simply banished. She and the duke had a falling out of some sort — I'm not sure what about — and he banished her to The Place. That's all. Unless something has happened in recent years, she's alive and well, and still living at the estate in Hampshire."

Livvie felt faint. Alex had most certainly told her the woman died his first year at Harrow. She knew she hadn't misheard him, she could never forget *that* conversation. He was very clear on the matter. He admitted to blaming himself for her death, for heaven's sake. "Caroline, I think you're confused."

Caroline tilted her head to one side, pursing her lips. "Alex told me that he'd been lead to believe his mother had died. He'd gotten a letter from his father's solicitor while he was at school saying the duchess had passed away. He was never allowed home after that, and when he came into his title, he returned to Hampshire only to discover his mother, very much alive."

Livvie felt the wind rush out of her. All those years Alex blamed himself for her death and was tortured by nightmares. She'd been alive the whole time! It didn't make any sense. And why hadn't he told her?

"As a mother," Caroline continued, "I cannot even imagine allowing my children to mourn me, to allow them to think I was dead. I don't believe he's ever gotten over her rejection, and who could blame him?"

Livvie didn't realize she was crying until a tear dropped onto her lap and she brushed the wetness from her cheeks. She couldn't imagine it either. Her poor, dear Alex. The last person she ever wanted to meet was his malicious mother. "I must tell you, Caro, that after that little story, you couldn't possible drag me to Everett Place to be near that woman."

Caroline examined her fingernails for the longest time, obviously contemplating something. Then she looked up at Livvie. "You are the Duchess of Kelfield, and you are the mistress of Everett Place. You have every right to be there, but the idea will eat at Alex. No matter how foxed he is or how hurt or angry, he won't want you or Poppy to be there. You'll have his attention, Olivia."

His attention. She had wondered countless times over the last fortnight if he ever thought of her. What would she say if she had those silver eyes focused on her again? How could she make him realize how much she loved him? How hurt she was by his defection? How could she make it right? "Caroline, I don't even know where to find him, to even let him know I'm leaving."

"Well—" Caroline shrugged— "I'm certain Staveley and James could scour the Town looking for him. One of them will eventually find him. And when they do, they'll inform him that you and Poppy have departed for Hampshire. I'm certain he'll come after you."

Or *she* could find him. After all, she knew the names of the bawdy houses he frequented. The gaming hells. Sarah Kane. Coleman was certain to know their locations. Though she knew Caroline would never approve, so she kept that idea to herself.

⚜

"You're a bloody bore. You do know that?" Marc asked as they stepped inside one of the gaming parlors at Mrs. Lassiter's.

The hell was dark and smoky, crammed to the gills with gamblers of both the highest rank and the lowest caliber. Over the last fortnight it had become as familiar to Alex as his own home, back when he lived in it. He preferred not to think about it.

Alex snatched a whiskey off the tray of a passing footman and downed it in one gulp. "No one asked you to play my nursemaid. In fact, I wish you wouldn't."

"You'd feel like a new man if you'd just tup *one* of these women who throw themselves at you." Then he grumbled under his breath, "God, *I'd* feel like a new man if you'd just tup one of them."

"Go to hell." He couldn't tup another woman even if he wanted to. Olivia was forever on his mind, and only dousing his brain in whiskey or brandy brought him the temporary peace he sought.

Alex stumbled slightly when he noticed an open spot at one of the card tables. Thank God. He wouldn't have to spend another night listening to Marc's unwanted, amoral advice. Without a second thought, he ambled towards the open seat and fell into it.

He blinked at the young man across from him. Lord Haywood? Alex widened his eyes, focusing on the fellow. It was Haywood. Sarah's new paramour. "What are we playing?" he asked, with only the slightest slur.

"*Vingt-et-un*," William Haywood answered. "You don't look like yourself, Kelfield."

"Bugger off, Haywood." Then Alex turned to the dealer and gestured himself into the game with the wave of his hand.

As the first card was placed face down in front of him, woman's hand slide along Alex's shoulders. He barely lifted the edge of his card. The Ace of diamonds. He'd always been lucky at the tables. It was a shame that luck didn't extend into the other aspects of his life.

"Five hundred quid," he informed the dealer and waited on his next card.

The woman stepped to his side, a blonde he'd never seen before, and she smiled. Alex wished that he cared. He raised his brow. "Yes, love?"

She bent down giving him an excellent view of her décolletage and whispered in his ear. "You are a handsome man, Your Grace."

"I know," he said, looking over Haywood's head to find Marc on the other side of the room, nodding his approval. Alex then glanced down at his freshly dealt card. The ten of clubs. He turned over his ace, showing his winning hand and said over his shoulder. "You should go back to the marquess, love. I'm not looking for company."

Alex gestured to a nearby footman for another drink and focused his attention back on the table, wishing Haversham to the devil. He didn't want some lightskirt to keep him company. He wanted the impossible. His wife. The life he had weeks ago. He amended his thought. He wanted the life he *thought* he had weeks ago.

Thirty-One

NEVER in all the years of his employment as the Kelfield coachman had Timothy Coleman ever been invited to tea with his employer. However, he now sat, uncomfortably, in a white brocade chair across from the Duchess of Kelfield, his mouth agape. Certainly she had not asked him *that*.

"I beg your pardon, Your Grace?"

The duchess sat forward on her settee and repeated her request. "You know all the places my husband has sought entertainment in the past, Coleman. I need you to take me on a tour of them."

Coleman swallowed hard. He wouldn't take a scullery maid to most of the places Kelfield had enjoyed in the past. He certainly couldn't take the duchess. She'd obviously lost her mind along with her husband's desertion. "I cannot."

"You can and will," she said, sounding more and more like the duke than herself. "Kelfield is gone, and I am your mistress. So, you'll do as I say, or you can seek employment elsewhere."

He swallowed again. "Your Grace, those places aren't suitable for you."

"But they're suitable for my husband?" she asked tartly. Then she rubbed her brow, and Coleman could see all the built-up tension on her lovely face. His heart went out to her. She really was a very lovely person when she wasn't threatening his livelihood. Then the duchess took a deep breath and pierced him with her hazel gaze. "Coleman, I'm moving the household to Hampshire. I don't know where to send a letter to His Grace informing him of this. And while I'm certain he'd learn of it from someone else, I have to be the one to tell him. I can't leave it up to others. So, I need you to take me to all the places he sought entertainment before we married."

He stared at her for the longest time, surprised he was even contemplating the suggestion. But he'd seen Her Grace over the last few weeks. She was suffering and he hated to see it. Still, he couldn't take her to bawdy houses and places of that nature. Firstly, it was completely improper for a woman of her standing. Secondly, such places were dangerous and he'd just as soon be sent to the gallows than allow the duchess to be hurt. And lastly, it was obvious to everyone that Her Grace was deeply in love with her husband. If they found him, she'd be more devastated that she was now.

"I can hire some men in your stead, Coleman," she said, breaking his concentration. "Off-duty runners, returned soldiers, or someone else, and I'll go with them on my own. But I'd rather not, as I trust you."

She would do it on her own, too, if the determined set of her jaw was any indication. Coleman's stomach twisted in a knot. "Your Grace, this is highly improper and I don't want to see you hurt. Why don't I go on my own and seek him out? I'll bring him to you."

She smiled for the first time during the interview. "Thank you for your concern. But I don't believe it will be that easy, Coleman, or he would have come home on his own. It needs to be me."

Coleman raked a hand through his graying hair, not ready to give in. But maybe he had a solution. "If I took you on this tour, the places we'd be going to can be dangerous. I could go inside the establishments. Then when I find him, I'll come back to the coach and escort you in. It has to be that, Your Grace. I can't let you go to these places and let you see inside if he's not there."

look of relief crossed the duchess' face and she took a deep breath. "Thank you. I think that might work."

Livvie had been overwhelmed with the amount of work she had to do. The entire household of cook, maids, footmen, Gibson, Mrs. Bickle, and of course Poppy and herself were packed and ready for their journey to Hampshire. She didn't know how long it would take for her and Coleman to find Alex, but when she did, she would have to act quickly. She didn't want him returning to Kelfield House and finding her there. It would be too easy for him to leave her again. She needed him alone in the country, where she would have all the time in the world to talk some sense into him. So Poppy and the staff would wait at the Golden Arms, a fashionable inn west of London, for her and Coleman to return before they continued to their ultimate destination.

She didn't want them going on without her as she had no idea what awaited them in Hampshire. It was still difficult to fathom that her mother-in-law was alive and in residence at Everett Place. The woman had turned her back on Alex as a child. Livvie wouldn't let Poppy face her alone. It was better for them all to arrive at the same time.

Besides, Caroline and the others had no idea that she intended to locate her husband by herself. None of them would approve. It was imperative they all believe she'd left Town, giving her the freedom to search in peace.

Outside Kelfield House, four traveling coaches were filled with bags and staff. Livvie and Poppy said their final goodbyes to Caroline, Staveley, their children, and the Carterets. It was a bittersweet moment.

Caroline embraced Livvie for what must have been the hundredth time. "Don't worry, darling, everything will work out."

It was the same thing everyone had said to her for months. When she learned she would marry Alex. When she was ruined in the eyes of the *ton*. When her husband left her, never to return. When he fought in that awful duel. When she learned she was pregnant. Livvie wasn't sure if everything would work out or not, but she was tired of waiting for it to happen on its own. Either way, she was taking her destiny in her own hands. She prayed for strength.

Livvie kissed Caroline's cheek. "Thank you. For everything. Once we're settled, I'll write. Say you'll visit."

"Just try keeping me away."

Then Coleman opened the coach door and Poppy piled inside next to Mrs. Bickle. Livvie hugged Staveley and smiled at the Carterets before joining her step-daughter in the conveyance. The door shut behind her, and Livvie took a deep breath. She'd never used subterfuge in her life.

Poppy smiled across the coach at her, and then scrambled to Livvie's lap. "Tell me again, Olivia. What is it like in Hampshire?"

Livvie snuggled Poppy close to her and smiled. "I haven't been to Everett Place, Poppy, but I've been through Hampshire when I've visited my cousin in Dorset. There are pretty country roads with lovely trees and wild grass. The people are very nice."

"Do you think any unicorns are there?"

Livvie kissed Poppy's brow. "I've never seen one. You'll have to keep your eyes open."

Which was, apparently, easier said than done. Just a few miles outside of London, Poppy was fast asleep in Livvie's arms. When the coach rambled to a stop in front of The Golden Arms, Livvie handed her step-daughter to Coleman who gently carried the girl inside the taproom and up the stairs to the guest rooms. Livvie followed them inside and overheard Gibson and the innkeeper.

"You don't know how long you're staying?" the man asked with a frown.

Gibson shook his head. "It could be a day or sennight, perhaps longer."

"Other guests will need a place to stay, sir."

"We've pre-paid the entire establishment for a month, Mr. Browne. The rooms are ours whether we're here or not. And you'll not sell them out from under us. The Duke of Kelfield will not stand for it."

The innkeeper blanched at the name.

Livvie smiled. Having the Kelfield name did occasionally have its uses. It was good to see that Gibson had the situation under control. It gave Livvie peace of mind to leave everyone here during her search. The young butler had come a long way in the last few months, and she had all the confidence in the world that the man would take care of their haphazard group while she was away.

Livvie walked through the taproom and up the stairs, finding Poppy still sleeping in one of the rooms, clutching one of her beloved dolls in her arms.

Mrs. Bickle stood watch over her. "Don't worry about the little dear, Your Grace, I'll keep good watch over her."

"I know you will," Livvie replied, smiling at her step-daughter's sleeping form, hoping to make everything all right for her. She blew a kiss to the sleeping child and descended the steps again, to find Coleman waiting for her.

"You are sure about this, Your Grace?" the coachman asked.

Livvie nodded and they were soon back on their way to London in a rented coach. After all, it wouldn't do to go through Town with the Kelfield crest emblazoned on the side.

⋆⟅⟆⋆

Night after night, their routine was the same. Coleman and Livvie would roam through the streets inside a hired hack. Coleman would enter an establishment that from the outside looked perfectly decent, but Livvie could tell from the other men she spied from the coach's darkened windows were far from respectable. Each night, Coleman would return with a shake of his head.

"It's the same thing, Your Grace. No one has seen him in months."

They couldn't keep going on like this. In addition to the anxiety it wrought inside her, they weren't getting anywhere. She was beyond desperate. "Coleman, tell the driver to take us to Drury Lane."

He nodded his head and gave the new orders to the hired driver, and then settled back against the squabs. "Are you sure about this, Your Grace?"

"Do you have any better ideas?" Not that she was happy at all about the prospect of coming face-to-face with Alex's mistress. With any luck he was at the performance and this could all be over with. But if they were together...Livvie couldn't think about it. Seeing him in his lover's arms would be sure to destroy whatever was left of her heart.

Once at the theatre, Coleman left Livvie in the coach, like always. In the dark, her nerves were on end and she wasn't certain if it was the babe she carried or the idea of Alex enjoying a tryst with Miss Kane that had her stomach tied up in knots.

It seemed as if Coleman was inside the theatre a lifetime. He was definitely there longer than he had been at any of the bawdy houses or gaming hells. Did that mean Alex was there? Was he berating the coachman for taking on this fool's errand? Livvie's hands fidgeted and she peeked out the window, hoping for some sign of Coleman.

Then he appeared from around the side of the theatre. His gait was purposeful, though his face was pinched. Livvie steeled herself for the worst as Coleman opened the door. "Miss Kane would like to speak with you."

Thirty-Two

LIVVIE was certain her heart stopped. "Is he here?"

Coleman shook his head. "No, Your Grace. I've searched the place over, but I haven't seen him."

"Then why does she want to speak with *me*?"

"I couldn't say. You don't have to see her, of course."

Livvie took a deep breath. Alex wasn't here. She wasn't certain if she was relieved or not about that. Sarah Kane wanted to speak with her? She stared at Coleman for the longest time. "What is she like?"

"I've always thought she was very kind."

Very kind. Not the words she was expecting to hear in description about the actress, though Alex had said as much. Livvie accepted Coleman's hand and allowed him to help her from the carriage. Perhaps the woman had seen Alex.

She followed the beleaguered coachman down the side alley to a back entrance where he rapped twice. A burly man opened the door, looking down his nose at Livvie and her servant. Coleman tipped his hat to the man. "Miss Kane is expecting us."

The burly man frowned, though he held the door wide for them to enter. When it shut behind them, Livvie shuddered. The corridor was dark and foreboding. Luckily Coleman knew the way, and he led Livvie through the place. Costumes littered the hallway and people rushed past them in every direction. Finally, they came to an open door and Coleman knocked.

From inside, Livvie heard movement. Then Sarah Kane stood before her, dressed as a medieval Scottish lady. Heavy cosmetics adorned her face, and she looked like a strange caricature. The actress smiled. "Your Grace."

"Miss Kane."

The actress gestured for Livvie to enter her dressing room and then shut the door behind her, leaving Coleman in the busy corridor. Livvie wasn't certain what to make of the woman, who threw off discarded gowns from a dingy settee.

"It's not much, but please sit."

Livvie did so, wincing when a spring poked her in the back.

Miss Kane sat in a seat and her eyes leveled on Livvie. "You have more fortitude than I'd given you credit for. I didn't think you'd actually come."

"Miss Kane, I am certain that you are busy. I only wanted to ask if you'd seen my husband." They were some of the hardest words she'd ever spoken.

With a warm smile, Miss Kane shook her head. "The last time I spoke to Kelfield was before your wedding."

Livvie was relieved, but her heart still sank. She was wasting her time here.

"But I do know where he is, or at least where he spends most nights."

"Where?" The words were wrenched out of her.

"Do you love him, Your Grace?"

Not that it was any of her concern, but Livvie was tired and emotionally drained. "More than life, though he doesn't believe me."

Miss Kane nodded her head. "I thought so, when I saw the two of you at the performance. He loves you as well."

Tears spilled down Livvie's cheeks. She was surprised when she heard herself say, "He's never said those words."

Miss Kane smiled sadly. "I'm sure he hasn't. That's not like him. But I could tell it the last time we spoke. And I could see it in his eyes as he watched you that night in the box and not the stage."

Livvie swiped at her tears, trying to be stronger than she knew how to be.

"He's in bad shape, Your Grace. Are you certain you want to find him?"

Livvie's head bobbed up and down, imploring the actress to tell her what she knew. "I've never wanted anything more."

"Will...er, Lord Haywood is a *friend* of mine, and he has seen Alex many times."

"Where?"

"Mrs. Lassiter's. She runs a gaming hell, and whenever Haywood has attended in the last few weeks, Alex has been there. Apparently deep in his cups and half out of his mind."

"But we've been there. They told Coleman he wasn't there."

Miss Kane snorted softly. "These aren't your sort of people. They don't tell the truth, Your Grace, and you shouldn't expect it."

"Mrs. Lassiter's," Livvie repeated, rising from her seat, her heart lighter than it had been in weeks. "I can never thank you enough, Miss Kane."

"Take care of him. Love him. I only want his happiness."

Livvie threw her arms around the actress' neck. "So do I. I will forever be in your debt."

Alex was right. Coleman was right. Sarah Kane was very kind. Livvie opened the door and grinned through her tears at the coachman. "Mrs. Lassiter's."

⁓✦⁓

Livvie stepped inside Mrs. Lassiter's entryway. Smoke billowed from the nearby drawing rooms, raucous laughter and high pitch twittering filtered into the hallway. She looked around with an elitist frown. This was certainly not a place she would have ever envisioned herself a month ago.

A butler stepped forward and looked her up and down. "Yes, my lady?"

"I'm looking for Kelfield."

The butler shook his head. "Sorry, ma'am. His Grace is not here this evening."

How many other times had this man lied to her and Coleman over the last few weeks? "I know that my husband is in here, and I'm not leaving until I find him."

The butler grimaced and stepped closer to her. "You're the *Duchess* of Kelfield?"

At her nod, he continued, "Your Grace, to gain entrance you must have been invited. I'm afraid I cannot let you in."

Livvie took a deep breath. "My good man, I have not come to make a scene, but I will make one if you turn me away. I just need a quick word with my husband."

"A quick word?"

"On my honor. I will leave after I've spoken with him."

The butler frowned. "Very well, Your Grace. I will ask the duke to see you."

Livvie waited for what seemed an eternity. Men she had seen in fashionable drawing rooms roamed past, some drinking, some smoking, most taking in her form with appreciative leers.

Finally the butler returned, and shook his head. "I am terribly sorry, Your Grace, but Kelfield will not leave his table."

"Then I shall go to him." Livvie didn't wait for the butler to stop her. She followed the path down the hallway she had seen him take before. As soon as she entered a small drawing room, she could sense him.

Alex sat at a far table, his back towards her. Livvie's heart flipped in her chest. Heavens, she missed him. Then she wanted to kill him when she realized that a giggling blonde tart was draped across his lap. This was how he spent his time away from her while she cried her eyes out over him every night!

Before she could stop herself, Livvie stalked up to the table and tapped the tart's arm. "I believe you're sitting on my husband."

The blonde's big, blue eyes widened in surprise, but Alex didn't even glance up from his cards. "Olivia, I told Peters I was busy at the moment."

"Unbusy yourself," she snapped back.

He dropped his hand to the table and flashed his silver eyes up at her. Livvie sucked in a breath. He was still so devastatingly handsome and she loved him with all her heart. Still this had to be done. It was for the best. And she didn't know how else to get through to him, so she kept her eyes leveled on his and held her ground.

Alex pushed the blonde from his lap. "Janie love, go on." Then he inclined his head to the other men at the table—two beady-eyed fellows and Lord Haywood. "Excuse me, gentlemen."

He clapped an unsteady hand around her arm and began to tow her towards the hallway, and Livvie feared he was simply going to throw her out without talking to her at all.

"Alex, stop! I need to speak with you."

"Yes, you've made that abundantly clear," he replied as his whiskey-scented breath assaulted her nose.

He pulled open a small parlor that was being utilized by a randy fellow and another blond. Livvie decided right then and there that she actively disliked blonds. "Who is Janie?" she demanded after Alex cleared the room.

"I have no idea. I only met the woman this evening. What do you want, Olivia?"

She folded her arms across her chest and tried not to cry. She tried not to envision Janie sprawled across Alex's lap, her hands twirling through his inky locks. "Do you have any idea how hard it is to find you?"

"Obviously I didn't want to be found. But since you've done so, what do you want?"

"I have had to search you out in bawdy houses—"

"I don't visit those anymore," he mumbled under his breath.

"Then I enjoyed a charming tour of gaming hells across London, and when I'd run out of hope I finally I went to Drury Lane to speak with Miss Kane, and—"

"Oh, God," he groaned, pinching the bridge above his nose.

"That awful butler here lied to me."

"Well, h-here I am," he slurred, raising his hands as if presenting himself as a gift.

Yes, there he was. Still the most handsome man she'd ever seen. Still the only man who could make her heart race with just his smile. But she had to do this. She couldn't keep wondering where he was at night. Hearing the gossip the next day. Hoping he'd come home.

Livvie squared her shoulders and took a deep breath. "I'm leaving you, Alex. I thought I should tell you in person, since I have no idea where to post you a letter."

"You can't leave me," he responded with a mocking laugh. "I've already left *you*, Olivia—hence the reason you've had a difficult time locating me." He slurred the last of his words, and her heart ached to see him like this.

She thrust a letter, explaining everything, against his chest. "You can read that if and when you ever sober up. I don't know when Poppy and I will return, but thought you were owed an explanation for our disappearance."

Even through the fog of his drunkenness, Alex's grey eyes narrowed to dangerous black slits. "You and Moore are not taking *my* daughter anywhere."

"Oh, for heaven's sake. Philip has nothing to do with this. I'm certainly not leaving Poppy with you. I love and care for her too much to allow her to see you like this."

"Where are you going?" he demanded.

"I'm not hiding from you, Alex. Just leaving you. Poppy and I are going to Everett Place. I have yet to see the house, but feel it will be a much more conducive environment for us than London is at the moment."

"Everett Place?" he echoed with a note of panic in his voice. "Absolutely not! Why would you consider such a thing?"

She hoped that he'd remember this conversation in the morning. Her plan relied on him remembering. "Because women in my condition are generally confined to the country. I figure one of us should follow society's dictates."

He blinked at her. "Your condition?"

Livvie rubbed her brow. She prayed this would work, because if it didn't, it was certain to kill her. "Don't follow me there, Alex. I'll forever wonder if you returned to me because you loved me or because of the babe. I don't want to live like that—never knowing for sure. I'm certain you, of all people, can understand that."

⚜

If Mrs. Lassiter's hell had come crashing down around him, he could not have been more stunned. *The babe?* Olivia was going to have his child? The air whooshed out of Alex and he had to struggle to remain standing.

"I'll send word through Staveley when... Well, after the blessed event." Then she reached up to touch his cheek, nearly scalding him with her fingertips. "I do so love you, Alex. I wish things had been different. Please take care of yourself. You look a mess."

And then she was gone. As if she'd never been there in the first place. Only the letter clutched in his hand and the lingering scent of lilacs were proof otherwise.

He blinked his eyes, trying to focus on the letter and broke the seal.

My dearest Alex,

I am not sure how things have turned out so badly for us, but I suppose we were doomed from the start. Our inauspicious beginnings aside, I have loved you with all my heart and soul, more than I have ever loved anyone, but I cannot continue like this. The anxiety of our separate lives is not healthy for me. Doctor Watts has been very clear on that matter. I cannot spend any more of my nights wondering where you are, if you are safe, and if you will ever return to me.

Though I know you will not believe me, I will love you the rest of my days, Alex. I only wish that it was enough to make things right between us. However, my wanting it alone is not enough. Since you have given up on me, it is rather clear that this battle is lost. I wish it had ended differently.

I hope Poppy and I will find peace at Everett Place, and I hope you find your own peace – whatever it might be. My thoughts and prayers are with you.

Your devoted wife,
Olivia

Devoted? An interesting word from a woman who was leaving him. No, he'd left her first. There was no mention of Philip Moore in the letter. No mention of his duel. No mention of their child.

Alex had never felt so empty in all his life.

Dear God, Everett Place! He couldn't let her go there.

Thirty-Three

ALEX nearly stumbled on his way to the front door. He dashed down the steps and stared blankly at the busy street. Carriages and hacks were everywhere. He squinted at all the conveyances, but couldn't spot the one that belonged to him. Where the devil was she?

It took longer than he expected to hail a hack. He barked, "Kelfield House," to the driver and sat back on the seat with a thump. A whirl of thoughts darted in and out of his inebriated mind. Olivia. Everett Place. Poppy. A babe. His mother. Dear God.

He closed his eyes as the hack traveled into Mayfair. He had to stop her before she went to Hampshire. She didn't know about his mother, and he'd really rather keep it that way. The old woman was spiteful and angry. Who knew what her reaction would be to Olivia and Poppy?

He should have said something when she'd told him her plans, before she escaped Mrs. Lassiter's—but his mind was in such a fog, especially after the mention of their child. Though, none of that was an excuse. He should have forbidden her to go.

The hack came to an abrupt halt. He paid the driver and started up the walkway to Kelfield House. Something was not right. The entire house was dark, as if it was in mourning of some sort.

He climbed the steps, waiting for Gibson to open the door, but it remained immobile. Alex turned the knob, but it was locked. He pounded on the door, but there was no answer. What the devil was wrong with Gibson? Is this how he took care of things while Alex was away? He would have quite the earful when Alex got a hold of him. The butler would be lucky to maintain his bloody post.

Alex stomped around to the back of the house. Everything was eerily quiet. He reached the servant's entrance, but it was locked as well. He pounded on the door, bellowing for someone to let him in. It was all pointless. The place was closed up tight. They were all gone.

Panic raced through him. How could she possibly be gone already? He rushed to the front of the house and down Park Lane to Upper Grosvenor. He was out of breath when he reached Haversham's home, but he wasn't about to stop. The butler, Simmons, opened the door, gaping at him as if he had three heads.

"Simmons," he panted, "have the marquess' coach readied for me."

"Your Grace?"

"Now!" he barked.

The butler took off at a sprint.

While Alex waited for the coachman and groom to prepare Haversham's conveyance, he jotted a note to his friend, apologizing for the theft and promising to make it up to him at a later date. When the driver was ready, Alex handed the letter to Simmons and boarded the traveling coach.

"Driver—" he began.

"Anderson," the driver informed him, as if he cared at the moment.

"Anderson," Alex growled, "if you get me to Hampshire with no stops I'll pay you a year's salary."

The driver's eyes lit up. "Of course, Your Grace."

Olivia probably had an hour's lead on him. With any luck, he could catch them. "Be on the lookout for my coach. If you can reach my wife before we reach Brockenhurst I'll double your salary."

They were off within moments.

Alex still couldn't understand how she had moved so quickly. One minute informing him of their child and the next she was gone without a trace.

The glow of a small lamp lit inside the coach, and Alex slipped

Olivia's letter out of his pocket and read it again.

She loved him? He'd spent the last month trying to get over her, with no success.

She wished him peace, but he could never have peace without her. The memory of her laugh and shining hazel eyes lifted his heart a bit. Why had he let her walk out of Mrs. Lassiter's?

Her letter was filled with pain. The same pain he'd endured himself this last month, and he cursed himself for not having realized it sooner, for not having sought her out.

Olivia fled him in the dead of night, *enceinte*...

He was suddenly enraged. She left in the dead of night? When Alex caught up to them, he'd sack Coleman on the spot. There was no reason to go fleeing off into the countryside in the middle of the night. It was too dangerous. The coachman definitely knew better. They could have an accident or be set upon by highwaymen, or any number of other terrible things. If one hair on Olivia's head was harmed, he wouldn't sack Coleman — he'd kill the man.

Thankfully Anderson took him at his word about the year's salary and raced through the night.

~~~

It was late when Livvie and Coleman arrived at The Golden Arms. It was such a relief to have found Alex, to have given him the letter. Now she only hoped that he would come for them. Livvie thanked the coachman again for aiding her over the last few weeks, then she climbed the stairs to Poppy's room.

Livvie unlocked the door and quietly slid inside. Moonlight illuminated the little girl's pretty face, and Livvie was so relieved to see her again. It felt like forever since the cheery child had talked to her about unicorns and handsome princes. Tomorrow they'd start for Hampshire, and Livvie prayed she'd done the right thing.

Tired and achy, she slipped out off her dress, threw on her nightrail, and climbed into bed next to her step-daughter. If all went as planned, Alex would meet them at Everett Place in a few days, maybe even tomorrow. Between now and then, she had to find a way to convince him to stay. She had to find a way to prove her love.

As daunting as that seemed, it was the first time in weeks that hope filled her heart.

Anderson drove straight through and only stopped once to acquire fresh horses. The sun was just starting to rise when Everett Place became visible on the horizon. With a throbbing headache from the previous evening's over indulgences, Alex stared out the carriage window at the baroque mansion in the distance. He hadn't been there since he was seventeen, right after his father had died of the pox—which was not surprising to anyone who knew the man.

Alex had wanted to put the estates to rights, so he'd ridden from London to Brockenhurst on his own. He never could have imagined what—or rather who—would greet him upon his arrival. His *dead* mother stood in the drive as he approached, angry and bitter. At first he'd thought that he must be dead himself, because people simply didn't return from the grave, and his mother was very clearly in front of him.

The shock had worn off quickly as she'd skewered him with her acidic words and biting tongue. He'd vowed never to return.

With every mile he traveled in Haversham's pilfered coach, Alex became more and more concerned about Olivia. He'd felt certain they should have caught up to her by now. But they hadn't seen a Kelfield coach anywhere along the way. How fast had Coleman driven his wife in the dead of night? Was the man unaware of her delicate condition? Traveling at those sorts of speeds was reckless. He'd have the coachman's head on a platter.

Alex closed his eyes, rubbing his temples, wishing he hadn't imbibed so heavily the night before. It would be so much easier to think clearly now.

He winced at the idea of Olivia arriving at Everett Place only to be greeted by his vindictive mother. She would be stunned that he hadn't told her, led her to believe the woman was dead. It would be one more thing to widen the chasm that existed between them.

He hated that chasm. Hated the time he'd spent apart from her. Hated that he'd hurt her so deeply. Everett Place grew larger in his window as they neared it. God, he hated it here. The awful memories still haunted him.

When Anderson stopped the carriage on the front drive, Alex threw open the door and raced up the steps. Before he could knock, an ancient butler with tufts of white hair pulled the door open. *Martin*. It had been nearly two decades since he'd laid eyes on the man, but he'd know the old fellow anywhere.

"Where is my wife?"

"Y-your Grace? We weren't expecting you." The old butler blinked at him in astonishment.

"My wife. Where is she?" Then he bellowed through the house. "Olivia!"

Martin shook his head. "Sir, no one is here, save your mother."

Alex stared at the old man. "What do you mean, no one is here? She left before me."

"What is all the commotion?" came a cranky voice from the top of the stairs.

Alex cringed at the sound. He could have gone the rest of his life without facing *her*. "Morning, mother." It was early. Shouldn't the old witch be in bed?

A gasp sounded from the level above, and then a series of slow movements down the stairs.

Moments later, Iris Everett, the dowager Duchess of Kelfield, came into view. She was older than he remembered, but of course it had been seventeen years since he'd last seen her and twenty-four since he'd last resided here. Her once ebony hair was now completely grey, knotted at her neck. Her brilliant blue eyes had softened to the color of a wintry sky. But her lips, pursed in anger, were just as he remembered.

"Alex?" she asked with a frown. "What you are doing here?"

Alex ignored the question and turned back to Martin. "They have not arrived?"

The butler shook his head. "I can't even recall the last time we had guests here, Your Grace."

Where could they be? They hadn't passed them on the road. Anderson had kept a vigilant lookout the entire night. Why would she tell him she was going to Everett Place if she intended to go somewhere else? And where else would she have gone?

For a moment he considered that she'd run off with Philip Moore, but it was only a fleeting thought. In the first place, taking Poppy along was not exactly conducive for romance if Olivia wanted to run away with Moore. If she wanted to be with the major, she could have abandoned his daughter and Kelfield House. There was no need to close it up tight.

Could she have taken a different road? He shook his head at the thought. There wasn't a better way to get from London to Brockenhurst. Coleman would have to know that.

"Who are you looking for?" his mother barked, increasing the vicious pounding of his brain.

Alex pinned her with his gaze. "Certainly not you, madam."

Then he stalked back outside to Haversham's coach. "Anderson, they're not here. She's not here. Have you any idea how we could have passed them?"

The coachman frowned and squinted his eyes, as if concentrating very hard. "I suppose they could have stopped for the night somewhere, Your Grace. We didn't stop at any of the coaching inns since Basingstoke when we got fresh horses."

Alex cursed himself for being a goddamn fool. Of course they'd stopped somewhere. Olivia wouldn't put herself or Poppy in danger riding through the night like *he* had done. There was nothing to do now but wait for her.

He heard his mother's foot fall behind him, and he pinched the bridge of his nose, willing his headache away. If he'd searched the inn yards and found his wife, he could have avoided coming *here* altogether.

"I've heard word you married. Is it your wife you're looking for? Or a troop of naked acrobats?"

Good God, the naked acrobats? That was more than a dozen years ago. Alex glanced over his shoulder at his mother. "I had no idea you were so interested in my exploits, mother. You never showed any evidence of it before now."

She sneered at him. "You are indeed Arthur's son."

"I don't think there's any question about that." After all Arthur Everett was the only *man* she'd ever taken to her bed.

The coachman covered a yawn with his thick gloves. "Do ya want to go the other way, Your Grace? Meet them on the road somewhere?"

Alex would like nothing more, but he shook his head. Anderson looked close to dead, and he didn't want to end up in a ditch along the way. "We'll wait here. Martin will see to it that you have a nice bed and something to eat."

As the butler directed the coachman toward the stables, Alex brushed past his mother, returning to the house. She was quick on his heels. "You can't stay here. This is *my* house."

"The house is mine, mother. You only live here thanks to my generosity. Don't make me reconsider it." He entered the house and threw open the doors to the study. Perhaps he could pass the time away by sorting through his father's things. That's what he'd originally come to do seventeen years ago, after the bastard's death, before he'd been blindsided by his mother's resurrection.

He felt his mother's presence in the doorway, but he didn't look up.

"What are you doing here?" she asked.

Alex blew away what looked like years of dust on the desk, revealing a ledger. How long had it been since someone had cleaned the room. "Your presence is not required, mother. Go do whatever it is you do and leave me in peace."

"Will you never stop hating me?" she asked softly.

For the briefest of seconds, Alex thought he noted a hint of sadness in her voice, but he shook off the thought. "My wife and daughter will arrive sometime today. If you'd like to stay living here, you'll treat them both with more respect than you've shown me."

She gasped slightly at his words. "You have a daughter? I thought you'd just recently married. That's what the papers said."

"One does not need to be married to father children, mother."

"I have a granddaughter," she barely whispered to herself.

Finally, he glanced up at her, only to see her lips trembling. "She is nothing to you, as you are no mother to me. I'll thank you to remember that."

"You and your father have made sure I could never forget it."

Alex shook his head and began thumbing through the old ledger. It was just an old account book. Nothing interesting in the least. "I am busy, mother."

She didn't say a word, but he knew when she walked away. Alex pulled open the top drawer and found a rusty letter opener and several fragile, old quills. Honestly, when was the last time anyone tidied up in this room?

The next drawer was filled with old ledgers, similar to the one he'd gone through before and equally uninteresting. However the bottom drawer seemed more promising as it was locked. What could Arthur Everett have kept hidden?

Alex retrieved the letter opener from the top drawer and stuck the rusty, old thing in the lock. Of course it didn't work, that would be too easy. He shook the drawer which rattled the desk, but it didn't open. However, it did dislodge a key that had been hidden along the edge of the desk.

It dropped to the floor with a soft thud

Alex shrugged. It was worth a try. He put the key in the lock. Though it was stiff, it did fit. Then turned it to the right and the drawer popped open. "What were you hiding, father?"

Thirty-Four

ALEX looked into the old drawer and was thrown back a bit. It was filled with letters. Hundreds of them. All addressed to him. None of them had ever been opened. He reached through the pile, picked one randomly, and broke the seal.

October 6, 1795
Dear Alexander,

I understand from your father that your school marks are quite good. I am not surprised as you were always such a bright boy. He did note, however, that your theological marks could be higher. Again, I am not surprised as neither Arthur nor I have been sterling examples for you. I do hope you will find your way despite your parentage.

Last week, Mrs. Dinks' sheepdog had puppies and your father allowed me to have one. Zeus is a happy little fellow, full of energy, and whenever he scampers about the place, he nearly falls over himself. I am certain he will grow into his name. If you come home for Christmas, I am sure you will adore him.

I keep hoping that you will come home on your next holiday from school, but understand from your father that you prefer to spend your time with your friends. Please consider coming home, if only for a few days, my dear son, as it has been forever since I've seen you and I do miss you terribly. I hope that eventually you can come to forgive me for my sins.

Love Always,
Mother

Alex stared blankly at the pages, in complete bewilderment. He picked up another letter and then another. All of them from over several years, all of them professing her love, all of them begging him to forgive her.

Clutching a number of letters in his fist, Alex staggered backwards. What was this about? What sort of trick was this? He steadied himself and stomped from the room, finding Martin in the hallway. "Where is my mother?" he growled.

The butler looked a little pale and he cleared his throat. "In the orangery, Your Grace."

Alex stormed off down the hallway, around a corner, and down some steps until he reached the orangery. He threw open the door, causing his mother to scream and drop her watering pot. He paid no notice to her state of shock and stalked towards her. "What is the meaning of this?" he roared, thrusting the letters at her.

His mother frowned, shaking her head. "I don't understand you, Alex. You show up out of nowhere. You rant and rave. You threaten to dismiss me. Now you've tracked me down to bark at me. What do you want?"

"Pray explain these mendacities, madam."

She scooped one of the letters off the floor and opened it. "It's a letter I wrote to you." Then she looked at him with a quizzical expression. "Have you kept them with you this whole time? I never thought they meant anything to you."

"You never sent these to me," he replied icily.

With an affronted look, she tipped her head haughtily in the air. "I most certainly did. Every week after Arthur sent you away. I only stopped when I got your letter telling me that you didn't need your whore of a mother and to stop pestering you."

Alex's mouth fell open. "Mother, I never received one letter from you, nor did I send one. I thought you were dead."

She stumbled backwards and would have fallen over completely, except that he steadied her. "Why would you think that?"

"Because father's solicitor sent me a letter saying so."

Tears spilled down her cheeks and she turned away from him. "No wonder you hate me so much. You thought I'd abandoned you."

"You weren't exactly welcoming when I arrived last time."

"I was hurt from the things you'd said to me, or thought you'd said to me. It was childish of me." She spun to face him. "Oh, Alex, I am so sorry. My dear son, all this time lost…"

All the time he'd spent away from her, thinking she blamed him, thinking she hated him. He stepped backwards. "Mother, I need some time."

⚜

Livvie smoothed her hand over Poppy's back as the girl stared out the carriage window. Her step-daughter had been so excited to arrive at Everett Place, she'd even bounced on her toes half the way to Hampshire.

"Olivia, do you really think Papa will come to visit us in Brockenhurst?"

She wished she knew the answer to that, and she didn't want to get the child's hopes up. "I've asked him to visit us. I don't know if he will, Poppy."

"It's so pretty. There aren't any buildings or theatres. Just land."

Hampshire was going to be a change for a child who'd only ever lived in the city. "Country life is bit quieter, dear."

"Ooo," Poppy nearly squealed. "Olivia, look. Do you think *that* is Everett Place?"

Olivia leaned over her step-daughter and peered out the window. A large, sandstone baroque mansion proudly stood in the distance, and her heart flipped. It had to be Everett Place. "I do believe it is, Poppy."

⚜

Iris found her estranged son sitting in Arthur's old study, reading one letter after another. She had thought her heart would break all those years ago when her husband had punished her by sending her son away.

250

But watching the painful expressions wash over his face was much worse. It was one thing for Arthur to punish her, but another entirely different to have done so to their son. What was left of her old heart was slowly crumbling.

When she sniffed away her tears, his eyes flashed to her in the doorway. He held up a letter. "You breed sheepdogs?"

Iris nodded her head. "Eighteen, nineteen years now."

Alex smiled tightly, holding up one of the letters. "1796." Then he dropped the letter in a pile and gestured for her to sit on the room's settee. "My wife, Olivia, is terrified of dogs. You'll need to make sure they all remain in the kennels while we're here. Her condition is delicate, and I—"

Iris walked into the study, her heart expanding since he was opening up, even if just a little, to her. "You're to be a father again?" She sat opposite him, studying his handsome face. She had missed seeing him grow into this man.

He nodded. "I'm sorry for what I said about Poppy. You are, of course, her grandmother."

"Please don't apologize. I can well imagine what you must have thought about me."

"All his lies. I don't even know you. I vaguely remember you from when I was a child."

"I'm certain I'm not even the same person anymore, Alex."

From the doorway, Martin cleared his throat. "Your Grace, a number of coaches seem to be headed this way."

"A number of them?" Alex echoed, rising from his seat.

Iris followed her son out of the study and onto the front drive. He seemed quite agitated, so she softly touched his arm.

"Your wife?"

"Yes."

⚜

He stood there in silence with his mother until four large traveling coaches came to a stop. Then hordes of people began filing out of them like ants leaving a hill. Alex quietly scanned the crowd of maids, footmen, and then he heard...

"Look, Olivia, Papa *is* here."

Then before he knew it, his daughter sprinted through the crowd and flung herself around his waist. "Oh, Papa. We have missed you. Are you going to stay with us here? Or do you still have business things to do?"

Alex snatched the girl into his arms and held her close. "No, Poppy," he choked, "I'm never leaving you again."

She tightened her arms around his neck and kissed him. "Olivia cried every day you were gone. She doesn't know I know."

Alex blinked back a tear of his own when he finally spotted his beautiful bride climbing out of one of his coaches. The air rushed out of him and he felt faint. He'd been such a fool to leave her. He kissed Poppy's forehead and then placed her back on the ground. "Let me see to her."

Then he pushed his way through the crowd, relieved to see a tentative smile tug at Olivia's lips. Alex picked her up and spun her around in the air, kissing her soundly in front of his staff, his mother, and his daughter. "You're never allowed to leave me again," he whispered as her feet touched the ground.

She laughed back a cry. "You left me."

"I'm a bloody fool."

"Agreed."

Alex held her against him, afraid that if he let her go, she'd vanish. "I'm not here because of the baby, Olivia. I mean, I suppose I am in a way. But I am here because I love you, sweetheart."

Tears streamed down her cheeks, then she buried her face against his chest. "I love you, Alex, and I was so afraid you wouldn't come."

He stepped away from his wife, a look of chagrin on his face. "You told me not to come."

Olivia blushed and chewed her plump bottom lip. "Yes, but you never listen to me."

Amazed that she'd played him, but so glad that she did, Alex threw back his head and laughed. "You crafty woman."

"I've missed you so desperately," she confessed.

"Me too. I can never apologize enough for what I've done."

"Don't be sorry. Just hold me."

Alex pulled his wife back into his arms and kissed her soundly again. It was so healing to hold her, to let her love flow into his heart.

"Papa," came Poppy's voice beside them.

He stepped back to look at his daughter, and discovered she was holding his mother's hand. Alex blinked at the sight, then took a deep breath. "Mother, you've met Poppy?"

"She's delightful," his mother replied.

"Olivia sweetheart, this is my mother —"

"Iris," the older woman clarified.

Alex looked into Olivia's pretty, hazel eyes, praying she wouldn't be furious with him for not being completely honest about his mother's current state of being. She did frown, but nodded her head in greeting. "Your Grace."

"Olivia, Livvie," he whispered, "there are some things I should have told you."

"Caroline already told me, Alex."

The lies that his father had perpetuated. "Caroline doesn't know everything."

Her eyes shot to his in question.

Alex smiled at his mother. "Why don't you take Poppy on a tour of your kennels?"

Olivia's muscles tightened at the mention of the kennels, and Alex caressed her back. "Don't worry, sweetheart, the pups are safely locked away."

His mother offered her hand to Poppy and her eyes glistened as the child accepted her without question.

On a settee in the study next to her husband, Livvie stared at the pile of unread letters littering an ancient desk. The mound was staggering. She was dumbfounded, hardly believing the awful tale Alex had just told her, and she brushed away a straggling tear. It was heartbreaking that her husband and his mother had been kept apart for nearly a quarter of a century due to the previous duke's lies. It was unconscionable.

Beside her, Livvie could see a line of worry marring his brow, and she shook her head, squeezing his hands. "I'm so sorry, my love."

His brow lightened and he smiled at her. "You're supposed to remain calm, aren't you?"

Livvie nodded. "Doctor's orders."

"I'm afraid I haven't made that very easy for you. How are you feeling, sweetheart?"

"So much better now that you're here."

Alex moved his hand to her belly and lovingly traced the small bump that had already formed. "Have you felt anything yet?"

"No. Caroline says I won't until the fifth month."

He smiled with relief. "I won't miss another moment. Not after realizing how much of my life has been spent wasted."

Livvie kissed his strong jaw, wishing she could kiss away all the years of suffering he'd endured.

"Olivia!" Poppy's voice echoed through the house.

Alex laughed. "She's still yelling through the house?"

"It's a hard habit to break, apparently."

"In here, Poppy," Alex called back.

Moments later Poppy and the dowager duchess stood in the doorway, then her step-daughter rushed to Livvie and Alex on the settee. "Olivia!" Poppy gushed, "Grandmama has lots of puppies. She says I have to ask you if I can have one."

Livvie's eyes flew to the soft blue gaze of her mother-in-law.

"They are very tame," the dowager said softly. "You can visit them in the kennels if you like until you feel more comfortable. Poppy says you plan to spend your confinement here, so you have time."

Livvie smiled. They all had time now. Time for Alex and his mother to know each other again. Time for Poppy to enjoy her grandmother. Time for Livvie and Alex to love each other without the spiteful eyes of the *ton* watching their every move. And time, apparently, for her to get accustomed to sheepdogs.

"I think I would like that."

Epilogue

June 1815 – Everett Place, Hampshire

LIVVIE had no idea how difficult it was to be a new mother *and* throw a house party. But after hosting friends and family the last three weeks at Everett Place, she felt guilty for all of her complaining about Juliet Beckford's party the year before. As lovely as it was to see everyone— with the exception of Cordie, since her friend's husband felt it would be too difficult for her to make the journey—Livvie was glad to have her peaceful home returned to her.

Lying on a soft blanket atop an Aubusson rug, she caressed her son's face. Tiny Lucien Everett, the Marquess of Brockenhurst, batted at her hair, cooing.

"Brock, my little darling," Livvie began, tapping the infant's nose. "You look more like your father every day. You'll be the most handsome boy in all of England."

Poppy flopped down on the blanket next to them, frowning slightly at her baby brother. "I don't think he looks like Papa at all. He's bald and chubby and doesn't have any teeth."

"All babies are chubby," Alex said from the doorway. "You were as well, angel."

"Was I as chubby as Brock?"

Alex stepped forward, as if he was seriously considering the question. Then he nodded. "Oh, Poppy, I'm afraid *you* were even chubbier than your brother."

When her step-daughter squeaked from horror, Livvie sent Alex the most annoyed look she could muster, which, while playing with their son, was not all that annoyed. "Pray, do not worry her over such nonsense. Poppy dear, only pay attention to half the things your father says."

"Ah, but the trick is knowing which half," Alex teased with a wink for his daughter.

Mrs. Bickle cleared her throat in the corner of the room. "Your Grace, it is time for the lad's nap."

Livvie smiled into her son's adorable face. Already she could detect just a hint of a mischievous sparkle in his bluish-silver eyes. She hated to relinquish him, but the child did get cranky if his schedule got disrupted. She kissed his chubby little cheek. "Sleep well, my love." Then she handed the child to his nurse.

"And you come along too, Miss Poppy," Mrs. Bickle said. "Your grandmother is waiting for you near the kennels to give Unicorn his exercise." All agreed it was a silly name for a sheepdog, but Poppy *had* been allowed to name the puppy. None of them should have been surprised.

When everyone else had finally left the room, Alex pulled Livvie up from her spot on the blanket. "I have a present for you," he said with a lascivious twinkle in his eyes.

Livvie grinned at her husband. "A present?"

"Hm." He quickly undid his cravat.

"How sweet of you, my love," Livvie responded with a saucy tip of her head, slowly crossing the room out of his grasp. "But I do not have need of a cravat."

Alex stalked towards her, a wolfish smile tugging at his lips. "Close your eyes."

"Absolutely not." She feigned indignation. "You see, I find Your Grace morally lacking, and I don't trust you at all."

He chuckled. "You're a very disobedient wife. Didn't you vow otherwise?"

Livvie playfully cocked her head to one side. "You paid no attention at all during that ceremony. So, you have no idea what I vowed to or did not, Alexander Everett."

He pulled her against his chest and covered her mouth with his. The evidence of his desire pressed against Livvie's belly and she sighed. She would never tire of his passion or his love. Alex's hands caressed her, sliding up her back, and then before she realized what had happened, a blindfold tightened around her eyes.

The cravat.

The devious duke.

"There," he said triumphantly.

"I was right not to trust you," she giggled.

Alex spun her around and placed his hands on her hips. "Follow my direction."

She didn't have much choice, not that she wanted to resist him anyway. He gently pushed her forward and then right, down a long corridor. When her feet reached a set of stairs, her back straightened. "Alex, where are you taking me?"

"It's a surprise."

He urged her forward and Livvie tentatively climbed the steps, listening to his direction. "Last one, sweetheart."

Then he led her down another hallway and a few more steps. Alex's hands momentarily left her waist and then she heard a door open in front of her. "All right," he whispered in her ear, "you can open your eyes."

Livvie ripped the cravat from her face and blinked her eyes open. In the middle of Alex's chamber stood a large, mahogany wardrobe adorned with a lavish, red bow.

"Happy Anniversary."

She recognized the wardrobe instantly as the one from Prestwick Chase. She could never forget it. Her life had never been the same since she climbed inside it. "Is that really what I think it is?"

Alex's roguish smile returned. "It took quite a lot of negotiating to get Beckford to part with it."

"It did?" she asked, still stunned.

"Hm." Alex wrapped his arms around her middle and nuzzled against her neck. "They wouldn't hand it over for anything I offered. Apparently it's some old Prestwick heirloom."

"Then how did you get it?"

"I made a deal with your cousins. They made me promise never to leave you again and make sure you were happy all of your days or they'll take the thing back."

Livvie's grin spread across her face. The two of them had never been happier in their lives. Neither of them would ever leave the other again. "They took a sucker's bet."

"They did, indeed."

About the Author

Ava Stone is a USA Today bestselling author of Regency historical romance and college age New Adult romance. Whether in the 19th Century or the 21st, her books explore deep themes but with a light touch. A single mother, Ava lives outside Raleigh NC, but she travels extensively, always looking for inspiration for new stories and characters in the various locales she visits.

Feel free to visit her at:
www.avastoneauthor.com
www.desolatesun.com

17537300R00155

Printed in Great Britain
by Amazon